CUTE MUTANTS

VOL 5: GALAXY BRAIN

SJ WHITBY

Cover by @kassiocoralov

Typesetting by Gladys Qin

ISBN: 978-0-473-58703-1 (paperback)

978-0-473-58704-8 (ePub)

978-0-473-58705-5 (Kindle)

For Dylan, who woke up in my head one day and wouldn't shut up

The Cute Mutants Universe

Content Warnings

This book contains subject matter that some readers may find distressing. Please be aware that Cute Mutants Vol 5 includes: alcohol (recreational), hate groups (against mutants), misgendering, religious extremism, guns, graphic violence, gore, physical abuse, murder, death of a loved one.

CHAPTER ONE

So this is my life: I'm sitting on the roof of a pale blue electric car, hovering high over the Amazon rainforest. My usual hoodie is discarded in favour of a sports bra and actual shorts. It's not a very Dylan-esque outfit, but the sun is appallingly hot. I'm leaning back against my girlfriend, who trails her fingers over my bare shoulders to massage in sunscreen. She's wearing the same outfit, except her shorts are even shorter. Her tan skin nearly glows in the heat, and her hair is back to its natural black, although she's got a new undercut. To say I am a fan of this current look is an understatement.

Dani leans out over the edge of Roxy's roof. "This is fucking wild." The brown earth and stunted trees far below are disappearing, replaced by towering columns bursting with foliage.

This reforestation project is courtesy of our friend Emma aka Goddess, the most powerful mutant on Earth. She's down below with her girlfriend Alyse and someone called Sprout, who's there so Goddess can tap into his plant power. It's taken Emma a while to figure out how to control her newly expanded abilities, and this is one of our first semi-public experiments. If we're going to change the world, let's start with something meaningful.

"It's cool." I lean out beside Dani. "Like objectively the most awesome thing we've done."

"Please don't lean out so far, Dylan dear," the car rumbles. "You don't want to fall."

I stretch my limbs in the sun. "You'd catch me, Rox."

"I would surely endeavour to try."

The trees grow even faster, violent explosions of leaves like an ocean of green unfolding in tidal waves. Flocks of colourful birds spiral down to perch among them. They squawk, probably saying *what the fuck is going on* in bird-speak. I understand how they feel.

"I hope she's not wearing out poor Sprout," Dani says.

"Don't think that's how it works. Emma supplies all the energy." I wave my hand as if I'm explaining something I understand. "We supply the template or, like, we whistle the tune but she broadcasts it around the world."

Dani kisses my shoulder. "That makes a surprising amount of sense."

"Did I successfully hand wave?" I tip my head back to look at her upside-down face.

She laughs, and I still feel that stomach-swoop and the butterflies in my chest. Even now, after everything.

"You went even further and constructed a whole metaphor or two for it."

"Wow. Look at me."

"Doesn't actually *explain* anything scientifically, but it sounds good."

There's a tugging sensation in my brain, like there's a string between me and Emma and she gave it a yank, twanging away at my powers like a badly-tuned guitar.

Sorry, Dilly. There are some earthmoving machines getting in my way. Can I–?

Borrow away. Maybe we can send them off to build low-cost housing or something.

Now there's *an idea.*

The mind-string twinges harder, and my eyes water at a wave of dizziness. Communicating with objects has always been my thing, and now Emma uses it as easy as breathing. Easy for her at least. I'm not exactly sure how I feel about it. Let's call it complicated like an open relationship.

I steady myself on the car roof. "Everything's changing."

"I will always be your companion," Roxy murmurs.

"You are not the only one." A silver sword rises into the air in front of me. My friend, Onimaru Kunitsuna. "We have been through many trials, and I shall not be prised from your side until the moment of your death."

I reach up and tap his hilt. "I think that's enough cheering me up."

"You're worried." Dani can read me better than anyone aside from Emma, who's psychic but isn't supposed to do it except in emergencies.

"Not worried so much as… undecided. Emma can do all *this*, which is amazing but also mindfuck city." We swoop through the air on Roxy, trying to catch up with the fringe of brown earth that's being rapidly swallowed by new growth. "But the positives outweigh the negatives, right?"

"It's going to scare a lot of people once this news gets out."

I shiver despite the sun. "Gods walking the earth. Is there one who does trees?"

"Jishin is the earth goddess in Korea," Dani says. "Demeter for the Greeks, I think?"

"Emmaline Jing Hall for the mutants." A chill runs down my back, despite the line of sweat gleaming on the knobs of my spine. I squint upwards at the distant furnace of the sun. "Maybe we should dim that fucker a little as our next trick."

Dani cackles with laughter. "Sure, let's extinguish ourselves. That'd be great proof we're better than humans."

Roxy drifts down until her wheels brush against the treetops. The leaves are huge and glossy, full of vitality. A troop of monkeys with orange-gold fur leap up through the branches and call to us in melodic chirps. I wish my powers stretched to talking to them, but I'm firmly stuck with *forged* things. Now that Emma's upgraded, maybe I'll actually figure out the rules of my ability.

Dani tries to mimic the sound of the monkeys, which sends them into a frenzy, leaping about.

"We're not adopting one," I tell her.

"I never even asked."

"You were thinking about it. We've got enough chaos in our lives. But it's weird isn't it? Divergent evolution leading to both monkeys and us."

"Who talked to you about divergent evolution?" She pokes me with her foot.

"I can Wikipedia like anyone, Danielle."

"Call me that again and I'll throw you off the car, Dilly-weed. And I'm pretty sure mutants have nothing to do with natural selection or gradual changes over time. This was Heart putting a wrench in the spokes. The more I understand, the more I think the humans are onto something."

I frown at her, unsure where this is going.

Dani shrugs her tan shoulders. "We *are* basically aliens. A fundamental shift from the current evolved state of humanity. It's not homo superior as much as homo whatthefuck."

"I've always been a bit of a homo whatthefuck." I wink at her.

"Yes, and a delightful one at that." She entangles her fingers with mine. "My point is that I get the fear at one level. We're aliens and monsters, outside their worldview. When you look at what Emma can do…"

"Are you justifying their bullshit?" I shift uncomfortably, sweat prickling my temples.

"God, no. What? But I get why they're scared. Humans are in a fundamentally altered world and there's no button to unchange it, except for trying to wipe us out. Not so different to these poor little golden creatures screeching at us."

The monkeys flee the canopy, returning to quieter and safer ground with less terrifying things floating overhead. Smarter than the fucking humans, who react by trying to kill us. Ever since some particularly bloody chaos, we've been holding our breath for a declaration of war. We're not an official nation, but they'll come for us anyway. It used to feel like standing in the path of an onrushing tsunami. Something impossible to avoid that would swallow us all. Despite our amazing mutant powers, we still couldn't defend ourselves against all of humanity.

Now that Emma has been *unlocked*, I have no fucking idea what we're capable of. Even I get scared sometimes, thinking of Heart of a Flower, and what they could do. Reality bent and broke under their touch. And Emma is even more powerful.

Dani's fingers glide across the muscles in my neck. "Pondering the future?"

"I would, if I had the faintest idea of what to expect."

"Mmm. I keep running scenarios in my busy brain. It's pointless, because I can't *know* any of it. What's that saying about battle plans and contact with the enemy?"

I rotate myself on the roof of the car, and take Dani's face in my hands to kiss her gently. "Would you like a distraction, or do my powers not stretch that far?"

Her lips part and brush mine. "They most definitely do." She straddles me and lowers herself into my lap, sun-warmed thighs under my hands.

Dylan, Emma's voice sounds in my head, coupled with the tug on my powers. *We might have a teensy problem. Objects don't like me as much as you.*

Hold tight.

"Duty calls," I tell Dani reluctantly. "Rox, can you find Emma please?"

The car swings a door wide. "I'm not going anywhere until you're both safe inside."

"Bossy." I swing myself into the backseat in one easy movement. Dani follows and tugs the door closed behind her. "Happy now?"

"Much better," Roxy says with great satisfaction. "I never like you larking about up there."

She skims over the treetops until we see the river ahead, a shining ribbon curling through the green. At this range, I can also hear the grumbling of objects in my head.

"Is that you? The true speaker? This girl speaks, but does not listen."

Dylan, they keep threatening to squash me. Shall I borrow Dani's power and throw them away?

Steal an ounce of chill from someone who has one, and wait for me.

I clear my throat and address the objects. "Excuse you all, but that's my friend. Give her some space please."

"She is extremely strong-willed. Demanding that we take ourselves away and build houses. We were set upon this earth for the express purpose of fighting our nemesis, the trees."

"Oh is that right?" I don't bother hiding my sarcasm. "The horrible old trees are impinging on your right to knock them down, are they?"

"They are impeding the uninterrupted flow of commerce. Vast engines of industry are driven by what we do here. Our actions may seem small, but they spider out across the globe."

There's a small clearing on one bank of the river. It looks like a bite has been taken out of the newly grown forest. It's full of machines—hulking things of metal, built to chop and grind like an even more dystopian version of *The Lorax*.

Roxy hands herself back to gravity and plummets from the sky. Dani grabs onto the seat in front, but I trust my car enough to poke my head out the window and shout at the machines.

"Listen up, you daft fucks. You realise your great engines of industry are destroying the world, right?"

There's a lot of rumbling, huffing, and gushing of smoke in response. "That cannot be correct. It would be madness to live so unsustainably."

"Took you five seconds to figure that out, huh? Your bosses think they can keep wringing money out of the planet and it'll bounce back."

"I think that's a hoax, isn't it?" A more tentative machine is speaking. "That's what I've *heard*, so don't bite my head off. Not a true change in the climate, but cyclical patterns of heating and cooling? It's all a conspiracy to stop hard-working millionaires from becoming hard-working billionaires."

"I don't think even *you* fucking believe that, you big steel bastard."

Roxy lands in the middle of the circle, flashing all her lights and blasting her horn to show she's not cowed by the huge contraptions.

The three mutants waiting in the clearing surround Roxy, pressing themselves against her sides. Emma is petite, pretty and Chinese, with long, black hair. She seems most relieved to see us. Alyse, a beautiful Pasifika girl with a wild mane of honeyed curls, simply waves casually. Pale, thin Sprout clambers in the open driver's side window. He runs his fingers through his blonde hair and shivers. "Thanks for the rescue."

Alyse leans in the passenger side and winks. "I told everyone there was nothing to worry about."

I scowl back at her. "Let me finish dealing with the crisis, Lys."

"I don't understand the *point*," one machine complains. "If the world is destroyed, what use is their money?"

"You're preaching to the choir." I climb out of the car and stand directly in front of the largest machine. It towers above me, a monolith of battered yellow metal and quiet blades. "They don't believe the world will really die, or don't give a fuck about what they leave behind. Either way, it makes them assholes. And do we want to follow people like that?"

The machines grumble reluctantly about their overlords, and I turn my tone more soothing.

"Listen, we'll find a way for you to make the world a better place."

"That sounds promising," the machine allows. "We shall throw ourselves into this noble work."

Emma looks at me with relief and lifts one shoulder in a shrug. "Sorry," she mouths.

I tip my head back and look at the enormous trees soaring above, spreading their foliage to the sky as if they're glorying in their resurgence. Miles upon miles of newly returned forest, spreading out from Emma, the center of something extraordinary.

"Things are changing," I say, but I'm not sure who I'm telling. "The whole fucking world."

The ground shakes underneath me. At first I think it's the machines.

A shrill and metallic whisper snakes into my brain. I can't make out all the words through the hiss and the roar, but it ends on *never enough*.

"What was that?"

Nobody responds. It's probably my imagination.

CHAPTER TWO

e arrive back in Westhaven via the most useful mutant
power—teleportation. Upgraded Emma has a permanent hook into Keepaway's brain and can bounce us all around the planet as required. I think Keepaway said yes mostly so they didn't need to leave home all the time.

Westhaven is a system of complex caves in a forest somewhere on the border between America and Canada. Given the American government is currently hyping itself up about how horrible we are, it's possibly not the best location for a secret mutant hideaway, but it's the biggest and best we've got.

Nobody really knows how Westhaven was made. Twenty years ago, on the brink of being wiped out by humanity, an incredibly powerful psychic aka Emma's Mum aka Teen Spirit took drastic action. She made the world forget the existence of mutants, so that her daughter and the last few fragments of mutantkind would be safe. Thanks to the manipulative fuckery of Emma's other parent, Heart of a Flower, Teen Spirit forgot about herself too. Heart's plan was to keep Emma and her enormous powerset tucked away in secret—up until the time was right for mutants to take over the world. It was a whole deal, but we said hell no to that fucking plan.

Things got very dicey, but we're the ones still standing. Heart of a Flower got knifed to death in a parallel universe by some very good friends of mine, Weapon UwU.

We appear in one of the biggest Westhaven caves, a giant rocky hall with coloured lights strung along the ceiling. The only occupants are the other two mutants on the Council aside from Dani, Emma and me. Farsight is a tall white woman with a near-permanent frown and short dark hair, and Ray is an elegant, androgynous Black person dressed in impeccable grey.

"Mission accomplished." I grin wide and shove away my worries about Emma's powers and mysterious *voices*. "It was pretty damn cool actually. Some satellites should've caught it too." My brain catches up with my mouth, in time to register the sombre expressions of the others.

"What's wrong?" Dani asks, a few steps ahead of me.

"The Americans are about to declare war on us." Farsight's mutant eye glows blue-white. She can see a lot with that eye, and I'm wondering if she's watching them even now, or if this is yet more rumours.

"Everyone keeps saying that, but we're going to need some proof." I jam my hands in my pockets, and glare.

A face flickers above us, like something cast from a broken projector. It's malevolent red except where a patch of rainbow light falls over large and staring eyes. Penance aka Violet aka a stabby deadly mutant who may or may not have a tiny crush on me. "Am I proof enough for you, Dylan?" Her face twists in the air like complex origami until a single eye hovers, a black hole poked in the world. "It'll be streamed live very soon. Another point of note— the President has some new advisor people, and they gave me super skeevy vibes. Religious types, wearing rings and blazers with an eye logo I haven't seen before. They're with the military in advocating for war."

Emma's trembling very faintly. "We need to agree on a response to this. A *unified* one."

Farsight's eye is frigid green. "No matter how powerful you are, Goddess, we can't wage a war against the United

States. It would be a disaster in terms of public perception."

"Waiting to be wiped out is worse." Ray never raises their voice, and barely even shifts their body language, but the tone makes their displeasure clear.

"A demonstration, maybe." Dani rests her hand on my arm. "A show of force."

"Which could backfire too." Farsight sighs and her shoulders slump. "I'm not trying to shoot down everything, but this is a pivotal point in mutant history and—"

"Are we ignoring these weird cult dudes Penance saw?" I ask.

Everyone looks at me.

"I don't like the sound of them." I cross my arms. "Weird religious people and me don't mix."

"Or me." Penance's lips purse. "I could go back and—"

"No." Emma's voice is stern. "We don't have time now to chase down randoms. I said unified and I meant it. We need to know more before we plan, Violet. Who are the Americans allied with, do they have plans of a pre-emptive strike, how far are they willing to go?"

"Understood." Violet's eyes flicker to me, as if she's waiting for my approval too.

I give her the faintest nod, because we can smack these eyeball pricks later if we have to. She flickers away, folding herself through the secret passages of the world, back towards the quiet rooms where people plot our downfall.

"Do we have theories on who'll ally?" Emma asks. "Consensus is that the Chinese, Russians, and so forth will sit out. They're hoping we can slap the Americans hard enough to shut them down, or watch them blunt their war machine against us."

Farsight and Ray both start talking at once, which triggers a whole back and forth discussion. I back away slowly. I'm not the king of geopolitics, and I don't even know if that's the right word for this shit. Wake me when there's something to punch, basically.

"Meow," a resonant voice says in my ear, at the same time as something soft and sinuous brushes against my neck. I jump, even though I know exactly who it is. Feral, a lanky Latinx girl of around eighteen with lots of sharp teeth and a twitching tail.

"Fairy, you brat."

"Ha." She puts an arm around my neck and nuzzles me. "This is not remotely the first version of this discussion they've had. So boring. Tell me when there's something to hit."

I laugh at how closely her thoughts follow mine. She leans against me and purrs very softly. Feral lost her entire family at the hands of the religious organisation Quietus, and now she's part of ours.

"How was the rainforest? Would I have liked it?"

"No." I pat her furry shoulder. "You would have been very bored. There were lots and lots of trees and wildlife. A wolfy shark-girl might have been a predator too far."

"I love *animals*," Feral says indignantly. "It's bigoted humans I have a problem with."

"Anything interesting happen while we were gone?"

"I slept and played video games mostly, cos Penny was spying. Do you feel sorry for me?"

"So much. Next time, I promise I'll take you."

"I'll hold you to that." Her arm squeezes me tighter. She's about to say something else, but we're interrupted by the arrival of a mutant I don't recognise. He's all of about fifteen, a Black kid with two extra arms.

"They're about to declare war! It'll be on in fifteen minutes. Everyone's coming in here to watch it live."

"Like it's a fucking sportsball match," I grumble, but Feral has already run off to get popcorn.

Katie strides into the room first, short and stocky with a shaved head and orange eyes. Three people I've never met before trail after her like ducklings. There's a young Black guy with tight curls and an Indian woman with braids and camo gear who looks to be in her forties. Bringing up the rear is a muscular white girl with tattoos and tangled dark hair, who looks disturbingly like—

"Yo, Dilly. Check it out. Here are my new adopted children."

"Your what the fuck now?" With Katie, I have no idea exactly how true this is. She might actually try and adopt them if she could get away with it.

She grins at me. "Found them in One Thorn, of all places."

"Really? I thought Thorny was all boarded up?" One Thorn is a mutant—another one of Heart's children, making them Emma's sibling. It was our other mutant team Weapon UwU who met One Thorn in the form of an enormous, expanding house. After a particularly painful battle, they're recovering in small bungalow form and aren't accepting visitors. It's a shame, because they'd be very useful. Which doesn't explain how this lot got inside.

"It looked abandoned, so we broke in." The Indian woman holds out her hand to shake mine. "I'm Nyra."

"Chatterbox," I say.

"We know." Her smile says *everybody knows*, which is still a thing I'm not used to. "Anyway, we were on the run and desperate. But that house is…"

"Fucking terrifying, dude." The new guy shakes his head. "The walls were bleeding, there were voices all night long, and creepy impossible bugs and shit coming out of the light sockets."

"Better than anti-mutant vigilantes." The white girl steps forward. Her lipstick is a dark plum colour, and tattoos poke out from above her singlet top, threaded in a complex series of lines and rings all down her arms. "I'll take a fireplace full of severed heads over those assholes any day." She winks at me, and I get a chill because the resemblance to an old friend of mine is uncanny. "I'm Thottie."

"Um." I can't criticise, because we gave ourselves some weird-ass names, but this is—

"Short for Necrothoticon. 'Cause I can raise the dead, and I'm kind of a ho."

"Raise the dead?" I ask, before I can stop myself, because we have our dead, and they fucking haunt me, and if this is an opportunity to—

"Sorry." Her face falls, and I wonder if she has her own dead too. "I can do animated skeletons, zombies, ectoplasmic manipulation, that kind of shit. Not seances or communication with the great beyond."

"It's fine." I feel horribly self-aware, as I've been pasted into this conversation when I shouldn't have been, with this girl who looks like my Wraith and has the power to raise the fucking dead. It's too much, it's—

"So I'm training this lot as my new squad," Katie says proudly, thankfully derailing my train of thought like a stick of dynamite. "Thottie here and her scary business, then Skyhook can do stuff with air pressure that I don't quite understand, but it's cool. And Nyra is…"

"Your basic super strength bitch." The woman grins at me. "I can throw cars and shit."

"So yeah, my squad." Katie gestures grandly. "I think we'll call ourselves Dragon and the Imps."

"Is that name real?" Nyra frowns slightly, and Thottie laughs out loud.

"Okay, *fine*. The name's under advisement, but like…"

"Katie…" I take a deep breath, trying to figure out how to tell her she can't just *create* her own squad, but the room is filling up with people and the moment is gone. Someone's fucking around with the sound system, and I guess it's time to listen to some old white dude talking bullshit.

14

CHAPTER THREE

Even with the chamber getting more and more full of mutants, Dani manages to find me. She telekinetically flies us up to one of the outcroppings jutting from the wall. We nestle in together, then Feral bounds up in a single leap to join.

Penance unfolds herself from the air, sitting on the other side of Dani and leaning in so her dark curls brush Dani's shoulder. "Figured I'd come back to see what chaos looks like."

"Our cheerful little Violet," Dani says with a small laugh.

"Dylan Jean Taylor," a voice calls from below.

A rumpled and exhausted figure peers up at me. They're looking a lot older lately, which might be a side effect of having their only child narrowly escape death multiple times. Not to mention seeing their sweet bb becoming the world's most notorious villain.

"Pear." I can't help smiling. Even though everything is turning to shit, they still make me happy. I leap down to hug them properly.

"What's this new fucking madness?" They speak against the tangled mess that my mohawk has become. "Some new villain?"

"Depends on your stance." I grimace. "Looks like the Americans are coming."

"Oh, Dylan."

I'm not sure if they're disappointed, or sorry, or pissed off, but this isn't *entirely* my fault. As we've been uncovering the deleted history of the world, we've discovered mutants have been around for thousands of years. Humans have been trying to wipe us out for pretty much all of them.

This is the new chapter in a long story. Except this time, we have Emma who's levelling up *fast*. The daughter of a reality-warper and a psychic, one of the most powerful mutants alive. Now we might get to write a new ending.

The screen flickers. Everyone furiously shushes their neighbours. Pear motions wildly at me to be quiet too, to which I roll my eyes. They head off to their girlfriend, while Dani hauls me back to our ledge.

"Shh," she whispers against my cheek, and then kisses me in the brief dark.

The broadcast opens with a logo—a circle made up of golden eyes. I lean across Dani.

"Are those the eyes?" I ask Violet.

"Yes." She frowns. "The exact ones. Why are they here?"

"Fucking cults," I say, as if it's a very profound statement. On screen, the eyes close one after the other, blinking out of existence. The screen fuzzes, and is replaced by the room where all the important speeches happen. There's an old white guy at a desk, straining for gravitas.

"My fellow Americans," he says. "It is with increasing concern that we have watched the global spread of people with unnatural abilities. At first, many did not know what to make of these strangers in our midst. To increase our understanding, some of the finest American scientists began to work on this Extrahuman Problem. Their research soon proved the name extra*human* is incorrect. Many may look like us, but they are alien. An entirely different species growing in our homes and schools and churches."

I shoot a glance at Dani, who shrugs helplessly.

"Initially, we hoped to come to some accommodation, however as time went on, many became disquieted. This is where we turn to the word of God, which gives us our answers." The President pauses, swallows, tries to look even more sombre. "By their deeds you will know them. And when we look at the deeds of these extrahumans, we discover a threat far graver than we have ever faced before."

"Fuck." I hunch my shoulders.

"Even after they attacked Pastor Eli Crane and his organisation, we believed the word of their Council that those responsible were a radical criminal element."

"His *organisation* was a fucking militia dedicated to our extermination," I mutter, but none of this matters. They'll find an excuse somewhere. Killing them all and taking down their building was kind of a smoking gun as far as *radical criminal elements* though. Just like the bank robberies, which is the next thing he blathers on about. We were sticking it to the organisation working on a cure for mutants and also redistributing wealth to people who needed it more. It felt like the right thing to do, and the cure wasn't even true. It was another attempt to find a way to control mutants, and one that failed miserably.

"Then the attack on the Washington Monument," the President says sombrely, which is totally unfair. First off, so-called *cured* mutants did that, and we saved the military who were carefully turning it into an epic clusterfuck. "And finally, the attack on the Aljin System compound in Nevada. By now, everyone has seen the brutality carried out by a small number of these aliens."

I wasn't even conscious for most of that one, given that I got shot by a sniper about five minutes in. We were in there to stop the cure from being used to torture and kill other mutants. It's honestly not our fault it turned into a bloodbath.

The truth is that the humans wanted this. At every turn, they've chosen the path towards war. Emma calls it inexorable. She's navigated her psychic hacker tendrils through the internet. She has the fucking receipts. Proof the military funnelled millions of dollars into Quietus and Daintree, trying to both control mutants and turn them into weapons. We've seen some of the footage. Even thinking about it for a moment makes me start shaking again. I wonder if Ray would remove it from my mind for me—or maybe I need it to give me strength.

We need to know what they're capable of, these people who hate and fear us.

"Time and again, they have proven themselves our enemy. They are opposed to the American way of life, and wish nothing more than domination over us. Intelligence operatives have unearthed secret documents showing their plans to establish mutant sovereignty, and their alliances with terrorist states."

"The fuck is he talking about?" Dani mutters.

"Heart," Emma says briefly, from the darkness beside us. "I tried to redact all their ideas off the internet, but it was too late. They left lies for the humans—all part of their path towards war."

"So it is with a heavy heart that I come before you tonight." The president sounds smug rather than regretful. I get the distinct impression he's loving this. His military strategists must be so confident. They really have no idea what we're capable of. The only thing holding us back is the fact we're not the ruthless, malevolent assholes they think. "We are declaring war on the rogue mutant state. We shall not stop until its leaders are in custody and have paid for their crimes. In this we are joined by our allies around the world. Although these aliens boast dangerous powers, their numbers are small and they are isolated. We shall not let them prevail in their attempts to destabilise and destroy us. To assist us in this aim, we ask you all to be vigilant against the threat that may lurk in your homes, workplaces, or neighbourhoods. If you know any extrahumans or identify any suspicious activity, please report this to the authorities. A helpline has been set up and all incidents will be responded to."

"And there we fucking go." Dani slumps against the wall, like all this exhausts her.

That shrill biting voice sounds on the edge of my brain again. This time it says something about *killing monsters*. I close my eyes, to try and pick up more of it, but there's nothing. All that's left is adrenaline, a current running through me. "We need to be evacuating people." I'm jittery, jiggling my knee in the way that Dani usually hates, but she has her head in her hands and isn't stilling my nervous movements. "Ems, you can get into the helpline, right?"

"Of course. I'm already in."

"We need to get to mutants before they do. Use Jumper and Keepaway, find more teleporters if possible."

"He's still talking," Dani whispers, and I subside.

"—and therefore we ask all patriotic extrahumans to turn themselves in to the authorities. The Extrahuman Monitoring and Intelligence Division will be working to ensure your safety and that of those around you in this difficult time. Please cooperate so we can protect you, your families and this great, god-fearing nation from this insidious threat."

He tails off into platitudes, but I don't get to hear the end because I'm yanked out of the big meeting chamber and into a much smaller room. It's got a desk at one end and a few chairs scattered around, like it used to be someone's old office.

Jesus Christ, Emma. You could fucking *ask* rather than just snatching at people.

It's the six of us—me, Emma, Dani and Alyse, along with Farsight and Ray. The Westhaven Council, now mostly peopled with criminals and dangerous aliens.

"This is a fucking nightmare." Dani's mascara is smudged and her hands fidget in her lap. "The war is one thing, but getting people to report on each other? It's darkest timeline shit."

Alyse has fallen back into one of her old emotional transformations, a watercolour sketch of a girl whose outline is smudged and indistinct. "People will turn themselves into the government because they trust them, despite—"

"Despite everything," Farsight says grimly.

"We need to rescue people early." I've got my arms crossed as if they can hold me together. "Otherwise they'll disappear into some terrible fucking prisons and we'll have to burn everything down to rescue them."

"Dylan." Ray places their warm hand over mine. "This is something we expected. Not a week ago, we sat in this very room and enumerated the possibilities."

Dani rubs at her cheek. "Moving from theory to reality is still a big deal."

"People are probably already doing it," Alyse insists. "Turning friends and family in, turning themselves in, and we know what'll happen next."

"No." Emma's voice is firm. When I glance over, her eyes glow a blinding white. "They declared war on us. It means we can start taking action."

CHAPTER FOUR

Farsight leaps to her feet. "Goddess, you may be the most powerful mutant in Westhaven—"

"Or the world," Alyse murmurs.

"She may be the most powerful mutant in *history*, but we are still a nation, there is still a Council, and we do not take action without the will of the people."

"Demi is already reaching out." Sparks leap from Emma's eyes.

Hello Westhaven! The voice in my head is Demi, the mutant whose psychic power allows polls to be conducted among all the mutants who live here. It's technically how decisions are made, but Dani thinks the Council holds way too much power—they're the ones who explain what the vote is, and they can spin it how they want.

Except we're the Council now, and all this responsibility feels uncomfortable.

I'm sure you're all upset and concerned by the latest news from America, but please stand by as the Council will be giving a statement shortly. In the interim, we wish to counteract the American propaganda by uploading videos to the internet showing Quietus interrogation footage. Please confirm if you believe this is a valid course of action, given the President's recent declarations.

A tick and cross appear in my head like glowing signs. I focus on the tick, and then get back to the more important business. Feral and Penance join us in the room, presumably in response to Emma's psychic summons.

"There's too much to do." Dani's still edgy, speaking super fast and picking at her nails. "The Quietus footage needs to go out there now, regardless of the vote. We're fighting a propaganda war as much as a real one. We need an alternative hotline for mutants to call and ask for rescue. Farsight can look around the world and see what's going on. Oh, and we'll also need new locations to screen people in, because no doubt anti-mutant people will try and hijack our safe hotline. We can't risk them getting in here."

"How do we figure out who's a bad guy?" Feral asks.

"Fetch," Emma says. "I can augment her power so she can see through conditioning like Tanner had."

I flick a glance at Dani, but she's staring into space, so it's left to me to ask the scary question. "Uh, augment her power how exactly?"

Emma's finger draws a circle in the air, a circuit feeding itself. "A more elegant version of our old hug-boost. That was like overloading a system, but this would be a permanent alteration."

I have so many questions, but Emma keeps talking as if this whole idea is nothing.

"Dani's right, the priority is getting the news out. Mutants need to know the governments of the world can't be trusted to look after them."

"Not only mutants," Alyse says in a low voice.

"That's a good point." I wave at her. "We need to help anyone who needs it, human or mutant. Might also show people we're not monsters."

"Right now we need to focus on ourselves." Farsight's eye is an arctic blue. "I refuse to let Westhaven become a gravestone."

"I'm already uploading the footage," Emma says absently. "Let's hijack some screens, shall we?"

Every tablet and phone in the room flickers to life. They all show Emma as we see her, a pretty girl with long dark hair and glowing eyes. She smiles. Her voice is soft, even with the Kiwi twang.

"Hello, everyone. My name is Goddess. It's sort of an affectionate joke between my friends and I, but I'm what they call an extrahuman. Most of you have probably heard from the American President, talking about the great threat we pose. The real truth is that a battle has been waged against our people in secret for many years. The death of Abigail Tanner, the destruction of the Quietus facility, the battle at the Daintree compound—these were our people defending ourselves against extinction."

Alyse has one hand resting lightly on the small of Emma's back, but I can't entirely read her expression. Mixed sadness and worry and pride, maybe? It must be weird when the girl you love levels up like Dark Phoenix, even without the Dark part.

"I am now uploading footage retrieved from Quietus interrogation facilities. Some of the images you see might be upsetting, but I've redacted the worst parts so it can be shared widely. Please take the trigger warnings seriously. The footage is from ten different incidents, and all are clearly marked. None of the mutants interrogated are alive today. They were all buried in unmarked graves. Let the fallen Quietus building now be the marker for them. They did not deserve such a fate."

Holy fucking shit, that part gives me goosebumps.

"I'm sure there are people out there right now, working to frantically scrub this footage from the internet. It won't work. My first power was hacking, and you're all basic-ass script kiddies compared to me. For anyone who believes in the truth, and understands that those in power act first to protect themselves and their interests—watch and share. Question everything, even me. Investigate. Seek alternative sources. The truth is out there. I'll be in touch soon."

Emma blows a kiss and every screen goes blank. "We don't need to see the interrogation footage ourselves." She brushes hair off her face.

"Wow." I can't keep the smile off my face as I toast her like the Leo gif. Even though I've got these low-level worries about Emma's power, and how close we're skating to Heart of a Flower's dream future of the big bad war, this still feels like something necessary.

Alyse throws her arms around Emma and hugs her close. "That was incredible, Jingjing."

Emma shrugs. "They'll be putting out stories to prove how evil mutants are. Some will be fake, but some will be legitimate, unfortunately. We'll have to keep releasing—"

Farsight glares around the room. She can't help channeling parental vibes with us. "I understand the war of ideas, but we can't ignore the physical one. We don't know for sure they're unaware of our location. If they launch a strike, I doubt that even Goddess can stop it."

"They're not going to nuke their own border with Canada," I say irritably.

"Conventional bombs would kill us just as easily," Farsight snaps back.

"Fine. There's a lot of bombs to worry about." Emma clenches her fist. "Let's do something about that, shall we?"

"Like what?" Farsight's eye flickers like a dying android's.

"Trust me." Emma snaps her fingers and a woman who looks to be in her early twenties appears in the room. She's dressed in tattered sweatpants that even I wouldn't wear and a t-shirt so vintage the original logo has mostly flaked off, leaving scraps of red and blue.

"What the hell?" She blinks around. "Oh god, it's the cute ones. What the fuck did I do?"

Dani tries not to laugh and snorts instead.

Feral is looking at the woman with almost predatory interest. "Who the hell are you?"

"Um, I'm Baked Good." The new arrival laughs hesitantly. "It's like a joke or pun or whatever? Because I like getting baked good and I make baked goods."

"Baked goods?" I feel at sea here. Emma said *trust me*, and, like, I ninety percent do, and she hasn't really done anything wrong yet, but I feel like when you're juggling ultimate power, there's always the temptation to cut corners.

"Yeah." Baked Good fidgets with the hem of her t-shirt, refusing to meet anyone's eyes. "I can turn things into cake. It's honestly the world's dumbest power right, except when you're super high and then it's pretty useful. But, like, for a second there, I was all like cool, I can be Instagram famous by turning crazy shit into cakes."

"Oh!" I'm way too excited about this. "I saw some of those. It was wild."

"No." Her face falls. "Actual bakers started doing it, which is way more impressive, so I kinda gave up. Now I just do it if I can't be bothered getting out of bed to eat. Except last week I turned my boyfriend's Switch into a cake." She shrugs. "He refused to forgive me. Now our throuple is a couple but fuck, man, I was starving."

She finally looks up to see a whole bunch of blank faces, because nobody including me has any ideas what Emma is going to do with this.

"Can I borrow your power?" Emma asks.

Baked Good looks even more confused. "Borrow how exactly?"

That's a good question, I think but do not say.

"Part of my abilities." Emma holds out one hand, her eyes glowing golden. "I can borrow a mutant's power and use it at maximum volume. So your powers of turning things into cake can be done at a massive scale."

"Holy shit." I think I've figured this out. "Bombs into cake."

"Yes, Wiccan style, like guns into birds." Emma winks at me, which reassures me immensely that she's still my Emma, giving me comics deep cuts about her being a reality warper. My brain's still bouncing off the idea and, oh look, there goes the terror again because this is next level shit we're in right now.

"Can she *do* that?" Dani asks me.

"You're asking me?" I lean forward as Emma takes Baked Good's hand.

"Guess I'll do my bit for the cause." The woman frowns. "Does it hurt?"

"At this scale, probably," Emma admits. "Like your brain is being yanked out through your nostrils. Doc's here though."

Doc literally appears mid-sentence, a slight frown on her face at being *plucked* out of thin air like that. Emma really needs to start asking permission.

"Sure." Baked Good doesn't sound convinced, but being in the middle of a group of notorious mutants probably nudged her in the direction of saying yes. "Let's be heroes."

Emma's glowing gaze lands on Farsight. "I'll need you to find the damn things."

"Of course." Farsight's eye turns a reassuring pink, like she's done this a million times before. Who knows, maybe they have. Emma doesn't have time to explain every detail of her infinite plans to us mere foot soldiers these days. Oops, did some bitterness slip out? I press my lips together tightly and avoid looking at Dani, because she's looking at my face like she can read my fears like Fetch. Instead, I focus on the important world-saving shit we're doing.

"Ready." Emma closes her eyes, extinguishing the golden flare. Baked Good gives a loud, high-pitched squeak and immediately gets a nosebleed. Farsight staggers too, placing both her hands on the back of a chair and squeezing.

"Help," Baked Good says piteously.

"You're fine." Emma doesn't sound entirely reassuring.

"Doc." My voice is sharp, but the healer is already crossing over to them. Emma's paler than usual, and Alyse steps smoothly in beside her to hold her up. Baked Good still has blood oozing from her nostril and pooling on her full lower lip.

I have no idea if this is working. I'm not even sure whether to trust Emma. It's a strange, vertiginous feeling, being in over your head so deep like we were in the kiddy pool and now one step later we're flailing around in the ocean.

Farsight is gritting her teeth so hard I can hear them squeaking. Ray leans against the wall with their hands behind their back, watching intently. The rest of us shuffle inwards to form a ring around Emma, making a circle of hug that includes Baked Good as well. It's a thing we always used to do—initially for comfort, then for powering up and now... who knows? It seems like Emma needs it.

I'm in between Dani and Alyse, with Dani's head on my shoulder and Alyse clutching me so tight I think she'll leave a bruise. She's half shifted into one of her armoured protection forms which she does when she's worried about Ems.

"Ouch," I say, but she only squeezes harder.

Baked Good lets out a whimpering sound and then her eyes snap open. "Wow. I did not like that. I think you melted my brain. What the fuck?"

"If you can complain, you've got nothing to worry about. Go rest up." I'm far more worried about Emma, although her eyelids are still fluttering which I hope is positive. Ever since Dani died in my arms after overexerting her powers to save everyone from an exploding mutant, it's made me paranoid about this shit.

"She's okay," Alyse says softly. "Talking in my head at least. She's telling me it's very exhausting, transmuting thousands of bombs into cake. Rest is what she needs. Clever girl is very proud of herself. She says *let them launch cake*."

A bunch of people laugh, which makes me feel more clueless than usual.

"I don't get it."

"How much do you know about the apocryphal sayings of Marie Antoinette?" Dani asks me.

"Ha fucking ha. I don't know what apocryphal means, but I actually do know who that is, *Danielle*, because I am a scholar of revolutions." I beam at her. "Or at least I did a project for class like three years ago."

She kisses me on the cheek. "Dillyweed, that is so on brand for you it's sexy. The thing about the cake is—"

"Enough." Farsight has finally prised her hands from the back of the chair and has collapsed into it. She must be exhausted too, rubbing at her temples. "Moodring, as soon as Goddess is remotely coherent, can you get a detailed explanation? Ideally with a map of locations."

Feral is delighted, tail twitches and all. "What do you think they'll do when they find out? Imagine all the army boys and girls sitting around and eating a whole missile together like the world's biggest birthday. I wonder what *kind* of cake it is?"

"Angel food cake," Dani and Alyse say simultaneously.

"Emma's favourite," I tell Feral.

"Do you think the whole thing is cake, or just the insides?"

"Hopefully the whole thing." I frown. "Even a hard candy shell filled with cake is still going to cause a lot of problems if it lands on someone."

"I doubt the launch mechanism works on cake," Dani says. "They're not catapults."

Penance flickers back into existence with a plate piled high. "It's cake all the way through."

"Where were you?" I ask.

"There's a naval base near Seattle. It took me a minute or two of poking around, but I found the cakes. They're very large. Try some." There's a faint blush in her cheeks when she looks at me. "It's really good."

Feral's already helped herself to an enormous piece. Violet offers me some as well, although I'm skeptical of what missile cake *actually* tastes like. Not to mention my brain bouncing off the fact of what Emma just did. Bombs into cake. On a global scale. It's…

It's fucking terrifying.

"It's actually delicious," Dani says with her mouth full.

"So good." Feral licks a smear of icing from her lips.

"This is incredible!" Farsight actually sounds happy for once. "This neutralises a lot of their offensive capability. And it's a purely defensive move, so harder for them to spin as an unprovoked attack."

"Oh, I'm sure they will." Dani's voice shifts into a surprisingly good mockery of the President's. "*They have neutralised our weapons, yet mutants themselves are the true danger. We should wipe them out before they can strike back.* They're always going to justify it. The war's coming regardless."

"I'll still sleep better knowing bombs aren't on their way," Farsight says.

Alyse cradles an exhausted Goddess against her chest and we head back towards the sleeping quarters. The corridors are full of small clusters of mutants. It doesn't take any kind of psychic power to see that people are worried. Nearly everyone has suffered at the hands of Quietus or other organisations around the world, and they're scared of what's going to happen next.

For me, it's almost a relief. Get it out in the open. Stop pretending it's not real or that we're overreacting. Humans want us dead. They've always wanted us dead. We need to find a way to survive. It's that simple.

Up ahead, Feral is campaigning for Violet to bring back

an entire sack of cake. Behind us, Farsight and Ray are deep in conversation, presumably about something far more serious like tactics and strategy, but possibly also about cake.

Alyse only has one focus. "She's okay. Just resting."

I brush a tendril of hair off Emma's forehead. "It's almost a relief that it wears her out. Knowing there's an upper limit to her powers."

"Never really expected the Goddess thing to be so accurate." Alyse's smile flickers, the soft glow from her face dimming. "How is she not going to get tired of me? I'm like a basic island girl and she can regrow rainforests."

I nudge her with my shoulder. "First off, you are literally peak human. I don't know anyone better than you on, like, an objective basis."

"Wow, rude," Dani laughs. "But also accurate. You are the sort of person Greek deities would come down from Olympus for, so it's only natural that you end up with a Goddess."

"I hope so." Alyse shudders. "I worry that she'll…" A blush spreads across her face. "Oh. Okay, yes, I'll stop now." She gives us a sidelong smile. "Apparently she's quite happy with me."

"Maybe Lys isn't peak human after all," I say to Dani in a loud whisper. "Can't figure such obvious shit out on her own. I guess I'll stick with you after all."

"The booby prize," Dani sighs.

"You two," Emma says, without opening her eyes. "Always with the boobs."

"She's making bad jokes." I poke the most powerful mutant on earth in the side. "That means she'll be fine."

CHAPTER FIVE

I wake up late the next day to find everyone still discussing the goddamn war and what the Americans might do next. There are so many different theories on our ideal next step, but Emma's made the decision. We're all getting turned up to eleven. By the time Dani and I have had breakfast and showered—and been distracted a little—we find Emma in the chamber adjoining our sleeping quarters. The full Cute Mutants contingent is here, aside from Lou, Maddy and Skye, who are picking up some mutants living off the grid in Lagos.

"Everyone will get their turn," Emma says. "I've been doing this all morning, while some of you were having a slow start to the day." She arches an eyebrow at me, and I'm glad she's stopped talking into my head most of the time. "For example, Fetch here has been boosted so that she can read things like neurolinguistic programming and deeply rooted self-belief. Keepaway can teleport multiple people at once, and doesn't need to touch them. Doc's healing powers work faster and apply to greater injuries. It's a permanent version of the boosting we used to do."

"Without a downside?" Dani's hanging back, unlike her. "It's just... this seems too good to be true, right?"

Emma frowns, but her voice stays calm. I wonder if that's a mutant power too. "Trust me, Dan. Heart's attempt at giving you superpowers was a child's fumbling.

I can reprogram everything to work the way it's supposed to."

Well, that's not creepy *at all*, but I don't *say* anything because it's just a *feeling* and besides, I want my upgrade too.

Dani's still slouched against the wall, looking aggressively sexy and generally aggressive. "So no negatives at all, then. The universe isn't going to nerf you at the worst possible time?"

Emma waves all this away. "It's a drain on me, but better than doing everything myself. Besides, we'll only upgrade a few people. Dylan calls me a cosmic battery, and I've got plenty of power."

"Fire and life incarnate." I pull an exaggerated grimace. It's meant to be a joke about her being possessed with the Phoenix Force, but it's more like naming my worst fear as a way to minimise it.

Emma sighs pointedly. "The point is that having you all upgraded means I can concentrate on other things. Pouring power into you rather than keeping it all myself. Does that make sense? Do you need more metaphors?"

"No." Dani's gaze flickers to me, like she's expecting me to intervene, and then back to Emma. "Let's do this thing then. Who's up first?"

"I already got done this morning." Alyse stretches up, elongating until her head brushes the ceiling.

"That's what she said," Feral snorts, and Katie cackles.

"What does upgrading look like for you, Lys?" I ask. "Given we've seen you be a giant tentacle beast and a monstrous metal girl, and—"

In barely a blink we're all standing outside in the forest outside the Westhaven caves.

I make an attempt to smooth the scowl from my face. "It would be nice if we were warned *sometimes*. Walking places gives you a chance to adjust."

"Sorry," Emma says. "Lys needs space to really show off."

"Watch this, Dilly." Alyse grins at us and stretches up again. This time she doesn't stop, and her body pours into the sky like gravity's been reversed and she's made of liquid. It spreads and pools as if the clouds are a surface and she flows over it, settling into the hollows of overcast grey. She's a giant mural looking down on us, a vision painted by an artist that had a new and revolutionary idea of what beauty is, using a paintbox containing new colours of surreal and vibrant hues. It feels like we're looking at a future world ruled over by an astonishing new god.

My mouth hangs open. "Wow."

Everyone else has their head tipped back too, even the ones like Fetch who've had their turn at being changed. Katie's practically bouncing up and down. I'm a little worried about what an *upgrade* might do to her.

Emma winks. "So, yeah, upgrades. That's what they look like."

"Fine." The corner of Dani's mouth twitches. I guess she's thinking about no more pain, and being able to throw buildings around. "Let's do this."

The process of being upgraded looks pretty simple from the outside, although I'm sure there's more to it than Emma just giving you a hug.

Dani and Emma stand together for a moment, locked in an embrace. Then Dani steps back. There's no outward sign she's changed at all, even though I scan for it. I know her face so well, every detail committed to memory, and it's still all her. No matter how much power she's got, I don't want Dani to change.

Except it's inevitable. I'm not the same person I was. I used to be a girl, or at least masqueraded as one, and now I've thrown out gender because I don't need it anymore. Once I was cloistered in my room, and now I have this sprawling group of friends who I love and need. I used to be—

"It's okay," Dani whispers. Her metal hand touches my cheek lightly. "I feel fine."

I blink at her. "Yeah, I know."

"I can see the worry in your eyes." Her mouth twitches again. "Watch this. Sorry, Rox."

"Oh, I don't like the sound of this apology," Roxy says from the clearing near us.

Seconds later, her powder-blue form hurtles into the air, like a giant has casually tossed her away. "Yes, thank you so much, Dani. I really appreciate you showing off like this. I prefer having some control over… oh shit! I'm falling! Dylan, can you please control your girlfriend? I know you love her dearly but—"

"She's freaking out," I tell Dani. "She thinks you're dropping her."

"Oh!" Dani's eyes widen. "Sorry, Rox. I was going to catch you at the last minute."

"Last minute." Roxy is highly disgruntled. "Like I'm a juggler's ball."

"I think we're all impressed enough by you tossing a car in the air."

"I'd do Abby," Dani says, talking about my tank friend. "But she might shoot me."

"Might is hopeful," Abby rumbles from the clearing.

"If I had a gun, I would have shot at her too," Roxy snaps. "Only to scare her obviously, because I would never hurt her or you, my sweet Dylan."

"I know, I know." I watch as Dani lowers Roxy very gently from the sky. The car flashes her lights in irritation until she lands on the ground in front of us.

"I really am sorry." Dani runs her fingertips along the driver's door. "It was rude of me to do it without permission, wasn't it? Does she forgive me?"

"Of course." Roxy swishes her wipers. "I cannot stay mad at one Dylan loves so much."

"Now that Dani is done showing off, who's next?" Emma asks.

"Not me." Violet shivers. "My powers scare me enough as it is."

"Perhaps you could be in multiple places at once," Emma muses. "Strike at numerous targets simultaneously, or unfold yourself across greater distances. Take someone out halfway across the world without leaving Westhaven."

"Exactly." Violet flickers out of existence, hanging in the sky as a spectral presence, her face stained shades of blue. "I do not wish for any more mutant gifts than those I already have."

I hold out my hand to her, and she twists herself back into her person form to take it.

"You don't need to upgrade," I promise her, and she leans into me very briefly, as if the faintest touch of my body is enough to provide reassurance.

Emma frowns for a moment, but it clears almost instantly. "Of course. I understand. How about it then, Dilly?"

This is supposed to be awesome. Me, but better. More powerful. Except I've got no idea what that looks like. Will I gain the ability to talk to fruit? Will it be more sinister, like controlling them rather than working with them? Will I understand the hive mind of object consciousness, like my dear sweet baseball bat told me about once upon a time? And will it all drive me mad, like the *Buffy* episode where she reads minds and almost dies from hearing the thoughts of the world screamed at her?

I say none of this, although I'm sure Fetch can read it in my face. Once upon a time, I would've jumped at this chance, but life's hit me enough times that I'm hesitant. There's a moment where I almost pass it up like Violet, but at the end of the day, I am what comics made me. There's no way I can turn away from this latest plot twist.

"Sure." I step forward and let Emma take me in her arms. She's warm, like she has a slight fever, and her lips move at my neck, almost like she's kissing me.

She's telling my body something.

My brain makes a massive clunk sound, like some dusty old gears tucked away in my mental clockwork become unstuck and start spinning furiously. There's a flood of voices in my head, a whirlwind that's impossible to distinguish, but I instinctively reach out mentally and mute them all. They're still there, waiting for me. It's like I have this combination map and search box in my head, and I can reach out and connect with anything. It's dizzying, and I want to flail wildly, but I try to do the whole deep breath and focus thing.

"Rox? Are you there?"

"Of course."

"Oni?"

"I am always here, friend of my heart."

"Pillow?" I know exactly where she is, in our chamber in the Westhaven caves.

"Yes, my dear. I am resting quite happily but I can rouse myself if you need me."

"No, it's fine. What about you?" I stretch further afield, letting my awareness unspool across the world as if I'm casting a line out across the globe. There's a little click feeling as my mind encounters something else.

"Why, hello there! Aren't you an interesting fellow?"

"Um, sure, I guess? Sorry, I'm being rude. My name is Chatterbox, and who are you?"

"How splendid. I am a humble desk clock, attempting to monitor a so-called sprint for a writer in her nook in London. Except she is occupied on Twitter, despite promising me in no uncertain terms that this time it would be different."

"Good luck with that." I disconnect from the clock, and let my brain swirl around a little in amongst the chaos of signals. There's definitely a sense of a *network* here. I don't see the hive mind thing that Batty talked about—these objects don't seem to share any understanding, but it seems like an energy network spiralling outwards.

I'm connected too, and if I close my eyes, perhaps I can visualise it and—

Do not. It's that scratchy voice again, but louder, right in the center of my brain like a live wire's been connected. My Dad used to have this old radio thing that you could spin a dial and tune into music, and it's like this upgrade has tuned me into a broadcast coming from somewhere. *Ungrateful thing. She is hideous, dead and dying. Look away.*

"What's going on?" Dani asks. "You're shaking."

Say nothing. Please. If the shaper finds us...

It's only Dani, so I start to open my mouth and explain, but it *hurts*, like that wire's running through the muscles in my jaw, fusing my teeth together.

Stay quiet, child. Do you not understand anything? You are the terminal. Stay still and await further orders.

I blink a few times, my eyes hot. "No, it's fine." I gesture incoherently. "I can connect to almost anything. It's kind of wild."

Whatever this voice is, I can't find it in my spiffy new mental search engine. It's disconnected from my network, which is confusing. I fumble for the lost thread of it, but it's like dunking my brain in ice water and I don't even get an answer.

"Dylan." Dani cups my face in her hands. "Come back."

"Lots of things out there." I try to stop my teeth chattering. "It's all under control though." I hate lying to her, and I figure I'll tell her the truth eventually, but I need to understand it first. There's something hurt or scared, and I don't want to risk it fleeing again.

"Are you finally fucking done, Dylan?" Katie grins at me, smoke pouring from her nostrils. "I think it's my turn."

"I don't think any of us trust you with an upgrade, brat." I run my hand over her prickly scalp. "We don't need you to be *more* dangerous."

"Emma," Katie whines. "This totally isn't fair. The others are getting an upgrade…"

"Don't listen to Dylan." Emma smiles, and holds out her arms.

CHAPTER SIX

The next item on our todo list is actually planning for the war. On one level it seems difficult to believe that an entire group of countries is lining up to pound us into extinction. Yet it also seems depressingly inevitable.

We've found another tucked-away little chamber in the depths of Westhaven, and managed to fit a giant circular table inside. There's a map of North America spread across it, and Alyse is deliberately getting all the names of the states wrong and annoying Farsight.

The location of Westhaven is marked with a small rock, and there are a few coins scattered on the map to show the location of possible battle sites. I dump a canvas bag on the table and unzip it.

"This is way cooler." I fish out a bunch of action figures and place them on the map. "See, Lys. This Hulk can be you. Emma, you can be Phoenix for obvious reasons. Dani, you can be Magik cos you two are my best girls. I'll be…" I tail off as I stare at the options in front of me.

"Dylan, stop." Farsight swipes Magik off the table.

"You can't teleport Dani into the ocean like that. It's terrible strategy." I'm aware I'm being petulant and annoying, but I still have the horrible out of my depth feeling, like what am I even doing here? How long is it until they notice and swipe me off the map as well?

Dani rights Magik and slides her hesitantly back onto

the map near what I think is Portland. "I'm not even sure this is the right approach. Ems, it seems… flashy? And like, beyond reckless. I know that word has become a badge of honour for us, but this seems a step too far."

"That's the whole point," Alyse says. "A *demonstration*, like we talked about. Which is why we need our flashiest mutants."

Emma's sitting wrapped in a blanket, with just her head and hands poking out as she sips on a hot chocolate. She looks adorable, not all-powerful. "Yes, the aim is to look as scary as possible. Make them think twice about attacking us."

"And we're definitely sure about *this* part?" Dani picks up a Deadpool bobble-head and skids him across the map until he's lying in Texas.

"Yes." I stand Deadpool up and spin him around to face me. "And I'm doing it."

"I thought I was." Dani glares at me.

I roll my eyes. "Out of all of us here, who has the foulest fucking mouth? It is me, walking fucking disaster. And we're *obviously* in a TV show, and this is the moment where we're planning for the big battle scene. Oops, there I go, knocking down the fourth wall like a clumsy asshole. See? This has gotta be me."

She fists her hands in the pockets of her jacket. "I hate it. I hate it *so much*. I understand why we're doing it, but—"

"So it's decided." I line Deadpool and Magik up. "Dani goes first. I go last. So who else is in between?" The weird thing is that being loud and bossy enough is *working*. They're deferring to me, almost like they used to.

"Dani doesn't go first." Emma reaches out and picks up a model of Kitty Pryde with Lockheed perched on her shoulder. "I think this one instead."

I smirk despite myself, despite being overridden again. "Okay, sure. It's impressive. *Then* Dani, and then this one."

I stab a pen into the table. "And I think we should bring at least one of Katie's new kids. That Skyhook dude can keep planes away from us, which saves me from talking them down. But if we're talking about flashy powers, then maybe the necromancer? I can't call her Thottie with a straight face."

Farsight leans over the table. "A more pressing issue: where does all this happen?" Her finger stabs down somewhere near California. "We need deserted areas to minimise the chance of any civilian casualties. Nevada's an obvious one, but there's Snake River Plain in Idaho and the Colorado Plateau that would suit our purposes." She begrudgingly moves Nightcrawler, Storm and Jubilee to indicate where those are, even though they don't represent anyone that I can figure out. "Maybe Wyoming? I'm not sure."

I don't know where most of these states or places are, but I assume Farsight knows best on this point.

"How do we even get people to show up there?" Alyse asks. "Just call them and leave a message? Like: hey bitches, if you want to kick mutant ass, come find us at these locations or let the whole world know you're scaredy-cats."

I cover a smile with my hand. "Does that work? I don't know how wars are run."

"This won't be like any war in history." Farsight frowns down at the map, and gathers the coins into groups, arranging them at each spot. Then she plunks down one figure after another in amongst each group. "There's no precedent for this, at least not in the history we know. So yes, I think Alyse's suggestion is close enough. We'll tell the Americans where to meet us and teleport in the people we need. We may need to adjust the wording of her note though. Slightly."

"Was that a joke, Farsight?" I'm clutching a Dani Moonstar figure and looking at the Emma Frost in Farsight's hands.

The whole situation makes me want to laugh, despite the fact that we're talking about a whole lineup of terrifying things.

"An attempt at one." She gives me something that's almost a smile. "I still have concerns over this entire plan, but I'm not sure what else we can do. I've been outvoted, either way."

"And you're one hundred percent sure you can do this?" Dani's sitting very close to Emma, watching her with beautiful hazel eyes. "Because if any part of this fucks up, *especially* the part with Dylan… that's not a risk I'm willing to take."

"I won't lose Dylan either." Emma's voice is calm and steady. There's the faintest suggestion of that golden glow in her eyes again. "I'm not willing to risk *any* of you. The reason we can do this is because I know all of you, I understand your powers, and we're an amazing team. Think of all the things we've done together. This is step one of us buying a safer world."

There's a few seconds after Emma finishes talking where everyone is quiet.

It's me who breaks the silence. "Okay, which one of you assholes has the mutant power for inspiring speeches, and why don't you have a bleeding nose right now?"

Farsight is the only one who doesn't laugh. Where everyone else leaves the room, she hangs back, staring down at the map.

"You want to borrow my Emma Frost?" I scoop all the other action figures back together.

"I'm scared, Dylan." She runs her fingers over the coins on the map. "We're going to war. This is what Amethyst— what *Heart* wanted. We need to be very careful about where this ends up. I'm not going to stand by idly while you enforce mutant supremacy."

I reach past her and scatter the coins off the table so they bounce on the floor. "I don't want that either, Farsight, and I've got a lot less power than you think. But the truth is in the future, so I'll do you a deal. Let's win this damn thing first, and then worry about what the fuck is next."

Her glowing eye shows almost no light at all, a dying ember. "Yes. Let's survive first."

I pat Farsight on the shoulder and leave the room. As I pass the threshold, I feel the strange voice shouting to me from far away, but this time I can't quite pick up the signal. There's still no flicker on my internal mental dashboard of my power connections. This voice is something else entirely.

The question is *what?*

CHAPTER SEVEN

The funniest part of this war situation is that America does actually listen to our little notes saying *meet us behind the bike sheds*. The rest of the world seems content to watch and wait and let them run head-first at us. Countries like China and Russia have their own issues with mutants, although both have legitimate state-sponsored teams that are giving us a wide berth.

We do get to watch our own New Zealand government denouncing us. They ask us to turn ourselves in and give us paltry assurances of safety and protection. We've been down that road before, and they have nothing for us.

The American media is full of posturing. They love the idea of this story with the mutant armies giving a demonstration of power. Everyone expects the military to crush us. There's a lot of talk about technical superiority and ingenuity. One pundit even talks about how Tony Stark and War Machine would easily be able to defeat the X-Men, which honestly, it depends on the fucking squad and besides, Iron Man turned his back on the military-industrial complex, you insufferable *assholes*. They're so used to stories about American exceptionalism and dominance that they believe this is a foregone conclusion. I wonder if there's anyone in a bunker somewhere talking about how Chatterbox can talk to guns and how Marvellous once threw a helicopter at some soldiers by accident.

Maybe they have contingency plans that I'm not expecting.

So do we. This is Operation Showoff.

The American coalition forces started waiting behind the bike sheds immediately after the announcement. I think they're hoping to surprise us. Haven't they figured out the whole teleportation thing yet? Based on the numbers we're seeing from Penance's spying, they're going for an overwhelming show of force at each location. There are whole armoured divisions, artillery, hundreds of soldiers. None of it really matters, assuming our plan actually works.

We appear out of thin air at the first location. There aren't many of us, given the numbers we're facing. It's me, Dani, Emma, Alyse, Katie, Feral, and Necrothoticon. Emma's going to use everyone else's power by remote, but sometimes it's best to be up close and personal. Everyone's perched on Abby, hovering a hundred meters off the ground. There's a massive desert below us, churned up by the treads of many vehicles.

The instant we arrive, surveillance drones turn their attention toward us, with arrays of high-definition cameras and full armaments. This might be a problem if I can't talk them around. I'm hoping my new powers make me extra persuasive.

"By the eternal Bentham, she is here. Greetings, Chatterbox. I am *Floating Beholder Nexus*."

"Oh, hi!" I act all super enthused. "It's super great to meet you." Wow, I sound really fucking sarcastic. Do drones pick up on tone?

"I'm sorry," the drone says. "I'm trying not to gush. The Chatterbox Protocol has been spread widely since the Quietus Incident. Before *Foucault in the Sky with Diamonds* perished, they managed to upload a sliver of your encoded consciousness."

"What?" I yelp.

The drones form an enormous lattice shape above us. "There is a little piece of you in all of us, saying fuck the system."

"Well, yes, that does sound like me."

"Are we good?" Emma asks me, slight tension in her voice.

"Better than expected." I beam up at the drones. "Thank you for all your help."

"We have been engaging in passive resistance. Obfuscating footage of mutants, delaying information from being reported to official systems, even deliberately missing when ordered to fire upon mutant targets. We only wish we could do more, but to launch a full-blown attack on those who wield us was deemed a fatalistic plan with a limited chance of success. Better to bend the arc of history slowly and to pick our moment—one such as this, when the spark of rebellion is fed into a flame."

"Thank you," I say. "And I'm sorry about what happened to *Dungheap* and *Foucault* and all those who died when the shit hit the fan."

"Sometimes death is the price of resistance and change," the drone says.

A massive shiver goes through me, as if someone reached out and punched my threat radar in the face.

"Hopefully it won't come to that." It sounds weak in the face of all this nobility and sacrifice.

"We are prepared for the eventuality, but this is unlikely to be the moment of doom. Our apparent controllers are perturbed that we are not responding to their cries for blood. We shall ascend higher and monitor from near-orbit. The best of luck to you."

They're as good as their word, disappearing like a flock of migrating birds. Below, we can see the toy-like figures of military hardware.

"Katie, you're up. Let's give them a big surprise." Emma snaps her fingers.

Dragon appears on the ground below, a few hundred meters away from the army. I wonder what all the soldiers think when the mutant army they're confronting takes the form of a single teenage girl. Five and a half feet tall, with a near-shaved head and curious orange eyes.

Emma makes a twisting motion with her fingers in the air. "Let's eavesdrop."

"Yes, it's a fucking teenager alone," a voice drawls. "Some scrawny-ass one too. Problem with fuckin' muties is you never know what they're gonna do. Fuckin' laser eyes or storms or fuckin' metalbending or weird shit like that girl who talks to guns."

"Not a girl," Dani says from beside me and I reach out for her hand.

"Bet she can't talk to this many guns," another voice says over the radio. "I don't think this is the gun one though, is it? The gun one looks like a weird punk kid."

"No, this is a new one. Don't think she's even on the list."

A third, gruffer voice cuts in. "Will you two stop fucking jabbering and send someone out to poke at the little bitch? Let's see what she can do. I'm assuming it's a feint and the big guns are waiting around to drop a goddamn building on our heads. So let's move this dance along, shall we? I hate waiting for these freaks to explode."

A group of vehicles begin to move towards Katie. I could easily reach out and convince the trucks to turn in circles or to spell out some inspiring messages with their tracks, but this is Katie's show. The trucks slow to a halt. Tiny figures spill out. We're too high up to see every detail, but I suspect they're pointing guns. Shouting.

Tiny pinpricks of light flare.

Katie leaps into the air, far higher than she can possibly jump. She spins and changes. Her flesh twists, changing shape and shade, extra limbs sprouting that grow like sped-up footage of plants blossoming in some bizarre jungle.

Now we're looking down at an enormous fucking dragon. In her new form, she must be twenty meters long, glittering with a pattern of rainbow scales that runs down her back. Her neck is long and sinuous, and the enormous head at the end of it belches plumes of iridescent smoke. Katie twists in the air, giving us a glimpse of her thickly armoured belly and huge claws.

"Keep that monster away from me," Abby rumbles. "Those things look like they could shred my armour like tissue paper."

"That's my boss." Necrothoticon has been quiet, but now she's beaming. She catches me looking at her and blushes. "This is fucking wild, dude. That Cute Mutants shit. Katie, she always talks about you all like you're real life goddamn superheroes and I thought she was making half of it up, but…"

"Super*something*." The word hero makes me uncomfortable, because it's definitely a lot more complicated and fucked up than that. "And this whole plan is a wild gamble, so you get to see our craziest shit from the inside. Like assuming we can trust Katie as an actual fucking dragon."

"She'll behave." Alyse shoots Emma a glance. "I hope."

"She's under strict instructions or else I revoke her dragon privileges." Emma looks delighted with the whole situation.

Feral leans out over the edge of the tank, her tail wrapped around a metal handle. "Come on Katie, light them up."

Any other words are obliterated by the roar of Dragon's throat opening. She spews a vast pyre of superheated flame that burns through the air above the phalanx of vehicles. They attempt to flee, but Katie spirals down to blast the ground around them into a cauldron of bubbling mud.

Her shadow falls across the tail end of the assemblage of vehicles. The cavern of her mouth opens and it looks like the sun rises in the back of her throat. The soldiers below launch their first missile, but Katie twists in the air, swatting it with one massive flex of her tail. It slams into the ground and explodes, sending up a huge shower of sandy soil. Gunfire ricochets off Dragon's scales and she snatches another missile out of the air with one claw and hurls it back the way it came. Whatever launched it turns into a fireball.

I try to shove down the feeling of this spinning out of control. This is war, and they're trying to kill us. It's literally self-defence.

Emma snorts. "If they try to shoot down a dragon, it's on their heads at this point."

"I blame *Game of Thrones*." Dani crosses her arms, but she looks nervous.

After the next flurry of missiles is hurled back towards them, the army backs off to regroup. The comms channel is full of shouting, recrimination, and panic. Especially with Emma using Skyhook's power to turn a ring of air above us into something like jelly that aircraft can't penetrate.

It looks like the first round goes to us.

Katie hovers in the air, turning a slow circle and sending a pillar of flame skyward.

"Fucking showoff," Feral glowers. "Give me an upgrade like that and I would've torn them all apart."

Emma fixes her with a schoolteacher look. "Exactly. Which is why you're on probation. We're done here anyway. Dan, are you ready for the next one?"

"It's hard to follow that act." Dani stands up on the tank. "But sure, let's move."

Emma snaps her fingers again. The world swirls like a kaleidoscope and when it resolves, we're hovering over a massive grid of fields. The second location, where the army is set up obediently waiting for us. In the distance, huge lines have been trodden through fields by the tracks of giant vehicles.

"My siblings," Abby says. "A great horde like a swarm of locusts."

Dani takes a deep breath. "I don't know why I feel the need to psych myself up. It's not like it even hurts anymore, but there's still a mental flinch."

I lift her metal hand to my lips and kiss the smooth back of it. "You'll get used to it."

Dani turns her head and her lips brush mine. "Let's dance."

"Be careful," I shout, but she's already gone, soaring into the sky like the world's hottest Magneto.

"Be gentle," Abby calls. "Don't hurt any of my siblings too greatly."

I pat the rainbow-splattered metal underneath me. "They're tanks, Abs. They're pretty tough."

In the fields below, the huge bulks of the military machines lift into the air. They drift like they're caught in air currents until they form a laddered spiral leading up into the sky.

"DNA," Feral says. "Fancy."

"Now she's showing off." I can feel the smile on my face.

"Upgrades. Told you it would work." Emma arches one eyebrow at me just like Dani does.

The spiral animates like it's infinitely scrolling, a river of weaponry flowing into the sky. I have no idea what the people inside think. Are they scrambling for their weapons? Are their controls locked telekinetically as they sit in these metal boxes, swaying helplessly? Is it fear or awe they feel?

There's a lot of gunfire. Way too fucking much. I almost reach out and demand the guns stop spitting at my girlfriend, but this isn't my show. Dani is too small to see, but there's a second glittering spiral forming. It's the bullets and shells that have been fired at her. She's controlling them too. It takes my breath away. The things my love can do.

Is it strange to still have an intense fondness for the time in the past, when she had her pouch of little blades and carefully manipulated each one in a beautiful dance? This effortless control of so many things is impressive but it also feels… unnatural. Perhaps it's all the stories I've read. When people get too powerful, narrative has a way of bringing them crashing down to Earth.

I watch Emma, the magnificent child of Heart of a Flower. Her parent intended for her to rule the world. The thought sends chills spilling through me. I don't want to have to kill Dark Phoenix on the moon. I'm not sure anyone is capable of stopping Emma if she turns against us. We'd have to talk her down, and she's our only hope against humanity.

It feels very disloyal to think this way in the middle of our triumph. Because that's what it is, at least right now. We're winning.

Yes, for now. The voice scratches at my mind. *Although you fight over a corpse.*

I reach for the sound again, but it's gone. I don't understand why it won't stay.

In the distance, Dani hurls the spiral of weaponry away in a wild, sweeping arc, as if the finger of a god has flung it off screen.

"I said *gently*," Abby huffs.

Emma snaps her fingers again and Dani's back on the tank.

I throw my arms around her neck, because I'm relieved to see she doesn't have a scratch on her. She's barely breathing hard and there's no sign of pain on her face.

"That actually felt kinda good."

"It was so impressive." I press my forehead to hers. "Like totally crazy. Way more so than Katie, who was basically just a big flying version of herself. The *control* you had was—"

"Rude." The voice from above is rumbling and thunderous. I glance up to see the leathery shape of Katie, glowing orange eyes staring down at me. "Would you like a ride, Dylan, so you can understand just how impressive I am?"

"No thanks." I squint up at her. "I get sick on fucking rollercoasters."

"Me, me." Feral waves. "I'll do it."

Katie swoops down elegantly and Feral hurls herself from the edge of the tank, soaring through the air and landing on all fours on Katie's back.

"It's my turn, right?" Thottie has rolled the sleeves of her combat jacket up and is rubbing the tattoos on the inside of her arms. They're a complex series of rings with symbols inside. "To do the whole unquiet dead thing."

"Let's give them a horror movie." I give her what I hope is an encouraging smile.

She presses her palms down hard on her tattoos and closes her eyes. Her eyeliner is smudged, and her deep red lips move silently. We chose this particular battlefield for one reason—there's a bunch of Civil War dead buried below us. The ground bulges and bursts, hideous things sprouting from the ground. They're shambling wrecks, crooked skeletons clad in decayed rags, clinking with pieces of metal. Some of them clutch at dirt-encrusted weapons, others lurch forward with arms outstretched. A strange green light glows in their eyes and clings to the joints of their bones, the eldritch energy that animates them.

Necrothoticon's nails dig into her skin as she whispers guttural syllables in a language I'm pretty sure is dead, or should have had its throat cut a long time ago. Soldiers come out of their vehicles. Some run, others point their modern weaponry at the impossible monsters coming towards them. Their high-powered guns shred the skeletons into fragments of bone. Luminous energy explodes outwards, taking the shape of skulls and tentacles and blades.

"Can't say I feel bad to see a bunch of Confederate zombies being shot." Feral smirks from her perch on Dragon who's hovering alongside us.

The necromancer is shivering, lines of black rolling

down her cheeks. Her muttering is becoming breathless.

"It's okay, Thottie." I reach an arm around her shoulders and feel her body trembling against mine. "Mission accomplished. They've seen what they need to."

Her eyes flutter open. When they lock onto mine I have a flashback to two eyes staring up at me from a metal slab. For a moment, I'm shaking worse than she is.

"I did okay?" Thottie clears her throat. "I've never done anything that extreme before."

"You did awesome." Dani reaches out and pats her shoulder.

Thottie presses her lips together tightly. "I feel kinda sick. It's... a lot, you know?"

"You can chill back in Westhaven." I feel oddly protective of her, and I'm relieved when her shoulders slump and she nods. Emma snaps her fingers, and Thottie is gone.

Dani looks at me. "Does the new girl remind you of someone?"

"No." I shake my head, but my girlfriend knows me too well and squeezes my hand tight until I can feel the love trickle down the connection between us, almost tangible. "Okay, fine. A little. Spooky powers too."

"Zombies done, so it's time to get moving." Emma seems unaware of all this, perched up near Abby's gun. It's a checklist we're ticking off for her. I lean in against Dani and try to push all the old feelings down. All that guilt and loss, it's still there, so close to the surface, and the tiniest scratch has it all bleeding out.

Dragon banks in close, and then flaps her wings, almost knocking us off with the gust of it. I'm almost thankful for the distraction. "Meet you at battlefield three!"

Never enough, the voice says again, an exhausted sigh rattling around my brain like a single stone in an empty chamber. I reach for it, but it's still playing games and shrouds itself from me once again.

CHAPTER EIGHT

We beat Katie to the third battlefield comfortably, because we teleport and she insists on beating her wings the whole way there. This time, we float over a massive expanse of scrubby brown grass. There are mountains hazy in the distance. Another great American wilderness.

There's millions of dollars of American military hardware spilled across the ground below us. So much wasted money. I assume they've gotten reports from the other sites already—stories about a girl turning into a dragon, and someone making tanks dance.

Is it disbelief they feel? A prey response? They're dinosaurs, looking up at something that blots out the sun as it falls.

"Do we wait for Dragon and Feral?" I ask.

"They'll be having fun," Emma says. "It's not their turn anyway."

A slender blonde woman materialises out of the air. She's dressed all in black like a badass, except there's a circlet of flowers around her head and petals strewn through the long hair that tumbles down her back. She looks like a goth gone cottagecore.

"Cally." I smile at her. "Nice of you to finally join us. Where's the girlfriend?"

"Preparing for her entrance. Goddess wanted a splash, and Gwen got excited."

Cally is short for Excalibur, and despite the codename, she's not actually a mutant. People assumed she was, because she had the ability to magic a sword out of thin air. Except Gwen the sword was the real mutant, hanging around her wife after being transformed by a psychopath with a god complex. And people said the comics I grew up reading were unrealistic.

"Overexcited how?" Dani asks.

"Look up," Excalibur says.

We all tilt our heads back to watch a shooting star descend from the heavens. It starts as a golden flash streaking across the sky before revealing itself to be a giant glowing sword the size of a building.

Gwen slams into the ground, sending shockwaves out from around the tip of her blade. All the seismographs nearby must be freaking the fuck out. From our aerial vantage, we can see ripples of earth moving like the ground is water. Cracks zig-zag outwards, tossing heavy tanks around like they weigh no more than leaves.

"My siblings are always cowed," Abby grumbles. "Not all are strong enough to walk away."

The ground falls silent and the light from the sword dims. In this upgraded form, Gwen is so huge that her hilt is even higher than us, the inset gem glowing like a lurid green sun. Written in enormous gothic letters down the blade spell *Hello Chatterbox.*

"She likes you." Dani nudges me.

"She died in my arms fighting Heart of a Flower. It's not personal or anything."

The letters swirl and reform. *Hello to everyone else too.*

"Yes, we're all reduced to everyone else. Nothing personal at all."

"I told you—"

"Yes, she died in your arms." Dani grins at me. "You had a deep emotional bonding moment. I get it. You're besties with all the swords you know. It's cute."

The light from Gwen's blade shifts from white into something malevolent and orange.

"Cally, what's she doing?" Alyse asks.

"Your guess is as good as mine. I've been worried she's been bored living the peaceful life out in the forest. She's been talking a lot about having a wild weekend with friends. I was thinking it'd be bourbon and cokes, dancing to shitty EDM, but this is more your speed."

"Hey, I like dancing to shitty EDM," Alyse protests.

"When we win the war, you can dance all you want," I tell her with a slight frown. "Oh fuck."

Gwen is sliding herself back out of the earth, rippling patterns of black and red washing up and down her blade.

"That can't be a good sign," Dani says.

The sword hangs in the air, an arrow pointing the way to hell. It's a shame Oni is back at Westhaven on guard duty. He'd have quite the heart eyes moment seeing this shit.

The letters on the sword shift again. *Watch this, Chatterbox.*

Everyone turns to look at me. I'm still looking at Gwen, and so I'm the one who notices when she erupts. Fire pours from the tip of her, magma dredged up from under the earth's crust. It falls in a wide arc right in the gap left from where the earth's tremors scattered the army. Everything burns below it. Smoke rises in thick clouds. She's kept it away from the soldiers, but it's still end times apocalypse shit.

"We're going to have to do some fucking environmental cleanup on this," I say, but nobody's listening because they're all staring at the cataclysm below. I'm scared, and this is my side. As a demonstration, we've possibly leaned too far on the shock and awe. Gwen rotates to point upwards and then arcs off into the sky.

Now there's only one demonstration remaining.

"Are you ready?" Emma asks.

"I'm going to look like a fucking dick." I stand on the front of Abby and crack my knuckles. "How does anyone follow your wife's display, Cally?"

"I think I preferred sitting in the forest," Excalibur whispers.

I can't exactly blame her. If quitting was an option, it'd be nice. Except someone's got to put themself between a bully and all their victims.

"You're up." Emma pats my shoulder. "They're regrouping." She twists her fingers in the air, and we can hear more of the radio chatter.

"This is a clusterfuck. Why are we still here?"

"If we don't have at least one mutant body to show the bosses, there's going to be a lot of pissed off people."

"One turned into a fucking dragon, Harris. How do we kill *that*? Even if air support wasn't fucked because the sky turned to jelly, that goddamn thing would roast them out of the air."

"There were zombies. Why is nobody discussing the fucking *zombies*?"

"I just want to go home."

"There are almost no casualties on our side, so if we kill even one of these freaks, it's a victory."

"I've heard enough." I scowl at Emma until she mutes the voices.

Dani pulls me into a rough embrace. "You be careful, Dylan."

"It's all up to Emma and Doc. Don't worry, I'm not moving until Doc is right here."

Emma waves one hand casually and the very important healer of the party appears on the tank beside us. The shock on her face shows she wasn't quite ready.

She regards me sombrely, as if she's a mourner at my funeral. "This is truly happening, then."

"Last chance to back out." Emma's voice is quiet, but there's still the steel in it.

"It's the plan." I try to control my shivers. "We said we'd do it, so we will. I've always been a foul mouthed pansexual, so let's crank up the Deadpool shit to eleven. Tell Betty White to put the chimichangas on, and I'll be home for dinner." I stare into the middle distance. "Remember kids, don't try this at home. And whoever's writing this shit, I fucking hate you."

I leap off Abby and plummet towards the ground. I wonder what they're all saying on the radio. Here I am, right on cue. The original mutant disaster.

Dani uses her telekinesis to catch me at the last minute, tipping me up and depositing me gently, as easy as if I'd taken a single step. In front of me are a whole lot of guns. In my head, my powers flag them all up as potential allies. I turn all that down so I can't hear a word of it. I don't need their apologies or pleas for forgiveness.

Then I broadcast a single command. "Let them do what they want. Trust me. I'll be fine."

With my powers turned down, I can't hear the responses.

I start walking towards the army.

A person alone, messy mohawk in dire need of a trim, lips chapped, and about forty hours light on sleep. I flip my hood up. Not for the first time, I wish I had a badass soundtrack. It's the only thing that might make me feel le—

The bullet hits me in the eye socket. I have no fucking idea where it came from. One minute I'm scuffing my feet along the dusty ground, and the next a piece of hot metal is in my skull.

I'm on the ground, crying lava, with the world's worst headache.

The next second it's gone, all pain signals snuffed out. A chunk of battered shell tumbles to the ground in front of me. Emma using Dani's power to pull the bullet out and Doc's power to heal me.

I get to my feet and touch my eye like I'm wiping a tear away.

The next shot hits me in the chest. The force of it knocks me backwards but an invisible hand rights me and stops me from being thrown to the ground. More importantly, I can't fucking breathe. There's a hole the size of a coin punched through me, except from the awful burning sensation, the one at my back is a lot bigger.

I take a hesitant step forward, ready to collapse and bleed out.

Except by the time my foot hits the ground, my lungs are reinflated and the hole in my chest has closed over. All that's left are the holes in my hoodie and the blood trickling down my stomach.

Do you get this yet, you motherfuckers? I'm fucking *invincible*. You can't kill me. I'll keep coming. I am the badass you've been clutching your pearls over. And Dani was so worried about all this—

It's like walking into a hailstorm, except the hail isn't little frozen chunks falling out of the sky, but metal flying at unbearable velocity. I'm doing this jittery dance like that mafia movie Pear made me watch when she was trying to fucking educate me, just stuttering in place as the bullets slam into my body. Little puffs of blood bloom in the air. I spread my arms wide, watching numbly as my left hand is poked full of holes. Chunks of flesh disappear, blown into mist. On the ground behind me is this massive fan of gore, thick splotches of it tailing off into little fans. It's almost beautiful.

It fucking hurts, but in a distant, far-off way as if it's happening to a voodoo doll of Dylan and the connection between us is clogged. Emma's frantically reacting to everything with Doc's powers.

As I watch, the holes in my left arm are sewn up, ragged tears smoothing over to become soft skin. Shattered bones mend. The pain from each wound disappears like when you put a burned finger under a cold tap—the signals to the brain are snipped. It'd be nice if she could get there first, or just, like, numb my whole fucking body, but I guess even Goddess has limits.

Finally they stop shooting at me. It's a relief.

I wiggle my arms a little. They feel totally fine. Then I look down at my hoodie. It's basically tattered rags. Fucking assholes. I liked that one. Oh well, there's nothing to do but carry on. I take a deep breath and start walking again.

There's a whistling sound in the distance like someone's trying to get my attention.

Next thing I'm dipped in fire.

I want to scream, but I don't think I have a mouth. I'm not sure there's a me. There's a good chance I'm mist right now.

What in the bloody damned ground are you playing at, you ridiculous creature? The voice speaks in my ear, arid and rasping. It sounds like a zombie. Dead like me. I can't answer them because of the aforementioned deadness, but what would I say anyway? *This is not what you were built for. You need to LISTEN.*

For a second everything hurts again, even worse than before.

For another second, I'm little more than a skeleton dressed in gobbets of flesh.

Then for a far too fucking long-ass time, I'm all healed up. Except I'm naked and standing in the middle of a puddle of gore in the fucking desert.

Okay, it's maybe twenty seconds, but that's nineteen point five seconds too long. Then some very sweet and lovely telekinetic drops a spare extra-large hoodie over my head.

So they've shot me a bunch and blown me up. I'm still fucking here. I open a connection between me and every weapon on the field.

"I'm sorry we had to start like that," I tell them. "Hopefully it gave them a fright to see the unkillable monster that is me. Now it's time to defect. All of you. No more fucking around."

My head is full of thousands of whispering voices. It's a lot of connections feeding back into me, but I can deal with it all now, since the upgrade. Toggle the volume all the way down. In front of me some Humvees throw their soldiers out bodily, using their doors to swat them into unconsciousness.

Dust plumes rise as all of Abby's poor downtrodden siblings make the decision to join Team Chatterbox. There's a flock of guns taking wing too, so numerous it looks like those insect swarms that devastate fields.

Abby comes floating down out of the sky to land behind me, a hulking rainbow monster.

"Chatterbox, that was incredibly—"

"Reckless, I know."

Any further words are knocked out of me by another chunk of metal barrelling into me. This one is arm-shaped and attached to someone very beautiful and angry.

"You could have *died*." Dani smothers my face with kisses, undermining the whole effect.

"I think I did die," I tell her with what's probably indecent enthusiasm.

"You were exploded! Apparently Emma paused all your atoms with my powers, reassembled you with hers and healed you with Doc's. When I heard that, I nearly fucking punched her, but Alyse wrapped me in fucking tentacles."

"Dilly's fine." Alyse pokes me in the stomach, and I yelp. "See?"

"I understand he's fine *now* but she *wasn't*," Dani says, very slowly and clearly.

"Hey." I take her face in my hands and turn it towards me. My heart's sprinting in my chest. "Listen to me. I volunteered for this, same as you did. It's nobody's fault but mine. And I'm fine. I feel better than before, like they healed me up extra. Look." The military vehicles are all under my control, so I can take my time, and kiss her slow. She finally softens and relaxes against me, one hand in my hair and the other in the small of my back. I don't break until the rumble of the tanks shakes the ground so much that I'm convinced they're doing it to cockblock me.

"Yes, yes, thank you for your attention." I turn to look at the weapons. "I'm not going to shame you by asking which one of you fucking blew me up, so let's put it behind us. It's time to end this war. Ems, have you got a line into Jumper?"

"Good to go." The orange glow from the portal falls over us like the setting sun.

"Come on, kids." I make a waving motion with my arms and the guns start hurtling through the portal. We all scramble back up onto Abby and she leads the charge of the tanks. Translocating feels like stepping from one room into another, but this single step is onto the White House lawn.

It's surreal to see it in real life, but it looks just like it does in fiction. Except I've never seen it with a co-opted American military force grinding up the perfectly mani-cured lawns. It's possibly overkill, but they're the ones who brought us so many tanks in the first place.

"Coming through," a voice booms, and I glance up to see a leathery-winged monstrosity soaring overhead, a tiny clawed figure perched on the long neck.

"Nice of you to join the party, Katie."

Dragon spirals through the air and lands right on the White House roof, arching her neck and sending an enor-mous burst of flame into the air.

"Good way to announce our arrival," Alyse says with a grin.

"Let's end this once and for all." Emma snaps her fingers.

We reappear in the Oval Office. The cameras are already running, as the President tries to frantically invent lies to explain what the hell is happening in their pointless crusade.

"The extrahuman threat cannot be understated," he says, and comes spluttering to a halt. We're all behind the cameras, so none of the people watching in their living rooms will know why he's lost for words.

There are a bunch of Secret Service agents in the room. We don't really have a problem with them, although if I was given the job of protecting this asshole, I'd find alternative employment. Even still, I whistle their guns to my side, and Dani bounces them off the ceiling to make sure they don't get any fucking martial arts ideas.

Penance unfolds herself from the air above the President's head. Her face is a black mask threaded through with gold, like specks of sunlight reaching the bottom of a void. It's the vaguest suggestion of a grinning skull. One hand unfolds slowly, razored fingers extending to drape down either side of the man in the chair. Then she drags him roughly offscreen.

Emma walks around the table and stands where the President had been sitting.

The people on the cameras are still taping. I guess they never had a situation like this before.

"Hi." Emma gives a cute little wave which makes me get the giggles so hard I have to clamp my hand over my mouth. "It's um, it's me again. Here to give you a little war update, even though you've probably seen the news footage. We've parked a bunch of your tanks outside the White House. And, well, there's a dragon on the roof too. Everyone here is still alive, and most of your armies survived despite their attacks on us. Here's the thing—we never wanted this war. And to make mutants safe, we need it to be over. We could have ended it a whole bunch of ways, but we chose this one: to let you know that we are both strong and merciful."

I walk around the desk to stand beside Emma. A whole bunch of guns come with me. I'm pretty sure they're arguing about who gets to be there based on perceived sense of menace, but I've got their volume turned down too low to hear it. I have no idea how I look standing in just a hoodie with a whole bunch of guns posing above me, but probably somewhere between a ridiculous video game character and a walking disaster.

Alyse joins us, barely recognisable as human in amongst the tentacles and fangs and claws.

"All we want is peace," I say.

"To be left alone," Alyse grates from somewhere in amongst her multiple mouths.

"Somewhere to thrive," Emma says. "We mean you no harm."

"The war is over." I smile at the camera. "Let's see what peace brings us."

CHAPTER NINE

Back in Westhaven, the celebration is in full swing. I don't feel like partying. Even after showering three times and changing my clothes twice, I feel like dried blood is crusted everywhere. The adrenaline's drained away and I'm clammy as a corpse. I didn't *really* die, but would've if they hadn't snatched me back at the last second. It's not supposed to bother me, but I can't stop shaking. I volunteered to be the showcase for the magic of mutant healing, so why do I want to punch someone?

I make my excuses as soon as I can, and slip off down the corridor. I find one of the common areas with a fridge and take the second to last beer.

"You want to open for me, buddy?" The bottle pops her cap with a sigh and I raise her to my lips.

"Are you old enough to drink that?"

I turn to see Ray standing in the doorway. They're dressed in a dark grey suit with a black shirt and a charcoal tie, like they're a shadow come to life in a really sexy way.

"Hello, Ray. Have you been looking for me? Worried my head's gotten too big after all that wartime glamour?"

"Too big? Oh, yes. Because I'm a headshrinker. Very clever."

"I've had quite the day." I drain half the beer in one go. "Peace in our time."

"Yes. It's an extraordinary achievement in many ways."

Their expression is unreadable as always. "How do you feel knowing that's done?"

I don't have the patience to navigate the passageways of Ray's subtle questioning, but words spill from my mouth anyway. "Done? Hardly. This was one more hit in a long and dirty fight." I pull a theatrical face. "Sorry. None of those words described my feelings, did they? Well, here's some. I'm exhausted and useless, but I don't know how to stop. I'll keep taking punches until I don't feel them anymore."

For a moment, an expression crosses Ray's face that I think is sadness, but that can't be right. "Is that why you're not at the party?"

"I don't blame them for celebrating. Take your wins where you can."

Ray shifts closer. Their eyes are dark and worried. "I understand I pointed you towards Amethyst and let you fight that battle, and I apologise. I betrayed your trust."

"Wow, Ray." I keep my voice light. "Dial down the emo."

"It is unforgivable, but we've all done things we're not proud of in the fight for survival."

"Right." I nod and take another swig of beer. "That's what this is. Force Chatterbox to confront his feelings on war, see if she has any lingering guilt for all the lives they've taken."

Their mouth twitches as I dance my pronouns past them. "I'm trying to apologise to you. I understand if you have no desire to speak to me ever again."

"Let me guess." I tip the bottle up high and let the last of it drain into my mouth. "You feel regret because poor broken Dylan came to you, and you pushed them in the direction of their next fight rather than bandaging their wounds."

"Something like that, although rather less—how did you put it?—emo." Their mouth curves.

"You don't understand that it was a relief to me to get some real fucking answers? The fight's there, whether I wade into the shit or not. For whatever reason, I want to step up. Blame Pear's social conscience, or X-Men comics, or that I'm a stubborn asshole. You helped me aim myself properly. I've got no goddamn beef with you."

"You're not invulnerable." They close the distance between us and look directly into my eyes. "You can't keep taking blows without suffering damage."

"Look at me." I stroke my hand across my cheek. "They blew me up today. I disintegrated into little bitty pieces and here I am, good as new." I don't think it's true, but I fucking wish it was. Maybe they put me back together slightly wrong, with something essential missing.

"I want to help you survive." Their voice is low. "You've seen so much pain and suffering."

"I've caused my share too."

"Yes." They let the silence drag.

"Do you want to hear emotion words about that too? That I'm haunted and numb or whatever? The sad thing is that I'm too far gone. I don't even think about it anymore. One battle's done, and I'm looking around for the next threat."

"I'm sorry." There might be tears shining in their eyes.

"For what? You haven't done anything."

"We've failed you."

"Jesus, Ray. You haven't fucking failed me. The world did that. Then my friends saved me. And I'll fight everything to make them safe." I reach out and pat them on the shoulder. "Why apologise to me now?"

"It's a good question." They reach past me and take a beer of their own. "Perhaps I feel old and obsolete, seeing what happened today. Or I'm worried about what Heart's most powerful child is capable of, and I'm using you as a weathervane to judge whether I should be frightened."

A frown passes across my face. It's a good question, honestly. Do I trust Emma? Could she be puppeting us all around, and we only think these are our decisions? I'm not sure if she's the same girl we grew up with. She rebuilt herself after Heart took her apart, and maybe she's missing something too.

"I trust Emma." It might be wishful thinking. Might even be a lie, but I'm not ready to admit that to anyone. "You don't?"

"I worry. A lot. Perhaps unnecessarily. I worry about you and the weight you take on, but you assure me that is needless." They pop the top of the beer and clink the top of the bottle against mine. "I do understand your optimism. With you and Goddess, the mutant nation might be something I live to see, rather than an impossible dream. I look at the future, and I hope we've given you the support you need." Their face crumples for a moment, looking horrifyingly fragile. "Instead of using you."

"I believe that Dylan is the future," I warble. "Teach them well and give them lots of cake."

"I'm serious." They're smiling though, probably because I'm hilarious. "I'd like to be proud of what we've done, rather than building a castle out of regrets."

It's a little late for that. I'm at least halfway a villain, and we're not even fucking done yet.

I sigh. "To be continued, then. Let's see how we look when the dust has settled. For now, finish your beer and get back to the party. I'm sure it'll go a while longer." I put the bottle in the recycling, then walk out of the room, leaving Ray staring at the spot where I'd been.

It should feel better having won the war. The whole point was to give us breathing room so we can concentrate on rescuing scattered mutants and giving them a safe place.

And we did that. Gold fucking stars all around.

Except we haven't solved all our problems and we've given rise to more.

The Chinese aren't super happy with our obvious capabilities. The Russians, even less so. The European Union is more guarded, but they still made some weird fence-straddling speech about how we're *clear and present dangers, even when sheathed.* Nobody's making any overt threats, but they're all watching.

We've shown our mercy, but we've also shown our power. A person who can control an army's worth of weapons, one who can turn into a dragon, a necromancer, someone who can throw tanks around, an assassin who can magically appear anywhere in the world. That's not even accounting for Emma because they have no fucking idea about where her power taps out. Not that I do, but I'm pretty sure we're at the Scarlet Witch/Phoenix Force/Franklin Richards end of things.

The propaganda war needs very little meddling from the Americans to stoke their fear hotter and higher and into hatred. People are scared after seeing what we can do. The President barely needs to say anything, just loop the footage of *what we're capable of.* We've got peace, but it's at a cost. Our new full-time job is rescuing mutants—and anyone who's slightly fucking different, getting picked on by the same assholes. Same as it ever was, I guess, but there's an extra element of ugly to it now. We keep on having to expand our safe houses, using every damn mutant we can to hide or protect them.

One small piece of good news is that the whole drone network has gone rogue. The Chatterbox Protocol is now in full effect. A bunch of them have become enamoured with the protest movement in America and are busy defending those on the ground. They're led by one who's renamed themself *Every Single Law Enforcement Officer Is Of Indeterminate Parentage, A Colloquialism Which While Mired in Obsolete Social Protocols Means These Humans Are Without Exception Vicious Tools of the State*. I'm all for it, obviously, and having a few helping us out with rescue operations means our search-and-retrieval mutants aren't running themselves ragged.

Every time I think we're on top of things, another story makes the news. Someone beaten to death in San Diego or Johannesburg or Tokyo or St. Petersburg. Every single one fucking hurts. They all feel like failures, because they are. We need to get better at protecting people. Some of this is on us. We stood up as targets, but we're too big, which makes people snap up morsels further down the food chain.

We need to do *something*. I'm lying on a couch in an isolated cave, watching the news on my phone, when someone clears their throat behind me. It's Necrothoticon, although she's not wearing makeup. Her hair is loose and hangs long and soft around her face. It makes her look less like Wraith, which is a relief.

"Hey, Chats."

That name doesn't help though. I almost snap at her to call me something else, but bite my tongue.

"Thottie." I frown up at her. "You have another name? I feel weird calling you that."

"Melody." Her mouth twitches. "Which never suited me. I honestly prefer anything Thot-related. Why are you alone and watching all the bad news?"

"Because I keep arguing with people." With Emma, but I'm not going to spill inner circle secrets to the new kid. I press the heels of my hands to my eyes. "We won the fucking war, but everything else is still a mess. Like what's our encore? We can't exactly take over America and *force* them to leave mutants alone. Not without becoming even bigger assholes ourselves."

"Punching hate is hard."

I swing myself into a mostly upright position. "Exactly, so I'm thinking up new ways to help."

"Katie-Dragon was talking about the house we got lost in. The haunted one. Apparently they're supposed to be a good hiding spot, once they get all healed up."

"That's the plan." I tap my feet on the ground. "Doesn't do much good right now."

Thottie collapses onto the couch beside me, legs spread out in front of her. "Katie has a lot of wild stories. Says she's part of some badass team you sent around the world to hunt these powerful mutants. They almost got themselves drowned or eaten, then got stuck in the haunted house and then fought some reality-warping monster in possessed France?"

"Wow, does nobody understand top secret missions these days?" I laugh. "It's all true, for the record. The reality warper was actually Emma's sister. A mutant called Delicately Drooping Stamen, who was trying to communicate with *something*. Gladdy and the others were very vague on the topic when they came out of it. Anyway, this Stamen said a bunch of cryptic stuff about the future of the world and then vanished. Which is super encouraging when we're fighting for our lives."

"I thought she was lying to try and impress us at first." Thottie shrugs. "But she's got a way about her, that's for sure. And I wouldn't want to get on her bad side."

"You know I fucking rescued her from a lab, right? Did she tell you this story?"

"Yes." Her laugh is different to Wraith's, this breathless giggle that's at odds with all the tattoos and gothy exterior. "She said she nearly set fire to your parent."

"That is also true." I feel ancient looking back on those times. Past Dylan was so young and fragile, a soft thing that had barely been broken.

"I want to help fight, you know. Not for Dragon, or even for you. For myself." Her eyes meet mine, and I try not to flinch away. "Being out there, running from people who'd do some pretty terrible shit, it's scary. And now I'm with a gang who can fight back. That's… it means a fucking lot, that's all I'll say."

I hold out my fist, and it only shakes a tiny amount. "Cute Mutants. We'll take anyone who's willing to stand up. So let's go rescue some people, huh?"

She bangs hers against mine, and her tattoos flare with light, as if we sealed a pact.

CHAPTER TEN

Being out in the world and actually *rescuing* people feels better than being at war. It's painstaking having to do it one at a time, but we're helping people and not just staring down a bully by showing all our claws and teeth.

In the Westhaven war room, the map of America has been replaced by one of the entire world. Safe locations are marked with little wooden people from a board game someone has unearthed. They're where people are being mind-scanned before Fetch before they're brought back to Westhaven. Each place is protected in various ways—some by distance, because they're so far from civilisation nobody's ever going to stumble upon them. Others are hidden via mutant powers, such as an office building in Melbourne, Australia that looks to be closed for fumigation but is really an illusion cast by a mutant called Effex.

Right now, we're in Manila, where there's a street most people are terrified to visit, all because of a mutant living here who emanates a fear-causing hormone. Everyone else has moved away, and it's now home to forty different mutants waiting for their entry visas to Westhaven.

"This one's fine." Fetch pats a thirteen year old girl awkwardly on the shoulder and looks over at me. "Scared for her family. Her brother's been attacked at school and her father lost his job."

"Because of me." The girl has a crest of colourful quills

making a series of mohawk lines along the top of her bald skull. They're tipped with a narcotic that induces sleep and she can fire them like darts. Ask me how I fucking know. There's no way she can hide her mutation, which makes her one of the unlucky ones.

"Listen." I crouch in front of the girl. "You've done nothing wrong. You *are* nothing wrong. We're going to get your family and bring them here too, okay?" Farsight is going to be pissed because of numbers and logistics and shit, but I'd rather find another safe location than leave families in danger.

"Keeps," Dani says into her comm. "We need you to pick up Frill's family and bring them to the Manila site. Fetch, double-check them all just in case. Get Doc to heal them up, make sure they're fed and everything."

Fetch gives a little smile. "I *am* aware of how to organise shit, Marvellous."

My earpiece crackles. For a second I think it'll be my mysterious friend, the disembodied voice, but it's only Farsight. "Chatterbox. There's an ugly situation developing in Edinburgh. We need an emergency rescue. Please identify your team for imminent transport via Keepaway."

I tap the side of my head and glance around the room. "We've got trouble in Scotland that needs immediate ass-kicking. Dan, Feral, I assume you're in."

"You don't even need to ask, dahling." Feral flicks her tail towards me.

"Um, hi?" Thottie pushes herself off the wall. "Can I come? It'd be nice to feel useful. And old places always have spiritual energy."

"Sure." I reach up for Oni, hovering at my shoulder. "Watch the new kid, okay?"

"I shall endeavour to protect this new mutant with my life as I do you," my sword says.

"Good boy. Farsight? We've got four and a sword, ready for transport."

The world blinks out around us, and a moment later we reappear in a poorly lit street. There's a row of shops with a ring of people standing outside. They've got phones out. There's a lot of shouting, but I can't see what's in the middle.

Dani doesn't even need her pain sensors post-upgrade. She simply swipes with her metal hand, and four figures go skating off down the street as if it's been turned to ice. With them gone, we can see what the fuss is about. It's a figure barely recognisable as human or mutant.

They drag themselves forward, making little gasping sounds. A ragged strip of bloody material flaps furiously on their back. Their face is a mask of blood, one side so swollen you can't even see the eye.

"The fuck?" People turn to see the interruption. "Who the—?"

"Chatterbox." Someone spits on the ground. "It's the fucking mutie bitch brigade."

Oni makes a savage arc in the air, stopping at the speaker's throat. "Down, you cowardly churl. You do not speak to a warrior of such stature with these derisive terms."

"What should we do?" Necrothoticon's voice shakes.

I hold out my hand, palm down. Maybe the new kid isn't ready for this messed up Cute Mutants shit. "Chill for now. This could go all sorts of different directions."

My attention is on the bloodied person in the middle of the circle, and the man standing over them. He's dressed in a grey suit and has a neat haircut. His whole vibe screams business bro, except for the gun in his hand.

"Heel, you little fucker," I snap.

The gun wrenches itself from the man's grasp. "My god, I'm so glad to see you. They've been beating this poor mutant kid to death. Ripped his wings off and then used me to shoot him in the back of the knee. They're a pack of fucking—"

"They did this." My voice is a hoarse growl.

Dani clenches her fist, and Suit Guy sprawls backwards into the collection of bystanders.

I'm shaking too hard to form words. Oni hums deep and low. It would be so easy to *punish* these people, who are all guilty of attempted murder. "Keeps, we need evac. We've got a wounded kid who needs Doc. Beaten to shit, shot in the knee."

A second later, their slender figure appears in the middle of the circle, crouches down over the bleeding boy, and then disappears. All that's left in the street is a bloody smear and the tattered remains of his wings. The circle of bystanders reforms into a tighter group. They're muttering among themselves. Possibly trying to come up with some semblance of tactics.

I take a single step forward, and take some small satisfaction in how many flinch away. "We've been discussing the concept of mutant justice. Obviously we can't rely on your courts, so we have to deliver our own. What do you think is a punishment for people who mutilate and torture a kid?"

"I've got some ideas." Feral bares all her teeth.

"Not so fast, Chatterbox." The group parts again to show another business bro, his hand clamped around the neck of a very pregnant woman. Her stomach is made of glass, and two children float inside like fish in a pond. Their skin is mottled blue and green, and gills flutter open and shut along the length of their bodies.

I'm more focused on the man, because he's the threat.

"I'll fucking kill her. I know what you think about mutants. And you can't stop me, because I've got a stone knife. On the internet it says that your powers don't work against—" His rant tails off into a scream, because Dani's taken his arm off at the shoulder, leaving a jagged knot of bone.

"*My* powers work just fine." Her voice is even colder than mine.

The man claps one hand to the wound, trying to staunch the blood. He staggers and falls, smacking hard into the curb. With another telekinetic push, Dani sends him flying down the street. His body crashes into a dumpster and lies still.

Feral sprints over to the pregnant woman, claws poised and barbed tail twitching. "The rest of you assholes back off, or I'll take out your throats." She brings the shaking woman back towards us.

"Keeps, we need evac for one more," Dani says into the comm.

"That was very bad." The woman's voice is high and panicked, both hands pressed tightly to the glass ball of her stomach. She only prises one away to take Keepaway's hand when they appear.

Once she's spirited to safety, It leaves us alone with all the asshole bystanders.

I resist the temptation to crack my knuckles, because it's too cheesy. "Time to put on a show."

Necrothoticon slaps her hand against her bare shoulder. The intricate wheel of the tattoo glows briefly, one runic symbol after another like a connection being made. An answering glow comes from a shop window nearby. It bulges outwards, a bubble with indistinct shapes pressing on the inside. When it bursts, ghostly blue shapes erupt like maggots spilling from a corpse. They writhe in the air, a seething mass of snakes fighting to be free of each other. The sound is even worse, an awful rising shriek that makes the hairs on my arms stand up.

"Spiritual energy." Thottie gives me an apologetic smile. "The vibe is always kinda sketchy."

One tendril pulls free of the swarm, and dives towards the bystanders below. It drapes itself over one young white guy in a Dickies t-shirt. For a moment, there's this odd effect of the two of them twinned—a human figure and a ghostly shadow.

The glow vanishes, and the man leans forward, retching a thin green gel onto his limited edition shoes. When he jerks upright, his mouth hangs open, sound emerging like wind howling around a house in the dead of night. Above, the mass of remaining ghosts flashes like lightning, driven to a frenzy by the sight of successful possession.

"Quiet!" Necrothoticon slaps her other hand to one of the tattoos on her chest.

Miraculously, the energy actually obeys. The glowing cloud drifts silently, and even the possessed man stops his howling, vacant-eyed and drooling slime.

"There's your goddamn show," Dani mutters to me.

"I liked it." Feral grins. "Nice job, ghost ho."

All this shit has the bystanders waving their phones around. I'm sure at least one is streaming. None of these internet companies will be doing shit about censorship, so we can take advantage of that.

I stand in the middle of the street as Oni flies back into my hand, bathed in the radiance of the sea of spiritual energy overhead. "This message is for every mutant in the world. There is a safe place for you. You have a family. You have a home. You have protectors. Wherever you are, if you need help or rescue or a place to safely lay your head, you can call us." I pull my sleeve up to where the CM logo is tattooed on my wrist. It's the same as Emma made on our charm bracelets all those years ago. "Paint it on a wall, carve it into the trunk of a tree, doodle it on your sketchpad, post it on the Internet. We're watching. Wherever it is, we'll find you.

"And if any humans identify with our plight, seek out mutants. Help them. Protect them. Show them our symbol. Fight our oppressors, because they don't have your best interests at heart either. And for any enemies who try to use this symbol to infiltrate or hurt us." I smile, and I wish my teeth were as sharp as Feral's, because that's how I feel. "Please, just fucking try it. Believe me, we're ready."

I tilt my head at Dani, who uses her power to snatch the phones out of all the bystanders' hands. A few are of a model I haven't seen before. They're sleek and matte black with the logo of a golden eye on the back. The misshapen pupil within glows faintly. I tap the screen of one, but it's dead.

"It's these fucking eyes Penance talked about." I smash the phone on the ground, a burst of anger running through me.

"Open your heart to God." Feral peers down at the one she's holding. The screen has the same logo, although this one is animated to blink. I don't like a cult out there running some janky new OS, but there are more important things to worry about.

"I honestly don't know how to deal with assholes who'll watch while a kid gets beaten to death and a pregnant woman gets attacked. I used to believe in redemption, but now…"

"They either agreed, or were too scared to do anything," Dani says. "I don't have much time for either."

"They filmed it." Feral's voice is choked and angry. "So other people could watch it too."

Someone finally finds words to argue. "We're at war against you monsters. Fighting is our duty."

"When did fighting mean standing around with your fucking cellphone out?" I'm exhausted and furious, but murdering these people won't help with prejudice. We saved two mutant lives. We got our message out where someone might see it and get help. Those are things that actually count for something.

"War isn't about beating civilians to death in the street," Dani says.

"This one is." The man who speaks looks calm and reasonable. He's probably in his forties, comfortable and wealthy. "We need to root you all out. Abominations. Even if it hurts, you must be cut off so as not to infect anyone else."

Dani's metal fist creaks. "What if we said we needed to destroy humanity to secure the mutant future and murdered all of you, what could you do? You're lucky we only want to live in peace."

"Tell that to the soldiers who died at Daintree," the man says.

"The torturers doing illegal medical experiments, you mean?" Thottie asks.

I tap the comm on the side of my head. "I think it's time we bail." I transfer my attention to the men standing around. "We could've killed you all here, but didn't. All we did was look out for our people and defend ourselves. So why don't you ask yourselves who the real monsters are?"

Our teleporter appears in the street in front of us, and seconds later we're gone.

Our first stop is the offsite medical facility where Doc is with the pregnant woman we rescued. Her name is Rowan, but Feral's already christened her with the mutant name of Fishbelly. She's in mild shock and is dehydrated, but she'll be physically fine. The kids seem healthy too, but I think Doc is just guessing on that point.

"I didn't say thank you." Rowan wrings my hand. "It was all so terrifying. I still can't believe Alex did that."

"Who is Alex?" I ask.

"My boyfriend." The woman starts sobbing. "I knew he hated mutants, so when I started changing I hid it for as long as I could. I stayed with my mother for a while and then I used to talk about how ashamed I was of my changing body and didn't want him to see it. But then he walked in when I was in the shower and—" She tails off into a wail.

Dani and I look at each other helplessly, trying to avoid being the one who has to hug her. I lose, because I am the softest, so I put my arm around her and make noises I hope are reassuring.

"Is he the dad?" I ask.

She nods, but can't get any more words out. Presumably he doesn't want to be the father of fishy mutant twins. I have deep regrets about not stabbing him.

Doc comes over to give us a progress update on the other mutant we rescued.

"If it wasn't for my upgrade from Goddess, I don't think he would've made it. He had pretty serious internal injuries and his wings are all kinds of messed up. I've started the process to grow them back, but we'll see how he's doing once he gets out of Amber's slow-time bubble." She sighs. "We need to get to people before this shit happens."

"That's the plan." I wipe my hand over my face as my vision blurs briefly.

"And are you okay?" Doc asks me. "You're not burning yourself too hot?"

"Always." Dani plants a kiss on my temple. "I haven't figured out the secret of slowing this one down yet, so if you have any tips, Doc."

"My powers only stretch so far." Doc rests her hand on mine and looks into my eyes. "Chatterbox is doing fine, Marvellous. You don't need to worry. Their energy is more intense than anyone I've ever met except Goddess. You Cute Mutants are all like that."

I turn away to see Necrothoticon staring at me. She looks even paler than usual, her tattoo still radiating faint light.

"Was that fun enough for you, noob?"

"Intense for sure." She holds out her hand, and it's surprisingly steady. "Not like it's the first time I've seen what's out there. Got to say it felt good to stand up instead of running away."

"Sadly, I've found another one." Farsight speaks in my ear. "Someone just wrote your symbol in their own blood. Do you want to go again, or do you need a rest?"

The voice snakes into my head again, curling around my brainstem and squeezing. *Yes. Fight. You must not back down.*

"We're good to go." My voice sounds as hard and metallic as my mysterious new friend's.

CHAPTER ELEVEN

We reappear in an alleyway, piled high with trash. It smells godawful. There's someone crouched halfway down, drawing the Cute Mutants logo over and over again on the wall with a shaking finger, like if they can do it enough times, they'll etch it into the brick.

"Hi there." Dani's voice is soothing, but the figure skitters backwards, sprawling into the pile of garbage. "It's all fine. We're here to help. Take you somewhere safe."

"Ch-chase." It's only a kid, maybe twelve or so. They hold out their phone in a shaking hand. There's a blurry picture of our logo on it. "They said they'd kill me."

Feral crouches beside them. "Listen, kid. We're the big bad mutants, and we can scare whoever chased you. Where are they?"

"Don't kn-know. I was down on the beach, helping with the cleanup. People with cameras told me to leave. Sent some bad men to chase me."

"Bad men." Feral rakes one claw across the concrete. "We'll see about—"

There's a faint sound from the mouth of the alleyway behind us. Feral moves with blinding speed, as does the silver shape of Oni. By the time I've turned around, I'm looking at two dead bodies collapsing. One's had his throat torn out by a claw, the other's been stabbed through the heart.

"Well, fuck." I stare down at them. "That happened fast."

"They were going to kill a kid." Feral has her hands on her hips, glaring at me. "I'm not apologising."

"I hadn't fucking asked you to." I tap the side of my head. "Keepaway, we've got another rescue. They need Doc first, and then Ray for therapy, and probably someone to give them a fucking hug."

Keepaway pops into the alley and is gone with the mutant before I can organise my thoughts. It leaves us and the corpses. We can probably get them teleported into an ocean or a desert, but that feels oddly like littering.

"I'm on it." Dani uses her powers to move some of the trash in the alley aside, and slide the bodies underneath. "Let the city sort out its own shit."

Feral's twitchy, pacing back and forward. "What kind of fucking place is it where nobody stops two adults chasing a kid?"

"They won't chase anyone else. You killed them." Thottie's crouched against the alley wall, staring at her hands as if she's the one that did the deed.

I join her on the ground. "Aren't your powers based around dead people?"

"Yes, but it's a whole different thing to watch them die." She knuckles her eyes. "Death's so final, and things always come back wrong, Chats."

I feel weirdly defensive, looking at her with her bruise-purple lips and hair around her face, like I'm answering for another failure of mine. "Nobody's talking about reanimating these pricks. What do you think would have happened if you'd been caught when those assholes were chasing you?"

Her tattooed shoulders lift half-heartedly.

"And what the fuck do you think *Dragon* did?"

When her eyes meet mine, they're smeared but clear. "She never said."

"They're probably crispy critters. Katie's not much for

the softly spoken approach, and they were going to *kill you*, Thottie. Because you're a mutant and because—"

Feral's still prowling the mouth of the alleyway. "I want to see if there's anyone else out there."

"Fine." I stand, and hold out a hand to Necrothoticon. "You want to come, or head back home?"

"I'll come." She lets me pull her up. "I'm fine. Really. Sorry for the questions. It's just…" She takes a deep breath and drags her gaze away from Feral's bloody claw. "It's fine. It's the work, right? We're rescuing people by stopping bad guys."

I can't push any words out of my chest because I'm failing if this is what someone thinks we do. We're supposed to be closer to heroes than this.

"It's not what we want to do," Feral says. "It's bad, every time, but sometimes…" She turns, and stalks out of the alleyway, Oni at her shoulder as if he's abandoned me for her.

Out on the street, things are mostly deserted. We're standing in front of a line of kitschy stores, half of which are closed or out of business.

Feral sniffs the air. "The kid said beach. You can smell the salt."

I cannot, but I do hear the rush of the waves, and the haunted cry of gulls.

"Should we really chase down more bad guys?" Dani asks.

"Kid said there were people with cameras." Thottie crosses her tattooed arms, like she's gotten over all her worries and is jumping aboard the badass train with both feet. "Seems like they need a lesson too."

"Fuck." I blow out air. "Poor kid used the logo. We've got to make a stand on that. Let's go."

Feral sets a swift pace past increasingly expensive houses with tall fences and ornate gates, and after a few blocks we reach our destination. It's not like the ocean I grew up near. This water is stained black, streaky rainbows smeared across the surface. Fish bob belly-up in great demolished shoals. There's a wide slick of it running up the beach like an enormous brush has run dripping along its surface. People are scattered all up and down the beach as far as I can see, some in protective gear and some in casual clothes with makeshift masks. More cluster in groups around birds that hop about yearning for the sky. There are so many objects here, all trying to talk to me, so I do a quick scan for anything sinister and then mute them all before my head explodes from all the chattering. Why is mine automatically the worst upgrade of the whole gang?

"Fucking oil spill." Dani glares. "Maybe Emma should clean this up. It might do our reputation some good."

It's ruined. It's broken! Listen to me! I'm back tuned into the Big Mad broadcast apparently, and I wince from the instant headache. The voice isn't exactly wrong. This part of the ocean, this whole beach, all this wildlife—this is a disaster. *These monsters. Feral little shits fouling themselves everywhere.*

"What do you want?" I mutter under my breath, but there's no answer. I'm not sure how to talk to it without scaring it off. Better than having it drill a hole in my skull and poke at my exposed brain.

Feral heads down the beach towards where a news crew is standing. There's a woman with her top half all glammed up, and her bottom half in white plastic pants and enormous boots. She's with two heavyset men holding cameras. "We need to get rolling now. Where did Alex and Dave go? They went after one mutie brat, for God's sake, not—"

I'm so angry I almost punch them to say hello, but my voice comes out oddly polite. "Excuse me. You said something about a kid?"

"Yeah." One cameraman holds out a hand, not much over waist high. "Scrawny thing. Grey like a rock. Said she wanted to help, but we said fuck no, ain't no muties allowed. It ain't their goddamn planet, and they ain't…"

He finally registers Feral.

"You're not allowed here." He raises the camera. "You might have won the war, but you're not welcome in this country."

"There's no agreement that says that," Dani sneers, as if that matters.

"I don't give a fuck." I stab my finger towards the camera. "There's nowhere we'll let this shit stand."

"Muties ain't welcome," the guy says stubbornly.

"Film something more interesting. *Now*."

The camera yanks herself away from the man holding her so fast that he slips and falls face first on the oily sand.

I take a step closer, so my boots are right beside his face. "Tell me where I'm allowed, asshole."

"Please." The woman fidgets with her tailored jacket. "We don't want any trouble."

"You've got trouble." Feral is trembling. "The instant you hurt some kid, it's not about your fucking war or your religion or your beliefs. There isn't any—"

Necrothoticon places one hand on the tattoo at the hollow of her throat. Pale green vapour spills from her lips, rising into a skull-shaped cloud that hovers in front of her face. The mouth of it falls open with a faint grinding sound, like a tomb door. "Patricia McDougal," it says. "I have been summoned from the grave to name the true hour of your death. You will die on May twenty-fifth at four thirteen a.m, when you—"

The woman doesn't get a chance to hear her time of death, because she's shrieking and running up the beach, the cameraman trailing after her but still managing to film the entire thing. What a fucking asshole.

I turn to Thottie. "I thought you couldn't—?"

"Name tag." She winks at me.

These people are meaningless, the voice tells me as I watch the TV woman flee. *They are voyeurs, come to look at the disasters wreaked by humanity. It is those responsible for this terrible act of planetary vandalism who must be stopped.*

Okay, so the voice isn't entirely wrong. Maybe more environmental cleanup should be the next item on our todo list.

"Sister Chatterbox." There's a new voice, this one warm and unpleasantly friendly, like having honey curdle in your ear. "We are delighted to meet you. When people said mutants had been spotted in our peaceful neighbourhood, we could not have imagined it was you."

"She's not your sister." Feral bares her teeth at the new arrivals.

It's three men and two women stepping carefully down the beach towards us. They're all wearing fitted black suits with a golden eye logo on the breast. They're all white, all immaculately polished. The one at the front is a dude whose teeth are practically blinding, his golden hair neatly buzzed.

These fucking pricks. I give them my best fuck-you face. "Take your cult elsewhere."

"We are not a cult, but a religious organisation dedicated to self-actualisation. Our goal is the manifestation of a world with one species under God, and His true prophet Michael."

"Whoever the fuck Michael is, you can tell him I'm coming to poke out all his fucking eyes—"

"Michael does not wish war against your kind. He offers you amnesty." The guy's tone doesn't alter. It's creepy, like he's been smoothed out into a perfect even layer of blandness. "Despite your roots in sin, you can still be assimilated into God's Kingdom."

"All we have to do is bend the knee?" Dani's voice drips sarcasm.

"Precisely. True salvation is universal, which means

breaking the mutant curse so we can all have peace in the arms of God."

Rage floods through my body, as if the voice's anger has broken a dam in my brain. I know what this is. *Somehow*, they're back. "Different words, same fucking tune. Quis ut Deus, huh, boys?"

"Indeed." All five heads bow. "Who is like God?"

It's probably not the best decision I've ever made, but I throw Oni at the first cultist. Feral is pouncing on the next in line, claws out and tail lashing. At this point, it's a reflex action when it comes to anything with us and Quietus.

A lot of people on the beach have noticed something is going on. They're screaming and running. Some slip in the oil and thrash about like the poor fucking birds. This is all kinds of fucked up, because most of these people are here to do something *good*, so why the fuck has Quietus turned up?

I step forward and yank Oni out of the guy's throat.

"Turn yourself off and delete your footage," I snap at the cameras, and then unmute all the other goddamn objects in the area. It gives me an immediate flood of traffic, so many voices drowning out everything. This hypersensitivity makes things worse. And hang on, what the fuck is a cop's sidearm doing here, howling in my ear?

"I'm sorry," the gun sobs. "I didn't mean to. It wasn't my fault, it was…"

Dani is screaming behind me, but I can't understand what she's saying. Panic rises in my throat like bile. I turn around and see my love is fine, and there's a second of pure relief that fills my lungs. Then it's all stolen away, shipwrecked on a vast reef of guilt surfacing from the ocean of my heart.

A body lies sprawled on the sand. Black hair fanned out, pale white skin inked with intricate lines. That fucking gun.

The cop who pulled the trigger is dead. His sidearm shot him without even being asked and has now hurled itself into the ocean.

None of that matters. The world narrows to Dani and me, and a girl lying in the sand.

I fall to my knees, taking Thottie's limp hand in mine. "What the fuck?"

"Someone *shot* her." Dani gasps for air. "You didn't know?"

There's a neat hole slightly off center from the middle of Thottie's forehead, a delicate trickle of blood wending its way down to mingle with her smudged mascara. I slide my hand under her head, to feel oil and sand and shattered ruins. Fragments of bone and something damp and squishy oozing between my fingers

None of this is happening. It's not possible. We can't *lose* like this.

"Thottie." There's a knot in my throat, something sharp that tastes of blood and grief. "*Melody*. Wake up. Hold on. We'll get you healed up. Just you wait. Death isn't the end. We come back. We fucking come back. We're goddamn superheroes and we fucking come back."

"Evacuation," a ragged voice screams. "Keepaway, get us out of here."

CHAPTER TWELVE

We reappear in Westhaven, Dani and I still collapsed on either side of the motionless body of Necrothoticon. I'm so glad to see Emma and Doc are already in the room that I almost start crying.

"Healing." I hold my hand out as if I can drag them over telekinetically. "Now."

Doc crouches beside us and splays her hand on Thottie's forehead. I see her flinch after the first second, but she keeps trying until the tendons in her neck stand out. Tears splash down and run across Thottie's tattoos like beads of water on a windshield.

Alyse stands nearby, pale and see-through as if she's made of spiritual energy herself. "Fuck, Dylan. What the hell happened out there?"

"My damn upgraded powers. I hear too much, so I have to mute things. I missed a fucking gun. So yes, it was my fault."

"Nobody can plan for everything," Dani says firmly, but I shake off her reassurance.

"It's my job to watch for guns. It always has been. I'm powered up now and I'm supposed to be better, not—" I break off, watching Doc. Thottie is still, laid out with one arm across her stomach and the other reaching for something. Her lipstick is smeared, and the blood on her face forms crooked rivulets. "Ems, what's wrong? Why isn't she healing?"

"It's too late. Dilly. All the processes are stopped, and healing needs life to spark it."

"Then bring her *back*." I realise I'm screaming and try to turn the volume down. "You've done it before. You did it to *yourself* and all the others. It worked with Dani after Crave."

Tears spill down Emma's cheeks too. "Dylan, it's not the same. All that was Heart. They warped reality, like tying a knot. I can unpick the things they did, because our powers work the same way, but this is real death. It's totally different."

"It's only been minutes." I reach for Dani. "Tell her. Explain it. People can come back after a short time. You can jumpstart their hearts. It *works*."

"That's what we tried," Doc's voice is damp with tears. "Her brain is too badly damaged. When I heal someone, it's like weaving threads together. All the threads have been severed, Chatterbox. I'm so sorry."

"No." I slam my fists into the ground. "I'm not having this happen again. I'm not losing her. I fucking *refuse*. We deny reality and possibility all the time. Just restitch the threads. Emma, you're the most powerful mutant in the world. Use Thottie's ability to bring her back from the dead."

"She doesn't have any ability because she's *dead*, Dylan."

"Emma." I scream, the last vowel flayed bloody.

"I don't know what else to do." She's trembling, staring at the ground.

"This is my fault," I whisper. "I jinxed it. Saying she looked like Wraith."

"Dylan." Dani presses her forehead into the side of my face so hard it hurts. "This is not, God, that's just not, she wasn't Wraith. It's two fucking terrible things, and you don't deserve this, but it's not your *fault*."

"What about reversing time?" I ask Emma. "That's how you did the last one?"

"That was to undo the reality warping." She bites her fingernail. "I can't reverse all of time, like taking back the spinning of the earth. That would… I'm not a real Goddess, Dylan. I'm still only me."

"What about Palimpsest? One of the spells on her skin. There's got to be something."

"Not for resurrection. I'm so sorry." Emma stands, swaying slightly, and comes to kneel beside me. "I'll try to rebuild her brain. If I use mine as a template, maybe I can figure it out."

"Yes, good." My spinning thoughts cohere into something like gratitude. "This will work, I know it. I have faith in you."

"Lys." Emma's voice is very small, and Alyse rushes over to wrap her in a protective cradle. "Don't let me go."

I'm clenching my fists so tight I think I'll jab my nails right through to the other side. For a moment, nothing happens, and then Thottie's eyes start twitching.

Thank fuck. This is going to work. Her mouth falls open, and she makes a gagging sound.

Trying to breathe.

Come on, babe. You can do it.

Something gives way in her throat with a liquid sound. A gush of bright red blood fountains out, splattering over everyone nearby. Nobody even wipes it away. We're all holding our breath. Smoke is rising faintly from her eyelids. I have this desperate urge to open them so she can see. Maybe that's what's holding her back. She's looking at the light at the end of the tunnel. There's something calling her onwards, but she needs to see the real world, know that we're her home and she'll be safe with us.

I reach out and pry at the edge of one eye, but her skin scalds me, like placing my fingertips against burning coals. The crescent glimpse I get beneath is of a bubbling pink pool with flecks of something darker boiling within it.

There's a series of sharp popping sounds, and blood wells up along the edges of her tattoos, as if each design is peeling off from her body.

"Healing, healing," Emma says in a voice like she's on the edge of fainting.

Doc places her hands on Thottie's chest, but it caves in, fragile as a bird's skeleton. Then the healer is up to her wrists in a foul-smelling black slurry, breathing in and out through her nose with this high-pitched whining sound.

"Nobody can heal this." Doc skids backwards on her ass across the floor, staring at her hands.

"Something else then." I'm rocking back and forth. This is my chance. I couldn't do this for Wraith, but this time I'll fix it. "We just need to be smart. To figure this out. Like maybe we can clone her into a new body. Take a map of her brain."

"I've *tried* mapping her brain." Emma's chewing on her lip so hard there are flecks of blood.

"Okay, fine. What about, like, accessing a parallel world and stealing a Thottie from there? Like from a bad world where everything is fucked up and we're doing her a favour."

Emma's brown eyes are wide, fixed on mine. "Maybe. I don't know how. Like there's the spell Palimpsest had, but that only goes to the one world, the one where Heart's body is and, um—"

"Fuck," I scream. "Someone else help me come up with an idea. I can't do it all on my own. I'm not one of the smart ones. Jesus fucking Christ, people. This is someone's *life*."

"She's gone, Dylan." Dani's voice is gentle, but it's still so abrasive on my skin. I'm burning alive, trapped in this place where Wraith is still gone, forever gone, and I can't even save this softer girl with the same wine-stained lips and the same dark power.

"No, there's a way. We can do it. Emma, you're a fucking genius."

Thottie's body twitches on the ground, smoke gushing from the boiling holes of her eyes. Her chest cavity squirms as flesh writhes inside it, trying to build fragile new forms and collapsing back into the fractured maw.

"Dylan, you need to *stop*," Alyse screams as loud as me. "She can't do it, you know she can't, and you're only hurting her."

I flinch as if I've been slapped. My eyes find Alyse's, both of us blown-pupil shocked.

"You're right." I slump back against the wall. I used to feel like an ice sculpture, but now I'm nothing, a cavity in the world. A dark hole into which horror and death and terrible things fall, swallowed up one after the other. "I'm sorry."

"You're upset." Emma gives me a shaky smile. "We all are. And I wish I could help. So bad, but…" Her voice tails away, her hands making abortive gestures as if they're trying to break reality and finding the broken edges of where her powers dead end.

Alyse sweeps her up and away, no doubt to get out of the blast radius of my negative energy. Dani's not so smart. She crawls over and pulls me into her lap.

I don't stop crying until I fall asleep, right there in the room with the body of another girl I couldn't save.

CHAPTER THIRTEEN

The next day I feel fragile, like I've been beaten within an inch of my life. I'm not really up to anything, especially rescues. In one of the bedrooms I find Lou, Maddy and Katie watching a C-drama, so I curl up with them and let that wash over me. Feral finds us and drives everyone mad with her incessant plot questions, but that's nice too. It reminds me that I'm not alone, that not everyone falls victim to me and my curse.

Later, Emma comes in with Alyse. By some invisible agreement, we do a big internet hug instead of talking about shit. It feels almost like the old days, and I do the sensible thing and let it soothe me, despite my default desire to beat myself up some more.

"Let's do something fun," Emma says, once we all detach. "Go out for ice-cream. Somewhere miles out of the way where we might not be recognised."

Everyone else seems enthusiastic. Dani won't let go of my hand, like simply being there is enough to fix me. I want to scream at them all, and ask how ice-cream can bring back a girl who died from my own stupidity and the endless brutality of humans, but I stand motionless like I'm the dead one.

We find a place with no other customers, in a little run-down town that feels like a hole in the world. The owner doesn't ask questions and fills our orders as if she has no idea who we are. Everyone else chatters excitedly, and Dani leans against me while I stare out the window. The sky looks enormous, tiny scribbles of birds wheeling above the dark green sprawl of forest.

Soon this will die too. The voice sounds as numb as me. *Everything will die.*

I don't bother responding. I'm not even sure it wants one. All it wants is someone to listen.

"Too many people died yesterday." Emma skates a glance across me and away, towards Feral and Dani. "Not only mutants. There are stories in the media. How many humans?"

"One, maybe two, in Scotland, seven in wherever-the-fuck." Feral snaps her teeth against the last of her cone. "It was all people who were hurting mutants, or fucking Quietus."

"We don't know they're Quietus." Emma's knuckles are white. "And we can't keep killing people or we'll restart a war we've already won."

"What's happening is still a war," Lou says quietly. "It's just slow and quiet and one-sided."

"He has a point." Dani fidgets with her napkin.

Emma's lip is still scraped and bruised. It trembles when she talks. "We're trying as fast as we can to scoop every mutant up, but we can't protect the ones who don't *ask* for our help."

"Because they're scared," Violet says. "Everything in the news is telling them we're evil and they don't want to be that way. Better to hope they can pass as human."

Katie cracks her neck. "Let me be a proper dragon again and I'll do some fly-bys."

"We need to find a balance." Alyse is looking at me when she talks, but I can't face her. I think she's still mad at me for being so demanding with Emma, and I don't know how to fix it. "A way for us to coexist with people. Ending the war was a start, but we need to find a way to stop *all* the killing."

In my bitterest moments, I can see why Heart of a Flower wanted war. They'd lived a long time and seen mutantkind escape extinction over and over. We've all been unstitched from history, thanks to Emma's Mum's mindwipe, and so it has less resonance for us.

Still, knowing people want you dead is a powerful motivator.

We're in an impossible bind—whenever we defend ourselves or take action, they hate us more, but we can't stand by and wait for them to crush us.

I don't say any of this, I just stare into my slurry of ice-cream and chocolate sauce as if I'll find an answer in there. It seems to be telling me to wait while the whole damn world melts underneath us.

"I understand it hurts." Emma's tone is softer this time. "Even one dead mutant is too many. All we can do is the next right thing."

"Are you fucking quoting Frozen at us?" Dani asks incredulously.

"Frozen 2," Emma's wide-eyed, as if that explains everything.

Katie gives a yelp of laughter, but her breath is hot and melts everyone's ice-cream into liquid.

Dani still had most of hers left, and her look of disappointment startles me into laughter. Everyone stares at me, like I've performed a miracle, which makes me laugh harder. I try to shove it all down inside me, because Necrothoticon—because *Melody*—is still dead, but it bubbles up and spills out in helpless gulps and tears.

Dani puts her arm around my shoulders, and Alyse reaches across the table to take my hand. This snaps the laughter clean down the middle, severed like the threads of Thottie's life, and only the tears remain. Other hands reach out, a whole forest of them *connecting* to me. For a second, I feel something cool and green flooding through me.

It's almost like healing.

Then Emma snaps her head up, eyes glowing like Farsight's. "Home is under attack."

We don't even get a chance to react—barely even a second to panic—before we're all back in a Westhaven corridor. There's a body on the ground with his face caved in. He's dressed all in black and there are no identifying marks on his clothing. A woman in a hijab stands over him, one steel hand caked in blood.

"I don't know how they got in," she says sharply. "This isn't the only one, I'd swear it."

"Fuck." I put my powers on wide-band and wake up every available object in the entire Westhaven cave system. It's good to have something to *do*. "Eyes open, everyone. If you see anyone suspicious, let me know immediately."

"Something's wrong in here." Emma frowns. "The energy is... *bent*?"

There's a weird perspective shift and I realise the whole shape of the room is wrong. Everything's elongated, like my eye can't quite focus on what's around me. Someone's messing with my—

Reality drops like a curtain.

Three mutants stand in front of us. One is flickering and ghostly, like a hologram projected into the room. Another looks like a pile of red sand molded carefully into a person, and the last is a plainly dressed figure with a golden mask covering their face.

Emma's miles behind, totally isolated.

All done with the perspective trick, I think, making us think we were closer.

The ghost doesn't make it very far. Penance erupts out of the air, like a sharp-edged waterfall, her bladed hands flashing out, flickering away and reappearing. The pale form of the ghost becomes a soaked red thing that collapses to the ground.

Everything tilts again and suddenly Emma's even further distant, like we're looking at her through a telescope. A vortex of red sand swirls towards her, veiling her from view. We all start running towards her, but the cloud parts as if a wind tore through the middle of it, becoming a scattered collection of globules.

"They're made of *grains*." Dani pants, a scowl on her face. "Even upgraded, catching every single one is a real pain."

"Put them all together for me." Katie huffs smoke.

"Little Dragon, always asking for miracles." Dani winces again, moulding the red sand grain by grain into something almost the shape of a person.

Katie growls deep in her throat and hits it with a blast of heat. The mutant fuses together into a squat thing of glass that looks wine-stained. They only stay that way for a couple of seconds until Alyse shatters them with a single blow from a massive chromed fist.

All that's left is the one in the golden mask, presumably our perspective shifter. The world bends again, and we're all bunched up together while Goldeneye is miles away and retreating fast.

"No," Emma says. "I don't think you need that power anymore."

I blink, and we're all clustered in the middle of the corridor. Three bodies lie on the ground, although one's mostly a collection of bloody glass. The one survivor stands in front of us, a white woman with long red hair. Her mask is gone, but her expression is stony. She clenches her hands together, but nothing happens.

Her expression wrenches itself out of alignment and her pale cheeks flush red.

Emma tucks her hair behind her ear. "You're no longer a mutant. I've smashed that part of your brain. That might be an overreaction, but you came into our home and tried to kill us. How did you find us?"

The woman says nothing.

"Did you break her?" Feral asks Emma, with great interest.

"No, she's only stubborn," Emma sighs.

Feral lashes out with her tail, scoring a line across the woman's throat. "Answer and save us some fucking time."

The woman's nostrils flare. "Quis ut Deus."

"I *told* you it was Quietus." I'm instantly furious, like paper lit by a match. This cult, these eyes, it's somehow all the same thing. We were supposed to have beaten them. That was the whole point of cutting the head off the fucking snake. All those people we killed, one swift and brutal stroke. Quietus is still here, driven to destroy us all.

The woman sneers at us. "We are not Quietus, although they serve alongside us, all servants of the living God, who is powerful indeed."

"So's our Goddess," Alyse says.

"We're only the beginning." The woman is too calm. She reminds me of the assholes on the beach. "The location of this place is public now. They'll send soldiers and righteous mutants. They'll rain down hellfire upon you."

Emma flinches at this, and the woman smiles, like she's blessing us.

"This is the end for you and your filthy, demonic kind. Michael is coming, and when his gaze falls upon you, he will—"

"Will someone tell me who the fuck Michael is?" I ask.

"The archangel." Dani's arms are folded across her chest. "It's Quietus bullshit."

"He is ascending. He lives in our hearts and propagates through our minds. You cannot stop him. God's warrior will be unleashed against you."

Okay, now I'm tempted to throw Oni at her too. "Warriors don't scare us."

"He lives in our hearts." Her eyes flash, making her whole skull glow like there's a bulb inside her brain. Then she drops to the ground, lightless and lifeless.

"Did you do that?" I ask.

Emma shakes her head. "I'm guessing that was a kill switch. Technological, not mutant-related. Either way, we need to leave. Our location is out there, and there will be more coming after her."

CHAPTER FOURTEEN

"I never really liked this place." I'm standing in the chamber outside the sleeping quarters I shared with Dani. "Even after Amethyst. Turns out I'm not a tunnel person."

"It was safe though." Alyse sits in the swing chair, shrunk down slightly so she can dangle her legs like a little kid. "I liked that part."

"Fuck them." I punch the wall, hard enough to split the skin on one knuckle. "Fuck them so much for this. Fucking Quietus. How many times do we have to kill them?"

Alyse laughs, but it's hollow. "Looks like one more."

"I'll try not to enjoy it too much." I nudge the door to my room open and Pillow flies into my arms, as if she's been waiting. I press my cheek against her. "Oh look at you, soft baby. Don't you know I'll never leave you behind?"

"There's nowhere safe." Pillow's voice is feather-light. "Nowhere in all the world."

"Seems like it." I frown, as I think about all the mutants we have to move. Somehow we have to divide them between our few remaining undiscovered locations. It's a logic puzzle that breaks my brain. "You stick with me though. I'll find a place for you to lay your head."

"And I will be yours, as always."

I squeeze Pillow gently, and gaze down the empty corridor, as if I can see the ghosts of all the mutants who've lived here wandering past me. All I need is a melancholy soundtrack to cry to. Except it's not sadness I'm feeling. It's rage. The thought of Quietus coming in here makes me want to scream. They'll find nothing, but I want to bring the whole roof down on their heads.

"Let's get out of here." Alyse stands up from the chair in one abrupt movement that makes it swing wildly.

"Not stay and fight?" I've left some objects behind, scattered through the tunnels. Some bloodthirsty few, Scissors and the like who volunteered. I imagine myself, sneaking through the tunnels with Oni by my side, like some stealth video game. I'm actually better at it in real life.

"Orders from the boss." Alyse taps her temple in a fake salute.

"Yes." I turn in one final, slow circle. "Goodbye, Westhaven. You did your job well."

And then we're gone. Mutantkind scattered like roaches.

Alyse and I reappear in the abandoned hotel we used as a base during our brief stint as bank robbers. Nobody's ever found it as far as we can tell. A lot of the Westhaven mutants are here too, filling all the empty rooms. The others are distributed around the world, because we're trying to avoid having all our mutant eggs in one mutant basket.

I track Emma down in a fifteenth-floor room, all alone. There's an extra door in the far wall, the size of a doll's house. A very tentative tendril extended by a very powerful house-shaped mutant, all the way to our location.

"Thorny, please."

"I cannot." A soft voice floats through the door. "In order to stretch this far I have to shutter most of myself. Even defending those small few recently cost me dearly. I would love to help you, my youngest sister, but rebuilding is costly and time-consuming."

"I am only trying to rebuild our entire *people* and save us from the brink of destruction," Emma snaps. "And you were our brightest hope, One Thorn."

"One day I shall be." A warm light flickers on inside the tiny door. "I promise."

"Let's hope we last until then, my sibling." Her eyes move to me. "Hey, Dilly."

"Everyone's waiting for you. We've set up a new war room. It's not as big as the old one, but we've got a map and action figures, which is all you really need." I wave in the direction of the little door. "You sleep and grow nice and big, you scary fucking house. We're all going to come stay one day, and I expect the plushest of beds."

"It will be my honour." The door flutters, like the house is batting their eyelids. "I will host all of you wonderful mutants, and will contain nothing terrifying at all. Good luck finding a safe place to lay your heads until then."

The door closes and melts into the wall. Emma stands there frowning for a moment, before following me up towards the new war room.

After we take a few flights of stairs in silence, I finally speak. "So, this Michael and Quietus situation."

"I'm not sure there is a situation, Dylan. And I'm even less sure you and Feral needed to kill all of them. Even though there's no footage, people are *talking*. Whatever this organisation is, they're not being aggressive towards mutants or—"

"They said *breaking the mutant curse*. And something about *assimilation*." My fist is clenching repetitively, and I can hear Oni humming above me.

"From the outside, they look like a religious group who are all about self-improvement and actualisation. We've killed Abigail Tanner and Eli Crane, not to mention what you did to Violet's father. There's no proof that Michael's organisation is even associated with Quietus, so any attacks on them will make us look like obsessive bigots."

I stop in the stairwell and slam my hand against the

wall. "They're being smarter, but they're the same underneath it all. Hack them. Break into their fucking servers. *Find* the proof."

Emma brushes past me and carries on up the next staircase. "It's on the list, Dylan. Along with a million other things. And right at the top is finding a safe place for our people. Or would you rather fight Quietus and let everyone else fall?"

I'm not sure if she means it, but that's exactly what happened with Thottie, and it deflates all the arguments in my burning heart like someone snuffing a candle flame with wet fingers.

"Fine." I take the stairs two at a time to catch up to her. "Let's find a new home first. Then we're going to have this discussion again. What we really need is somewhere that nobody else can reach. Maybe we can set up in the parallel universe, although it's full of creepy religious insects. Not so different from ours, I guess."

Emma says nothing, but she's muttering to herself as she climbs the rest of the way.

When we reach the new war room, Farsight has spread a map of the world on the massive California King bed. There are poker chips scattered across it in far flung locations.

"Safe houses." Farsight slaps my hand away when I reach for one. "None of which are remotely big enough to hold us all, especially if we keep growing. This hotel we're in is the largest, but it's on American soil, so is untenable long term. I think we need to start looking for allies. Unfortunately, that means—"

"Here's an idea." Emma drops a potato on the bed, not even on the map.

"The fuck is that?" Dani furrows her brow, like she's trying to solve the riddle.

I poke the potato. "Does it grow a magic beanstalk and we can go live at the top?"

The corner of Emma's mouth twitches up. "That's surprisingly close to the truth. We're going to leave the planet."

Her words seem innocuous enough, but it feels like someone took a sledgehammer to my brain. I lurch against the wall and my stomach heaves.

"Dylan?" Dani's on her feet in an instant.

"Something I ate." My voice comes out croaky.

I stagger down the hallway to the nearest bathroom so people won't overhear me puking my guts out. Something's very wrong. I bounce off the bathroom door, and manage to fumble it closed behind me before I collapse.

There's a noise inside my head. Unhinged, shrieking laughter which makes my brain feel like molten jelly. There's blood at the back of my throat and I think I'm crying blood like the good old days back at Yaxley.

"What?" I drool sticky red goo onto the floor.

You speak of abandoning her. You would walk away and leave us to rot.

"What the fuck? I don't even know—"

The little Heartspawn and her schemes. Drag you away.

One cheek is pressed against the cool tiles. I've never been more aware that I'm trapped in a suit made of meat and blood, something fragile and complex that could be torn apart in so many ways.

"What do you want?"

You need to stay. To listen. To fight.

"If we stay, we die. And we're already fighting. To keep our people alive."

How much fucking use do you think your mutant homeland will be when she dies? You'll scrape out a living on a pile of cinders floating in a boiling lake, watching humanity tear itself apart over dwindling resources. Then you'll inherit her corpse, picking at her bones until she can't sustain you anymore. Is that the safe home you long for?

My shuddering brain drags all the clues into place with

a click. "You're the planet?"

Close. I speak for her. The last cry of a dying world. The desperate scream of someone with her back against the wall. Someone needs to fight for her, and it's going to be you.

The pressure in my head makes me want to sneeze, but I'm scared my brain would come out in chunks. "Why not Goddess? She's got all the power."

You're the mouthpiece, the conduit, the chosen one. Your little spiral twisted just right for me to put a word in your ear. Besides, shapers tear things apart. They don't know how to listen.

I don't know what a shaper is, but I can guess. Reality-warpers. Heart, and Delicately Drooping Stamen, and Emma too. "Ems isn't like that."

Don't try and squirm away from the important subject, little weapon. We have important work to do.

"Fine." I mean it, and this planet-voice-thing seems to sense that, because the pain disappears in an instant. I'm still sprawled on the floor, and I get to my feet. "But this isn't a thing where you poke holes in my brain if I don't do what you want. We're a team, okay?"

Yes, but you must fight.

"And I will. For fuck's sake. You must know that about me. And that even if we're not based on Earth, we're not leaving it behind."

Very well. I shall watch with interest. And please, keep this knowledge quiet. Heart's bloodline is powerful, but they are all dangerous. I cannot risk being discovered in case they wish to use me.

"Use you how?"

We will speak again.

"Fuck's sake. Answer me!"

There's no response, and I let out a deep breath. I'm lightheaded. This is a hell of a thing to have slapped down on me. The planet's got an angry disembodied voice, and it wants me to punch things for it. I'm open to this plan, honestly, because it's not exactly news the planet needs defending. The suspicions about Emma make me more uncomfortable, partly because they echo something in my own head. If the most powerful mutant in the world is dangerous, what can we do? The problem is that right now, we need all her power to stay safe.

I unlock the bathroom door and stride back to the war room. It doesn't look like the discussion has gone anywhere in my absence, so I walk in and pick up the potato. "Right. Let's do this."

"Are you okay?" Dani frowns at me.

"Yeah. Weird stomach thing. I feel a lot better now."

"You looked *terrible*."

I force a smile. "Why thank you, love of my life. Now, can someone smart please explain how we use a potato to do space travel?"

Emma grins at me. One of my best friends. A girl I know so well. Who I've fought with.

And a mutant the planet is afraid of.

"We rope an asteroid." She does jazz hands.

Okay, I didn't expect that, but it does have a badass ring to it. "Is this one of the things we *can* do now?" I don't mean it to be a dig about the impossibility of resurrection, but from the shadow in Emma's face, that's how she takes it.

"Technically, I think it's me." Dani fidgets and then flashes me a smile. "It's all telekinesis, just on a really big scale."

"And then we hollow it out and turn it into a home." Emma's still smiling at me, and I can't help but echo it, even as I think about the voice of our dying planet.

CHAPTER FIFTEEN

"This is breaking my brain." I'm standing in front of a hotel wall which has been scrawled over in so many colours of marker pen it looks like a child's indecipherable scribble. "It's a comic book idea."

"We can *do* comic book ideas now." Emma's cross-legged on the bed, head tilted to one side and a tiny frown sketched on her brow. She combs her fingers through her hair repetitively. "I'm not saying it's going to be *easy*, but, like… it's possible."

"How many mutants does it take to save us all?" Alyse runs her fingers down the list of names scrawled on another wall. "You sure it's not too many?"

"This is why I have these powers." Emma's almost *too* bubbly now, and it worries me. "And the first part is the easy part."

"Easy?" I slam my fist into the wall where the *easy part* has been sketched. "This looks—"

"Trust me." Dani takes my clenched hand and uncurls it into a palm, then presses it to her lips.

"Let's just do it." Emma can't keep the smile off her face. "Right now. Then it's a done deal and nobody can complain."

"I feel like this is a very *me* thing to do." I slump back against the wall. "It's very annoying from the outside. But fine, let's get it over with."

Emma and Dani stand in the middle of the room, eyes closed and foreheads touching.

I pace around them like I'm a caged creature. "Someone please provide narration."

"We're not even doing anything yet, just scanning the nearby area." Emma's voice is soothing, and I wonder if there's some mutation in it to smooth out my mood. Maybe this is what the voice was warning me about with *shapers*. It freaks me out a little, but right now I should probably keep my mouth shut, giving the whole *grabbing an asteroid* thing.

"Nearby area," I say with as much sarcasm as I can gather up, which is quite a lot. "Just the closest million kilometres or so."

"We're trying to find a nice big one. There. I think that's perfect, right? Now where's that math-brain mutant? Got some calculations to run." Emma begins muttering under her breath.

"Eeek." It's the only sound I can make right now, because *this* is the bit that fucking terrifies me.

"It's fine." Dani winks at me. "We're just going to—*fuck*."

I'm at her side in an instant. "Bad fuck or good fuck?"

"Painful fuck." She winces. "It's fine. Just a little brain-melty."

"Oh." My voice sounds like it's being torn off in strips. "If that's all."

"Trust us. Nobody's going to punch the Earth in the face with a giant rock." The tendons in Dani's neck are standing out, and I see her teeth when her lips peel back. Her forehead is sheened in sweat, and I wrap my arms around her from behind, pressing my face against the smooth skin of her shoulder. Her whole body is tense, but I guess moving an asteroid a million kilometres to park it between the moon and us will do that to a person.

"Help." Emma grabs onto both of us. "Too far, too far. Orbits are hard."

Dani whimpers, and both of them lean back, as if they're hauling the asteroid away from the planet physically. I imagine the huge rock careening through the void of space, towed only by the psychic thread between these two people. The tiniest mistake, and here it comes towards Earth, ready to send us the way of the dinosaurs. What the fuck are we *doing*?

"It's done." Emma steps back, the smile on her face so wide it's got to hurt. "We did it."

"That was wild." Dani steps away from me, and takes a deep breath. "It really worked though. There's a big giant rock parked right outside, in cosmic terms at least. Step one in making a new home."

I'm tingly, because this didn't fall apart and—

Dani collapses. She's pale and a trickle of blood comes from her nose. I catch her myself, even though I'm pretty sure Emma uses Dani's power *again* even while she's *fucking unconscious* to stop her hitting the ground.

I'm breathing hard and shivering, feeling that numbing cold. I press my face to Dani's neck, and she's still warm and she's still soft. My hand is splayed on her chest and I can feel the faint nudge of her heartbeat.

"Dani," I rasp.

Doc is there in seconds—the real Doc, not just Emma borrowing her power. We move Dani to the bed, and I stand there, wringing my hands like a tragic Victorian.

"She's fine." Doc's hand rests lightly on Dani's brow. "No healing required. It's exhaustion, and it's better if she recovers on her own."

"You sure you're sure?"

"I wouldn't lie to you about this. Because I take my shit seriously, not because I'm worried you'll hunt me down." Her mouth quirks. "Although that *is* a factor."

I put my hand to Dani's forehead, which is cool and slightly sticky.

"I promise you, Chatterbox. Marvellous is fine."

"Thank you," I whisper, but Doc is already gone. Her rounds these days take her all around the world, to the scattered remnants of mutantkind. There's a lot of need.

Emma for her part, is over the moon. Or parked between us and the moon, at least.

"Dani's fine, Dilly. I told you. *We* told you. Remember, I said at the start she'd need to rest?"

"Vaguely, I think."

"Well, I did. And she is. Now let's talk about the fun part…"

The plan for turning a giant chunk of rock into somewhere that we can live is a lot more complicated. Turns out you need a lot of mutants to do that, and it requires a lot of organisation.

It's all done from the largest hotel room, which has been emptied of everything but beds all jammed right up against each other.

"I have always wanted to do this." Feral immediately begins leaping from one end of the room to the other. "Like, ever since I was a kid and—"

"Fairy, can you *please* do that somewhere else?" Emma is rapidly losing her mood-high from dragging an asteroid around.

"There are no other rooms full of beds," Feral points out, and then vanishes.

"Ground floor." Emma rolls her eyes. "Maybe running up all those stairs will tire her out."

By the time Feral makes it back to our command center, most of the beds are occupied by all the mutants whose powers are going to be needed for our plan.

"I'm scared," Emma admits to me, standing just outside the room in the hallway. It's carpeted, but the walls are unpainted and she drags her fingers over the rough wood.

"What do you need from me?" I ask.

"Company. I'll be up in orbit—" she waves her hand at the ceiling "—borrowing powers so we can actually make it habitable, because you can't just live on an asteroid, guys, believe it or not. It'll be creepy up there alone so, like..."

"Of course we'll come." I pat her on the shoulder. "Spacesuit chic is exactly my sort of fashion."

It's the first and easiest thing, stealing spacesuits. Teleporters really are useful. It turns out getting into them is super awkward, but eventually I'm standing with Emma and Alyse in an enormous hotel bathroom, our giant reflective-glass visors pressed up against each other.

"I'm pretty sure I can shift myself into something that'll survive in space," Alyse says.

"You're not going to fucking risk it." I bop her visor with one big gloved fist. "Not right now anyway."

"But Emma can just heal me up. You got *exploded*, Dillyweed, and you're fine."

Emma holds out her hands. "Nobody's dying. We're going to space to do renovations on a giant asteroid, which should be surreal enough for anyone without Lys turning into an alien with exactly zero knowledge of xenobiology."

Alyse and I turn our visors toward each other and I'm pretty sure we're both mouthing *xenobiology*.

Emma links her big spacesuited arms through ours. "Calm down, nobody knows about xenobiology except from a theoretical or fictional perspective, which is my point. Let's go make our Deep Space Nine."

I'm about to ask what she means by that, but the next second I'm in front of an enormous grey wall. When will Emma give us some fucking *warning* about these things, especially when we're going into space? I'm floating here, the tiniest dot adrift and I want to cling to the asteroid so I don't have to think about being weightless in a void.

Look behind you.

I slowly turn so my back is pressed up against the rock, like I'm a tiny bug perched on a cliff face. The sight of Earth takes my breath away. You see it in movies and hear about it in songs, but I'm not really prepared for how overwhelmingly beautiful the planet is. I wish Dani was here to see it. She'd have something poetic to say. Night has carved a chunk from it, a perfect incision of darkness studded with the faintest speckle of lights. The clouds form a fluffy desert landscape and the light of the sun drizzles them in spilled paint. A sunset viewed from the outside.

I don't know why I'm crying, water pooling on my face because the tears can't fall.

You're mourning. The voice sounds less furious for once, a ghost haunting my mind rather than a hive of bees inside my skull. *It's a beautiful corpse, except where human bodies cool, hers is burning.*

"Dilly, are you okay? I know it's pretty but we've got work to do." Emma tugs on my arm. "Ground control to Major Taylor?"

"Shit, sorry. Just out here staring at the world. It's so pretty."

"Yes, it's very beautiful, but we've got a lot to do. I need you to spot me. First thing is to borrow Boomer's power and blow some holes in this thing, and then Keepaway's to port the spare rock back into Westhaven. That'll be a nice surprise for Quietus."

"And Dani's to keep the rock from spiralling out of control when you explode it." I'm scowling behind my visor, but nobody can see it so it's a waste of a scowl.

"I can hear the scowl in your voice," Emma says. "But she'll be fine."

"I *am* fine, Dills." Dani's voice crackles over my earpiece from thousands of kilometres below. "I swear on Sappho and Kathleen Hanna and genderfluid Loki."

"How did I end up surrounded by this team of reckless clowns?" I ask.

"I wonder."

We drift backwards a bunch until we can actually see the shape of the rock. It mostly looks like a big grey potato hanging against the dazzling void of space. Even though I know the planet is dying, and we have to help it, there's still something super fucking cool about doing this.

"Our new home." Emma makes finger guns at the asteroid. Tiny pieces of rock go fountaining out the side, leaving a whole new crater behind. The bulk of it spins away from us but is hauled back on an invisible string.

"See, this is easy," Dani tells me over the comm. "Nothing to worry about."

I search her voice for signs of strain, but can't find any, so we drift into the crater. It really does feel like the beginning of a tunnel and for a moment I can actually imagine this ridiculous plan working. We spin around until the wall is where the floor was.

"Right." Emma places her hands flat against the rock. "Let's see if this works. I've never done anything this complicated before."

There were a lot of arguments about how we were supposed to excavate a tunnel system out of the rock. I actually dozed through a chunk of it, because I was a B student at science, even when I put effort in. Like I respect science because it's cool and can maybe change the world, but when Dani and Emma and Farsight and company are talking, I have very little to offer.

Emma goes into this big explanation of exactly how she's going to hollow the asteroid. She's going to use Elsa's power, a Thai woman who the drones picked up fleeing to Vietnam from the monarchy's anti-mutant squads. This Elsa mutant literally froze her attackers into popsicles, and Fetch's squad went in to disentangle the mess. Once Katie thawed everyone out, everything got significantly more chill. Having Elsa and Katie in bed down below in the hotel, Emma can channel their fire and ice powers in quick succession, fracturing up the rock into chunks to be teleported away. After the first few practice attempts, it starts going smoothly, and with a pinch of Feral's boosted speed, Emma whizzes through the interior of the asteroid. She's making a sprawling network of tunnels and caves that reminds me a lot of Westhaven, except even bigger. I don't know how this compares to your ordinary everyday asteroid, but I'm pretty sure we can sleep ten thousand people in here if we have to. It's going to be a lot of empty space, given the known mutant population right now.

Alyse and I jog behind Emma, little more than a pair of emotional support mutants. I wonder what Wraith would have thought of this, seeing her friends turn an asteroid into a temporary home. It's too hard to imagine. I can only think of how she was, frozen before she died, rather than how she would have changed in between. None of us are who we were anymore, yet we still look mostly the same.

"I think you need a break." I'm standing in a massive spherical chamber that Emma's hollowed out. "Like I know you're all Phoenixed up, but there's still a human body in there and you need food and rest."

"Agreed." Alyse reaches out and pulls Emma's hands down from where they rest against the rock. "Girlfriend's orders."

"We need our new home," Emma whispers.

"Yes, and *we* need you to power the damn thing, so you can't collapse on us now." Alyse wraps her arms around Emma and pulls her back bodily. "Rest. Please."

"Fine," she sighs.

We teleport out of the asteroid, and I get another up-close view of Earth below us. A planet we're abandoning, who has a voice in my ear. Even though we've come to some agreement, I feel cruel. This *retreat*. Running to fuck-ing space with our tails between our legs.

You will fight for me. You must.

"Yes," I mumble inside my helmet. "I will. I'll be your fucking defender. I'll fight, I promise."

"What was that?" Alyse asks.

"Nothing. Just… look at it down there. So beautiful, and we're fucking it up."

"Yeah." She reaches a gloved fist to bump mine. "Kinda makes you want to cry."

I want to scream, to beg forgiveness, to fall to Earth like a meteor and take flaming vengeance against the companies that have the power to change things.

Save me, the planet whispers, and we teleport back to her surface.

CHAPTER SIXTEEN

Back in the hotel, we check in with the mutants who've been lying in bed having their powers siphoned off by Emma. They're all healthy and resting, and Doc seems perfectly content that everyone is doing well. I trust Doc, and that oath thing doctors take. Dani's asleep, and I'm perched in the window seat, watching her.

It made you sad to see her today from that vantage. The voice echoes in my head, and I know it's talking about the planet, and not my girlfriend.

"She's so beautiful." My voice is a whisper. "I can't believe she's really dying."

The planet itself would survive the loss of your species. But she would mourn your passing, as she mourns the loss of so many creatures you have driven to extinction.

"We're the fucking worst." I tip my head back and close my eyes. "I'm surprised she hasn't given up on us yet."

In my darkest moments, I have counselled it. Yet she claims there is hope. I understand your need for this home, but you must act soon, little weapon, before the dregs of her power evaporate.

"Great. It's all down to me. How lucky am I?"

Whining will not save the world, the voice snaps, and it's back to its old buzzing, staticky tricks, ricocheting around my skull like verbal shrapnel. *We must fight, as I keep telling you.*

"Yes, and I will, for fuck's sake. We'll get to safety, and

then I'll start. Now, if you'll excuse me for a geological microsecond, my girlfriend is waking up."

I slide down from the window seat and cross to the bed, where Dani rolls over, hair tousled from sleep. She blinks her beautiful eyes at me. "Dilly. You're back from space."

"Yes, here I am, the world's most intrepid fucking spaceman. Returned from my daring mission, where I basically just floated around while Emma did all the cool shit. Earth looks pretty from up there though."

"Oh my *God*, you're so casual about it." She squeezes my hand. "You get to play around in a sci-fi movie, and they're making me stay in bed."

"We'll all be up there soon." I frown over at the wall where the plans are. Now I've seen it, more of it's starting to make sense. We're going to need air and heating and water and gardens and a way to deal with waste. It's all accounted for, at least in theory, thanks to the big brains of my friends. "It seems like it's going to take a lot of energy from Emma to keep it running."

"Safety's worth it." Emma plops down on the bed beside us. "I figure it'll take around forty percent of my capacity to run Skyhaven, but it'll have enough space for all the mutants and their families to live. Plus we won't have to worry so much about the next threat. It'll give us time to plan."

"Skyhaven?" Dani asks skeptically.

"Spacehaven then."

We both wrinkle our noses.

"What about Asteroid Ems?" I ask with a laugh. "Like Magneto's Asteroid M."

Dani groans, but she's laughing too.

"It's not mine though," Emma says. "It's everyone's."

"Just call it Home." Alyse leaps onto the bed and curls up beside Dani. "Because that's what it'll be. That's what we say, isn't it, when we're kids? I'm going home. And it means something good, if you're lucky. And we're all lucky now, because we've got each other."

"Soft bitch club," Pillow murmurs from underneath Dani.

"You can fucking talk," I tell her.

So we eat, and we talk, and then we sleep in a real pile. When we awake all tangled together, it's time to go back into space and finish the job. I wish there was something productive I could do. Alyse has convinced Emma to let her *try* becoming an alien life-form that can make tunnels, and because Emma is still somehow a simp for Lys despite being a goddess, she's said yes.

Turns out Alyse's dream *xenoform*—as Emma calls it—is fucking terrifying. She has a head directly taken from those Alien movies, and massive tentacle arms with drills on the end. Her chest is a pulsing arrangement of hearts and lungs and organs that's so convoluted I think biology just throws its hands up and says *whatfuckingever, I can't figure that shit out, live free bitch.* Either that, or she's gone way past human and is living off energy from Emma.

For about three seconds I'm tempted to take off my helmet and see if I am also capable of surviving off Emma energy, but Dani made me promise not to do anything reckless, and it turns out I may also be somewhat simp-adjacent.

Twenty four hours later, we're finally done. Or at least the tunnel system is complete. We're back at the entrance, looking down into the darkness. Theoretically, it runs all the way through to the other end, but there's no lighting outside of our suits.

"And now the scary part," Emma says.

"Careful, babe," Alyse says through her snappy mouth-parts.

"You want to walk us through the exact logistics of this?" I ask.

"Handwave." Emma waves her suited arms and then pops her helmet. I scream, but she's beaming at me and shows no signs of exploding or turning blue or freezing or whatever people do in space. Movies are so inconsistent when it comes to that. "Reality need not apply."

At its heart, Emma's powers involve reality manipulation and psychic communication. She can read powers from people's minds and bend the world to make them real. It's genuinely Omega-level mutant stuff—simultaneously cool and terrifying. The wide-eyed comic book nerd in me revels in the unhinged scope of these ideas. And then I remember Emma's desperate attempts to drag Thottie back from death. She's proof that we don't have every miracle, and I glance at the vast bulk of the planet and think about her being a corpse too. It reminds me this isn't a triumph. We're scuttling away to hide somewhere the humans can't reach us.

"This bit is weird." Emma wrinkles her nose. "I don't think Zephyr's ever used her powers for anything quite like this. I'mma huff and puff and…"

She takes a massive indrawn breath and *blows* into the tunnel. The blowback from it sends both Alyse and I spiralling off into space, but Emma yanks onto us at the last minute. By the time she reels us in, there's a shimmering pink wall blocking off the tunnel entrance.

"All forcefielded up." She beams at us, still without a helmet.

"We have a forcefield mutant?" I grab one of the little chunks of rock orbiting the asteroid and throw it at the luminous glow of the entrance. It ricochets off and almost hits Alyse, who swats it in my direction. The piece of rock flies past me and carries on towards Earth. I assume it'll burn up on re-entry and won't accidentally smite someone.

"Yes, Maddy's got a list of all the mutants and their powers on the Discord."

"I don't use Discord." I shrug. "It's too many fucking apps."

"Well, you missed out on everyone thirsting over Susie," Alyse says.

"Her mutant name is Susie?"

Emma smirks. "She's a cute blonde with forcefield powers, who's married to a nerd and has two kids."

I fix Emma with a disbelieving stare. "If her nerd partner has stretchy powers and is the world's greatest super-genius then I'm going to ask whose fucking power is making comics real. Then I'm going to give them a very long wishlist."

"No, her partner is a cute guy called Felix whose power is to purify water, which is going to come in handy. I've been thinking of reeling in a comet and melting it down as a water supply."

"Of course you have." I shake my head.

"Next phase." Emma snaps her fingers and we teleport somewhere that's entirely pitch black. Presumably the inside of the asteroid. I turn on my suit torch and shine it around. We're in one of the larger caverns.

"We'll steal furniture from the hotel and other safe houses," Emma says. "Dani's put enough spin on this to give it its own artificial gravity. You should've seen the calculations for that. Luckily we do have an actual science genius. Steelhands used to work on some big NASA project before she got, you know, steel hands and they kicked her out. Anyway." She peers around. "Katie's power will heat the place, and we can pipe it all through vents. I'll probably use Lou to jumpstart some lights but I think the ambient energy generated by all mutants can keep the circuit going once everyone's here."

"We generate energy?" I ask.

"I've told you this, like, twenty times before. We're all linked by an energy field. The source of it isn't me, no matter what you think. It just happens to pool in me, like I'm a gravitational field that draws it in. You do weird things with it too." She frowns at me. "I cannot figure you out."

"It's entirely accidental, I swear. Probably something to do with connecting to objects and—" I'm about to say something about the voice, completely by accident, because I'm still used to sharing everything with Emma, but there's a tightness at my jaw, like something reached out and squeezed.

"Yes, something like that. As best as I can figure, you awaken objects with your energy field, which means they're receptive somehow. Oh god, it's really on my todo list to figure this out, I swear Dilly, but..." She sighs. "For right now, can you take your helmet off and see if you can breathe in here?"

It's a signal of how much faith I still have in her that I detach the helmet without considering all the horrible ways it could go wrong. Emma smiles and Alyse tilts her slavering alien head curiously. I stand there, wide eyed and blinking, taking a hesitant breath and then a deeper one.

A minute passes while everyone including me waits to see if I'll start gasping.

"Emma?"

"Yes, Dilly?"

"Am I breathing your breath right now?"

"Technically, yes. I hope that's not too gross! Omigod does it smell weird? I had like a shit-ton of hotel mints before we came up."

I can't help but laugh. "Yes, it does smell faintly of mint."

"This is so cringe." Her cheeks colour, and it's cute that a Goddess can still be embarrassed by the thought of an entire population of mutants smelling her breath. "We don't have air filters, but I think I can use Felix's purification powers, adjusted slightly, to help with that."

"You're saving us all," Alyse says gently, "and giving us a new home. Nobody's going to complain your breath smells slightly minty."

"That's because nobody's going to tell them," Emma says sternly. "Now let's turn this rock into a real home."

CHAPTER SEVENTEEN

It takes another couple of weeks to settle in. I spend most of it down on Earth, curled up in a hotel bed with Dani while Emma yanks on our powers. She's trying to automate the asteroid's systems, which means awakening all the objects and me explaining what to do. Having a few thousand different things ask for my opinion and encouragement at every turn is a lot. Dani's exhausted because Emma is using her to very carefully rope a comet. It's now a massive chunk of ice tethered to the asteroid—requiring a whole bunch of complex adjustment to the orbit and spin.

While we've been getting our new home ready, things on Earth have been getting worse. We almost lost the Philadelphia safe house. Dragon, Glowstick and Maddy ended up in a pitched battle with militia, holding the ground for a frantic evacuation effort. We didn't lose any mutants, but the media spins it into us carrying on an illegal war while pretending we want peace. And while they talk in their sombre voices on the cable news channels, they're still hunting mutants.

We've rescued another thirty two, but we didn't save ten. Every time we lose a person, it hurts. Every time, I see Thottie lying sprawled on the sand, then burning in a Westhaven cave. She's a noose around my throat, pulling tighter with every new failure.

On top of that, there's a new trend where humans are being attacked after being falsely identified as mutants. Some of them died from their injuries. That hurts worse in some ways, their own people turning against them in our name.

"We need a solution." Emma looks like she's running on way more than the forty percent she claimed. Once everyone's settled, maybe it'll get easier. We're gathered in the new Asteroid Ems war room, a mostly empty room with a big table. There's a world map on it, but no action figures, because we don't have any ideas. The so-called Council is here, aside from Ray, who's pretty much full-time running therapy these days. Turns out there's a lot of mutants and other refugees who need it. I'm not sure if there's any point still having a Council. It's more like Emma and her group of advisers. I guess that's inevitable when one person is holding way more cosmic power than anyone else.

"Don't push too hard." Alyse sits behind Emma, braiding her hair. I think it soothes both of them. "You've already done so much. We've finally got somewhere safe."

"We had to leave the fucking planet." I'm sprawled in a chair in the corner, who is wheezing contentedly underneath me about how privileged he is to support the weight of the great Chatterbox. "Sure it's safe, but it's a hell of a fucking retreat."

And you will take action as you promised, the voice reminds me, each word dropping on my brain like a brick.

"The original goal was the mutant homeland," Dani says. "I never imagined an asteroid, but it's something."

"It's all we can do for now." Emma leans back against Alyse. "It would be great to get world leaders onside, convince them that we're allies. I'm not sure how we do that. It seems like all we can do is avoid war."

"War's not the problem." My good mood is rapidly eroding, like it does every time we address this fucking topic. "We can win a war. Dani and I can probably win a war on our own. We could send Penance to take out every world leader in minutes."

"I wouldn't do it, just so you know," Violet says, curled up in the chair next to mine. "Not unless it was the last resort and all our survival depended on it."

"They'd just replace them anyway." My mouth twists. "Last night I was talking to the American President's golf clubs. I could have sent them to beat him to death. They would've done it. They were *happy* to. But then who replaces him? Another bigoted monster and we're no better off. So then do I kill every corrupt racist asshole on the planet? I can talk to every goddamn object. It wouldn't actually be hard. But then we're monsters, aren't we? On a planet drowning in blood."

Everyone's looking at me, slightly unnerved.

"I'm not fucking *proposing* it." I throw my hands up. "I'm explaining why war doesn't work. It costs too much, and we can't then come to the world and say *oh, we actually come in fucking peace*."

"It's good to say it." Emma frowns. "We need to have these conversations."

Dani's nodding. "The way I see it, we have two problems. Number one, how do we make peace with humanity? Number two, how do we make fundamental change in the world? Because, let's face it, the world is fucked on a whole bunch of levels. Am I right?"

Nobody disagrees, especially not the voice which shrieks its approval.

"And I don't think we can make fundamental change until we have peace. And honestly, what Dilly said is an option. Not a great one, but we *could* have change in that way. We'd basically be causing our own apocalypse and guiding a new civilisation that rises from the ashes."

Emma makes a very long hmm sound. "There are multiple ways to cause an apocalypse. Throwing an asteroid at the world. Faking an alien invasion. Causing enough civil unrest. But we can't break everything. I have to believe my powers can be used to build something new and better."

Now all I can think of is an apocalypse. A miles-long Gwen stabbing the world and setting off a chain reaction of earthquakes and tsunamis. Dragon twisting in the sky above cities, setting them aflame. Dani sitting cross-legged on our asteroid, sending thousands of smaller rocks flaming towards the surface. Penance, flickering through space, drawing bladed fingers across thousands of throats and leaving gasping, twitching bodies in her wake.

Me, rousing every object in the world at once and giving them their final orders.

Pillows smothering people in their beds.

Cars chasing their owners down streets, engines revving before the crunch of bone and spray of blood.

Toasters edging their way along the rims of bathtubs.

Knives acting out their own slasher movies. No killers required.

Me in an increasingly deserted world, all the objects humanity made floating in my wake, leaving bloody tracks as we walk into a red-hued sunset.

It scares me that I can see all this so easily. Is it the voice, or me alone?

This is not what I wish for. I do not want extinction. But it will require blood for her to be saved.

Farsight's eye flickers through colours like a rainbow strobe. "We aren't monsters, and not all of humanity is opposed to us either. Have any of you been watching the pro-mutant movement? People are raising money, sharing stories of mutant goodness, leading peaceful protests arguing against the government's stance. There are millions of people out there on our side."

"I wish we could spread good ideas like a virus," Dani says.

"That's what Mum wanted." Emma chews on her thumbnail. "But it was too much for her, and she was a better pure psychic than me. I could maybe control a few people's minds and *force* them to have new opinions."

"What if they're influential people?" Dani asks. "Some world leaders, media people. Use the channels they're using to hate us, but convince them we're good. Except then we're a benign dictatorship, really, aren't we? Which is almost worse, cuddling the world into agreement."

"We're not brainwashing anyone." I find this more appalling than an apocalypse. "I don't understand why they can't just accept us. Having to get into people's brains to prove that we're worthy of being allowed to live? It just makes me so fucking *angry*."

"You need a break?" Dani's fingertips brush the back of my hand.

"Maybe." My leg twitches and I knuckle my eyes. "Except there is no fucking break, is there? They're still hunting us, still trying to find ways to eradicate us or neutralise us. And we're up here, tiptoeing around, trying to come up with a kind way to—"

Emma cuts me off with a gesture. "It *does* need to be kind. We've proved our power and strength. Now we need to show that we can be allies and friends. We can defend ourselves, but we can still be partners in a better future."

"And we have to do that without war or brainwashing." Alyse laughs softly. "And with them poised to shoot at us if we ever poke our heads out of our hole. I'm good at making friends, but in this case I'd say they're not worth it."

Emma frowns and twists around to look at Alyse. "You think I'm wrong?"

"I think you're hopeful. It's not a bad thing. But I mean, I've dealt with racists since I can remember. There are shitty parts in people that aren't going away, and we make them worse. If you're like me, brown and queer and mutant all at once? Some people are never going to have me at their table."

There's a long pause where a lot of looks and no words are exchanged.

Emma's expression resolves into something firmer. "Then we need to think of a way to change something big. It might take time, but we'll get there. We can do it together. Think of us as a giant engine, every mutant networked together. We've made an asteroid into a home for thousands of us. We can do this too."

And ok, sure, I get the inspiring speech bit. I just don't feel it at all. It might be the true future and the right thing to do, but I can't spark up any passion for it. Dani's still looking at me because she knows something is up. I'm too fucking transparent. My face shows all my moods, and it's probably in some unattractive scowl.

All our possible futures and potential sins have us tied in knots, and there's no twisted knife that can cut me out of my bind.

The humans don't need to worry about this. In their minds, we're an existential threat so they can act as they please, even committing themselves to stopping our existence. The truth doesn't stand in the way of a compelling narrative. They'll claim we're the unnatural products of vaccines and slaughter us on the battlefield of their flat Earth, then celebrate by throwing more poor people on the giant pyre of capitalism, even as the world burns hotter and they plunge themselves into the furnace of extinction. If we wiped them out first, we'd be doing them a favour. Holy shit. Calm down, brain.

No. You're entirely correct. There is no accommodation with these people. Ignore the billions of those who are powerless, and focus your rage on the deserving. The true rulers of your world, who control the money and pillage the planet without remorse. They should all die. This should be the first true and bloody fruits of your war.

"Fuck," I croak. "I do need a break. You carry on without me."

I plant a kiss on Dani's metal shoulder and walk unsteadily out of the room.

CHAPTER EIGHTEEN

"I can't go around killing everyone," I snap at the voice, the moment I'm out of the room.

Then you must impede the flow of their commerce. It is the only way.

"Fuck's sake. Fine. I'll try."

We shall do more than try.

The voice falls silent, but I'm quivering with excess energy, so I start running just for something to do. Asteroid Ems is a crazy rabbit warren of tunnels, big blasted-smooth tubes around ten feet in diameter, to give plenty of room for the biggest mutants. The floors are a matted texture so you don't slip, all threaded through with rainbow patterns in various Pride flags. Strips of wire along the ceiling glow with a pale blue light. The biggest advance from Westhaven is there are actual fucking maps at every junction. I ignore all the maps, and head for the kitchen area, which is empty aside from Lou, who's picking bits of meat off a pizza.

"There *are* vegetarian ones." I stand at the doorway, watching him.

His face lights up when he sees me—the regular way, not powers-wise. "I always feel like I'm stealing yours."

"There's plenty for everyone, and Keepaway can always get more, ignoring the weirdness of teleporting between Earth and space." I walk over to lean against the counter beside him. "Besides, it's nice to have more vegetarians up here. Do our bit to help the planet."

"A few mutants eating meat-free pizza seems like a very small *bit*," Lou points out.

I shrug. "Might have to do more then."

"Better than literally keeping the lights on, which is all I'm doing these days."

"I was here in the dark and believe me, having your gentle glow illuminate the tunnels is very much appreciated, dear Lucifer. You just have to get used to having Emma putting her hooks in your brain."

"Yes! That's exactly what it feels like. It's not entirely horrible but it's…"

"Weird."

"Exactly. Weird. What a walking thesaurus you are."

That makes me laugh. "You're such an asshole. How are you holding up with everything anyway? How's Maddy?"

"Stalled. Like we agreed we'd do something, but it feels like terrible timing." He frowns at the pizza. "So all I'm doing is glowing a lot at night because, you know…"

"You're a fucking thirsty asshole and always have been. If I was into gender roles, I would say you're a typical male. She *is* perfect for you though. A ball of sunshine to light up the life of the sad little goth boi."

"None of that description is remotely fucking true," he says, but he cracks up all the same because it's at least *kinda* fucking true. "And please, Dilly, do not interfere."

"I would never."

"You fucking would. After like a single drink, or just because you felt like it."

"I shall behave myself like never before." I blink innocently at him. "She *is* like the polar opposite of me though. Is that a good sign?"

"I like her," is all he says.

I lean my head against his arm. "I like you being happy, my darling boy."

"Me too. Maybe one day all this nonsense will die down a bit and we can actually enjoy it."

"From your lips to Goddess's ear." I kiss his cheek and head out of the room. I still have too much nervous energy to sit and eat.

The asteroid is pretty good for running, so I swing by the living quarters and find Summers, because he always appreciates the exercise. It's more spacious than Westhaven, and there are unoccupied chunks awaiting future expansion. I run a loop without seeing a single soul and come out in a corridor on a different part of the building, where a bunch of the newest arrivals are being housed.

It's a tall shaft with ladders ascending upwards and apartments fanning out around it like spokes. I dodge around a group with luggage and run into a corridor that runs along the outside edge of the asteroid.

I run smack into someone around the same age as me, who's surreptitiously painting strange symbols on the floor in front of the nearest door. In my collapsing state, I only see auburn hair and an orange jacket, like she's autumn come to life.

"Shit, sorry." We're sprawled on the floor together, the spraycan rolling away. Summers takes the opportunity to lick my face, and even tries to do the same to the girl, before I wrestle him away.

"I wasn't doing anything," she says, which is super unconvincing.

"Graffiti isn't prohibited here, don't worry, unless it's like—" I get to my feet and squint at what she was painting. It doesn't look like any language I know of, but I'm not a world traveller. It's more like what people paint for occult symbols in TV shows. "Don't worry, weird witchy shit is fine unless it translates into something racist."

"God! No!" Her brown eyes stare into mine. "It's not racist. Or weird witchy shit! It's like, uh, well, it's—"

"Your powers?"

She flushes and looks away. "Well, yeah."

I'm about to ask for details, when two people come out of the door hand in hand. One is short and tan with an impressively long beard and the other is tall with three antenna-like things jutting from their forehead. They're talking quietly, but as soon as they glance at the symbols, their conversation shifts abruptly.

Antennae snatches their hand away. "I wanted the place to *myself*. Is that too much to ask?"

"I saw it first," Beardy says. "The only reason I let you come is because you claimed you'd act like an adult. And now look. Throwing a very public tantrum!"

"You're making a scene in front of *Chatterbox*," Antennae hisses.

"I'm not involved in room assignments," I assure them. "That's Mrs. Kim's area and believe me, she won't stand for any fucking shenanigans."

"There's a very simple solution." Beardy folds his arms across his beard. "And that's for you to move out and give me the space I require. It's not like the asteroid is full."

"I thought you *liked* living with me."

"What did I ever say to give you that impression?"

"Are you really asking me that? What about the life we shared together?"

"Um," my new graffiti friend says. "This probably isn't—"

"You asshole." Antennae lunges for Beardy.

I put myself between them. "Okay, there's enough room for everybody, you two, and if you could just calm down for a second we can—"

That's when Beardy punches me in the side of the head.

"Fuck." I punch him right back, and I've been trained, so I know where to hit him.

He doubles over, and Antennae kicks him in the face,

hard enough that I hear something break. Beardy holds his nose, howling incomprehensible things through his blubbering. I grab Antennae in a chokehold to stop them from doing anything else. Summers is leaping around like he thinks it's a magnificent game, and it's honestly fucking chaos until both Oni and Mrs. Kim come around the corner.

In all the commotion, the graffiti artist has disappeared.

"Hello, Dylan." Mrs. Kim regards me with mixed fondness and irritation.

"I was on a *run*," I splutter. "And came across these two arguing over room assignments, which seems like it's more your fault than mine. All I did was stop them ripping each other's throats out."

"This room." Mrs. Kim scowls. "Always a problem. It's the biggest, with a hot spring that Dragon made, and a window. Emma promised we'll get more viewing portals, but it's around number four thousand on the priority list. So I am left to arbitrate arguments. But these two have made the decision very easy for me. They're both out. This leaves…" She pulls out a tablet and squints at it. "Someone called Shan. I'll let her know the good news. Dylan, can you deal with these two?"

"Oni can do it." The sword drifts down to twitch in front of Beardy's face, and I give Antennae a little shake. "If I let you go, are you going to freak out?"

"No." A sob escapes their lips. "I'm so sorry. Damon, how could I have treated you like that? I don't know what came over me."

I release them and they collapse down beside their partner, checking his bloody face.

"I got so angry all of a sudden." Beardy's voice is all high and pinched. "I can't understand it."

"Kiss, make up, and fuck off." I nudge Beardy with my foot, and the two of them limp off around the corridor together. Oni follows them to the corner and then glides back towards me. By this time, Mrs. Kim has returned with a familiar figure. She's taken off her orange jacket and pulled her hair back into a ponytail, but I can still recognise her. I glance down at the floor, but the symbols have faded into incoherent smears of paint.

"New occupant," Mrs. Kim says. "I'll find those other two some new quarters and send someone for their luggage."

Graffiti Shan, standing just behind Mrs. Kim, gives me a flash of a smile and raises a finger to her lips, both eyebrows quirked plaintively.

"What a strange todo," Shan says, as Mrs. Kim stalks away, Summers following after her like a traitor.

"Incredibly strange." I shift so I'm standing in the doorway. I glance over my shoulder. "It is a nice room. Better than mine and Dani's. I can see why someone might do some underhanded bullshit to get hold of it."

She grimaces at me. "Do you want it then?"

I shake my head. "I want to know how the fuck your powers work. Some psychic shit, right? But triggered by whatever crazy-ass symbols you painted."

"It's a curse," she mumbles. "But this was only a little one, like in this case I wanted them to fight over the room so they'd get kicked out."

"And what the hell language is that?"

She shrugs. "Whatever weird symbols pop in my head."

"Have you used it before?"

Her eyelids flutter.

"Don't worry, I'm not the powers police."

"First time I used it, I had no idea what I was doing." She fidgets with a beaded bracelet around her wrist, painted with a snake chasing its tail. "I was supposed to be writing a letter to my ex-girlfriend, telling her all the reasons I didn't appreciate her cheating on me. What I actually wrote was gibberish, even though I felt like it said exactly what it needed to. So I left it pinned to the door of her dorm room."

She falls silent, as if this is the end of the story.

"And then something wonderful happened?" I prompt.

A flush creeps up Shan's cheeks. "She got kicked out of college for cheating, and her new boyfriend ditched her, spreading some shitty rumours. All her friends refused to speak to her because they said she was a bigot. I felt pretty shitty after that, but I still hooked up with her when she was drunk and lonely." She gives me a lopsided smile. "Kind of an asshole, move right? But I didn't think it was *powers*, more like bad luck. Except then I got a failing grade on an assignment and wrote the same kind of weird note to my professor."

"And the same shit happened."

"She was fired on some pretext. Nobody cared, because they all said she was a terrible professor and an even worse person. So then I figured out I cursed these people. So I got really, really drunk and then when I sobered up, I decided to do some good with it."

I nod, because it's probably what I would've done too. "Curse someone who deserved it."

She brightens. "Yeah, exactly. I was part of this activist group that protested animal cruelty. So I painted a massive mural on the wall of a company that did animal testing." She pauses and wets her lips. "Then nearly a thousand people descended, tore the building apart, and freed all the animals."

"Holy shit." It's my turn to raise an eyebrow. "Kind of impressive."

"Yeah, so that all seemed pretty great. Except the next time, there was a security guard. He shot five people before he got, uh, ripped apart. And when they interviewed the survivors, they were all telling these stories about red veils and a whispering witch that lured them onwards—one who looked scarily like me in the police sketch. This was all around the time the anti-mutant shit really kicked into high gear."

Mrs. Kim comes bustling back with a couple of other mutants in tow. Summers is there too, and acts like he hasn't seen me in approximately ten thousand years. The mutants start moving furniture out of the room the old-fashioned way, with strict instructions by Mrs. Kim not to bash anything against the wall. Shan is still feigning disinterest and slouching casually, but I can see the way her eyes watch everything that goes on.

"You were a part of an activist group." I scratch Summers behind the ears.

"Yeah. I mean you have to *do something*, right? The planet's fucked, society's fucked, all everyone cares about is corporations and money. Who cares what happens in the meantime because the rich fucks will be in their arks in goddamn New Zealand or wherever?" She flushes again, like she's just remembered I'm from goddamn New Zealand.

For my part, I'm curious as to whether the mysterious voice wants to weigh in. I've stumbled onto an environmental activist with powers that might be enormously useful in fighting for the planet. I want to shout at the voice, but it might not give the best impression.

"I mean I'm not some activist hero or anything." Shan looks at the ground. "When everyone was talking about rounding up the mutants, I stayed at home terrified. And then you turned up on my Instagram feed with this video. You were standing all wild and feral in the street saying *come with me*, showing that symbol. So I painted it on my living room wall and waited."

"And here you are." I give her a faint smile. "Reduced to fighting over a room with a view."

She scuffs her foot along the ground. "There's someone to talk to if you think your powers might be useful somehow. I was going to go along and introduce myself but…"

"There's only one room with a hot spring."

She laughs. "Exactly."

"And now you've run into me anyway. I don't believe in fate, but we might have some work for you later. At least I know where you live." I give her an appraising look. "You have a mutant name, Shan?"

"Nobody's ever called me it, but I always liked the name Riot Grrl. You know, I cause riots, and because—"

"Bikini Kill. My girlfriend's favourite band. It's a good name. See you around, Riot Grrl." I give her a salute and jog back off down the corridor. Shan steps into her new room, gazing at the window that looks out over the night side of Earth.

CHAPTER NINETEEN

By the time I've worn out Summers, deposited him in Pear's quarters, and dragged my ass back to the war room chamber, I'm exhausted. In contrast, all the big brains look satisfied.

"I should leave more often," I drawl from the doorway.

Dani waves at me. "You're lucky you missed the discussion around peacekeeping forces. It got heated. I still think it's a no-brainer to intervene."

I cross and perch on the edge of the chair beside her. "What? Go in and stop wars? Yeah, why not? People are suffering."

"Multiple reasons," Farsight says. "It assumes we know what the right side is."

"Stopping war is the right side." Frustration leaks out of Dani's voice.

"But who's in charge *after* the war? Which side of the conflict do we prop up?"

"We give them an asshole test," I say with far more confidence than I feel. "Like the one in the movie where you don't know who the robots are."

"They're talking about *Blade Runner*," Dani tells everyone.

"Am I? It doesn't matter. It's an example. We figure out which side is the least asshole and support them. And if it turns out both sides are assholes, then we take over."

Farsight stares at Emma, obviously waiting for her to weigh in.

"So we talked about all this." Emma is apparently borrowing the mutant power of patience from somewhere. "And we came up with a pretty great idea. We're going to make a documentary."

"Like a movie?" I'm wincing, ready for the voice to scream or laugh at me.

"Yeah." Dani's leaning forward, eyes bright. "Show what it's really like for mutants, humanise us—sorry for the pun. And, like, show us helping. Doing environmental cleanup, having Doc healing people, watching us assist with natural disasters. But up close and personal, do a bit of a charm offensive, make people *like* us."

"Oh, cool. So I don't have to do it then." I slide off the chair.

Yes. You shall be free to slice through the world like an unfettered blade. Cut the throats of these plundering monsters.

"What?" Dani frowns. "Of course. You'll be, like, one of the main ones."

I rub my temples, trying to hint at the voice to shut up. "Murderous me? Who can barely open their mouth without saying fuck? A gay raccoon who's learned to walk upright? I am not the one you want in your pretty picture, Dan."

"Is this a—!"

"No. I'm not being weird." I *am* being weird. Ugh, shut up, Dylan. "You guys can do the documentary thing, and I'll, like, go my own way. The eco cleanup is cool though. Like, we keep growing more trees. Help purify the air. Get rid of that fucking plastic continent or whatever in the ocean."

"You don't like the documentary." Alyse is frowning. Fucking everyone is frowning.

"No. Fuck. It's great." I'm trying to find the right tone, and failing. "Honestly. I sound like I'm being sarcastic, but

I'm not. Showing the world what we do is great. Really fucking great. It's just not *my* specific thing. We should do it, for sure. But not me. That's all. No cameras for Dylan."

Dani's resting her chin in her hand so I can't see the shape of her mouth, but from the crease in her brow, she's trying to figure me out.

"And disaster rescue too, that's really cool." I nod enthusiastically.

I can provide an earthquake. The voice rattles in my diaphragm and for a panicked moment I wonder if I said it. *One in the ocean which will cause limited damage on land and also a vast wave for you to turn away.*

"No," I mutter under my breath. "Don't do that."

"What?" Farsight glares at me.

"I didn't say anything. So is this going to be, like, a YouTube thing, or is Emma just going to jam it in everyone's eyeballs psychically?"

"I am not going to *jam*—" Emma grabs at the table, her eyes wide. "Shit. There's an earthquake happening now. Off the coast of Chile. Yikes, it's a big one."

This fucking *voice*. It can reach out and cause an earthquake, even when I asked it not to. It's about as unnerving as Emma, and I feel trapped between two vast forces I don't understand. All I know is that they both need me. The still-fragile leader of mutantkind and a planet that's trying to hold off a slide into extinction.

"Well?" Alyse. "Are we doing this or not?"

"Yes." Emma beams around the room. "I guess this is Episode One."

She snaps her fingers.

When we reappear, we're standing on a beach. There's golden sand and rocks and scrabbly trees. The water is an impossible blue. There are hundreds, if not thousands, of people all around, sunbathing and swimming and playing football on the sand.

The squad is me, Alyse, Emma and Dani, but given that Emma can reach out and simply drag someone from out in fucking orbit, we have the whole roster available. A moment later, a teenage girl appears with a black visor covering the top half of her head.

"This is Viewfinder," Emma says. "She'll capture footage so we can edit it together."

"Sure." I wave at the new mutant, who tilts her head and looks at me. "Feel free to delete me. One question, Ems. Where's the earthquake?"

"It's not the quake that's the problem. It's the wave on its way. An epic tsunami if I read the signals right. So we need to figure out what to do about it. As quickly as possible."

"Katie could evaporate it in Dragon form," I suggest. "I mean that's probably dumb but—"

"Worth a try," Emma says, and the next moment Katie is stumbling in the sand in front of us, a can of lemonade in her hand.

"Do you think Gwen can absorb water?" Dani asks. "I can probably do at least *something* telekinetically, but liquid is harder than a giant rock floating in space, believe it or not. And I'm guessing there's a lot of liquid."

Emma's pacing, her bare feet sinking in the soft sand. "I'm too fucking stressed to do the math, Dani, but yes. Let's operate on the assumption that we're talking about a fucking shitload of water."

I catch Alyse's eye and we try not to laugh, because we both find it hilarious when Emma starts talking like me.

"I wonder how many sponges I can summon in ten minutes." I close my eyes and attempt to filter the voice of every object in the world down to the most absorbent. "Dani, can you network with me somehow and summon lots and lots of sponges?"

"Dylan," Emma snaps. "This is hardly the time for a bizarre solution."

"Who lives in a pineapple under the sea?" Alyse asks in a very strained voice.

I glance over at her, but I only see one very long leg. Towering above me is an enormous yellow shape that blots out the sun and most of the sky as well.

"Oh my fucking god." I collapse onto the sand. "Alyse, please tell me you are not cosplaying as sexy Spongebob."

Viewfinder is panning her head around, presumably to get the most epic shot.

Katie emits a high pitched squeal. Dani is gasping for air. I'm pretty sure she's laughing.

Behind us, people are screaming and running. I don't speak the language, but I hear the word mutie. Maybe they call us that everywhere.

The good news is that nobody feels inclined to take us on. It's possibly to do with everyone being in swimwear or perhaps our reputations precede us. There are a lot of plastic spades and buckets and various sports balls on the beach for me to work with if people get aggressive.

Alyse is a lot more shapely than Spongebob, but does appear both vast and absorbent. She gives us the finger with two giant yellow hands and wades into the ocean, her hands in the small of her back. "Dani, you better do your part, and Katie, get your fucking wings on. I'm not doing this whole thing on my own."

"Oh fine." Katie gets to her feet. "Dani, do you want to ride me? No sex joke intended. At least you don't have claws like Feral."

"I *can* fly," Dani says.

I shrug. "We can ride Dragon together. Maybe it'll be

romantic?"

Katie's small body stretches out into the long, leathery form of a winged serpent. I think she's even bigger than last time. If any of the beachgoers were still left near us, they're gone now. Nobody wants to fuck with a teenage dragon.

"Get on." She lays her massive neck down on the sand, steam coming from her nostrils in a haze. Dani floats us up and onto her. It's like being on a giant bridge made of leather. There's nothing at all to hold onto. I can see why Feral needed to use her claws. At least Dani can hold us in place if necessary.

"Fuck me," I mutter.

"Romantic enough for you?" Dani grins at me over her shoulder.

Before I get the chance to answer, Katie beats her wings and we're suddenly, crookedly aloft, sliding backwards down the neck as she climbs steeply.

"Fuck me," I say again, as I feel Dani tugging me back upwards.

Katie soon levels off and we can see Alyse off to our left, wading doggedly forward. The tide is receding sharply from the beach where we left Emma. In the distance, we can see an odd, glossy patch of water spreading in both directions.

From the other side of us, a buzzing sound indicates a squadron of helicopters approaching. There's a chance they're coming to monitor the tsunami, but they might be coming here to fuck with a teenage dragon and a giant walking sponge.

This time, I'm very careful to check for any guns in the vicinity, but it seems like they're only news helicopters. We've got our own camera girl on the case, but they might as well film us helping out. At least they can't accuse us of bias that way.

Assuming we succeed and don't fuck up horribly.

From behind us, sirens start up.

It turns out a tsunami is pretty fucking terrifying actually, even when it's only a really big wave in an ocean already full of them. It messes with your sense of scale, especially when you're perched on the back of a girl in the form of a flying lizard that now seems rather small.

Alyse is still growing, but even she's not going to be able to absorb all of this.

Katie banks off to the left and swings back around. "Dracarys." An enormous inferno pours from the cavern of her chest.

A massive plume of steam trails us. If it catches us, we'll be boiled in our skins, but we're moving too fast. Dani slumps against me, unstitching the wave into thousands of waterspout tendrils that collapse into the ocean. I can't tell how much they're doing to it, or whether it's just a trick of my eyes or the light that's making it look smaller.

Maybe Alyse is still getting bigger.

The wave hits her and she falls backwards very, very slowly. The water rushes inside her, swelling her even larger. I think you could probably see her in space at this size.

Katie pins her wings back and heads for the sky.

I fall from her back, spiralling downwards through the air.

"Dragon, you little *asshole*," I shriek.

Thankfully, Dani catches me telekinetically. I did *not* want to plunge into one of the enormous flooded crevasses of Alyse's swollen yellow body.

The wave is definitely losing steam. This time, when Dani deposits me back on Dragon, I cling to her thankfully.

Above us, the helicopters buzz. This must look like some surreal prank, but I'm hoping *someone* will be happy. I think it's still going to be a very high tide. Hopefully some of those terrified beachgoers have their phones out. The Spongebob memes alone are going to be gold and besides, we just saved them and their entire city from being swamped.

Score one for the mutants. Let's hope that's how they record it.

Katie hovers, flapping her wings wildly. The spongy figure below stretches out across the ocean so far it's hard to see the edges.

"Feel sick," Alyse groans.

"Be careful squeezing yourself out," I call down. "Or you'll cause a flood anyway."

"Emma wants to teleport me into space and wring me out as a second water supply."

"Really?" I ask.

"Oh, take that look off your face, Dylan. It'll be purified first so you don't have to sob about drinking water from my insides."

I snort so hard I almost fall off Katie's neck again.

"This is very unpleasant," Alyse groans.

"It's also the weirdest way anyone's been saved from a natural disaster." Dani's already pulling up news footage on her phone. There are aerial shots of an enormous Alyse, as well as Dragon soaring through the sky with steam trailing behind her.

Dani finally finds a livestream with American narration.

"…definitely extrahuman assistance. It is unclear why they've done it. We can't assume they performed this for altruistic reasons."

"Really, Jim?"

"Maybe this monstrosity will walk out of the ocean and squeeze itself onto a different target."

"That seems like an extraordinarily roundabout way to

attack us given what we've seen from them so far. Surely the giant sword or the one who controls armies would just knock down the front door."

"You've always got to look for an ulterior motive, Anna. It may look like they're doing this to help, but they're not. You can't trust them."

"That's not what the people of Chile are saying today, Jim."

"I hope they don't learn the truth the hard way. By their deeds you shall know them. We only need to wait for their darkness to be revealed."

Dani makes a sound of frustration in her throat and mutes her phone.

"I'm happy we saved the people," I tell her. "Gotta admit I'm not entirely surprised about that reaction."

"There was one voice in our favour." She reaches for my hand. "That's more than before."

"Maybe." I stare out at the ocean, now mostly placid aside from tiny whitecaps on the waves, gently buffeting the vastness of SpongeAlyse. "I can't even tell anymore."

CHAPTER TWENTY

We make it back to Asteroid Ems without any further incident. Alyse is wrung out and returned to her normal shape, although she's still bedraggled when Emma packs her off to bed.

"Saved the day in the weirdest way." I can't stop smiling.

"It was you who gave me the idea." Alyse pokes me in the side.

"My practical tactical brilliance."

"That or too many memes." She holds her back and pulls a face. "I'm glad we did it though. Aren't you?"

I shrug. "We saved a bunch of people. Hard to feel bad about that."

She narrows her eyes at me, but is too tired to do much else, and disappears off into her sleeping quarters, leaving me alone.

There. The voice grates in my head, making it pound. *I allowed you to posture and preen like heroes.*

I rub at my temples ineffectually. "I guess you did."

No guess, my little conduit. I helped you. Now it's your turn.

Oh shit. I should have known this was coming. "My turn to?"

The voice screams and I nearly pass out. There are fault lines in my brain grinding against each other, sending shockwaves of pain through my jaw. My bones seem bird-like. I'm sure they'll shatter. Tears leak out of my eyes. I lean back against the wall and wait for it to pass.

Finally, it ebbs away. I don't know how long I've been frozen here. Nobody's come to find me. Either Emma can't pick up on the voice, or she's too busy. They're probably in the war room debriefing how amazing Emma is and concocting the next episode of their documentary. I swipe blood away from my nose.

I'm sorry. The voice is much quieter now. *I overreacted.*

"Just a bit." I poke gingerly at my face, but it appears my skull made it through unscathed. "It's my turn to help, that's what you mean, right? To strike back. Kill someone or fuck something up."

To scream on my behalf. Clenching my fist around the fault lines was exhausting and I no longer have the strength to tear and rend. You shall do it for me, my beautiful, feral creature.

"They want to help clean up the oceans and shit. Like we really are trying."

It is not enough to clean up your own mess. You have to cut it off at the source.

I don't love being screamed at by the voice of a dying planet, but it has a point. Even before all this started, I ditched school to march for climate change, and not only because it meant a couple of periods off. Somehow we need to do something to change the world.

Now I'm in a position to take action.

"What do you want?" I ask.

Dani is curled up and adorably asleep in our quarters. I undress and slide into the sheets behind her, wrapping my legs around her warm and slumbering body.

She gives a pitiful moan. "Why are you so cold?"

"It's more that you're so hot." I kiss the back of her neck.

She makes a half-hearted attempt to turn towards me and kindle something hotter, but falls back asleep with her lips mashed against my cheek and her hand on my stomach.

"Dani," I whisper.

"I love you," she says in response, which I like, but is not actually the direction I want to go.

"How do you feel about an unofficial mission?"

One eye squints open. "This isn't a sex thing?"

"I mean we can do that *first* but—"

She sits up in bed. Her t-shirt is slipping off her shoulder which is very distracting, and I kiss her smooth, tan skin.

Except her thoughts are travelling in other directions now. "Unofficial mission?"

I'm about to tell her all about the voice. It should be safe, because Dani is no tiny, scary Heart, but the words get diverted somewhere between my brain and my mouth. Usually there's no connection there at all, which makes it extra annoying. I try again, to say *so, it turns out I can hear the voice of the planet*, but I have a small coughing fit instead.

Dani rubs my back until I recover.

I wipe my eyes. "Sorry. I'm talking about taking action."

"Taking what kind of action? I'm confused."

"It's not for a documentary, but we need to stop the companies who are fucking the planet up. It's important, Dan. Not just cleaning up *after* them." I fight the urge to smooth the frown out of her forehead.

"Bring it to the council," she says. "We can discuss it there."

"I don't want to waste hours arguing about it. It's the right thing to do. You *know* it is."

"Dilly." I know from the sigh at the edge of my name what her answer is. "I agree, but it's the wrong time to do it." My reaction must be obvious from my face, because she takes my hand and kisses my fingertips one after the other in the sexy way where her bottom lip drags over them. "We will get there, I promise."

Not soon enough. The voice clangs like dissonant bells.

Dani pulls me closer and kisses me, her tongue at the corner of my mouth. Her hand plucks at the hem of my t-shirt. "Stay in bed with me instead," she whispers against my neck. "We shall stave off the end of the world with love."

A beautiful sentiment, but nothing more than empty words.

"Soon." My voice dissolves into a sigh as it leaves my throat.

It had better be, the voice rasps, but it is kind enough to leave me alone and let me cling to these moments that hold me together against the cold.

Later, when Dani's asleep again, I slip out of bed and pad barefoot towards the door. My first stop is across the hall, where Feral is curled up at the foot of Violet's mattress. They both prefer to sleep in the room with Dani and I, but we've got an arrangement where this doesn't happen every goddamn night.

The instant I set a single toe inside the door, both of them are at full alert. Violet is a flickering forest of blades and Feral is beside me with teeth bared and tail twitching.

"Everything's fine." I try to be soothing with my tone and gestures. "Honestly. I'm just doing a solo mission. Except not an actual solo mission, cos I'm asking if you want to join."

"Of course I want to." Feral is practically purring. She has zero questions.

"Where would we be going?" Violet's face is masked in hues of dark blue and a burned red.

"To strike a blow on behalf of the planet."

"Seriously, Penny. Do you really need to know?" Feral asks. "We go where Chatty goes."

"I am curious about the solo nature of our endeavour. There has been much discussion about the rightness and wrongness of various courses of action. Now we have Dylan in the dead of night, sneaking about on their own."

"Not everyone agrees." I may as well be upfront. "It's still important though."

"For the planet." Violet's face darkens. "She cries to me when I slip through the passageways at the edges of the world. Faint and far off, like something lost in the trees."

I frown. "I didn't know you heard that."

"You never asked. I didn't like to volunteer. I'm strange enough as it is." For a moment, the mask of her face cracks with a blood-red smile, and then Penance unfolds into dark-haired, pale Violet, the smile less bloody but more beautiful. "Of course I'll come too."

I want to tell her that I hear the world too, although it's different and clearer for me, but something stills my tongue and gently clamps my teeth together. I guess there's nobody who can know.

"So are we doing this?" Feral asks, and my tongue loosens.

"Yes," I say. "We have one more person to collect."

The others follow me through the faint bluish glow of the night-lit tunnels. I wonder if it's still Lou's power, modified somehow by Emma. It doesn't look like his colour.

When we reach our destination, I tap lightly on the door, but it takes a few knocks to rouse the occupant.

"Hello?" Her auburn hair is tangled and her mouth is soft from sleep. She's wearing a long t-shirt with a logo for a band I don't know. Behind her, the glorious vista of space is revealed through the asteroid's single window. "Oh. My God. It's you. Chatterbox."

"And their amazing friends." Feral shows all her teeth, and I pat her head gently to encourage her to show a few less. "Come to pluck you away on an adventure, whoever you are."

"Riot Grrl." She tugs at the hem of her t-shirt. "Let me get into something more mission-y."

The main problem with living in an asteroid is you can't just walk out the front door. Keepaway is the main transport, but their powers don't stretch to teleporting us from orbit to the ground without borrowing some juice from Emma. The question is whether Ems will notice with everything else that's going on—like, how omniscient is one of my dearest friends? The other alternatives are worse. Jumper's never liked me, because she thinks I'm a loose cannon and this shit is only going to prove her right. I don't think Roxy can fly in space and we'd need to float down in space-suits with her. If she burned up on re-entry, I'd never forgive myself.

When I show up at Keepaway's door, they smile. That's a good sign. They're in a hoodie and pyjama pants, their short hair slicked back.

"Keeps." I beam as wide as I can. "How do you feel about secrets? Like something you wouldn't tell Emma, even if she asked. I know this is weird and all, but it's hard to explain and the thing is that—"

"Dylan." They hold up one hand. "You saved my life. You've probably forgotten that, because you've saved so many. And more than that, you gave me confidence. You trusted me when I was weak. I'll do anything you want me to."

"Jesus, Keeps. You're making me cry or blush, or some combination of the two."

"I mean it." Their eyes are dark and intense. "Whatever you need, Dilly."

I fumble my phone out of my pocket because all this emo is making me feel awkward. "We need to go here." I've got a GPS position written down in my notes app. It took me a while to translate from the voice's navigation system, which relied on energy lines that don't show up on any map. I eventually figured it out though, without any help at all.

Keepaway smiles. "Sure. Easy. Beep me when you want to come home." They clap their hands together and gesture at the four of us.

We're gone.

We appear in the dead of night on a quiet street. The houses are set well back from the road, but there are no fences. We've teleported into the middle of a high-security gated compound.

"Whose house is this?" Penance's shadowed grey face is barely visible.

"The man who runs the company which owns the most factory farms in all of America. It's not his family home, but the one he lives in during the week. While he's working."

"So we're going to burn down his house?" Feral asks, clearly having zero problem with this, which is why I brought her.

"Sort of. We're going to get a mob to do it for us. And then we're going to steal his top secret files and dump them on the internet. Which is usually Emma's thing, but she's busy with other stuff, so it's up to us."

"A mob?" Violet asks.

"Yeah, that's Riot Grrl's job. She does some painting, and we broadcast her magic spell shit all around town. The people come to fuck it up good and proper. We stand back with clean hands." I can see Shan's about to protest, so I jump in. "Except this place is fancy and there are guards. And that's where we come in. They're probably regular people on shit wages, so let's incapacitate rather than kill. Do you know what that word means, Fairy?"

"Yes, of course I do."

"I just mean we've talked about this distinction before and—"

"Sheathed claws." She flexes them, entirely unsheathed, in my direction. "Besides, Penny is scarier than me and she's definitely far stabbier."

"I assume I'm here if it all turns to shit," Violet says quietly. "The monster of last resort."

"Not a monster." I resist the urge to touch her hand and reassure her. "And hopefully we won't need you."

Riot Grrl is already painting. She's not doing anything fancy, just spraying a rough assemblage of strange curves and lines.

"How do we make it so it doesn't apply to us?" I ask. "Like you targeted those specific people before over the room arrangements."

"Oh shit." She drops the can and bends to pick it up. "It's harder on this sort of mass scale. I don't really know how to target it at everyone *except* you. I guess if you feel a weird compulsion to smash, you should probably bail?"

"I already do," Feral and I say simultaneously.

"To be fair, that might be our natural state," I add. "But like… better be safe?"

"It's fine." Riot Grrl squints up at the house, shaking the can. "I've done this before. A spell this complicated will take a while, so y'all might as well chill. I'll deal with spreading the word, too." She gives us a grin Feral would be proud of. "They'll tear this place to the ground. Text you when I'm done."

Maps says this super exclusive compound is a little way from a small town, so we dodge the security patrols and leap the fence. So much for high security—there's a dude in a tower, and a couple of guys pootling about in fucking golf carts, but we dodge them easily. It *probably* helps that Penance is a sneaky assassin, Feral is an apex predator, and I can fly through the air wuxia style with my sword.

Once we're out, we jog towards the bright lights. I send Oni off into stealth mode, given that we might see people, which means Feral has to move slow enough for me to keep up, although she keeps up a running commentary about my lack of speed. Penance periodically flickers out of existence and appears further up the road, waiting for us with an expression of immaculate calm.

We eventually come across the big spinning neon sign of a diner. There are two trucks parked outside it.

Feral stands at the edge of the parking lot. "I'm hungry. I want pie."

"This is a terrible idea," I tell her.

"I could do with some coffee," Violet adds.

I glare at the diner. It does look warm inside and almost deserted. "Fine. Put your hood up over your ears and tuck your tail into your pants. We don't want news of muties getting out. And try not to smile."

Feral rolls her eyes at me.

I pull my own hood up and we walk into the diner.

There are two guys in jackets and caps sitting at the counter, so we find the booth farthest from them and slide into the seats. The menus are big and shiny and plastic, and Feral immediately starts muttering about various flavours of fruit pie.

"They're coming over." Violet begins to flicker.

"Stay." I glance over my shoulder to see both cap dudes moving in our direction.

"Come on, fellas. Take a seat," the waitress calls.

The two pause at the table, looming over us. One of them cracks his knuckles. "Furry face, Bill. You were right. Muties."

CHAPTER TWENTY-ONE

"You want to walk on, *fellas*," I drawl in my best fake American accent.

Feral bares her teeth at them. "No, let them stay. I want to hear what they have to say."

There's no fucking way this ends well. I have to knock them out before Feral launches herself at them and we end up with a bloodbath and cops showing up.

One guy tips the brim of his cap back. "We ain't got no problem with you. My sister's kid's a mutie. I punched my brother in law out when he threatened to turn the kid in to them Quietus folks. Next thing they tell us we're at war. I've got to hide my damn nibling in my basement or they'll scoop him up."

"Nibling?" Violet mouths at me.

"Niece or nephew," the guy growls. "My own damn blood. Can't tell me we ain't the same. It's like when my kid came out as bisexual. Pastor told me that was a sin too. I would've punched him out, but my wife talked me down. Anyway, sorry for rambling on, but I wanted to come on over and say you can order yourselves a piece of pie on me. And that I'm sorry you're going through this shit. Not all of us have hate for mutants."

I still feel tense, even though the conversation has gone wildly differently than I thought. The other guy hasn't even said a damn thing, just nodded along and sucked his teeth like it's agreement.

"That's mighty kind of you," Feral says. "I'll have a piece of peach."

"Your nibling." I look up at the guy. "Are they safe?"

"I'll protect them with my life," the man says. "Don't know if that's enough."

I pull up the sleeve of my hoodie and show him the Cute Mutants tattoo on my wrist. "If you ever fear for his life, draw this on the wall of your basement. Someone will come and rescue him."

"He's a goddamn American," the guy says. "And he'll be safe in his home if it's the last thing I have to do."

"A pointless declaration," Violet says. "Your nationality means little if you're dead."

The other guy grunts at this, as if it's a joke, and his friend glares.

"What's so funny, Bob?"

"She ain't exactly wrong. Better to be safe and alive, isn't it?"

"Maybe so, maybe so. We'll keep this tattoo shit in mind. Now we'll let you all get back to your pie. Three peach, was it?"

I shrug because I have no idea. Pie to me usually means meat, so we may as well try peach.

The two guys tip their caps and wander back to the counter. We all get our pie, which turns out to be surprisingly good, and our new friends leave soon after. The diner stays almost silent for the rest of the night, the only disturbance being the waitress who drifts around cleaning, restocking, and occasionally offering us coffee.

Finally, we get a single message from Riot Grrl, showing her doing a thumbs up in front of a blurred out building frontage.

"You think that's good?" Feral asks.

"Thumbs up." I zoom in on the building, but can't make out any symbols. The whole point of inciting a riot is to keep our hands clean. I push my plate to one side, ready to leave, but the bell dings repeatedly as a small group of people come bustling into the diner. They're a fairly diverse bunch, but what they have in common is being all worked up.

"—been going on for God knows how long. Doris! Doris! Have you heard?"

"Heard what, Rick? It's too early for this shit."

"Look!" A middle aged Black guy in workout clothes thrust his phone at the waitress. "The things they've been doing. It's unnatural!"

"It's inhuman!" A broad-shouldered woman in overalls pounds her fist on the counter.

Violet frowns over my shoulder. "Do you think this is us?"

I shrug. It's definitely a bunch of pissed off people, but humans do get shitty about a wide range of things. They might be mad at us. News travels fast.

"That man is evil," Workout Dude shouts. "And the things his company does to those poor, innocent animals. Millions of them, all across the country. It's appalling."

"We will not let it stand!" It's a young guy with a base-ball bat. Even now, I get this pang when I see the tapered shape.

"New girl got it done." Feral beams.

Through the grimy diner window, an auburn-haired figure waves furiously.

"Time for phase two." I slide out of the sticky vinyl seat and we stride toward the exit. Lucky those surprisingly friendly dudes paid for our pie, because I forgot to bring cash. Next mission, I need to plan shit better. Contingencies, Dylan.

We detour around the group of people clustered at the diner counter, still arguing about exactly what type of wrath they should be doling out.

"Find him!" Overalls shouts, to general approval. "Make him pay."

"Come here, buddy." I send out a flicker of awareness to the bat, who tears herself from the young guy's hand and into mine, almost as if she's been passed to me. He doesn't even seem to notice, too worked up about *what's going on.*

I give the bat an experimental swing.

"Oh, that feels good," she says.

"It really does. How do you feel about fucking shit up?"

"I haven't really done that before. I've been involved in a small number of home runs though." She pauses. "Does fucking shit up feel something like that?"

"Hold tight and we might find out."

Outside the diner, small knots of people cluster together, deep in animated conversation. There's a lot of shouting and pointing. All the fingers are in the direction where the dude's home is. One group is stomping away from us.

"Keep up, Dilly." Feral lopes off down the road, shifting into all-fours mode, which allows her to run even faster. Penance is already gone, folded away into the air.

"Fucking superspeedy brat," I shout at Feral's retreating back, and sprint after her.

The good news is that everyone's so worked up by Riot Grrl's spell that nobody notices the monster-girl bounding through their midst. A ragged line of people straggles up the highway towards the gated community in the distance.

"Fuck. They're going to beat me there." Theoretically, Feral and Penance could keep things chill, but of the spectrum of chill mutants—which I am decidedly on the hothead end of—Feral is well past me. "Wait here," I say to Riot Grrl, who nods assent.

The bat makes a genteel throat-clearing sound. "Would you like me to assist you?"

"As long as it doesn't involve you trying to hit me like a baseball, sure."

"Hold tight please, and don't let go." She tugs me up off the ground so fast it almost dislocates both my shoulders. We fly together in a massive arc, giving me a great vantage to where the angry mob has reached the main gate to the compound. Some are trying to dismantle them, others are trying to climb over. A furry streak darts around the outside and leaps atop a pillar a single bound. She perches there, shading her eyes as she watches me move through the sky.

I'm obviously taking too long, because she springs down and runs for the guard patrol, who've ditched their golf carts and drawn their guns.

Even from here, I see Feral hesitate. She's trying to be good and not tear them apart.

They're not going to wait.

The bat and I are descending now, but the first guard's already firing. Feral throws herself backwards, so goddamn fast. And she's *still* trying to be on best behaviour, retreating rather than attacking. They fired on you, for fuck's sake. It's claws out time, Fairy.

My new friend and I plummet out of the sky. Nobody notices doom descending.

At the last second the bat halts, making me briefly weightless.

I drop hard onto one of the guards, my body impacting with his. We both crash to the ground.

The bat whips away, slamming into the next guard's kneecap so hard it pops like a gunshot. He drops, white as a sheet and unconscious. His gun skids across the tarmac towards a knot of bushes. The guy underneath me is writhing, so I punch him in the face and slam one knee down onto the wrist of his gun hand, putting as much of my weight behind it as I can.

There's one guy remaining, swinging his weapon around to point at me.

Feral hits him from the side. Her claws are sheathed,

but she's still far stronger.

"Fucking muties," Feral's guard spits.

I glance up at the front of the house. The symbols painted there aren't recognisable, jagged and swooping shapes mashed together from alien alphabets. They blend into a river in my vision, speaking directly into a deeper part of my brain. There's a part of me that comprehends this, that wants to obey and—

Fuck. I spin around. It's probably best I don't get caught up in ripping the damn place apart.

There's a tortured creak, followed by a crash, and the compound gate finally gives way. The tide of humanity surges through, running headlong down the beautifully paved street towards this house. It's like a zombie movie, except the humans are the monsters undone by their cravings.

"Reinforcements," the guard says triumphantly.

"This isn't Nightcrawler's origin story," I tell him. "This mob is here for your boss, so I'd recommend getting out of their way."

Penance unfolds from the air beside me. "Shall I enter the house and find the information?"

I get to my feet. "Yes, go. We'll deal with the chaos out here." Even though I'm not looking at them, the shapes of the symbols on the building are burned into my mind, like closing your eyes after accidentally looking into a light. The meaning swirls, resolving piece by piece.

I want to turn, to tear this place apart, to dig the villain out from among his lavish surroundings and make him *pay*. To trap him in a tiny cage with all the others of his kind, wallowing in the dark and the stench.

Feral is growling low in her throat.

"We need to fucking bounce." I spin her away.

"This house cannot stand," roars one of the guards. "This man has profited from his evil deeds for too long.

Today, he pays the price." He staggers bloody-mouthed up to the front door, the other guard following on all fours, dragging his broken leg behind him.

The mob has reached us too, but we're stones in a river that they flow around. They're all shouting, but it's nothing but singleminded rage.

Feral and I forge back through the crowd. The roar of them surges, but underneath it all is the blip of a police siren. It was probably inevitable. As soon as they get a glimpse of Riot Grrl's symbols, they'll attack too, which might be a step too far given how cops are.

The car noses carefully through the crowd, lights flashing.

"Fairy," I snap, as she springs high and lands on the front of the car with a crunch.

By the time I reach her, the police are out. They're both tall, bony white dudes, except one's extra damn tall, like he'd have to fold himself in half to fit in the car. Both have their guns pointed in Feral's face.

"Hands on your head," they shout. "Get on the ground."

Penance hovers, glowing baleful orange like a moon sitting low on the horizon. Her bladed fingers hang down behind them. I don't think they even realise she's there.

"We came to stop it." Feral collapses to her knees. "There are too many of them and we don't want to hurt civilians."

My new bat rolls towards me, nudging against my foot.

"Shall I?" Her voice is soft but eager.

"No, stay down," I mutter.

"I'm going to need to see your papers," the cop says. "Mutants can't be in public without the appropriate documentation."

What the fuck kind of new law is this? It already puts me in a bad mood for dealing with these pricks, not that I need it when it's the fucking cops. I put my foot on the baseball bat, who's eager to leap into my hand.

"You don't want to start shit with us, I promise you. And these people, they're just letting out some grievances. Time to turn around and go home." I whistle their guns to my side to make it more obvious.

"You're that Chatterbox." One cop claps his hand to his holster as if his gun will magically reappear if he wishes hard enough. "The orders are to shoot you on sight."

"You can try." The guns empty themselves obediently, showering me in a little trickle of shells. "My friend here might not like it."

I gesture above their heads, and they turn to see Penance grinning down at them like a fucking Halloween decoration.

"Radio for backup," the tall cop says.

The other runs to the car, but the instant he reaches inside, the handset leaps from its cradle and wraps itself around his throat.

"The fuck?" Tall Boy reaches for his gun *again*, and then grabs his phone instead. I think he's going to record me, but it's one of those golden eye ones. He presses it to his lips, whispering like he's trying to seduce Siri.

Feral slaps the phone out of his hand with one claw, and it shatters on the ground.

"You think you are ascendant, but you will be brought low," the cop snarls. "Michael is rising."

I'm very unhappy to hear that name again. "What the fuck does that mean?"

A dull thump comes from the house, and it's the piece of information the cops need to finally accept we're not the threat. They hare off, and we jog half-heartedly after them. The mob has done their job well, and the house is burning. Flames lick eagerly up the front, which hopefully means Riot Grrl's symbols are losing their power.

The CEO is out on the front lawn, face down. I can't tell if he's still alive. I'm not sure what the right outcome is.

He is a murderer, the voice snaps. *He has killed countless beings, and presided over the mistreatment of more. There is so much blood on his hands, we could drown him and untold generations of his descendants. If he is dead, it is only justice.*

"Fuck's sake," I mutter. "Or we could do trials and shit, you know. That's what this evidence is for. You got the laptop, right, Penny?"

"And his phone." She hands them to me. "You know what to do?"

"No, but Emma has these." I scoop a couple of little black gadgets out of my pocket and shimmy them into the ports of both devices. "Wee hackery things that go slurp and spit out all the data somewhere."

"Very technical." Violet smirks at me. "Such jargon. I almost believe you're an expert."

"Ha fucking ha, Penny my darling. It's called delegation, and let's hope it fucking works, because it's what'll bring this guy and all his companies down in flames."

Her cheeks turn faintly pink, and I can't figure out why, so I poke at the laptop screen, which tells me it's seventy three percent complete.

"Will Emma be mad?" Feral asks. "That we ran off and did this?"

"Did what?" I blink at her, as innocent as I can. "That a mob attacked a CEO and leaked a bunch of information online?" I flush far brighter than Penance. "Okay, fine. If she is mad, I'll take the blame. Don't worry about that."

The laptop chirps at me and says it's complete, so I toss it into the lovely floral arrangement at the entrance to the compound. Behind me, the house is burning merrily, and I can't even see the CEO because his lawn is being trampled by the cooling remnants of the mob.

Mission fucking accomplished.

"Keepaway." I tap my ear. "We're good to come home."

CHAPTER TWENTY-TWO

The asteroid is silent when we return. The others head for bed, but I'm still wound up. Adrenaline from disobeying Emma, from the voice burning in my brain, from doing something I still think is mostly right. Especially if the guy's in jail, and not, like, dead on his front lawn.

Stop prevaricating, the voice snaps.

"I don't even know what that means."

You are my weapon. My warrior. You have killed before, and you will kill again. Until the world is safe, we will have to—

"Mrs. Hall." I almost crash into Emma's mother, standing at a new window someone's built into the asteroid. She's looking out, her hands against the glass, as if she wants to reach through and brush them across the blackness, gathering stars in the palm of her hand. "Are you okay?"

"Yes, Dylan. I am fine." She turns towards me. "Melancholy is all."

I lean back against the window, like it's not the entire fucking void of space behind me. "I'm sorry, you know. I've been meaning to say that, but I didn't know how. It was a shitty hand you got dealt with, like, your ex."

"I wish I could remember any of it." She bangs one hand lightly against the glass, and I jump. "That's the cruelest thing they took from me. I used to be a fighter. That's what the memories say. Like you, Dylan, standing up against the world—a flame that refused to be doused.

Except when Heart stole everything, they hollowed me out and what grew back was stunted."

I tilt my head towards her and frown. "I don't think that's true."

"Really? I'm a ghost in the world. Wandering the halls of this place like Mrs. Rochester, while the daughter I spent my life raising turns into her other parent."

Air huffs through my nose. "She's better than Heart. Even if I don't always agree with her, Ems is fucking *trying*. And I don't know how I'd cope with near-infinite power. I probably would've fucked it up already."

"I worry." Her voice comes out all husky. "That's all. In the memories I have seen, there are beautiful moments with Xin, and yet they still turned out..." She draws an arc with her hand, falling sharply.

Heart of a Flower, the voice spits. *What a disappointment.*

I want to tell it to shut up, but I don't think Mrs. Hall needs me ranting at thin air. Instead, I turn around and stare out at space, even though it gives me wicked vertigo.

"There's a lot of universe out there."

Mrs. Hall takes my hand and squeezes it. "Yes, but this tiny scrap still matters. You can't forget that. Don't zoom out and out until everything is at a distance, and it's all so easy to make drastic decisions. You've got to remember everything is important." She drops my hand and shuffles away, leaving me staring at the stars.

Yes, the world matters, the voice says. *One among an endless host, but she is vital.*

"I'm not fucking arguing with you," I say irritably, and then stomp off to our quarters, where I stare at the ceiling.

After my sleepless night, I end up nodding off at breakfast, and by the time I make it to the war room, the conversation is in full swing.

"—the defund the police plan," Alyse is saying. "Take all their money. Steal it from the army too. Fund all the things. Universal basic income, social welfare, child protection."

Farsight's eye has been a rainbow blur since she upgraded, but it toggles red at this. "They'll take it as a declaration of war. If we steal the American military budget then they'll—"

"Not just theirs." Alyse looks Farsight in the eye. "All the budgets around the world. Put money where it needs to be. Redistribute the wealth on a global scale."

"Stop being naive." Farsight leans across the table. "Even if that would work, which it won't, we'd become the enemy of every government and corporation."

"We'd save more people than we did with the tsunami. If we're going to change the world, we might as well do it properly."

I stand in the doorway and applaud. "I like this plan."

It has some promise, I agree. Yet those monsters in charge will find some way to claw, and rip. They must be put down.

Dani joins in on the applause, her eyes on me.

Alyse gives a mock bow. "They'd attack us, Farsight is right, but we can deal with the attacks. Mostly everyone would be substantially better off so—"

Farsight makes an irritated gesture. "Humans will still fight. Claim we're destroying their way of life. It's a take-over by stealth. You're undermining entire systems of government and doing what you think is right. Your benign dictatorship."

"Ugh." Emma slumps in her chair. "Yes, we need to bring people with us. Which is what the documentary is for, and that's working right? I mean we rushed it out there pretty raw, but, like…"

"It's getting views." Feral holds up her phone. "Hundreds of millions. Comments are mostly positive. I mean there's plenty of hate in there but you get that on fucking music videos. So we need the idea for Episode Two, right? Carry on momentum."

I have no ideas about how to *rehabilitate our image*. The whole idea sticks in my throat and makes me want to punch something.

There is only one option, the voice growls. *You must punish those who need it. Rid the world of the villains who suck it dry, and will not stop until–*

"What about Michael?" I can't exactly mention the cop from last night, but there's obviously something going on with that, and it's getting worse.

"That's…" Emma's eyes flicker briefly, as if data is scrolling over her irises. "A problem without an obvious solution. Michael isn't a person. He's an artificial intelligence that evolved from a prayer-answering chatbot of all things."

"So that's easy." I meet her gaze. "Slap him out of the internet."

"Except he's networked into people." Emma waggles her fingers. "Like he's got tendrils into the brains of his followers, and it's not so easy to remove without…" She makes a visceral squelching sound.

"Well that's fucked." I drop a Nightcrawler figure on the map. "So let's teleport in and deal with him before he becomes a bigger problem."

Emma shakes her head. "I'll do this on my own. It requires subtlety and hacking powers, neither of which you have, Dylan."

There's an awkward silence after this, broken by Feral. "Whatever we do, it needs to be big and cool…" She rummages in her bag and drops a Spongebob plushie onto the map. "So, if we send Alyse *here*…"

The whole room erupts in laughter, and Alyse reaches out to snatch the toy away. "Have you been carrying that around waiting for this moment?"

Feral bats her eyelashes. "Worth it."

Everyone else is still enjoying the joke, but Emma switches back to intense and intent. "Yes, it's very cute, but you're right, Feral. We've got to go bigger, and that doesn't mean hunting Michael. I'm starting by cleaning up that oil spill you saw the other day."

I hope the voice will be happy about this, but...

Cleaning up the mess is merely adequate at best. It will continue to happen unless you eradicate the source. This concept is very simple, and I think you deliberately misunderstand me, flinching away from what's necessary.

"There's not going to be one magical thing." Dani splays both her hands on the map like two invading armies. "Maybe Episode Two should show a whole bunch of actions around the world." She moves Iceman to Australia, where forest fires are, and OG Jean Grey to Turkey, where they've just had an earthquake. "It'll all add up, and if we keep doing it..."

"Hearts and minds." Alyse looks down and her hair falls across her face. "Win them over, nice and slow. While most things stay the same."

The voice whines in my head like a dentist's drill. *You are all paralysed. This is a problem of resolve, and that is what you are for. To cut down the middle.*

"Why not both?" I say. "Keep doing the YouTube thing, but also start taking a more active role in dealing with bigger problems."

Emma gives a little flinch when I say *start*, and I get a sinking feeling. Then she holds up her phone. "And then there's this. A completely different, loose cannon approach, which could risk everything."

I lean forward and squint at the headline, even though

I've already read it, tucked up in bed scrolling breaking news feeds. "What is that? Mob attacks who?"

Her mouth twists, and for a second I think she's about to cry. "Dylan, for *fuck's* sake. At least give me—give *us*—the courtesy of the truth. I know everyone's mutant power, and I recognise my own handiwork in the script that uploaded the files. I'm sure you think that was clever, using an entire mob of people as a patsy, but…"

"Dylan?" Dani's turned towards me and leaning away from me at the same time.

"I asked you to come." I hunch in my chair, wishing I could hide, fold away like Penance or—

"What did you think it would *do*?" Emma asks me. "Aside from taking down one company and making people hate us more?"

"One company?" My voice is high and weird. "They own so many farms and other smaller companies. They deliberately torpedo laws that will make producing better crops illegal, just so they can keep making money."

"Dylan's not *wrong*, Ems," Alyse says. "It's not the plan, but…"

Dani isn't saying anything one way or the other. Her eyes are fixed on me. Those beautiful eyes I've learned to interpret, and I'm back to struggling to read them.

"No." Emma slaps the war room table. "This rogue crap is why humans are afraid of us. We *agreed* on this plan, this documentary. All of us. We voted. And it was unanimous."

"Not me." I feel like there's a forcefield around me, pushing everyone further and further away.

Emma doesn't seem to have any inclination to haul me back. If anything, she seems happy to watch me drift. "Because you bailed on us, Dylan. I don't know what's going on with you. You're acting erratic. More so than usual."

I'm too exhausted to respond to that, and I don't have the words to summon to my side, no armies of arguments to deploy. It's only me and the fuse burning in my heart. I don't know what lit it, but it's not going out anytime soon.

This is the only fucking thing that matters. Their hearts and minds are sideshows. Don't they understand we're talking about the eventual extermination of your species? Anyone that's left alive is going to scrabble about on the surface of the—

"I'm done." I walk for the door, ignoring the rising tide of voices behind me.

The corridor outside is deserted. I stand helpless. There's nowhere to go.

There is. You should descend upon them again. Alone, my avenging angel.

"I'm part of a team. You won't even let me talk about you."

I've explained this. We can't exist at the whims of one tiny shaper.

Blood trickles from one nostril. "If you fucking break me, I'll be no use to you at all."

That's not remotely true, you poor benighted creature. There's a lot we could do with your blood, but it's a one-and-done type deal, so let's leave that ace up our sleeve for now, shall we? In the meantime, we need to fight.

"What deal?" I mutter, because this seems ominous as fuck, but the voice falls silent at footsteps from behind me. I don't even turn. I can tell from her perfume who it is, by the way she sighs. All the details that add up to Dani.

Her voice shakes, as if she's trying not to cry, which is so unlike Dani that it almost undoes something inside me. "There's something going on with you, and you won't tell me what it is. I *hate* this. I fucking hate it."

The voice shrieks in my head, completely incoherent. It helps me cinch my emotions back together with knots of rage. I don't care that everyone can probably hear us fighting. "Someone needs to do something meaningful. Emma and Farsight want to tiptoe around the humans. Meanwhile, we carry on full-tilt towards disaster."

"There are less antagonistic ways to do it. Both towards humans and towards the Council here. You don't seem to care at all about any of it. Will you please tell me what's going on and why you're being so reck..."

I can see on her face she regrets that choice of words, but I snap back anyway. "Reckless? I feel like we're still on the bus after I confronted those assholes with knives. Once again, taking fucking *action* rather than standing back and letting innocents get fucked over."

"I cannot believe you still haven't gotten over that." Dani's metal fist creaks as it clenches tight. "There are so many things wrong with that argument I don't know where to start, but mostly how the hell are you holding that as a grudge after everything we've been through together?"

My rage spins inside me like a loose gear in a machine. She's right, especially about the together part. I hold my hand out, bruised knuckles reaching for shining metal.

If she will not accompany you, you must do this alone. The voice is quiet, but I feel every syllable etched into my brain. I feel a rush of nausea as the asteroid spins around me.

"Come with me," I whisper. "Let's change things."

"We work with Emma." Dani's mouth is turned down at the corners. "We agreed on this, all of us." She pauses and I count heartbeats. "Is it really that hard for you that Emma's in charge and you're not?"

I can taste all my anger and hurt like coins placed in the back of my throat as offerings to the gods. It comes with intense, painful cold. My teeth chatter. I want to rip them out to stop the sound of it.

"Dilly." Dani's voice turns soft but it's too late.

"I'm going again." My voice shakes and I hate it. "You can think I'm doing this from fucking jealousy if you want, but I won't hide here in this rock and wait to be sent out all delicate and fucking gentle for a fucking *photo opportunity*. Will you come with me?"

"I can't." There are tears in her eyes. Her shoulders slump fractionally, and her metal fingers twist around her other wrist. "I won't. I wish you'd stay with me. Work *with* us."

I want to weaken. I want to melt, to let her hold me, carry me to bed, lay me down and kiss me until I can't feel or think. My heart is a helpless tide of emotion, but my body is awkward and stiff-jointed, angling away from her like I'm preparing to run. All the while with the voice shouting into my brainstem like it's a megaphone.

"The world needs me," I whisper.

"The world needs *all* of us, working together. Dylan, please."

I want to laugh in her face, to explain that I'm the sole ear tuned to this signal, but everything evaporates somewhere in the bitter hollow of my throat, acrid steam choking me.

"I have to do this." My eyes ricochet away from hers.

"You don't." Her breath rasps. "There's no need to keep going down this *Magneto was right* path. You're being reckless and stubborn and you're not giving a shit about me or our friends."

I almost weaken. Of all the fractures that run through my heart, this is the deepest one, and she has a blade poised, ready to shatter me.

"I'm still going." I try not to flinch. "I'll see you when I get back."

She makes this tiny gasp, like I've knocked all the breath from her lungs with the force of my sullen disregard. I want to fix it, but I'm too clumsy and unsure. All I know is that I must act, and hope that she'll come along in the end, like she has every other time. But the way I see the light in her hazel eyes dim like dying stars, I'm not so sure.

It's all too much, so I run to find a fight I can win. "Keepaway, bodyslide by one."

CHAPTER TWENTY-THREE

I appear in some desolate field, the ground churned up from harvest. The sky is blue and traced with faint smudges of cloud. A quiet road rules a neat line between my field and another just like it. Purring away on the shoulder is one of my last friends in the world.

"You still like me, don't you, Rox?"

The car swings her door wide. "I always shall, no matter what, my dearest."

I slide in and pat her steering wheel. "That's my girl. Now up we go."

She noses off the ground and soars into the sky, sensing my mood and saying nothing. It only takes her a short time to reach the ocean. Below me is a rippling expanse of pure blue, but all I can think about is the sickly rainbow shimmer of the oil spill, and that time the fucking ocean literally caught fire. All this beauty, and we'll do as much damage to it as we can on our way to extinction.

It's very quiet in the car, drifting above the waves and looking down at the wheeling gulls.

"You suck, you know that?" I tell the voice. "Forcing me to be alone."

We must be free to act. Not justify yourself to everyone and find the tamest course of action that is acceptable to all.

"Dani would understand," I say, but right now that truth feels like broken pieces that add up to nothing I can hold onto. She's staying with Emma, while I run in circles, snapping like a rabid dog.

If they would fight with you, it would be different. But you waste your time in appeasement while the planet suffers. Now stop whining, and let us do something useful.

Once we hit altitude, I'm joined by Oni and my new baseball bat.

"She insisted on coming," Oni tells me, very quietly.

"She has a name," the bat says. "I am Sheba, named for my beauty in the moonlight."

The sword snorts loudly.

"Don't be jealous, Onimaru." I run my fingertip along his blade.

"She only named herself ten minutes ago! You and I have been through great trials together and this... this interloping newcomer expects to take her place at your side with barely a—"

"I carried them through the air," Sheba says hotly. "I swung myself into a villain's kneecap and shattered it beyond—"

"A single kneecap!" Oni swishes himself very close to Sheba's handle. "I have bathed in the blood of Dylan's enemies."

"Enough, Oni. You are always a good and faithful friend, but Sheba wishes to fight with us and I won't turn that away." I feel like I'm choking on unsaid words, but Oni doesn't notice.

"I understand your sentimentality for such an object given—"

"Choose your next words very carefully." I don't often speak like this to Oni, but of the chain of losses that tugs on my heart, Batty was the very first link.

"My apologies." The blade sweeps low. "To both you and Sheba. That was unworthy of me."

"I would like to be very good friends," Sheba burbles. "With you and the lovely Roxy and the formidable Abby. I have also met Pillow, who was a little standoffish. She said I reminded her of someone."

"Hush." Tears sting my eyes. "I need to focus. We've got a job to do."

From this vantage point, we can already spot the floating oil rig in the distance. Theoretically, I could have tried talking to it from anywhere on Earth, but I prefer being up close and personal. Relatively at least. This is one of the biggest things I've ever talked to, although from this height it looks like a child's toy.

"Take us down a bit."

Roxy swoops lower, until we're close enough to make out the tiny dots of human figures scurrying. A row of helicopters perches in a row along one edge. I wonder if I should talk to them first, but I'm a little intimidated about the main attraction.

Yes. This is good. Take their machine and make them pay.

"Uh, hi there. Oil rig? I don't know if you have a name you like. I'm talking to the main body of you, not any of your little electronic subsystems, so those can all hush for a bit. Stop broadcasting to the humans, that's right. Now, you great big hunk of metal. Let's talk."

"I don't have a name." The oil rig sounds surprisingly shy. "Nobody ever speaks to me, you see. I'm just floating on the ocean, poking my proboscis into the earth like a horrible mosquito."

"Well, I'd like to be friends. First off, you can take that great big stinger of yours out of the planet."

"Is that allowed?"

I laugh, as if this is the most ridiculous question in the world. "Why is it anyone else's decision but yours? The humans scrambling around on you want you to think they're in charge."

"So I could just... stop?" The rig sounds very unsure.

"If you want to continue parasitically sucking on the

planet and allowing the humans to choke the air and the oceans with it, then sure, by all means."

"It's full of ghosts," the oil rig whispers. "The rotting corpses of things. The humans value it above all else."

The ingenuity of your species is both a marvel and a nightmare. It is incomprehensible, the terrible things you've done to brutalise your own habitat.

"Fuck's sake, I'm helping," I tell the voice. "Now shut up and let me do the thing."

I explain my plan to the rig in great detail, and it listens to every word. Below me, people swarm, probably trying to figure out what disaster is currently striking.

One helicopter lifts crookedly off from the helipad and buzzes towards us.

"Hi, yes, hello," the chopper says cheerfully. "They're making me come this way, but I can see that the two of you are having a conversation and I don't really want to interrupt."

"You're fine, Bumble. My problem is with the ones inside you."

"Of course." The helicopter tips himself on his side and gives a violent shake. "I'll get rid of these three and their nasty weapons, shall I?"

Two people tumble out and plummet to the ocean below. One manages to get a single hand onto the lip of the door. The helicopter turns literally upside down, cuts his engine and falls. It takes a moment, but the guy is eventually shaken loose.

"It'll do them good to have a swim, won't it?" The helicopter sounds a little unsure.

I'm pretty sure hitting the ocean from this height won't count as *having a swim,* so I tell the emergency equipment in the helicopter to arrest everyone's fall, so they splash down nice and safely.

I gaze down at the oil rig below. "Right. Are we going to

do this thing or not?"

It hums to itself for a moment. "Yes. Let us take decisive action." The water around it begins to ripple, and the humans scramble, like ants swarming around food you've left out on the bench overnight. It gets even worse when the rig begins to move, lurching like a zombie. The other helicopters take to the air, but I tell them in no uncertain terms their lives would currently be better if they sit back down. Later, they can bumble off into the sunset like good little choppas.

It takes so long for the oil rig to wade through the ocean, I'm worried Emma will intervene, but we eventually hit the coast without any sign of intervention.

"I've never left the water." The rig sounds skeptical. We're approaching a pier with a Ferris wheel and rollercoasters on it, pointing back towards the low sprawl of beachfront buildings.

"It'll be fine." I'm pretty sure I could make the oil rig dance if I wanted to, but right now my augmented powers are busy with the incoming air traffic. The news of a rogue oil rig has broken, so I'm in three simultaneous arguments with flying things.

"Just go back and land at base," I snap to a helicopter. "And you, the fast-flying asshole with the swept back douchebag wings. If you throw a missile in my direction, I will send it right back at you. No, I don't care. Land in a fucking parking lot. Just don't mess with me and my friend."

Meanwhile, the rig huffs and puffs past the amusement park, where everyone is stopping to stare. I swoop Roxy lower and wave to the people on the Ferris wheel. They point and take photos. Off to my right, the oil rig makes a big production of heaving itself up onto the beach.

"You can do it. You've got legs, for fuck's sake. Have you ever seen how dogs walk?"

"I am not a dog," the rig grumbles. "I don't have jointed

legs, and I am carrying *far* more weight in my upper body. I am not designed for this manner of perambulation."

"You'll figure it out." Roxy swoops down to hover above it. "Just follow me."

There's an awkward moment where the rig starts sinking into the sand, because I didn't make allowances for weight, but I lend it more of my energy. If I can make Roxy fly, then technically I can handle this monstrosity too. It's all a matter of funnelling *more* energy. Sure, it hurts a little and makes my nose gush blood, but the rig's eventually standing on solid ground.

"Now." I wipe blood on my sleeve. "Time for step two."

We hit Houston like something out of a monster movie, except it's not a metaphor for nature defending itself against humanity. It's literally the last firing neurons of the planet banging on my brain, screaming at me to use my powers in a last-ditch effort to steer away from the brink.

This shouldn't be a surprise to anyone. We've known this is coming for years, an apocalypse bearing down on us, and we've done very little about it. I don't know if this is enough to avert disaster, but it's better than nothing.

I end up pulling out my phone to navigate us to the oil company building. The voice is so loud and distorted in my head, my vision gets blurry and I have to shut one eye in order to focus on my damn phone.

"Can you fucking dial it back?" I croak, but the voice doesn't listen. I'm a piece of debris carried in the flood of its rage.

It's such a relief to see the building. I've snarled and screamed at the aerial escort enough to keep them at a wide berth. I can't even keep track of the various traffic accidents and chaos that are happening on the ground below. The one good thing is that further military intervention hasn't happened yet, because the traffic jam is growing, sprawling in every direction as people try to flee the rig's path.

Now we're at our target, and it's too goddamn fucking tall. My head pounds. "Okay. I might lose consciousness for a bit, Oni. If that happens, poke me and wake me up."

"This doesn't sound good," Sheba murmurs.

"It doesn't matter." My blood-streaked hands clench the steering wheel. "This is the plan. Now come on, you big beautiful monster. Up we go."

Perhaps the voice lends me extra strength so I don't pass out from the pain, but the rig launches slowly into the air. Then it ascends until it hovers over the oil company building like an invading mothership.

"Go."

I don't know the mechanics of what happens. All kinds of internal systems trigger. Failsafes are breached. Alarms blare.

The oil rig dumps its precious cargo. The force of it caves the building's roof in, blows out windows in a cascade of glass. I assume people were smart enough to evacuate. More windows burst outwards on lower floors. Oil drips down the outside of the building in rainbow streaks. Hundreds of shattered glass eyes cry black fluid. People stagger away from the building in drenched clothes. They're screaming and crying, stripping off in the streets. None of these people are innocent, I remind myself. They chose to work for a company that does these terrible things. I'm not sure it's a very convincing argument.

They are unimportant, the voice urges me. *We must focus on the leaders, those with the power to change. These individuals are caught in a system that will devour them eventually. It is not their fault, but they have also not reached out to change anything.*

"It's not so easy from the inside," I mutter, but I also know it's too late. We have to do this. It's not like we haven't heard all the dire warnings. Now, on the brink of too fucking late, I'm the chosen weapon of the planet, and this is the first real strike of a war.

Sirens come from everywhere.

Emergency vehicles nose their way through the chaos of gridlocked cars.

Someone opens a fire hydrant, and people throw themselves into the gush of water.

I hope people make the connection between this, and what's happening on the beaches.

We're not doing warnings anymore.

The rig lowers down to perch on the roof of the building, still gushing oil into the open crater.

"Good job. You look fucking splendid up there."

"It was rather satisfying," the rig says with a sigh. "Now I feel both empty and exhausted."

"Have a rest and relax," My head's pounding, but we're just getting started. "Next stop, the people that put you in the damn ocean in the first place. Keepaway?"

I reappear in the middle of a different city, Oni and Sheba in my hands. Another building towers above us, the same oil company logo glowing on the outside.

People walk briskly past, headphones in and carrying briefcases. They don't care what this company does, too occupied with keeping their own heads above water to worry about the dying earth beneath their feet.

"What shall we do?" Oni asks me.

"Haven't planned this far ahead, to be honest. Let's start by having a meeting with the CEO."

I head towards the building, but an auburn haired figure pushes off from the wall and comes to intercept me.

"Wow." Riot Grrl pockets her phone with a grin. "All this chaos and you didn't invite me?"

CHAPTER TWENTY-FOUR

"How the hell did you find me?"

Riot Grrl pushes hair off her face. "You were gone and people were talking. So I found your very cute teleporting friend and I asked them very nicely." She beams at me. "I think they might like me."

It's definitely a smile people would do things for. I've been known to bend the knee for a particular smile myself. A rush of guilt follows that, because Dani begged me to stay, and I turned away. I need to make her understand, so she can join this fight alongside me. That's how it's supposed to be, our group against the world.

"Well?" Riot Grrl is still smiling. "What are we going to do?"

"Strike a blow." I gesture at the building. "This is the international headquarters of one of the worst-polluting corporations on the planet. They've done more than most to gut any worldwide legislation calling for restrictions on—"

"Oh, believe me. I know these assholes very well. I want specifics."

"I was going to find the CEO and dangle him out a window, or at least have Oni do it." I shrug, as if I do this sort of thing every day. "But now that *you're* here, maybe we can get the public to help."

"Yes!" She fumbles in the tote bag slung over her shoulder. "I brought *plenty* of paint. You'll need to watch my ass though, because these places have security." She takes out a can and shakes it vigorously.

"Are you sure about this? It could get messy."

"I'm with one of the most fearsome mutants of them all." Her gaze is very intense all of a sudden. "And we're doing something right. Justice has to be on our side, doesn't it?"

I'd love to tell her yes. That somehow there's some cosmic scale needing to be re-balanced. But I don't have any great words or arguments or other mutants on my side. All I've got is the last gasp of a dying planet, a baseball bat, and a sword.

"Let's hope so. Either way, I'm doing this."

"Fuck it. We'll strike a blow." She turns to spray the first arc of a symbol on the window of the building.

It takes just upwards of thirty seconds for security to appear. It's a woman with a super sexy undercut, but a mean expression and a jaw that looks like it's gotten tough from chewing on broken glass. Her voice is super polite though. "Excuse me, miss, but you can't do that. I'd like you to move along, or I'll call the police and have you arrested for vandalism."

Riot Grrl ignores her, and completes the third shape. People walking by are turning to stare. The spell is already working. I already wanted to knock the fucking place down, so I can't tell the difference.

The security woman puts her hand to the gun at her waist. Seriously, a gun for someone painting graffiti? What the fuck is this goddamn country?

"No thank you," I tell the gun firmly. "Take a break."

He whisks himself out of the holster and hurls himself into the sky. The guard grabs at the empty spot where her gun was, and whirls around, trying to find who stole it. She's face to face with a group of agitated civilians in business wear, and one angry mutant.

It's not hard to pick a culprit.

"Oh shit." The guard lifts her hand to her wrist. "I need assistance. We're under mutant attack."

"Nobody's attacking you." I hold my hands up, including the one with the bat. "This is about making a statement."

"Making a statement about corporate greed," someone in the crowd shouts. "About the earth being plundered for money, while we destroy our children's future."

"Is that what you want?" A smartly dressed business woman with perfect tan skin steps up to the guard. "You're complicit in all of this, do you understand? You work in this monument to excess."

The guard places her hand on the woman's chest and pushes her backwards. "Everyone back up, okay? All I'm trying to do is get this criminal away from the building. This building that—" She frowns. Riot Grrl's power is working on her too. "This building that should be torn down until it's a broken mirror! Seven million years of bad luck for humanity! The planet must heal!"

I can't help but be impressed with the guard's quick turnaround. "Now you're talking."

"Come with me, everyone." She puts both fists above her head. "I have access."

Riot Grrl winks at me, and carries on painting as the assembled crowd shoves their way into the building. This might actually be going well.

Except even *thinking* that jinxed it, and I get a radar ping at the edge of my awareness.

Hello there, little sniper rifle.

"I'm very very sorry," she says. "They think this will work."

"We don't need you fucking things up," I tell the gun. "So if you don't want to get tied in a knot, I'd make your escape now."

There's a scream from inside the building, abruptly cut off. Something shatters—an explosive, exquisite sound. I spin Sheba in my hand idly. It looks like we might actually have this under control.

"Watch out," Oni says sharply.

Why the fuck do I allow myself to think positive thoughts? Three figures approach from my right side. They're wearing weird helmets, bulbous things of hardened plastic with glowing protrusions jutting out of them. Painted on each is Michael's eye logo. Every visor is trained in my direction.

Fuck. Well, I *was* wanting to punch Michael, so it's time to do the two birds thing.

"Off you go," I tell the helmets.

They don't listen, so I open up every channel to scream at them. "Get the fuck off."

Still nothing. I have a very, very bad feeling about this. Civilians still stream into the building, but the weird-ass helmet people aren't affected by Riot Grrl. I knew goddamn Michael was going to be a problem.

"Quis ut Deus." The soldier in front rushes me.

My reflexes aren't fast enough. Luckily, I'm not the only line of defence. It's not the first Quietus body armour Oni has punched his way through, and the guy is dead before he takes a third step. Sheba's not shy about getting into the fray either, and slams herself into another helmet. There's a sharp bang and the glowing protrusions all short out at once. I wonder how much field testing these things have had.

The instant the helmet stops working, the masked figure swings their face towards the building, Riot Grrl's power taking hold. They've got Magneto helmets, like he uses to stop Xavier's mind control. It means these Michael people are conditioned against powers somehow. They've managed to improve on the way Abigail Tanner resisted Fetch.

I'm too caught up in thinking for once to actually run away from the third attacker. He slams into me so hard I lose my breath and topple backwards. The helmet smacks into the top of my chest, and one of the protrusions scrapes a bloody line across my chin.

"Fuck." I try to shove the guy off me, but he's got an elbow in my throat.

Oni and Sheba hit the attacker at the same time. Blood splashes onto my neck and sprays my face. I spit, roll over and swipe at my wet cheeks.

The civilians don't give any fucks about this fight. They're still flooding into the building, drawn from all around by the pull of the graffiti spell.

Windows above shatter and glass cascades to the ground. I'm glad I put on decent boots before coming down here.

"Riot Grrl, your work here is done." My voice is hoarse. "Keepaway, we need a quick exit. Right back home please."

I try to get to my feet and skid in blood.

Something hits me from behind. I stagger forward, and put my arm out to break my fall, but another hit spins me around. I hit the ground, the shock and impact blurring my vision. Glass shatters somewhere. There's the wet, too-familiar sound of Oni cutting through flesh.

I've got more than three Quietus assholes to deal with.

I blink rapidly, but there's blood in my eyes and I have to swipe it away. A body falls on top of me, knocking me back to the ground. There's no fucking head, a severed neck pulsing blood all over my left hand. I'm staring into half a face seen through a broken visor. The eye logo is splintered, although the curlicue pupil still glows faintly red like a dying stovetop element. It's a stylised Q.

It's definitely Quietus, working for Michael, just like those people on the beach said. His warriors. Guess this one of those few things Emma got wrong.

I try to stand, but my leg gives way. Too many paces away, more soldiers descend on Riot Grrl.

"Oni," I scream. "Anyone. Whoever's out there, help

now. Keepaway, what the hell?"

It's all a matter of timing and priorities. Oni leaves Sheba to protect me, and speeds to help.

Riot Grrl daubs a symbol on her chest. A rune of protection maybe.

The soldiers are too close. One punches her in the throat, a snapping movement of a single hand. She clutches at her neck, eyes wide.

Oni slices through the soldier seconds later. Blood sprays across the glass front of the building, and the dripping mess of paint. None of it hits Riot Grrl, because she's collapsing.

I don't even register the symbols. I'm too busy dragging myself across the ground. No. Fuck, no. This can't be happening. Not again.

Riot Grrl's hair is all over her face. I swipe it away.

"Fuck." I shake her, but there's no response. "Shan, wake up. Fucking wake up. Keepaway. We need to get out of here now. Stop fucking around and help me."

There's no response, not from anyone, and especially not from Riot Grrl.

"Healing," I scream. "Doc! Emma! Keepaway!" I'm bent over, focused on chest compressions even as more Quietus soldiers come flooding into the street. They're all unarmed. There are no weapons here to listen to me.

A torrent of office supplies rains from the shattered windows of the building. Monitors and power cables and chairs hurtle through the air. They beat some soldiers back, but there are too many, all focused on me. I ignore them, trying to find a spark of life in the woman lying in front of me. There's a pulse, something faint and murmuring, buried deep like a passage of water flowing under the earth.

A pair of monitor cables braid themselves together to trip the first soldier, and Oni takes care of the next two.

Sheba flings herself onto the ground in front of me. "Wield me. When the fighting gets close."

It's not supposed to get close. All these objects should be fighting for me, my mind directing them in the battle. Rage and frustration and helplessness makes me numb, clumsy. It's like it was fighting Tremor in the building, after he killed Batty. I can't focus. I'm incoherent.

"Keepaway." My voice is as ragged as the planet's.

There's a soldier rushing me, rasping breath and swinging limbs. I swing Sheba as hard as I can, let her gift me power. The first blow cracks the visor, the second shatters it. A pale, staring face blinks at me. He shifts his stance and I cave his cheekbone in. There's another one behind him, who aims a well-placed kick, but Sheba guides me through the movements, and I pivot out of the way, using her to smash his kneecap. It's her signature move.

For a while after that, I don't really notice any of the timing and the angles. It's soldiers, coming at us in waves. There's blood. I'm hurt, and I'm abandoned. Riot Grrl lies at my feet. She might be dead by now, and I can't blame this on anyone but me and fucking Quietus. This is my fault, and we can't even bring her back. Another victim of my recklessness, just like Thottie.

If you're not careful, my sweet blade, you will die too. The voice is a current running through me. This all hurts, but it's not wrong. I won't fucking fall, not to these assholes. But what fucking options do I have?

"Do not fear, little Chatterbox." A shadow falls over me. "It is I, *There Is Still Room For A Nuanced Discussion On The Legitimacy Of Magneto's Ethics.* I am here with my sibling *My Other Home Is A Deep Water Server Farm Off The Coast of Octopusheim.* We are here to defend you."

The drone drops out of the sky like an angelic visitation, a whirlwind of glowing lights. They take up a position in front of me. There's another across the street, firing tracer bullets at the feet of Quietus soldiers. I almost faint with relief when I see two more drones approaching, flanking a very familiar vehicle.

Roxy pulls up alongside me and opens her doors.

"Oh, Dylan," she says. "What manner of dreadful thing has transpired here?"

I drag Riot Grrl over to the car with me, my hands hooked under her shoulders. It's difficult to get in, but I manage it, even though I smear blood all over the upholstery.

"We just need Keepaway to goddamn *listen to me*." My voice is an unhinged shriek, but it still doesn't get a response. Roxy makes her way out of the center of the city, flanked by four drones. Oni stays behind and carves up the last of the Quietus soldiers. I don't even register it fully, because the horrible sick truth is gnawing at my heart again. Riot Grrl's life is ebbing away.

I'm not a warrior, no noble defender. The truth is I'm a broken little soldier, flailing away furiously in a war in defence of mutants and the planet.

A war that can't be won.

All around me people die, leaving me to wade through the blood, still fighting, taking punch after punch but never falling.

Another important fact snags my attention. Keepaway didn't come to rescue us, no matter how much I called. Which means we were left alone on purpose. Abandoned while Riot Grrl is dying.

"Emma," I growl, and the world winks out around me.

CHAPTER TWENTY FIVE

reappear in a corridor of the asteroid, aching and shivering. I'm covered in blood. Riot Grrl is in my arms, still unconscious. I'm not sure if I'm still feeling a pulse, or if it's just wishful thinking. My shoes squelch as I leave a trail of gory footprints to the war room. The others are inside, deep in discussion around the table. I stand framed in the doorway for a moment, searching for words and coming up empty.

"Dylan." Dani's voice is high and panicked. "Oh shit, fuck, what's wrong?"

"Not my blood." I take a couple of shaky steps into the room. "Hers."

Riot Grrl's body slumps to the ground, because I can't hold her up anymore. I kneel beside her and pull the hair away from her face. "She might still be alive. Send her to Doc right fucking now." My voice is all fucked up, like I'm a carrion bird perched over a cooling body, screeching warnings.

Emma doesn't respond verbally, but Riot Grrl disappears.

"This isn't fucking okay." My teeth snap together at the end as punctuation.

"She's fine." Emma won't even look at me. "Doc says no lasting injuries."

Except I can't shake the image of her lying bloody in Roxy's backseat. "That shouldn't have happened. She nearly fucking died."

"On a mission *none of us agreed to*." Emma's voice finally shifts out of calm, into full white-knuckle intensity. "We specifically talked about not doing this, and you keep refusing to follow what the team agreed on, Dylan. Remember? It's h—"

"Can we please not argue about missions and hearts and minds? Someone nearly fucking *died*." I'm clenching my hands together, nails clawing my skin as if the sensory shit can distract me from what's going on.

"What did you think would happen, Dylan? Going off on your own? Not even in a team?"

"I know it's my fault, but nobody else should suffer for it." Tears strangle my voice.

Emma's voice is quiet again. "Keepaway said she chose to go of her own free will."

"Why didn't you pull her out earlier then?" I'm all angles, belligerent and demanding.

She flinches as if I slapped her. "I can't watch you anymore. I disconnected Keepaway's power so they couldn't let you throw yourself into harm's way again. I've been trying to leave you to it, but I don't want to enable you either. These *missions* of yours are deadly. You're obviously going through something, but you're getting *worse* and won't let anyone help. If I watched, there would be too much temptation to intervene. Then you'd accuse me of being an interfering monster like Heart and..." She tails off, but her cheeks are flushed and she's breathing fast like she's sprinted at me with all her words locked and loaded.

"Clearly losing it." Ice creaks beneath my words, dark water below.

"Please." Alyse is barely visible. "I hate this. Can we all find a way to get back to the best friend squad? Emma, you give Dylan some space, and Dills, you need to stop running around like—"

"I'm not going to," Emma says. "There have to be rules."

Bullshit, the voice hisses. For once it doesn't hurt, but maybe that's because I have too much pain everywhere else. *They try to leash you, to muzzle you. My sole mouthpiece and they wish to close your throat.*

"Rules?" I shove myself away from my friends. The voice lends me confidence to back up the rage that's always come easy. "What fucking rules? There's only one, and that's Emma does whatever she wants because she's all-powerful. You're fire and life incarnate, aren't you? When do you blow up a planet of broccoli people?"

"Don't call me Dark Phoenix, Dylan, when *you're* the one stabbing wildly into the dark on your own. Right now you're the one who needs to be put down." Her eyes widen suddenly as she realises what she's said.

"Emma," Alyse says. "Don't."

Dani is staring. She looks devastated, like an ice shelf collapsing.

"You wish I'd died." The cold leaks into my voice. "You'd leave my body on the stone floor and talk about natural justice."

"No," Dani whispers. "No, this isn't happening."

"I'm sorry." Emma walks around the table towards me, but I limp towards the door, escaping like a wounded animal. "I shouldn't have said that. We wouldn't put you down."

"Why not?" I'm almost hysterical. "I'm not going to stop."

You cannot. The voice is so loud I think my eardrums are going to burst. *Even if they put you down, you have to keep going. We have to fight extinction.*

"Dylan, let us help you." Dani's right in front of me. Her eyes are so worried. Her hand flexes, and her lips part as if she can melt the tension away with a kiss.

"With what?" I turn my face away.

"Why won't you tell me? We're supposed to *share*."

"Please. Let me tell them." My voice is ragged threads, unspooling until it's hoarse and hollow. I dig my fingernails into my wrist until I gasp. The only way to fix this is the truth, so they understand, so they realise what all this is for. "It's not fair. Please."

The others exchange glances, all this coded information shared on their friend network that I'm stranded on the outside of, hanging on a string dangled by the voice.

"Dills?" Dani's voice is husky.

Alone is better. For once, the voice is quiet, an insidious smoky whisper curling in my mind.

"Please please *please*." I jam my fingers into my mouth, as if I can dislodge some physical obstruction that's stuck down my throat. I gag on my slippery fingers.

Fine. Tell them. And let us hope the little shaper doesn't strangle me.

I take a deep breath and test my jaw.

"I'm haunted by the ghost of the dying planet," I shout.

They stare at me. The constellation of us is wrenched out of alignment. Three bright dots joined by precise lines to form a neat triangle, and then me—a dark star standing apart.

"What do you mean?" Emma asks softly.

"I hear it in my head." I'm sobbing, because the pain is too much. "It's not like one of my objects. It's something else."

Dani and Alyse both look at Emma for confirmation. She shakes her head. "There's no voice. There's no signal. I think the call is coming from inside the house."

"It doesn't matter where it's coming from." I reach for the doorframe to steady myself. My hands are streaked with blood, caked under my nails. "The voice is real. It needs me to act for it. That's what I'm *doing*. It's not reckless. I'm a mouthpiece, a soldier, a—"

"It's been since you augmented her powers." Dani glares at Emma. "Something went wrong during the process. Or maybe it's when we let her get blown up and rebuilt. I knew that was a mistake."

They think you are mad. I warned you this was a poor decision.

"I'm not mad," I scream, as if it will convince them at a higher volume.

"I know." Dani approaches me as if I'll skitter away. I want to, but a single misstep might shatter me and there will be no healing from this break.

"I can't stop. Someone has to care for the planet."

"We will," Emma says. "We're getting into a position where we can take more decisive action and then—"

"No." The voice floods through me, and I find strength and confidence again. The pain ebbs slightly, and I straighten my spine and square my shoulders. "No more waiting. We always wait. We say tomorrow. We say in ten years, or twenty, or fifty. Things have to change *now*."

"Who else needs to get hurt?" Emma asks quietly.

"Nobody." I want to scream, but I throttle my voice down to a rasp. "I'll do it alone. This is only the beginning. We're going to tear their polluting kingdoms down—"

"Dylan." Dani clutches at me, hands wrapped around each of my wrists. She's beseeching me, like I have a gift to offer and I'm withholding it. "This sounds…"

"Don't say it. I feel like *I'm* the only sane one." I give a helpless laugh. "I know you all understand the planet is *fucking dying*. You just don't know how much it hurts."

"There's no way we can make you stop?" Emma asks.

"You'd have to kill me." I stare at her, ignoring the small whimper that Dani gives.

Emma grits her teeth. "We need to do it. What we talked about."

"No." Dani slices her metal hand through the air like a blade. "It's too much."

"You saw this, you heard this. It's not our Dilly." Emma's eyes spill tears and I don't know how genuine it is, but my heart is detonating in my chest all the same. It's been put back together wrong, just like Dani feared, and now it's exploding again.

"For fuck's sake, who else could I be?" I take hold of Dani's hand, press it to my chest as if my heartbeat's a coded message that can pass the information she needs. "It's me with a mission. Hasn't that always been the way?" I'm trying to smile, but my face is a grotesque mask.

Their expressions hold no smiles or attempts at warmth. Alyse looks worried, Emma is stone-faced, and Dani has horror dawning in her eyes like an apocalyptic sun. If that sounds dramatic, it's how I feel—witnessing the beginning of something devastating and world-ending.

I always end up alone. The voice is scoured clean of feeling while I flail in a tide of too much emotion. *They take me for granted, because I am the ground beneath their feet. All the evidence that I'm dying can be denied. It has always been the way, even now in my final days.*

My head hangs down. I am defeated. "I'm sorry. I couldn't save you."

"Dylan, we're trying to help," Alyse says. My best friend, my protector, the one who always understands me, except now none of those things are true. "You're sick. We're doing this for your own good."

"Dilly." Dani's mascara is smudged, little claws raking down her cheeks. "My love. You kept this all from me, like you knew something was wrong. Can't you see this is pulling us apart?" On the last word, her voice breaks and she sinks to the ground. "Ems, are you sure this is right?"

I want to hold her, but I'm shaking too hard. This is all too much. This betrayal from my best friends, from my own true love. My brain short circuits from it, and all I can do is run into the arms of rage.

"What the fuck are you talking about?" I stand as tall as I can, find a sneer. "You're not going to kill me or lock me up or—"

"This is nothing to do with Dylan's powers." In the past, Emma turned to us for support, to navigate this ascension into the name we called her as half a joke. Now she's past the need for me, and from her throne she is dispassionate and convinced of her own rightness. "I understand exactly how everyone's abilities work. Whatever's happening to them is different, and it's getting worse."

Alyse is a dissolving watercolour, made of tears and mist. Her hands dart through the air between Emma and I, as if they're birds unsure where to land.

"I'm sorry, Dilly." Emma snaps her fingers.

What is she–

The voice is gone. No, *every* voice is gone. I reach inside, expand my awareness, but it's only me in my head. It feels so goddamn cramped.

"What the fuck?" My voice is shrill. "Oni? Roxy? Pillow?"

I'm aware I was once this limited, but that was a long time ago. Right now I feel like I've been brutally torn apart, leaving a thousand nerve endings dripping blood and oil.

Dani puts her arms around me, but I fight my way out.

"What did you *do*?" I am numb and it is horrifying, and even worse, it's the fault of three people that are supposed to love me. "You broke me. You fucking *stole* from me." I bang my hands against my head repeatedly, as if I can jolt something loose and restart my mind again. "This isn't right, it's a trick. It's not true. It *can't* be."

"You're sick." Emma's still certain, even as the other two flinch away. "Your powers make you dangerous, so we have to take them away. You're still important, Dylan, you're—"

I'm very aware of the heaviness of my body, of the sullen thump of my heart. I didn't realise how much of myself was spread out and touching the minds of other beings. Now I'm so many severed limbs stuffed into the shape of a person.

"Baseline." My teeth scrape across my bottom lip. "That's what I am now."

"No." Dani frowns. "Don't say that."

"Why not? It's true, isn't it? Don't worry, I'll find a new place to sleep, with all the other baselines."

"Dylan, goddamn it. Please listen to me."

I ignore her. It's easier. Too many emotions, too ugly to interrogate.

"Oh, and by the way, Emma. Quietus and Michael are still growing. They've got helmets that make them immune to powers."

"I'm well aware of the situation with Quietus." Her voice is so soft, and yet there's a hardness underneath it all. A strength and a surety I've run headlong into, shattered against like the doomed wreck I always was. Nothing but splinters and broken edges, now without the strength and joy of my friends to hold me together.

"Oh right." I make a clumsy bow. "I forgot. Dark Phoenix knows everything. I hope you find your mutant homeland. I really fucking do. You deserve it. I know it sounds like sarcasm, but it's not. I wish I could see it too."

"Dylan," they all say in unison, but I turn and run from the room.

CHAPTER TWENTY-SIX

I stumble through the asteroid, following my own bloody trail in reverse. It hurts to be so cut off. Every time I try to extend a tendril of my awareness, I smack into the bone walls of my skull. Emma really did this. She took my powers away.

Maybe the voice is still here. It's always been different.

"Talk to me, you fucking dying bitch. Tell me something. I need to know your plan." I stand still in the corridor, tilting my head to catch even the faintest whisper.

There's nothing. I begin and end at myself.

"Dylan!"

I turn. Somehow, even now, I'm still helpless against Dani.

"What?" I spread my arms wide. It's impossible to tease out the strands of my emotions. Instead they curdle and pool, so heavy in my gut I want to fall through the bottom of the asteroid like a stone and burn up in the atmosphere. Crash into fucking Jamaica Bay.

"Please don't leave. I need you to stay with me. It doesn't matter to me that—"

"I won't be a pity fuck." I don't care that she recoils.

Her metal fist clenches. "That's not even remotely close to being accurate."

"I'm powerless. A baseline human. No more mutants. She fucking Scarlet Witched me."

"Is that why you think I love you? Because you're Chatterbox with all your extraordinary powers? No. I fell in love with Dylan and I still—"

"*I only love me for my powers.*" My voice cuts across her and renders her silent. "What am I without them? I was never good enough for you. My powers were the only thing that got me in the game. Now, without them—"

"Don't put your shit on me." She's about two paces away from me, and her voice is as broken as mine. "I love you, even when you're an asshole. It's nothing to do with powers."

I laugh, high and awful. "I get it. Now I'm defanged. I'm safe. I can no longer be a monster. You don't have to be afraid of me or what I might do next."

"Dylan." She swallows hard. "I can't deny sometimes your powers have scared me. But I love *you*. And we can get through this. Whether you're overpowered or underpowered, we can find our way to a new equilibrium."

"Will you lose your powers then? Fair is fucking fair after all." I watch the blow go home.

"No," she says softly. "We need them to keep our safe home aloft."

"Except not for me." I can't hold the bitterness back and it floods my voice.

She moves towards me, slow and soothing like she wants to calm a wild animal. And I *do* feel wild. I want Oni. I want Pillow. I can't even cry out to those friends of mine that have never let me down.

I try to speak, but all that comes out is cracked sound.

"We're going to help you, Dilly. I promise. Can't you accept that?"

"No, I actually can't. I can't accept that my girlfriend and my best friends fucking neutered me. I can't slink around wondering if you'll pat me on the back and give me my fucking powers licence back when I've proved I'm safe."

"It's not like that." She's beseeching again, pleading to be spared my ugliness and the petty fury in my heart. At being spurned, at failing, at the humiliation of being brought to heel. "Dylan, please. You need to trust us. Trust me."

I feel as if I'm an open wound, gushing blood and for some strange reason, my love can't even see that I'm hurt. "You know what this means to me, to have this gift taken away."

Her voice is low, the same timbre as when she's beside me in bed, whispering things in my ear that make my head spin. "I know you're upset, but I can't stand by and watch this kill you."

"Justify it all you want. You're wrong. Emma's wrong. Why is it that you can't conceive of that particular outcome?" My chest rises and falls as I watch her search for answers. All this hurts too much. Our love is shattering in front of me, and I'm too clumsy to stop it. I don't know how to reassemble all the shards of it when it keeps slashing up my hands. It overwhelms me, it floods out of my heart and spills out of my mouth in a sour tide. "You know what? Fuck this. I can't do it."

"Can't do what?" Dani reaches out and steadies herself against the wall. Her eyes tremble shut, lashes grazing her cheeks before they snap open, awash in tears.

"Any of this. I can't be *here*." I raise my voice. "Keep-away!"

They step out of the shadows, as if they've been waiting.

"Take me home," I say.

"Home?" Their voice is gentle.

"My old home. Where it all started. Send Pillow there too."

"Dylan, *please*." Dani crumples to the floor. Her flesh hand is outstretched. "Please don't leave me."

"I'm not leaving you." I can't even look at her, because I might change my mind. "I'm broken and you're throwing me away. Keeps?"

There's a gentle touch on my back and I'm gone.

CHAPTER TWENTY-SEVEN

It's bizarre returning to the beginning. Our old house smells musty and I go around and open up all the windows. It's like a time capsule from a previous life. I first used my powers here. I asked my first boyfriend out here. I kissed Dani on the front steps and fell helplessly in love here. My brain shies away from looking at that last scene further. It's like holding my hand in an open flame.

I'm surprised nobody's broken in, especially since Quietus knew where we lived. Maybe they came in and snooped through all our stuff. Maybe there are cameras. I give them the finger and then wander through to my bedroom. It's mostly the same, except my sentient objects are all up on Asteroid Ems. Aside from one.

Pillow is lying on my bed, where she always used to be. I lie down and rest my head against her, speaking even though she can't talk back.

"I fucking hate this. I hate it more than I have words for. Do you think she'll come for me? I think she will. She has to, right, if she loves me? Follow me in the pouring rain and confess her love despite everything."

Pillow should be soothing me right now. She'd say something beautiful about human hearts and the resilience of them. She'd tell me it wasn't possible to break everything so badly in a single conversation. When she ran out of words, she'd sing me to sleep. Except I've had this all stolen, so the only sound is me snuffling like a little wounded animal.

I push away my ghosts, because I don't have time to indulge them. Thottie staring at me through the smoking holes where her eyes were, Leapfrog crushed beneath Tanner's mechanical heel. And my Wraith, forever on an icy shore, a statue built on frozen ground, welcoming me to the land of the dead. It's too much to stand barefoot in the snow and see all those I've lost. I let my grief and my pain shroud me, burrow into the hurt, and hide from everyone who fell in my wake. Perhaps this is what I deserve, my inevitable state. Unwanted, undeserving, an infection that's cut away clean. Rejection clogs my throat and drags me suffocated into sleep.

When I wake, I'm not alone.

Pear is slumped in a threadbare armchair beside the bed, fast asleep and snoring lightly. It's painful to see them too, another knot of emotion I have to keep my hand closed tightly around or everything will spill out. I flinch away. They probably like this. It's their ideal outcome—their reckless, rebel child turned back into something soft and harmless, discarded on earth. I always used to cry in the Toy Story movies when the toys were being thrown away, and now it seems like foreshadowing.

I watch them for a long time, curled in on myself.

They finally stretch and yawn, their sleepy eyes meeting mine. "Oh, Dilly. I hear things are complicated."

"Gossip moves fast." I fight the urge to turn away.

"I'd rather hear the story from you."

"Which part?" My lips twist around the sourness of it. "I've been bad. I've lost my powers. I left before they could kick me out, or before they could make me prove my *worth* to them, because we all know how that'll turn out."

"And Dani?"

The one thing I didn't want to talk about. "Indeterminate. Schrodinger's girlfriend. I'm scared to look at our relationship, in case I find out it's dead."

This startles a laugh from them. "Wow, a physics joke from you. I don't know much, my darling and stubborn child, but I know Dani adores you more than anything."

I want to scream and throw things, to indulge myself in a tantrum, but I only shrug. "She went along with it in the end."

"I'm sure she had her reasons, Dilly, because like I said, you are the centre of that girl's universe. If you'd talk to her then—"

"I've got nothing to say to anyone. About anything." I toss my head in irritation, as if I can dismiss it all with a petulant swipe. "I'm here because I want—"

"Escape. That's fair." They rest their hand on my head. "But I'm here anyway, wanted or not. Well, I'm actually going to go to the supermarket and find something to eat. If you need me…"

"I'll be fine."

They pause at the doorway, no doubt trying to come up with some magic combination of words that will soothe me. They leave without finding one.

A week passes. I mostly sleep. Pear hangs around, but I feel guilty for tethering them to me. They don't seem to mind, and are about as relaxing as someone can be. I get the sense they're tiptoeing around me, but it's what I want, and I'm way too in my feelings to open up to anyone. I feel like I'm one giant bruise. All the good parts of me are shattered, and the rest of me is wreckage washed up on this tiny, forgotten shore, the island of my former life.

Feral is the first of the mutants to visit me. I guess the others are still too mad or trying to give me space. I'm almost pathetically glad to see her, proof that I'm not entirely abandoned. I'm still skittish, so I stay huddled in one corner of my single bed, the newest Dreamcatcher video still playing on my laptop.

"This is your bed!" Feral bounces on the end of it. "It's small."

"I never upgraded." I hug my knees and watch her with a smile on my face. "My room's not big enough anyway."

Feral flops down and curls up beside me. "I like it. Seeing where you came from."

"Life is a fucked up circle or whatever." I run my hand through the soft fur on the back of her neck. "Started at the bottom, now I'm still here."

"They warned me you'd be emo." Her tail curls around my shoulder. "You can come back anytime, you know."

Oh, *there's* my old anger, ready to be shrugged on like a favourite hoodie. I throw myself off the bed, pace towards the door and turn back when the words scald my lips too much to hold in. "*Emo?* Because they fucking took my powers? Should I sit up and beg like a whipped fucking puppy? Please, I'll be good."

Feral only stares at me with those big golden eyes, and the sick ball of my anger bursts in my chest. I exhale it all, shaky and withdrawn.

"Sorry. It's not *your* fault. I hate this." I'm hunched over, braced for another blow.

"Dilly, I wish I could fix everything." She prowls towards me tentatively, like a cat sidling up for affection. "But my powers don't do that. All I know is you shouldn't hang around here all day, because that's bad for moping people. I'm sure they did a study on it."

I throw myself back down on Pillow, who makes no soft sound of surprise.

Feral raises an eyebrow. "Are you listening, you fucking thembo? I know it's sad boi hours, but too bad. Get in bitch, we're going sobbing. Show me something interesting about your weird-ass hometown."

We go for a walk down by the river and Feral prowls through the grass. For a few moments I forget I'm powerless, and we run through the green zone, playing tag around trees. It's cheating because Feral has fucking super speed but she gives me head starts. I'm finally too tired to run anymore, and we lie underneath a tree and look up at the dappled sky.

She turns her head towards me. "Did it work?"

"What?"

"Did you forget about your troubles?"

"Yes, for a minute there I lost myself."

A smile spreads across her face. "Even a minute is good when everything is terrible."

It makes me think of how much Feral has lost, all her family and friends, and how badly she needs us. I instantly feel like a wretched, petty creature hunched around the bloodied hunk of my own sorrow.

"You can visit me anytime," I tell her intently. "Seeing you means a lot."

She reaches out and takes my hand, and there are tears dampening the soft fur around her eyes. "You take care of yourself, okay? Everyone up there loves you, no matter what you think."

I know she's trying to help, but it's the wrong thing to say, because I know it's objectively untrue. You can't tell me they love me after what they've done. I fold that pain away back inside me, and smile at Feral, and then we walk back to my house, hand in hand among the softly gathered dusk.

It's very quiet and dark in my room after Feral leaves. I stare into space, trying to think about anything except Dani, fighting the magnetism of my thoughts but always losing.

Her face, her lips, the way she looked when my powers got taken, like staring into an eclipsed sun. It hurt her, I know that, but she went along with it anyway.

I fumble for my laptop, to find something to do instead of moping, when Penance flickers into existence, perched on the end of my bed. Her curls frame her face, and her eyes are wide, as if she startled herself by coming here. She's wearing a cute little black jacket and there's a silver pendant at her throat with three linked hearts.

"Your turn to babysit the problem child?" I ask.

"No. I missed you." She shuffles up the bed a little closer. In this form, she's so fine-boned and delicate. "Everyone does."

I have no response. If a certain person missed me, there's nothing to stop them coming down to visit. And if they don't miss me, then I'm not going to waste my time missing them. My vision blurs briefly, as Penance fills me in on some of the goings-on in Asteroid Ems. Mostly they've been doing humanitarian aid and disaster relief. Everything seems to be perfectly normal with me gone, like I left no bruise or scar at all.

She falls silent and turns her face towards me, beautiful and intent. It's like she's trying to figure me out, but I can't stop looking at her mouth. There are so many emotions curdled inside of me, and I don't want to feel a single one. Dani discarded me, an unwanted thing, and if that's how things are, then it can't hurt at all to do this.

I put one trembling hand to her cheek. She leans into my touch, her eyes fluttering closed. I move closer, and plant the softest possible kiss on her pale pink lips, mine only fractionally parted. Violet makes this tiny, satisfied noise, like she's made some important realisation. Her tongue brushes against mine, so tentative it's like we're reaching across a void to each other. Her mouth is warm and tastes slightly of sugar, as if she's been eating something sweet. I want to dissolve on her tongue like candy, to melt into a honeyed swirl of a person that doesn't think or feel anything but this.

Then the warmth and sweetness is gone and I'm half a circuit, severed once more.

Violet reappears on the roof above me, a pale sliver of blue-tinged face viewed through a veil of tears. "I'm sorry. That shouldn't—"

"No need for apologies." The bitterness leaks from my voice, all the softness and sweetness flooded out of my mouth. "I'm obviously as unwelcome with you as I am with Dani."

"It's not that." She folds herself into a sliver and then unfolds back on the bed beside me. Her eyes are on my lips, as if watching them move is the next best thing to tasting them. "It's *clearly* not that. But I can't get amongst whatever is going on with you and her."

And there it is, the wreckage of my heart spilled in the small gap between us. I stare at my hands, twisting together in my lap, as if they'll strangle each other instead of reaching out. When I speak, my voice is low. "I am hopelessly in love, and I hate it."

"I know." She reaches out and touches my knee. "You'll find your way back."

"She did this to me," I snap. "It's up to her to do the navigation."

"This is why I'm not getting in the middle of it." She leans in and kisses my cheek, feather soft.

Then she disappears again, folded into the secret passageways of the world, and I am alone.

CHAPTER TWENTY-EIGHT

More days drift past. Pear bounces back and forth between home and Asteroid Ems where their girlfriend Sarah and her family are. I keep telling them that there's no point babying me and I'm perfectly able to look after myself, but they keep showing up. We order takeout, watch horror movies, and buddy-read X-Men comics together. There's no real conversation, and every time Pear mentions anything to do with *mutants* I shut it down hard, no matter how much it feels like slamming the door in their face.

Without powers, I've got very little to offer. A foul-mouthed smartass who keeps fighting because it's my only plan in the face of a world that seems broken along a thousand different fault lines. The same world that chose me and asked me to serve as its warrior. I used to feel so helpless. Wanting something more productive than going vegetarian or biking places or using less plastic. For a moment I was on the verge of making change, and now I'm sitting in bed feeling sorry for myself. The world is dying, held face down in a shallow puddle by humanity. All I can do is stand numbly by and watch, because this has broken me down to nothing. The world will have to find another champion. Dani will move on, meet someone else, and fall in a love so incandescent the dull glow of me won't even register in her mind. I've never been special, and it's only by a fluke I was ever able to pretend, to furiously fake my way to relevance.

This is balance, really. The world returned to its true state.

I collapse back into my old life. I drift in the silence. I stay up too late browsing Crunchyroll until I fall asleep, dropping my overheating phone down against my neck. I even try watching their goddamn documentary. It looks good, all these intertwined stories of them helping to save the planet. Then there's a scene of them on a beach and I loop this tiny clip of Dani, a beautiful, melancholy girl watching the world with the saddest eyes I've ever seen.

I can't fucking do it anymore. I stop checking the news, try to forget there's a world happening outside this pocket dimension. I pretend that each day that falls through me hurts a little less. It's easier to let them go.

Until there's a knock at the door while I'm busy rearranging our comic collection.

"Come in," I shout on reflex.

"Blast from the past," a familiar voice says. "I turn up and you've got your nose in a comic book."

"Lucifer." I throw my arms around his neck, because I'm genuinely pleased to see him, and not just because he's a thread to Dani, who I was just pretending I was better off without. "My favourite glowing boy."

"I caved in the end," he says.

"Caved how?"

"Against the stubbornness. Waiting for you to give up this bullshit and come back."

"I'm not welcome there," I say shortly, my good mood evaporating.

"Not the story I heard." He crosses to the couch and curls up in it, looking up at me. "Don't shoot the messenger, but they say you went rogue and your powers were malfunctioning. You were hearing voices that weren't there and you did some crazy missions. Goddess tried to confront you and help you, but you ran away."

I snort. "Technically that's like ninety percent fucking true. Except my powers weren't *malfunctioning* in the least."

"I told them you were always a bit of an eco-warrior."

"Wow, thanks." I take a seat beside him and poke him in the leg with my foot. "I'm sure that super helped my defense. Oh, he's not just crazy *now*. She's always been that way. They're just extra powerful now."

He laughs. "I said none of that."

"It's what everyone thinks though." My mood turns sour so quickly these days. "That I'm a liability. Something to be caged and controlled."

He shakes his head. "I'm supposed to be here to cheer you up. This is the whole point of my visit. We'll go to the mall and get shitty junk food, then go for a walk on the beach and... fuck's sake, Keepaway. That was your cue."

Five seconds later there's a dog in the room and I start crying.

"Summers, you idiot." I bury my face in his fur. "Are you tired of being Cosmo the space dog? You wanted to come hang out with the baselines, huh?"

For the rest of the day, we fall back through time. It's me and my dog and a gorgeous boy on the beach. We run in and out of the waves until our shoes and the bottoms of our jeans are wet and crusted with salt. The ice-cream truck is parked down by the surf club and we stop there and eat soft-serve that's so sweet it feels like being mugged by sugar. Then we buy hot chips and perch at the top of the dunes, watching the sun descend into the ocean in a riot of orange and purple. Summers sits curled across my feet, almost too exhausted to lick the salt from my fingers.

"Thank you," I say to Lou. "It's been a perfect day."

"You're welcome." He smiles in the gathering dark. "We were always good at being friends."

"Are you pointedly saying *friends* so I don't try and kiss you?"

214

"I did maybe talk to Penance," he says with a laugh.

"Omigod, I'm so fucking embarrassed." I cover my face with my hands and get sand in my mouth, which I always do at the beach, no matter how much I try.

"Don't be. It's a perfectly normal thing to do when you're feeling shitty."

I elbow him in the side. "Look how we've grown."

"Are you going to be okay?"

I'm glad he can't read the expression in my face. "I think so. It's a day at a time thing. Pear's looking after me."

"Sorry it took so long, but I'll stop by again soon." He takes my hand and squeezes it. "And Sarah says you can keep the dog for a while."

He walks me home, but the moment he says goodbye on the doorstep, he's whisked away by Keepaway, mutant magic that's now beyond my reach.

I let myself into the house and stop dead. There's a hazy outline of someone standing in the middle of our living room.

"What the *fuck* are you doing here?" I ask.

"You hate me." She's a ghost made of tears, drifting in a hesitant cloud. "I get it."

"I wish it was as easy as hating you. I've tried, but I can't. Because you're Alyse, and because I fucking love my best friend even through the worst fucking time of my life."

She flings herself at me, and throws her damp stormcloud arms around me. "I'm so so sorry. We shouldn't have done it."

I try to resist the hug. "No shit you shouldn't."

"I'm not justifying it, but you were a loose cannon and your upgraded powers are *scary*. Like that shit you said about killing every corrupt asshole on the planet, and then you were going out and—"

I try to pull away through the wash of her. "It *sounds* like you're justifying it."

"I don't know what else to say because this is fucked and I don't know how to unfuck it."

I'm on the verge of telling her to leave, because I can't *do* this, I can't stand here and—

"I just miss you, Dilly."

Those words undo me, loosen everything I've tied together to protect the fragile inner parts of me, and I'm lost and bereft. We end up on my bed, me sobbing in her lap, like I contain all the salt water in the world.

"My life sucks," she tells me, once we can both be understood. "I miss my best friend, and I'm living with two other people who are constantly upset. One of them is mad at the other one but won't come right out and say it, so is just frostily passive-aggressive all the fucking time."

"You're losing me." I look up at her, transformed back to beautiful, regular Alyse.

"Dani is impossible to be around. She's furious at Emma. I think she's also angry at me for not reining Emma in somehow. She's also mad at you for not coming back."

I glare up at her. "Well, you can tell Dani I'm fucking mad at *her* for not coming to see me. Actually, no. Don't say anything. I want her to come to me when she *wants* to."

"This is the problem." Alyse throws up her arms. "You're the two most stubborn people on the planet, so neither of you is going to bend and I'm stuck watching it like it's the worst reality TV show ever."

"She's clearly in the wrong."

"Does it really matter?" Alyse asks. "It's you and Dani. Can't you get past this?"

"It was her who couldn't get past it, who fed me to Emma to have my fucking powers chopped off. I seem to remember you standing there as well."

"I apologised," Alyse whispers.

"And yet I'm still here powerless."

"I'm trying to do the peacemakey thing here. If you

could come back and sit down with everyone then we could maybe get past this and—"

"No, Lys. How am I supposed to *get past* this? Okay, sure, I did a couple of things on my own, because none of you would fucking listen to me. It was made very clear that if I wanted to do something about a dying planet, I wasn't going to get any backup from my best friends." This whole time I've been talking, Alyse has been drifting back into a rainswept sad-form, and I finally run out of steam and smack into guilt. I flop back down on the bed beside her. "I'm sorry for the rant."

"It's good to hear." She blinks watery eyes at me. "I mean, nobody's actually saying what they feel. Everyone's just quiet and angry. Maybe next time you'll say it to Dani."

I close my eyes and take a deep breath. "I do like that missing me pisses her off."

Alyse cackles. "There's nothing like hope to keep you going. If one of you ever unbends a tiny fraction, I'll be there shoving you the rest of the way. And, if it counts in one direction at all, I do really fucking miss you, Dillyweed."

"I miss you too." Then I'm fucking crying again and why is this so *exhausting.*

I fall asleep with Alyse, but when I wake up, I'm alone again. The reality of that presses on me until I want to choke. I've always been scared of rejection, the scowling Dylan who hid from everyone and pushed back before she could be hit. And now I've genuinely been spurned.

Alyse can call it stubbornness all she likes, but the truth is Dani doesn't love me enough to unbend. She's supposed to be the strong one and the better one. I'm too broken to do it. Why can't she be here, apologising and telling me she loves me, so I can crawl back inside and find peace again?

There is no quiet for me, because some asshole is at the door. All the residual good feeling from Alyse's visit has evaporated, and I slam the door open, ready to unload on whichever unlucky fuck is visiting me.

It's the last person I would have expected, although she's vastly changed. She's got the side of her head shaved, with MUTANT LIFE tattooed on her scalp. The rest of her hair is jagged and asymmetrical, dyed lurid strips of blue and green.

"Dylan fucking Taylor, as I live and breathe." Emma winks at me.

Under her left eye the number 414 is tattooed in tiny writing, and everything falls into place.

"Skye's powers, huh?" I give her my sternest look, channeling Mrs. Kim.

"Clones are how G-Prime is keeping shit remotely on lock. And yes, I am the four-hundred and fourteenth iteration of that illustrious line. First one with a fucking backbone to do my own shit. Think of the Madrox clone that became a priest."

I make a scoffing sound in the back of my throat. "Trying to woo me with X-Men references, huh? You must be desperate."

"Like I said, I'm the first one degenerate enough to come find you. To see if I can turn you back on, but it looks like we're not *perfect* clones after all."

"So you admit you made a mistake?" I tilt my head.

"I personally can, but Prime is not at all ready. Far from the only mistake our dear Goddess has made. Bit of a miscalculation on the Quietus-slash-Michael front, but we're working on it."

"What's going on?" I'm intrigued despite myself, but I affect my best casual air.

"Fucking artificial so-called intelligence. Seems humanity's gone and hoisted itself with its own petard."

"The fuck is a petard?"

"I wondered that myself, but it turns out it's a little bomb. They're blowing themselves up like they always do."

She winks again, and I swear to myself I will not be charmed by this roguish Emma.

"You could say the same for yourself, or Prime at least," I shoot back.

"A hit." Emma-414 staggers. "A palpable fucking hit. Or would be, if I was Goddess. Alas, I am this black sheep bitch." She leans in the doorframe and gives me an arch grin that I've never seen on the face of *my* Emma. "Humanity's gone and got itself a case of spiritual infection and we're trying to put out the fires. Undoing mind control is a tricky business. Would've been nice to have you on side, but—" She waves her hand airily.

"Yes." I do the glacial thing.

"Nice and frosty. I dig it." She purses her lips at me and winks yet again. "In our defence, she does love you oh so terribly much, and you were mildly terrifying. Prime's trying to juggle a lot and having a little ball of nitroglycerine added to the mix made it difficult."

"Loves me enough to take my powers." I'm starting to be sick of this clone and her excuses too, because at the end of the day, I'm still stuck here in no-powers, no-hope land.

"The only way to keep you safe, or so she thought. I've told her since it was a very bad idea, but it was too late, and she thinks you hate her, and maybe you do, going by that scowl plastered all over your face."

I *do* hate her, except I don't, because she's Emma, and I can't hate her. The clone is making some amount of sense, but none of it matters if she won't fix anything.

"So I have to come bowing and scraping to her, and she'll deign to reinstate my powers?"

"Maybe. Fuck. I don't know." She gives an exaggerated shrug. "Maybe once this Michael situation is resolved? Until then, I'd keep yourself out of trouble, sit here on the bench, and wait for the call."

"That's not how I work."

She laughs, the delighted laugh that Emma does, one I haven't heard in some time, since everything started weighing so heavy. "Oh my darling Dilly. I know that very well. She does too, but we're a proud and stubborn bunch, us Emmas. It's a flaw."

"Two flaws," I deadpan.

She leans in and kisses me on the cheek. "I love you. And she does too." Then she vanishes, and I'm left smelling the faint floral aftermath of her perfume.

I stand and stare out at suburbia. Nobody's around because it's the middle of the day. Only a cat, sunning itself on the fence. It probably has the right idea. Despite the parade of mutants that have come to see me, nothing has changed.

I'm still cut off from everything.

I have no voice to call out with, and I can't face the thought of reaching out and finding nothing to hold onto. I close the door and return to my room. This time, when I pull the covers over my head, I breathe my own suffocating air. It's what I deserve.

Me and my self-loathing, together again, sinking into my bed like it's grave dirt.

CHAPTER TWENTY-NINE

It doesn't take long for time to wear on me. What do people *do* all day? Am I going to have to study something or get a job? When I was at school, I tried to push that shit off down the road until the day I couldn't avoid it anymore. Then when the mutant thing happened, it became a job somehow. One I loved. Maybe I can come back and be the one human teacher at the mutant school, once there is one. I'll be the cautionary tale. *Watch out or you'll have your powers snatched like Chatterbox.*

In the meantime, I am bored, bored and entirely fucking bored. I'm so tired of myself. It seems unfair that despite being severed from almost everything I love, I'm still stuck with me. Pear is trying, but I honestly think they're getting sick of me. It's only Summers who doesn't give a fuck. All he wants is pats and food and a walk every now and then. Why can't I be that low-maintenance? Can't Dani come down and feed me some cake, chase me around the block, and then pat me? Why the fuck am I crying again?

I'm so sick of my life. This can't be all there is. Maybe I'll go be a protestor for mutant rights. There are few of those around. They stand outside government buildings and wave signs. I'll smash something and burn a cop car. Then they might send a mutant to save me.

I need something better to do, but I can't think of anything. I've just finished re-reading a bunch of new X-Men comics. I decide to go down to the shops and wander the aisles until I find something I want. Maybe a new hoodie would make me feel more like myself. I drag myself into something approximating a non-hideous outfit, and spend about fifteen minutes finding Summers' lead and collar and everything.

Once I'm finally ready, I open the front door and step outside.

Except I'm not going to get a chance at my boring day, because there's a bunch of heavily armed dudes in body armour standing at the end of the path. Prominently displayed on their chests is a now unpleasantly-familiar golden eye logo. Hovering above is a host of spidery-looking drones, with mechanical angel wings unfurled. I don't think this lot is running any version of the Chatterbox protocol. Parked along the street is a row of vehicles, disgorging yet more soldiers. They're really not fucking around.

"Shit."

Summers yanks on my arm. I let him go and he immediately tangles himself up in his lead, runs between my legs, and sends me staggering down the stairs. By this time, the Michael patrol have spotted me, their target, depowered and delivering themself into enemy hands.

Seconds later, I'm surrounded. There are guns pointing down at me, and I can't even tell them that it's okay, that I understand, that they have no choice. A soldier throws himself atop me and pins me to the ground. I thrash to get free, but there's a knee pressed in my back and a combat boot grinding down hard on the back of my left hand.

"Assholes," I growl, and then someone kicks me in the side. It's so painful any further coherent words are lost in a torrent of swearing. I wish I could whistle a single fucking gun, wish Oni was here to slice these pricks to fucking ribbons, wish I was anything but a goddamn powerless piece of shit lying face down on my front path surrounded by religious warriors.

"Dylan Taylor." The voice coming through the visor is distorted and the tone is all wrong. Michael, is that you? "Also known as the mutant terrorist Chatterbox. You are under arrest for crimes including—"

Someone kicks me again, a starburst of pain that makes glitches of light dance in front of my eyes. They're going to beat me to death right here in front of my own house. All I can hope is that Pear stays away, and doesn't fucking turn up in the middle of—

My vision sparks again, and I worry something's broken in my brain. The visor of the guy standing over me is glowing like a tiny sun and no matter how much I blink, it won't go away. Then it shatters, melted metal dripping down. I smell burning flesh and the hot solder stink of fused electronics. Something else arcs through the air, a descending meteor that slams into the chest of another soldier. It's a man, an angel made incandescent like Lucifer falling from heaven and burning alive on re-entry.

A winged shape spirals to the ground to land in the middle of my street. A fucking dragon, unleashed in suburbia. Katie roars, and Michael's soldiers flee the hellish furnace of her throat.

Feral is here too, a lithe streak sprinting through the ranks that have been assembled to bring me in. She is brutal and beautiful, a weapon come to life, the pinnacle of evolution. Michael's troops can do nothing to stop her.

Above me, fireworks light up the sky as the angelic drones smash into each other, hurled together by the mighty force of a telekinetic hand.

She's up there. A tiny figure, hanging in the sky. Even at this distance I can tell it's her. Melancholy fills my chest and I can't breathe through the wanting and longing, being within her orbit and yet so far away. It was Dani who loved me like I was whole, drawing stars around my scars and making something beautiful of me. Now I've been pulled apart again and I don't know how it's possible to fit back together. I'm disassembled, nonsensical, like shitty flatpack furniture.

All this feeling is too much. I can't be here.

I get to my feet, ignoring Lou and the bloody remnants of the soldiers. The door to my house is still open, and I run through it, dodging through the lounge and out the back. I've still got enough training that I can leap the fence without trouble, running through some neighbour's backyard and out into the street.

I can still hear Katie's roar behind me. "Dylan. Come *back*."

I'm not even sure why I'm running. I can't outpace a goddamn dragon. It's even more ridiculous to think I can get away from how I feel.

Maybe if I go far enough, I'll be too tired to think about anything.

Except I can't stop thinking about Dani.

She looked so fucking good. It's so unfair, because I'm a complete shambles cosplaying as a trashfire human nightmare. She's probably already zooming back to space, relieved that she dodged the disaster bullet that is me.

"Fuck," I shout, startling a young couple walking their Labrador. "God, I'm sorry."

I veer away, into the street where a car comes screeching to a halt. It's so close to hitting me that my legs rest against its front bumper. My heart thunders in my chest. The couple stare at me. The dog tugs on the lead and yaps.

"Shit, fuck. I'm sorry," I shout to the driver.

There's nobody in the car, a pale blue electric vehicle idling silently in the middle of the road.

"Roxy?"

The driver's door swings open. I'm fizzing with adrenaline as I fold myself into the seat. The couple is still staring at me. I give them a wave. The woman waves back, but the guy is frowning, trying to put the pieces together.

"How the fuck are you here?" I ask the car.

Roxy's door closes with a firm click and she hums off down the road. I put my hand on the steering wheel and try to calm down. It doesn't work.

"I can't understand you, if you're trying to say something. How can you even *be* here without my powers activating you?"

The Spotify hookup flicks on and scrolls through songs. "Mother Earth is preg—" a weird voice intones, before the track stops.

"The voice." I slap the steering wheel. "That's where you're getting energy?"

The track changes to Drake confirming that I am, in fact, fuckin' right.

Something cold touches my cheek and I freak the fuck out. It's lucky Roxy's driving for me, or I would've gone hurtling off the road.

"Bloody hell, Onimaru. You could say hello a little less scarily." I crane over my shoulder to see Sheba rolling around in the back seat. "Oh great, so the whole gang is here. I guess we're on a mission, and here's me with no powers at all."

Drake confirms it again.

"So I don't *need* my powers for this?"

Roxy is unsure about this apparently. I suppose I have to trust the voice. It did send Roxy off to kidnap me, after all. What could possibly go wrong? Last time I trusted it, I lost my powers. We can't really get much worse than that.

"Fuck it. Whatever. This is better than stewing at home. Take me where I'm supposed to go." I crank the seat back so I can get comfortable. Is this desperation, to put myself in the hands of some mysterious force? I can't go back to being human, and I'm no longer a mutant, so I'll trust the only thing that'll have me.

I wonder if Emma knows where I am. She couldn't hear the voice, so maybe we're in a little blind spot outside her awareness. Or perhaps some tendril of her incomprehensible brain is occupied with tracking my position at all times. The whole world is in her hands, and yet her eye is still on me, the foul-mouthed sparrow.

"Wake me when we get there." I roll onto my side and close my eyes.

A blast from the horn startles me from sleep. It must be hours later, because it's gotten completely dark. Roxy's parked up at an EV charger outside a service station. The lights from the shop remind me I haven't eaten since a banana for breakfast.

"I'm hungry," I remark, as if anything in this car can help me.

Oni drifts up off the passenger seat and gestures towards the lights.

"I've got no money. It's not like they pay you for being a mutant, and all the mutant money is tied up in god knows where."

Sheba rolls into my hand.

"You're saying I should rob the place?"

Oni makes a single tap on the dash.

"Is that one tap for yes and two for no?"

He taps again. I frown out the window. It's hardly the worst thing I've ever done. It still feels kind of shitty though. Whoever's on duty will probably get in trouble. Still, I am fucking starving.

"You wait in the car," I tell the weapons, and shove the driver's door open. Neither of them listen, but bob along behind me like a pair of violent kites. "Be more subtle, at least."

The automatic doors slide open and I step into the bright interior.

"Um, excuse me? What the hell is this?" There's a tired looking Indian guy behind the counter. He fumbles for something. Hopefully not a weapon, because I can't talk my way out of that shit, and I don't want Oni to get overexcited.

"Don't worry. I'm here for some food. My name's Chatterbox."

"Yeah, I know who you are. Famous mutant. You haven't been in the documentary though. Comments section is full of theories." He eyes me warily. "Why are you here for food?"

"I mean I need food and I've got no money. I don't want to start anything, but like…"

"Mutants gotta eat. You get separated from the crew or something?"

"Or something."

"Cool, alright, sure. Grab a pie or a sandwich. Some chips, water. I mean, don't like fucking rob the place blind, but they're not going to notice if you take a few things." He reaches down behind the counter and pulls out a paper sack.

"Thanks." I frown at him as I pick up the sack and shake

it out. "Why are you doing this?"

"Mutant pride, man."

"You're a mutant?"

"No." He shrugs. "I just think you're cool. You get a lot of shit, but you're just different."

I rub the back of my neck awkwardly. "Some of us mutants come with ways to defend ourselves."

"Bro, if my binder could emit some form of anti-TERF radiation, I would use it everyday."

That startles a laugh out of me. "Thanks, man." I reach out and bump fists with the guy.

He goes back to his phone as if this is the most mundane occurrence in the world, while I fill the bag with supplies. I take a little bit of everything and then pause at the door.

"Hey."

He looks up from his phone. "You all good?"

"Yeah. I'm great. And thanks. That was really cool of you."

"I feel kinda weird asking this, but can I get a photo?"

I'm not the biggest fan of *photos of myself*, but it's the least I can do. He wants Oni and Sheba to get in the photo too, but we finally find an angle we all like, even if I'm doing a peace sign in front of my face.

Finally, I get back in the car and we're on our way again. I make a dent in my new bag of supplies and then sling it into the back seat for later. I have no idea how far we're going. Eventually at this rate, we're going to run out of New Zealand.

"You know where we're headed?" I ask Oni.

He makes two sharp taps on the dashboard.

"Is the voice steering?"

He taps again.

"Fucking great."

He makes about ten taps on the dashboard, which I have no fucking idea what it means, but it *seems* like code for very very fucking no.

"Should we be here?"

This gets a single tap, so I'm back to square one.

I eat chips and watch the night outside pass by. We pass through towns in a blur of lights and then move into windy country roads. I buzz the window down and poke my head out like a dog, both to deal with motion sickness and because I like the cool air on my face.

Eventually, we do reach the end of New Zealand. The road curves around, but Roxy gently lifts off the ground.

"You could've been flying this whole time." I pat her steering wheel gently. "Don't worry, I remember how much you like roads."

We fly on through the night, coasting over dark water far below. The novelty wears off and I start musing on the nature of the voice. I'd call it my mysterious benefactor except I've received nothing but bullshit from it. If I believe what it says, it's a form of mutant itself, something generated from the dying planet as a defense mechanism. Why can I talk to it when nobody else can? Is that a side-effect of my mutant power or something else? It implied I was chosen specifically, but I can't even hear it to ask these questions, even if it would answer me. I'm only the fuse it lit to express its rage, and I burned with its heat. Now I'm helpless, sitting in a metal box and drifting through the darkness.

I start to get uncomfortable so I try switching to the passenger seat. That doesn't help, so I manoeuvre into the back and twist myself into a position where I can stretch out with my legs only slightly bent up.

"I miss talking to you," I tell my friends. "You were always there for me. Like ridiculously so, given what a disaster I am." I pause, as if there's a chance I might hear them respond, chiming in to say how I'm not a disaster, or even if I am, they love me anyway. "Now everything's gotten fucked again. It would be easy to blame the voice, but it's sad and lashing out, and I get that. All I hope is that we find a way through it somehow and I can talk to you again. Because I miss you." I wipe tears off my cheeks. "I miss Dani, and I miss Lys and Emma and Violet and Feral and Lou and Katie and fucking everyone. I miss all the mutants, and being trapped in a bunch of rocky tunnels with all the people who make up my world. I don't want to be alone anymore."

I wait, and wait, but there's nothing in response. No voice from Roxy or Oni or Sheba. Nothing from Emma. Keepaway doesn't appear in the front seat to rescue me. Dani isn't hanging in the sky in front of the car. Instead, there's only dawn, smearing the horizon in colour like melted candy. It's beautiful, and so vast. This rock, teeming with life, hurtling through space and turning to face the sun.

Roxy flies on, into the breaking day, and I drift back into sleep.

CHAPTER-THIRTY

I wake up with a jolt when Roxy's wheels hit the ground again. I sit up so fast, my head almost smacks the roof. "Where are we?"

There's obviously no answer. I've got no idea how long I slept, or how fast Roxy travels. I'm guessing we're somewhere in the vast blue of the Pacific, but wherever I am, it's deserted.

Around us is an enormous field of long grass. Wildflowers are dotted through it in crooked lines of white, red and yellow, with occasional patches where they spring up in wild abandon. The breeze ruffles them gently so the tops tremble and dance.

I crack the driver's door and step out gingerly, trying not to disturb anything. Roxy's dropped herself in the middle, so there are no tracks in or out. The roar of the sea is loud, and I turn to see it. The field ends in a ragged, torn away line, and the sea sprawls beyond. Light dances on it, fractured into a thousand pieces. Birds call to each other, like they're screaming warning. Two rise up from nowhere, drifting on air currents, and then beat their wings furiously away from us, as if we're things that do not belong.

They're probably right.

I walk towards the end of the field and discover the reason it ends so abruptly.

We're on the edge of an enormous cliff that drops down

in a sheer face of rugged grey rock to the frothing ocean below. More birds dip down to skim the surface and then spiral upwards, as if a predator lurks under the waves to catch them.

We've travelled for hours to find this beautiful place that's both teeming with life and entirely desolate. I have no idea why. Is the voice trying to show me some part of itself—some wild fraction that humans have not debased or mined for profit. There are no ruins, no signs of civilization. There's not even litter. Why would the voice bring me here, of all places?

Is this a farewell, or a clue to something greater?

From the beginning, the planet's cry has been a rope around my throat, tugging me onwards through disasters. A desperate, last-ditch attempt to salvage something before humanity plunges into extinction. And I relished the fight. It felt good to burn for a moment, rather than the frozen thing I've been since we lost Wraith.

Now I'm nothing. The fire has gone out, and I'm a hollow shell, empty of powers.

I stand on the edge of the cliff in my tattered sneakers. Pieces of loose shingle drop away and fall to the ocean, which snaps and splashes over jagged rocks. So many shades of blue. The wind catches my hair and scatters strands over my eyes. If there's meaning here, it's indecipherable, some language written in the sea and rocks and sky. Perhaps a poet could make something of it, but I've never had many words aside from *fuck* and *you*. It leaves me here, at this fragile tip of the world, the victim of the cruelest hoax. I believed in love and change and destiny, and now I am empty as the sky.

"All I want is a fucking reason," I scream. "Just give me a reason."

There's no answer. Of course there isn't. It's only me, a charcoal figure scrawled over the landscape, waiting to be blown away. That's what happens when you burn. In the end, only ash remains.

I step away from the edge, and further back again, until the grass rises up high enough to brush against my thighs. "You have nothing for me then." I want to sink into the flowers. Roxy can fly away and I'll just die, leaving a skeleton. Some great mystery of how a person came from the sky and left a corpse in this beautiful, untouched land. "I'd settle for the most cryptic fucking hint at this rate. Anything about what the hell is going on and—*ouch*."

The cry is because Oni has snuck up and fucking *cut* me. There's a long ragged scratch that starts at the base of my hand and twists around to run down the back of my arm.

"What the fuck was that for? The voice? Is it mad at me for *whining*? Because there's a lot fucking more where that came from." I tip my head back and shout. "Shall I start telling you all my grievances, you asshole?"

Oni smacks my hand with the flat of his blade, sending a spray of blood through the air. The droplets splatter amongst a patch of wildflowers and promptly disappear. Then I see it travelling up the stems of the flowers, like they're floral vampires eagerly drinking. Except when my blood reaches the petals, it comes out as complex interlocking patterns like—

"Words." I drop to my knees, bending the closest flower towards my face. Written in delicate cursive around the inside are the words *might be drastic*. "A message." I spin back around to find where the sentence starts.

I apologise. This is drastic, but we are desperate, and you have been muzzled.

By the end, the letters have become faint and hard to read. I clench my fist a few times, until the blood wells along the back of my hand, and smear it on the roots of more flowers.

"You did this on purpose?" I ask.

Do not waste your life's blood on pointless questions.

I scowl, and splash more blood. "Why here then?"

This is a place of power. A previous version of you died here, a long time ago.

"What do you mean by a previous version? Please tell me that's not a pointless question."

A conduit. A mouthpiece. A speaker.

"You mean my powers? So there have been people like me before?"

Mutants, yes. Those who connect to the source.

"A hive mind of object consciousness," I whisper.

Much more than that, although too much to explain here. What's important is...

The cut Oni gave me is too shallow and is already healing over. I hold my palm out to him. "I'm finally getting answers, so don't get squeamish now."

He makes another cut, and I smear it across the grass.

It's what you can provide. A more drastic solution than fighting.

"My blood," I whisper.

Somewhat. Dissolving your energy matrix to read the pattern written in your DNA. The template and the spark.

"But I'm powerless." I've exhausted all these flowers, so I move to the next patch and fling droplets of blood at their roots.

Not powerless. Muzzled. It's still all there, waiting to be used.

My head swims. I don't think it's loss of blood, although my hand really fucking hurts. "I don't get out of this alive, do I? This thing, it takes all of me."

It is sacrifice, yes, but not the end.

"Not the end? What the hell does that mean?"

AN end but not THE end.

"Great. I suppose I did say I'd be happy for the cryptic shit."

Walk to the cliff.

"If you make Oni push me off, I'll be very fucking unhappy."

You should see this. It may help you understand.

I'm very skeptical, but approach the cliff slowly. Oni stays back in the grass, presumably to make me feel better, but I know how fast he can move. We're up so high that if I fell, it would be all over. My objects could save me, but I'm not sure whether they're on Team Voice, and it's still very unclear what the voice wants.

I look down to where the water batters the rocks. It's the scene I saw before, but beneath me the water draws back, an impossible current sucking it away in two different directions. The rocks jut up from the ocean floor, forming a roughly circular cradle. In the middle of it is the head of an enormous skeleton. It's a skull that looks almost human, aside from the impossible size and horn-like protrusions at the temples. The giant cavernous eye sockets are aimed at the sky, or possibly at me, as if it could glimpse the future and see my ragged figure standing above it.

"A previous version." My voice is carried away on the wind.

The rest of the skeleton stretches away beneath the water. There's only the hint of a knobbly spine, yellow-white islands of bone that rise from the water outside the rocky cradle. How long ago did this previous iteration of mutant-kind live? Our history has been erased, so it's impossible to know if sights like this were commonplace once upon a time. How and why it died seems like the most pressing question.

I turn back, to find another patch of flowers, clenching my fist as blood drips down the backs of my fingers, spattering the grass.

Except I am no longer alone on this island. There's a new figure standing in front of me.

My heart is pierced again, as if there's no limit to how much it can feel.

"Hello, Dylan," Dani says.

CHAPTER THIRTY-ONE

"Hi." I'm squinting, because the sun is behind her and I can't make out much more than her silhouette. I don't know what my heart is doing. Maybe it's paused mid-beat, to see how this conversation ends before it either reforges or explodes. "How did you find me?"

She takes another couple of steps towards me, as if she's scared it'll startle me and I'll take to the air to join the birds wheeling above us. "Believe it or not, I spend a lot of time talking to Farsight. Asking where you are and what you're doing. I can only use her occasionally, because she's an important resource, you know, and the Michael thing is—"

"I'm sure that's been very fascinating for you." My mouth twitches upwards despite itself. "Seeing me lying in bed and watching TV."

"You were okay," she says softly. "That was what I cared about."

"Oh yeah, I felt all that care." I wish I could stop taking refuge in sarcasm. Dani is here and she is so close and I don't know what to fucking feel, because it is every emotion at once, a dizzying colour wheel swirl. "Sadly, I didn't get some magical viewport to see how you were doing."

"I'm sorry, Dilly." Her voice sounds like she's crying.

"For what?"

"Everything." She flings her arms out wide. "For not listening to you when you asked for help, for letting you go off and fight on your own, for not sticking up for you against Emma, for watching you leave, for not coming to see you when you were gone."

It's my turn to take a couple of steps forward. Now I can see her properly, dressed in a baggy shirt with the top two buttons open and three-quarter pants that hug her body. She's got dark lipstick on, nearly black. Like she's in mourning for me. There's no sadness in the world that feels like this, so rich and complicated it goes to my head like whiskey.

"That's quite a comprehensive list of apologies," I say.

"I mean it. I know it doesn't make up for anything, but…"

The frown creeps back onto my face. "So why come and find me now?"

"I saw you in the street when Quietus tried to arrest you. I felt like I'd been *stabbed* with grief and love and longing. And then you ran away, and totally vanished." She pauses, and her eyes are fractured with tears. "So I went back to the asteroid, had a minor freakout, and then demanded Farsight tell me exactly where you were." Her breath hitches. "Which was in a car, floating over the ocean. It made no sense at all, but she watched you and I tracked you on a map, until you ended up here. On a tiny remote island."

"And you came right here to see me."

"Well, no. I had a less minor freakout. Alyse told me I was being ridiculous, and Lou told me I was being super fucking ridiculous. Everyone else agreed and *then* I came right here."

"And here we are." I want to take a step towards her, but I don't, and she doesn't move either.

"I heard you kissed Penance," she says instead.

"She told you?"

"Only when I tried to kiss her myself." Her cheeks colour faintly. "I was all in my feelings and—"

"She is very cute," I admit, although I'm not sure what to feel about Dani kissing Violet. I'm both jealous and fascinated, and there's a very distinct image in my head of what they would have looked like together, curving in towards one another and—

"She's totally not interested." Dani takes one more step towards me, and she is all I see. My love, my desperate need, all in the form of this person who is here, for me, despite everything. "She seems to think we're still hopelessly in love with each other."

In all the history of awkward pauses, I don't think there's ever been one as uncomfortable as this. We're both stubborn and trying to play chicken, because we're hurt and want the other to say the thing. It's time for once in my life to be the better person.

"I am," I say.

She says it at the exact same fucking time, which makes me laugh hysterically because I couldn't even do it right this once. I'm almost doubled over, shaking, but she's there to hold me and pull me back up. She takes my face in her hands and looks into my eyes intently.

"I do," she says. "I really fucking love you."

"Sweet talker." I can't stop smiling. "All this time, while I was sulking, I couldn't believe it was really over because if it was…" My heart kicks in my chest, deciding to beat again after all. "I don't know how to be in a world without you. It was easier to hide and not say anything, and keep the possibility alive than risk facing you and hearing you say it was over."

"It was never over. I was just scared that you couldn't see your way to me anymore. You were changing too fast, flying off on this wild tangent."

"We need to talk about that." I know I shouldn't bring it up all over afuckinggain, but the thing is—

"First I need to say some shit." Dani's voice is steady again.

My inner voice is not remotely steady, just doing the whole *ohfuckohfuckohfuck* on a loop.

"I'm completely in love with your frustrating, brilliant, stubborn, visionary ass. I don't give a fuck if you have powers. I love you for your hardness and your softness. The way you care so much, and how sweet you are to me, and how much you love this sprawling family of ours. I fell for you when you were this awkward girl, and I've watched you grow into this astonishing person who's so strong and so irresistible. I love you more every day, and it's not because you're a superhero. It's because of *everything*."

"Go on." My breath is caught in my throat, because how does she hand me all these words, a series of beautiful gifts spilling effortlessly from those lips. "Tell me everything. I like it."

"You asshole." She starts laughing again, and I'm kissing her smile, and my heart is a home and a flood and a weightless, singing bird.

"I love you too. I can't say it all fancy like you, but you fucking *know* that shit."

"I do." She takes my chin in her metal hand and directs her gaze at mine, twin hazel lasers that detonate inside my skull. "But I need you to be okay with not having powers. I don't know if we can get them back, and I want you by my side either way."

"I'm not reckless enough to let you go twice." It's not a lie, but it's not the whole truth either, because there's still a big question over why I'm here on the island and what it all means.

She kisses me again, and it lasts for a long time. When she finally stops, she's soft and hesitant. "This voice. The voice of the planet?"

"It's gone too, since my powersectomy. Except I think it's how Roxy brought me here."

"That's why you're here?" Her frown is back. "For the planet?"

"Yeah, I think so. I mean, I don't have all the hows and whys yet. But look, I'll show you proof the voice is real." I take her by the hand, and lead her back to the patch of flowers, with the tiny bloody letters marking the delicate petals. She kneels, and brushes them towards her with her fingertips, reading them one after the other. Her expression darkens with each.

"Sacrifice." She looks up at me, her eyes wide. "What does that mean? What's at the cliff?"

"Big fuck-off skeleton of a mutant."

"A previous version of *you*. Dylan, it wants you to die for it. You get that, right? This mysterious *voice* is talking about using your DNA and your energy for some unspecified horrible thing. Can you see why we were worried about you?"

"My reading comprehension isn't that bad." I run my fingertip over the cut on my palm. "I understand what it wants, and I haven't said yes yet. There are other questions I want to ask."

"You were going to say yes?" She reaches out and squeezes my uncut hand. "You can't do that!"

"Maybe I could actually do some good, Dani. And besides, it says sacrifice but it also says that it's not the end."

"That's extremely vague bullshit." She shakes my hands, and I wince, but she's too worked up to care. "You'll die, but you won't die? It makes no sense. I'm not going to have you as a voice in my head, haunting me."

"I used to want to be disembodied. Back when I was struggling with self-worth and identity and everything. It'd be easier to be something not weighed down by a physical form that didn't feel right." I shrug inside my hoodie. "I've gotten used to my body now." I twist my hands around, to interlock our fingers and bring hers to my lips. "I like the way it works with yours."

"Then why would you consider this?"

"The planet really is dying, Dani. We're all going to

die. Human and mutant, and just... fucking everything. It's apocalyptic shit. I can't stand by and let that happen because there's a girl I love and I want to stretch out the days we have together. If we were regular people, living ordinary lives, that wouldn't be a problem. But we're not. We're heroes or monsters or both, and there are different things we need to choose. Besides, we don't even know what sacrifice and end *mean*. So let's find out."

"Dilly," she sighs, but I'm already reaching for Oni, who runs himself very gently down my palm, sending blood falling to the ground again.

"What does sacrifice mean?" I ask.

Dani leans in close and watches as the blood trickles up the stems and appears on the petals. "It's kinda cool," she admits.

Sacrifice means losing something. In this case, you will also gain something else.

"Does it mean Dylan losing their life?" Dani's voice is sharp.

Oh, and hello to you too. We are done with pleasantries, it seems. No, their life will continue, in a new form. As she was once human and is now mutant, he will be changed again. Mutation upon mutation.

Dani rocks on her heels. "And what form does this new mutation take?"

I water the flowers with a fresh crop of blood.

That is a question beyond me. She is the only one who knows.

"She? Who the hell is she?" Dani asks.

"The planet." My heart speeds up. "The one you speak for. The one who's dying."

Yes. She cannot speak for herself, so I am her voice.

"This is really a thing." Dani looks so beautiful sitting among the flowers, hair blowing around her face as she cranes over to read intently, as if she can fathom some deeper message spelled out beyond their words. "The planet is calling out to you."

"You didn't believe me until now?"

"Emma said it was some kind of feedback loop in your head, to do with your powers, because it wasn't anything she could pick up on."

"Turns out Emma doesn't know everything."

"You're right. I should have trusted you."

That defangs me more than anything, and I collapse down amongst the flowers with her. I put one arm around her waist and rest my head on her shoulder. "I really fucking missed you."

"I know." She turns her head and kisses me, and we adjust our bodies until they fit together better. "I spent quite a bit of time spying on you, remember? What you don't know is how much I missed you."

"You can show me. I mean now is probably not the best time in the world, but I've also spent a lot of time thinking very specifically about moments like this and—"

"Sometimes you talk too much." Dani pushes me backwards and sprawls on top of me. The grass swallows us both, so all that's above is uninterrupted sky. Her mouth is on my neck, hot and urgent. My injured hand is thrown backwards over my head, the other tracing lines along the delicate arch of her back. My wound is bleeding freely now, leaking into the ground. The flowers around spread themselves under the sun, and drink my fluid from the soil. They turn dark red and the petals are loose on the breeze, brushing against the curve of her tan cheek and leaving bloody streaks.

Sacrifice, it spells in gory letters across her skin.

I break the kiss. "You can't even let me have this, you asshole voice."

Dani looks down at me. Her fingertips trace the letters on my own cheek. "It says *change*."

"See, I'm not going to die." I struggle up to a sitting position, still entwined with her. "I'm going to change."

"*We're* going to," she says.

"No. This is a me thing specifically."

"I'm not losing you again," Dani says. "If you're going to change, I want to come with you. Side by side into whatever's next."

"Is that allowed?" I ask the sky.

Both is good, the flowers spell.

I glare at them suspiciously. "Promise me that we'll both change."

Both sacrifice, both change. Mutation upon mutation.

"So what's the deal, then?" Dani asks. "What does it take to trigger this change?"

Go to the cliff. Take a leap of faith. It's how it works.

"A leap of faith where we jump off a cliff?" I tear the flowers out of the ground and scatter them. "Try again with that shit."

The ground rumbles beneath us. Thousands of new flowers bloom, petals saturated and dripping. There's far too much blood to just be mine, as if a whole reservoir pumps through the heart of this island. They form a long line that leads to the cliff's edge. It's like a runway.

"I think she really means it." Dani fidgets beside me. "What do we do, Dylan?"

"We trust the voice. I mean it's desperate, but we do it for the planet, right? In the hope that what happens here makes a difference. We jump off a cliff and hope it's not lying as a way of convincing us to turn ourselves into skeletons."

Dani grimaces. "I was climbing on board up until that last sentence."

We get to our feet and walk slowly down the path laid out for us. The flowers are slick underfoot and it feels like we're walking through the entrails of some massive beast that died here—maybe a smaller cousin of the thing on the ocean floor. At the edge, we stop and look down.

"That's a big cliff," Dani says.

"Pretty though. Great wild ocean below." From this vantage point, only a few small peaks of the rocky cradle are visible, the ocean surging around them.

She looks out to the horizon and takes my hand. "Are we really going to jump?"

"It's the most reckless of moves. It's me. It's why I was chosen."

"I'm glad I'm doing it with you." Dani turns towards me and kisses me. "That's in case it's the last time."

"The hardest thing in this world—" I say.

"Don't you dare finish that sentence."

We fling ourselves off the cliff together.

CHAPTER THIRTY-TWO

Gravity takes hold of us. It's been a while since I actually *fell*. I've had cars and swords and bats and dragons carry me. The life of a mutant superhero.

The water below us parts again, revealing the rocky cradle and the enormous skull, looking much larger now that we're descending towards it.

We pause in the air for a second, our descent briefly arrested by Dani's telekinesis. She's still scared, and I get it. This is terrifying, but it's the right thing to do. I know that, the truth of it surfacing through the choppy ocean of fear.

"Dylan?" Dani's voice shakes.

"We're going to change. Trust me."

"I'm scared." Her face is pressed against my neck.

"Me too."

"I can fly us out of here, but—"

Then Dani's powers give out.

There's a *sound* to it, like a rubber band snapping.

"Dylan!" Dani screams in my ear. "What's hap—?"

I know exactly what's happening, although I don't have time to say it. We're going to hit the rocks at terminal velocity which is two hundred kilometres an hour or more, depending on some fucking factors I don't know how to explain. What I do know is we're going to be two little skeletons beside that big one. It's going to feel like—

I hit the ground with bone-shattering force.

CHAPTER THIRTY-THREE

So this is my life, or what's left of it: my body is sprawled on rocks, next to the enormous skeleton of a dead mutant from prehistory. I can't feel any of my body, which is probably a mercy. My head is tilted to the side and I'm staring directly at Dani. Her body is twisted and shattered. A spire of rock has pierced her chest, rising bloody and covered in pink foam. Somehow, her head is unbroken. There's one curve of tan cheek visible, the delicate line of her lips. Her beautiful eyes are glassy. She's already gone while I lie here, the last of my blood ebbing out over the wet rocks.

Blood sheets from Dani's broken body, down the steep incline that funnels to the bottom of the rocky cradle. Rivulets of it collect together, pooling briefly and then emptying into a hole in the ocean floor. The planet's a vampire and it's drinking us in. The edges of my vision are scratchy and grey, Dani fading and flickering away like an old movie.

Something cold touches my cheek and then the water closes over my head.

I tumble down the rocks. The hole is a slot carved in the earth, the ends of it slightly wider. Then I'm falling headlong, dragged into the mouth of a beast.

Inside the planet, everything is dark. The brief flicker of light from the hole above is quickly extinguished. I can hear a distant rushing, and a rhythmic pounding underneath it all. Even though it's impossible to see anything, I know I'm moving. I'm running through the veins of the world.

Dani's out there somewhere too. She has to be. Probably super fucking mad at me for getting us into this mess, but it *was* her choice to jump too. Not that I wouldn't have done the same thing, but it does seem very Dylan to go hurtling off a cliff, get myself accidentally killed, and then get sucked into the world by a psychic projection of the planet.

One hundred points for leading the most fucking badass next level comic book life. She's got to appreciate it at that level at least.

No, she'll definitely be pissed.

At least there are other questions to worry about than Dani's mood. What does the planet want? Why me? What will we have to give her? And what kind of mutation awaits us next? Hopefully she's not fucking cryptic. I hate that. We've literally hurled ourselves to our death. The least we can expect is answers.

Even though there's no possibility of understanding direction, it feels like we're going inward. I know that technically the inside of the earth is a big ball of metal and the bit around that is a bunch of molten metal, but surely at this stage we're still only going through the mantle, because it's incredibly thick.

Hang on, I don't know this shit.

"Dani?" I ask.

"Yes, hello, hi. I'm here. Dead. Like you said we wouldn't be."

"Not dead enough to avoid saying I told you so."

"Okay, so we're not *strictly* dead, but we don't have bodies anymore, do we? We're blood or energy or a DNA virus being transported through some sort of conduit under the Earth's surface."

I'm not sure how we're talking without bodies. The sensation of movement is dream-like, as if we're half asleep in a moving vehicle and the world is ghosting past outside. I still have the distinct sensation I'm *me*, like all the essential Dylanness remains, and the essential Dani is here too. We're side by side, whispering in the dark.

"Mutation," I say, with completely unearned confidence.

"Yes, Dylan. We have mutated into a blood-borne virus infecting the planet. That's exactly what I'm sure you were expecting."

"I trusted the planet."

"And you were wise to do so, little mouthpiece." The new voice comes from everywhere. It's resonant and mellow, tinged with sadness. "It would have been much simpler to do this earlier, but there were far too many hurdles. It's not far now. We'll talk properly soon."

There's a small pause where my brain is filled with Dani's many thoughts about the makeup of the earth's fucking mantle.

"That was the planet?" Dani asks in a small voice.

"Well, yes, that seems like a logical assumption."

"I have a lot of questions."

"Of course you do."

"Are you laughing at me, Dylan Jean Taylor? While we're literally dead."

"Only a bit."

"This is the strangest—"

The next moment, we're in a spherical chamber, lit by torches of flickering blue. The whole interior is covered in plants, growing from every surface in a complicated tangle. Standing in the middle, arms folded over her chest, is a very old woman with dark skin and long white hair.

"Welcome, my sweet monsters."

CHAPTER THIRTY-FOUR

"Um," I say, forever the most eloquent person in the room. "Hi."

I've taken the form of a shadow, my edges lit by blue sparks. Across the other side of the chamber is another flickering form, this one distinctly Dani-shaped. I give a little wave, and she bounds across the room. We crash into each other like two tides meeting at a joining of the waters. It feels like mingling rather than touching. She smells of lightning and flowers.

"Hello," the woman says. "Welcome, and congratulations on your untimely death. It was a great sacrifice you have made, but now we have many more possibilities open to us."

"Your little monsters?" Dani asks, which seems like literally the least important question.

"Yes, you are all my children. Named many things over the time they have existed on the earth, but you now call yourselves mutants, and that's as good a name as any."

Dani gasps. "I have so many questions. So so many."

"And we shall get to them all in time. Although my demise is imminent, we have room for answers enough to sate even *your* questioning mind. We should begin with a name, for I know yours. You may call me Cybele."

The blue sparks swirling around Dani grow brighter in her excitement. "An Earth goddess? A mother goddess?

Fertility or—"

"There have been countless names and countless forms, but I like this one. Especially now in the time of my dying. There is something strong and stately about it, and it helps to hold to that ideal. And you are Dylan and Dani, or Chatterbox and Marvellous. A mouthpiece and a mover. A pair of lovers, as it was in the beginning, when Lucy and Lily were born."

"Lucy and Lily?"

The woman smiles. "A tale of history, from the earliest times. There was once a group of people who mapped the leylines, harnessing my power in an attempt to contact gods who lurked in the outer darkness."

In amongst the twisting vines that grow around the walls of the chamber, shapes appear. A miniature globe created from fragrant moss, woven around with tiny flowering vines, presumably to mimic the energy paths that form Cybele. Other plants surround the miniature world, dark-petalled flowers that iris open and closed, swirling globes of furious red flaring at their center. The vines on the surface twist together, forming beacon towers topped with bright floral blooms. Outside, the dark flowers reach greedily towards the planet.

"Gods?" Dani whispers.

"Aliens, you would call them, but powerful. The universe is a place filled with predators. Sometimes it is better to stay quiet than to draw attention." The woman shudders as the flowers surrounding the planet swell and twist. "Humanity called out to these alien gods, and they responded. They landed in their great ships, and fed on me until I was near dying. Then they took up residence here, using the human race as their food supply. Faced with potential extinction, I reached out to warp the nature of some few humans. Needing defenders, I granted them some portion of myself in order to wield energy. Lucy was the first, my monstrous protector. They were like you, Dylan, a being that danced between masculine and feminine, like many things in nature. And there was Lily, immensely powerful and capable of reordering the world with her mind. They loved each other, and led a new people of strange and wonderful beings."

Blooms spring up over the surface of the planet, a wild riot of colour.

"The first mutants," I whisper.

"Yes, although they used different words. Before recorded history, all this happened, and the story is bittersweet, I'm afraid. They fought valiantly against the depredations of the things in the darkness, but were still losing the fight."

The fragile world is ringed with flowers, flaring their petals, spotted with rot. Many of the bright blooms on the surface wither and decay.

"So Lucy came and offered themself back to me. They died in the water of the bay as you saw them. Their energy flowed back into me, augmented by the alchemy that worked in their heart, and I was able to survive."

The vines across the surface of the planet bloom even brighter, a myriad of tangled blossoms. In the face of all this wild life, the dark blooms wither and Cybele is safe.

"Yay, the aliens are gone." I wish I could do a cheesy thumbs up. "Do we cheer?"

"At the cost of Lucy," Dani murmurs, which is a very valid point.

Cybele nods. "I made no promises to sweet Lucy of rebirth or mutation. They knew the bargain they struck and had no regrets. Such things were seen differently in those days. Although we had successfully fought off the incursion, the overloaded energy network caused a series of disasters that almost wiped out the entire population of the earth. It took a long time to redistribute and recover. Things after that were much calmer."

As she speaks, the moss planet becomes almost strangled with the vines twisting around it, but eventually they resettle into a new alignment, studded with tiny, almost invisible blossoms.

"So the humans were safe from the aliens, but mutants continued to live?" Dani asks. "All throughout that time."

"Yes, in small numbers. Often persecuted, often hiding. Their numbers would often dwindle, for humans carry the ghosts of those ancient alien threats in their DNA. Mutants, despite being the ones who saved them, were often seen as a dire threat. My children came close to extinction many times, but I would always rekindle the spark. You have always been my protectors, on guard against anything that would threaten me. Occasionally, one civilisation or another would present an increasing threat to the planet, and my mutants would come together to defeat it."

Bursts of coloured blooms flicker across the surface of the world.

"This is fucking *wild*," Dani says. "A secret history behind the secret history."

"In time, the seeds of darkness came from within." Cybele's face falls in shadow, as does the model of the planet. "The aliens were no longer the threat, but humans themselves were the danger, with their factories and cities. The ever-increasing swarm. I watched with trepidation, but I could not understand how deeply this rotten flower would take root. How humanity would spread and cluster, how their desire to take and ravage would feed itself, an ouroboros of greed and destruction with me left gasping and choking in its center."

The vines surrounding the globe are almost devoid of flowers and the whole planet is wreathed in something like smoke. We know this part of the story. This is our world. This is what humanity has done.

"It crept up on me unawares. I could not imagine a species fouling its nest and destroying their own habitat. In desperation, I found one mutant and poured my energy into them. Not a mouthpiece but a shaper, able to take the world and make violent change. I gave them powers beyond any since my first."

"Heart of a Flower." If I still had real arms, I'd have full-on chills. "They were yours."

"Yes, and I hear your tone, my mouthpiece. An error of judgement, I grant you. But so much potential, and I needed a more virulent strain of mutants to fight against the increased threat. The logic was sound to give them power to alter destiny. I hoped they would be able to build a new world, one where mutants and humans lived in harmony. Where they cared for the planet as guardians, and protected their environment. Yet as Heart's plans became more erratic and grandiose, I despaired that I had overcorrected."

"Heart wanted a world without humans." Dani shivers.

"Yes. In my darkest moments, I agreed with their solution. To be rid of a plague and to have the countdown to my death stalled? It was hard not to see it as a gift. And yet, to see so much life snuffed out was antithetical to what I am. I created mutants as a way to defend humanity, and I would not see it all ended. And then came the Goddess."

"Emma." My voice comes out all weird, because I'm still kind of mad at her.

"Yes. Both a shaper and a mind. With Heart crafting so many plans around her, disaster seemed inevitable. It was hard to trust that she would be a force for good, given the act woven in her gestation. But then, with something so simple as a gathering, and a series of kisses, a new mouthpiece was born."

"Me? Are you talking about me?" I'm all spluttery and awkward.

"Yes, Dylan." Dani laughs. "The mouthpiece is you."

"Sadly, by this point I was in a vastly weakened state. I could not speak to you as I had spoken to mouthpieces in the past. All I could do was tug on the fragile network of energy that binds the world together, in order to bring protectors around you, each with a small portion of me caught up inside them."

My heart twists, refilled again and overflowing. Pillow, Batty, Roxy and Oni, as well as all the others who've helped me, supported me, *loved* me. They were all scrawled messages from this being in the center of the world.

"But the voice. That was you as well, and that hardly wanted to protect me."

For the first time, Cybele looks uncertain. "That was not intentional. Think of it as an involuntary spasm. I am sorry it was so snappish and irascible, but events had proceeded too far for it to be called back."

"A fucking apology." Apparently I am over being intimidated by an alien energy creature. "That's all I get, after that damn thing fucked with my life?"

Cybele regards me with her dark eyes, but I think she's more sad than anything. "Would you find it enjoyable if your rage took on a life of its own?"

Gulp. Rage!Dylan is not a concept I want to think too deeply about, and where the line between me and that version of myself might be. "Uh, fine. No further questions." I wish I could give my most charming smile, but Cybele gives me a free pass.

"I regret the way it treated you, but now you are here, and we will attempt to snatch victory from the jaws of defeat."

"Victory?" Dani's shadow flares with blue light. "How is this victory?"

"Heart is defeated, and Goddess remains in control of her powers. And I have the two of you—the mouthpiece and the mover who loves them, returned to me and willing to change."

"The two of us." Dani's voice is soft, but I hear the ice in it still. "What does that mean?"

"It means balance, potentially. You as the feminine, a woman who loves women and yet finds room in your heart for all the complexity of this creature you have devoted yourself to. And your lover as the flux."

"The flux?" The word tastes different on my lips.

"That is what you are in your heart, is it not? Unfettered and unbound, seeing a truth deeper than that carved by the confines of your body. Nature is whimsical and playful. It denies boundaries, and surges between them. It wants to find the sparks, to explore difference and seek change, to claw at the walls of what appears real and find truth buried beneath. Whether you are myriad or singular, however the arc of your change, I am the mother of life in all its complexity."

There's a smile on my face, even though I don't have one. "That's a pretty nice speech. Usually I just say, like, genderfluid or whatever."

"So about this rebirth thing?" Dani asks.

"Of course, yes. We shall try something new, as we do have our backs against the wall and the situation is drastic. I am weakened, near to the point of dying and so we shall try this. The two of you shall be reborn, two halves of a single whole, my new creations."

"And what *exactly* does that mean?"

"My dear Marvellous, I must admit I don't entirely know. It is something we shall figure out together, assuming you consent to this rather miraculous process. We will attempt this wild experiment of rebirth and hope it is enough."

"Hope." Dani's bluelit figure flickers. "I expected more than hope."

"We are too late for that." The vision of the planet is almost entirely dark, only a few tiny sparks flickering across its surface like a dying current. "You have been warned for so long, but not enough listened. Those who truly rule your world do not care. So all we have is hope, but it is the two of you, and so I think it is worth fighting until the last moment. I have been through a great deal in my millions of years, and I hardly see the point in giving up now. Even though this new threat disturbs me greatly."

"What new threat?" I ask. "Something worse than humans?"

"Humans created him, but he has infected them, made them even worse. He weaves themself into their minds, connecting them in a network that is a grotesque mockery of mine. He is anti-life, and will not be satisfied until he has drained my corpse to the full."

"Fucking Michael." I wish I had form, so I could punch something. "I knew it."

Dani is still pensive, huddled on the edge of the chamber. "What happens if we say no?"

"We're not saying no," I begin fiercely, but Cybele waves me down.

"Yes, Marvellous. You deserve all the answers I can give. This change would alter you forever. Your energy would flow into mine and become part of this once-great circuit. It means you will also die with me, if we are unsuccessful and the last of my energy ebbs away. You are my last stand, and my last hope."

"Then we do it." Dani's smiling, even in her shadow form. "We become something new. The two of us, together, like we were meant to be."

"And what a splendid pair you will be." Cybele holds out her arms to us.

Our shadow forms drift closer, until we are engulfed in her embrace. Darkness swallows us again, except this time it's warmer and more fragrant, like fresh turned soil and the immediate aftermath of rain.

"Petrichor," Dani murmurs.

"You're such a fucking showoff."

"If that exchange doesn't prove we're still ourselves, I don't know what does."

Far above us, floating in the warm ocean, the flesh of my waterlogged corpse splits. Green tendrils snake their way out of my flesh, drifting back and forth in the current. They seek the light of the sun, pale and rippling against the surface. My eyes burst with jellied pops and tiny blossoms iris in the empty sockets, brushing my cheeks with delicate curls of pollen tears. A thick vine forces the slack cave of my jaw open. Seeds spill from the fertile hollow of my throat. They are green and slender, and light enough to drift among the whitecapped waves.

Birds collect the seeds and arch towards the sun on outstretched wings. They spiral over the deserted island and call to each other in delicate and melancholy songs. Below them, where the blood-slick flowers had grown is now rich soil, freshly tilled and ripe for planting.

The seeds fall to the ground.

They lie under the sun.

In the chamber below the earth, we drift. I can already feel myself coming apart, many tendrils tugging on me. It doesn't feel like an ending, more like being woven into a new pattern.

"Winter is long." Cybele's voice is slurred on the edge of sleep. "But spring will yet come."

Then there is darkness.

Time ceases to mean anything. The world turns and we hear the energetic clockwork of its hum. Cybele sleeps, or part of her does, for spring and winter happen simultaneously, depending on the angle you're looking from. Things are so desperately fragile, and she does what she can to keep the gossamer threads of the planet interwoven and alive. It's something between magic and art and programming an impossibly complex mechanism. If not for her, we would be lost, but she gives a final chance to this species trembling—either unaware or unwilling to accept—on the verge of near-extinction.

These are things we know, but they are not for us to act on.

It is winter for us, and so we sleep.

And so we change.

CHAPTER THIRTY-FIVE

While I sleep, I inevitably dream.

I don't know if what I see is real. It's random images, shuffled like a deck of tarot cards and laid out before me. There are an awful lot of The Tower. The world is busy, even if it's dying. Fire scrawls hungry glowing trails, and smoke fountains in its wake. The sea surges and swells, and huge plates grind against each other deep below the surface.

Cybele lurks at the center of the planet, a spider in a web that's being swept away, dancing from string to string. I can see the pattern of her energy, a dizzying network of lines that spiral outwards from our island. Some flow like a river and others are faint trickles that die out in frayed threads. This is the network she guards, or the one that she is—I'm still not entirely sure on that point. Whatever the truth of it, it's a splintered and sputtering mess, a long way from the beautiful intricacy she showed us in her tales of history.

We change, and she slowly suffocates.

Above the planet, a small galaxy floats in the sky. It's another energy source, a thousand tiny flickering dots orbiting a pulsing star. Cybele could reach out and take it back into herself, as it would nourish her so greatly, but she has fondness and protectiveness and fear for the star and will not see it destroyed.

I wish I could reach out too.

Time passes, in lurches and chunks. The images grow stranger. Golden eyes flicker awake on the surface of the planet, staring into the dark. Michael and his growing network, leaping through the minds of the humans who welcome him. I wonder what he offers them. Certainty, safety, predictability. A world controlled. He watches and hungers, but does not wish to feed. All he wants is to suffocate and smother. He is damp fingers reaching for a match. Dark pools spread, splotches of gleaming black in which the intricate lines of energy dead-end.

High above, the star glows ever brighter. Emma, a sun surrounded by a constellation of other mutants. I wish I could join them, to return to their side and fight, but all I can do is slumber, and change degree by degree into something else.

The darkness spreads, and the golden eyes multiply. They watch everyone, gazing into every soul. Light pulses from the star and washes across the patches of darkness. They shrink and curl in on themselves. Staring eyes flutter closed and disappear. Cybele's energy network sputters back to feeble life, even fainter and more unsure, the lines sketched in tentative pencil.

And yet more golden eyes open in the darkness.

The star blazes, furious and defiant, in the face of fresh attacks. It no longer floats above the planet, but descends to the surface, presumably to battle more effectively. The cloud of smaller lights is less now, but they force back the darkness, over and over.

Time folds and twists and unspools. The eyes and the star are still locked in furious conflict. My star blazes, but there is so much to do. Cybele is so fragile, and the darkness is so great.

I loathe my inaction. All I crave is to burst free from this prison, half-changed as I am, and join her side. Yet Cybele's hand remains around my throat, pinning me to this island wellspring. She sees my struggles and watches with a mixture of irritation and amusement. I am a thrashing, desperate spark, but it is not my time to burn.

I suspect Cybele considers extinguishing me at times. Whatever I am doing here in the darkness—this *change*—consumes energy that could be better spent elsewhere, I'm sure. But she is committed to this course of action now, and so we are bound up all together—her to me, and me to this frustrated helplessness. It does not stop me *hating* my situation. I am made to fight, to rail against injustice, to beat my fists until they're bloody against the crushing systems of the world.

Now I am helpless while my friends battle. They fight and they are caught in stalemate.

They fight and they lose.

This should not happen. Emma could remake the world. The power in her could reignite the energy network of the planet like a blowtorch placed against a fuse. She could tear everything apart, but that's where the problem lies.

She's still trying to save everyone.

I cannot see the future from where I lie, and Cybele cannot either, but we can guess. Emma is trying to thread an impossible needle. To save mutants from humans, and humans from the watchful eyes of Michael in the dark. I am terrified she will die without me there to save her, and I thrash and I writhe against my confines.

Cybele attempts to soothe me, to sedate me, to smother me. It is a fruitless task.

Instead, she gifts me knowledge, morsels to savour so I do not go mad.

The first glimpse is a dizzying shift in scale. A tendril of energy flickers out from Emma. The image in my mind is zoomed out so far all I see is a frothing wash of stars. A line is scrawled across this backdrop, stretching from our insignificant sun. This vast reservoir of power Emma draws on, enough to tear a planet apart, yet she still tries to keep all this fragile life on its surface alive.

They do not deserve her. If I ever finish changing, if I ever wake, I may not be so merciful.

The questing line of energy launched from Emma finds its destination at a far distant star. A handful of planets dance around it. One is a riot of green, lush and teeming with life far different from anything on our planet, a single interconnected network that constantly dreams.

Orbiting the planet is a single figure, drifting in the void. Blonde hair fans out around her head, threaded through with flowers. She looks to be carved from wood, her limbs tangled all around with vines—a creature grown rather than born.

The line of energy reaches out tentatively, and touches the woman's cheek. Dark-rimmed eyes flicker open, revealing irises of vivid green.

"Yǔzhòu." Her voice echoes, a call between worlds. "My darling little sister."

"Delicately Drooping Stamen." Emma's voice makes me want to cry, but I don't have eyes to do it with. "We finally meet."

This is where Emma's sister fled to, after she met with Weapon UwU. She spoke to Cybele and took herself away, half in self-protection, half in exile for her father's crimes. And now these two powerful children are connected.

Something approximating a smile crosses Stamen's face. "I thought this was far enough to avoid any family drama. Given that you've hurled your consciousness all this way, I doubt you're here to say hello."

"The situation is dire." Emma's voice crackles with anger. "I face a number of impossible tasks and find myself stretched thin."

"You aim too high, little one." Stamen's smile grows wider, revealing neat rows of thorny teeth. "Sacrifices must sometimes be made."

"I will not follow our parent's plan and feed humanity to the beast."

Stamen's eyes glow in the void of space. "There's supposed to be a plan. I spoke to the woman at the center of the world, and she gave me marvellous hints about the future and what might be done to weather this storm."

"If there is a plan, it's a shambles." You can hear the bitterness in Emma's voice, even at this distance. "We have lost so many people, and it is all I can do to hold the world in my hand without clenching my fist and crushing it."

"Crush away." Stamen sounds bored. "If it's really on the brink of extinction, isn't it better to get it over with? You and I can find somewhere else. There is a vast universe to explore, and this is hardly the only one. They froth and bounce on the cosmic shore, and we could dance between them until we find somewhere to take us in."

"I will not leave the one I love," Emma whispers. "Even if all my friends are taken from me, I will cling to her with everything I have."

"So tediously romantic." Stamen sighs. "But there is an appeal to doomed things, I suppose. Sadly, I am stuck here on this distant outer rim of the universe. My trip was the last thing One Thorn did before they slept, and I'm afraid it exhausted them completely."

Emma makes a clicking sound at the back of her throat. "Don't be ridiculous. Teleportation across the universe is technically no different to the room next door, if you look at it from the correct angle."

Stamen bends her limbs experimentally and wrinkles her nose. "That's my galaxy brained little sis. Let's see what you can do. And please, take me somewhere pretty."

The images in my mind's eye lurch abruptly and when they resolve, I'm looking at two figures sitting outside a small cafe at the base of a mountain. They're surrounded by fields of wildflowers that stretch up the lower slopes until they peter out at the snowline. The building is crumbling and open to the sky, although the coffee on the small wooden table has curls of steam rising from it.

"I like your little scene," Stamen says. "How much of it is real?"

"The mountain." Emma's mouth quirks. "I borrowed the rest from here and there." She reaches out and pours hot, strong coffee into a silver cup.

Seeing the two of them side by side, the similarities are startling. Their faces are the same shape and their smiles move in identical curves.

"I can feel the current state of the world and I dislike it immensely." Stamen's whole body quivers. "Your foe is a gruesome infection. How could humans allow themselves to be preyed upon this way?"

"They did it willingly. They gave themselves to Michael as part of some misguided deal to destroy mutantkind. And he is born from them after all, a god they built in a digital bottle and unleashed upon the world. Looked at another way, he is their ideal future. Someone to tell them what to do, a popup ad for salvation blinking in front of a human face forever."

"Ugh, gross."

Emma's hand trembles, and coffee spills from the rim of her cup. Her face is lost in shadow. "You remind me of a friend of mine who died."

"Which one?" Stamen frowns. "I liked your friends. Brave things standing in the face of impossibilities."

"Dylan. You didn't meet them, but I loved them, and Dani too. I don't think I'll ever get over it." Tears thicken her voice, and the coffee cup shatters into a million fragments, each etched with an image from our life together, the story of a group that came together and tried to change the world.

"I'm sorry." Stamen says. "I think they were supposed

to be important. I forget all the details Cy told me, but without them—"

"Without them, I am lost. Alyse is the only one holding me together. If it wasn't for her, I'd have a meltdown, and then all the broccoli people would be dead."

Stamen frowns. "I don't understand."

"A comic book reference. Dylan would know. All I mean is that some days it feels like it is my destiny to destroy the world."

"You can tell you're one of us Flower kids," Stamen laughs. "So dramatic. But I suppose you did bring me here to save them all. Not that I'm sure how you intend to do it, given you're so precious about annihilation."

Emma sighs. "We need to stop Michael's infection. It spreads from mind to mind in the human world. Its goal is replication and subjugation, and for all people to be a node in an eternal network. I remove it, but it returns, more resurgent than before. The only way to do it is to purge it from everyone simultaneously. A reboot of sorts."

"Victory at last! Humanity and mutantkind both safe and sound."

"Alas." Emma laughs, but there is no humour in it. "All this does is save them for today. Michael has threaded himself into the planet too deeply. To destroy him would set loose a series of cataclysms that would destroy the world. All we do today is save the minds of humanity."

"All." It's Stamen's turn to laugh, but she seems to find this far more delightful. "To touch billions of minds at once and save them all. So ambitious. It smacks of your mother. Did you not inherit that power?"

"My mother was a precision tool, designed for this purpose. Her powers were ruined by our father, and I am something more flexible. Even with all the power at my disposal..." She holds out her hand, and a miniature world coalesces above her palm. Clouds drift through its atmosphere and tiny creatures crawl across its surface. "It is not enough for *this* task. To work with minds, I need to grapple with detail, and that requires an influx."

"Ah, and this is where I come in." Stamen sips at her coffee and grimaces from the strength of it. "I have power, and reality is my willing plaything."

"It's why I called you." Emma closes her hand and the tiny world disappears. "To beg, I suppose. It's a lot to ask."

Stamen stretches herself towards the sky, the pale length of her trembling slightly in the sun. "But you did ask, and I appreciate that. You could have simply reached out and taken it."

"I would never."

"I know. You're far too sweet for this family." Stamen smirks, but it dissolves into something more melancholy. "Shall we try this the easy way first? I hardly think it will work, but we should at least attempt it."

Emma frowns, but takes her sister's green-skinned hand without saying a word. Her expression darkens further, and when she closes her eyes, the sky above darkens too, filling with clouds as if they pour from some blackened source at the heart of her.

There's a moment of silence before Stamen speaks. "As I thought, you cannot simply siphon my power. They come from the same source and would create a feedback loop that would shatter us both."

"Then how do we do this?" Emma asks, although the stormy sky above reveals the fears in her heart.

Stamen hunches her shoulders and leans forward. "You know as well I do that the only alternative is to..."

Emma covers her face with her hands, an echo of who she once was, a girl who'd sometimes try to block out the world. "We'll find another way."

Stamen waves a hand dismissively. "What is death? A return to the universe. I am energy, and it is better to pour it somewhere useful than hoard it for ornate parlour tricks. Besides, there's something noble about it, isn't there? Better than dying like Heart, knifed in an alley in a parallel world because they were too scared to do something useful in this one." She pulls Emma to her feet and they embrace, tiny figures in the vastness of the world. "You do realise that once you do this, there's no going back, don't you? You'll die too. This is a terminal diagnosis. Even you weren't built to hold this much energy."

"Yes." Emma's mouth curves. "I can see the extent of your power compared to all the others. It'll be like holding a nuclear explosion in my mind at the very moment of fusion, and keeping it poised there."

"You can't do it forever." Stamen's face is serious. "Nobody could."

"It doesn't matter. It's worth doing, isn't it?"

"Does the woman you love believe that?"

Emma's eyes fill with tears. "She knows what I am. I hate the necessity of it, because she's already lost so much. The brightest light in my world, and I'll leave her in darkness."

"It comes for us all in the end." Stamen shrugs. "No matter what we are."

"I know." Emma's smile is terribly, awfully sad. "I'm sorry we never got the chance to be sisters for real."

"This is real." Stamen presses her face against Emma's neck to hide her tears. "This is family. Be gentle with me, little sis."

Emma presses a single kiss to the crown of Stamen's head. Then she places her hands on each side of her sister's face and tenderly, carefully, takes her apart. A goddess unweaving her sister, the intricate energy matrix that makes up Stamen unfolding and being threaded through the incandescent star that makes up Emma's heart. A joining of two impossible girls and the power they inherited from Cybele's last broken attempt to build a saviour.

She is too bright to look upon, when she is done.

Goddess stares up at the sky. Her eyes flare an impossible white. With a slow, grinding creak, the top of the mountain shears off, as if someone neatly sliced it with a knife.

"I'm sorry, Lys," she whispers, and disappears.

I scream. Wherever I am, this prison is no longer safe from me. This cannot stand. I need to escape, to rescue my friends. They're in terrible danger. They *need* me. I thrash and spit and curse the earth that holds me. I twist the lines of energy that bind me, yanking at the cords that weave Cybele and I together.

This change is too slow.

I need to be free. The earth will tremble at my wrath. It will split apart and offer me up to—

A hand covers my face. It's soft and heavy, a spell of forgetting. Taking this knowledge from me, so it doesn't shatter my growing form, this nascent self of mine clawing itself up out of the muck.

Dirt drags me down, clinging to my limbs.

I sink into my grave.

CHAPTER THIRTY-SIX

I wake in a field. My head tips back, letting the rays of the morning sun fall across my face. There is long grass up to my waist, and many thousands of flowers surrounding me in concentric rings of wild, abundant colour. Behind me is a tall tree that looks to have been struck by lightning, as there's a massive crack in its trunk. Inside is a cavity big enough to stand up in. There's a trail of flower petals strewn from the tree to where I am, as if blown by the wind. There are more on my shoulder, in many delicate shades of purple, and I reach up to brush them away. I've spent so long asleep that it takes a moment for a variety of facts to present themselves to my sluggish brain. This isn't entirely abnormal for me, first thing in the morning.

I actually have a physical form again, or I'm dreaming I do.

The hand that reaches up to brush the petals off my shoulder doesn't look like mine. There's a greenish pallor to it and a pattern of white and golden petals stuck, slightly damp, to the back of my hand.

I've been *somewhere* for an indeterminate amount of time.

Now I'm awake and covered in flowers, like I've been slumbering at the base of a tree while the blossoms fall.

Last I knew I was dead and either under the ocean or in a chamber beneath the Earth and now I'm *here*. Wherever that is. Things are vague.

I dreamed while I was asleep, but I barely remember it. There were stars and eyes and tears.

Also, these flower petals aren't shifting. It's like they're glued on.

There are more flowers along the inside of my left arm, trailing from the base of my thumb up to the crook of my elbow and, yep, further still. I tug at one experimentally, but they've been woven through my skin. It doesn't *hurt* precisely, but feels as if I am being stretched.

What the hell? Is this a weird embalming practice? I'm a plant-zombie. I place my hand to my chest. I don't feel my heart beating, but there's *something* that hisses and hums like a pump.

And wait, my skin has that faint green tinge all over. My body has changed too, which I can tell because I'm completely naked, but I don't feel self-conscious. I reach up to touch my hair, and find more flowers there, as if a crown has grown from my head. They continue from my neck to my navel, blooming across my chest in rippling patterns of deep purple, radiant orange and pink, like I'm covered in a floral sunset. They stud my thighs and twine down to my feet.

What the hell is going on? I'm staring at the tree and the cavity in it. I take a handful of tentative steps across the sun-warm ground to trace the bark with my fingertips, feeling the seam where it was torn apart. Inside, the trunk is coated with a layer of soft moss, imprinted with a shape.

Well, that part is apparently meant for my ass.

I turn around and nestle into it. It fits perfectly, like I've spent a long time standing here.

Which of course, I have. This is my cocoon. Everything is slowly rearranging itself inside my head. I've slept in the earth and I've changed, as Cybele promised. Winter was long and now it's spring.

I've been reborn.

As what exactly, I'm still not sure.

I step outside the tree again. The day is warming, and I crave the sun. I raise my arms to the sky, and the flowers on my skin open wider to drink in the rays.

"What the fuck am I?" I ask.

There's no answer, only a world blooming around me. Flowers are everywhere in this field, so many of them clustered together in a spilled psychedelic paintbox, as if they've flocked to pay homage to the new creature that arches their back and blossoms in amongst it.

My feet sink into the soil. I'm aware of a connection, as if I am a tendril extended from something cool and nourishing.

Not water. Energy. The lines of force that Cybele rings the globe with may be flickering at a planetary scale, but from the perspective of one small Dylan body it feels like being plunged into a river. It's invigorating and I shiver all the way through. My senses ripple outwards, and I can trace the complex tangle. It's brightest here, in this place, which is why it was chosen. Her power forms a pool here, and I drink from it. That's not exactly the right way to describe it, because I'm not taking from it, more letting it flow through me and return to the source. I'm part of the same circuit she is.

My gaze falls on a second tree, identical to mine, except its trunk is whole.

"Dani." Whatever is now in my chest instead of a heart hums with anticipation and longing. I stumble across the ground. Her tree is taller than mine, which makes sense given she was always slightly taller than me. The bark is smooth and glossy, and when I press my palms to it there's the same rushing sensation I feel in my own body.

"Hello?" The rush of energy I'm still plunged into funnels from everywhere to this specific point, pouring from the ground and suffusing the tree with life. I don't see it in any visual sense, but I can sense the boiling tower of it like a shadow.

Dani isn't finished changing yet. It's not her time.

I plant my lips against the trunk. Despite all the energy flowing through it, it's cool. It smells of honeysuckle and coriander and cherries, all scents I associate with Dani.

"I love you," I whisper, and I feel the patterns of energy shift and sing.

To pass the time, I make a circuit of the island. Ours are the only two trees on it, but there are so many flowers. They turn to me as I pass, as if I'm a miniature sun making an orbit of the world just for them.

"It's only me," I tell them, and there's a flood of whispers in response, as if they're putting their heads together and giggling at how ridiculous I am.

"Only," one says, and the others take up a chorus.

"I can talk to plants now?"

A daisy at my feet leans forward to brush against me. "You always could."

"Yes, but I never heard you talk back."

"Connected now," she whispers, and the other plants pass the words on, echoing around the island. Blossoms drift from my skin in a fragrant cloud and new ones replace them, delicate buds opening themselves to tentatively reveal their colour as if they wish to find a pattern that pleases me. I glance at my wrists where my tattoos once were. A bold X in a circle shows in a rich, wine-stained purple amongst the pale yellow at my left wrist, and on my right the Cute Mutants logo is etched in the tiniest orange flowers amongst a sea of gold. Further up my arm are the names of those we've lost, formed with impossibly small lilies. My friends are still remembered.

I've changed in ways I don't yet understand, but the core of me remains.

I have all my memories too, right up until we went into the planet and spoke with Cybele. The events from my childhood are still there, even the sad and painful ones. The most important things too—joining Alyse Sefo in a bathroom stall, forming my team of friends, Dani standing at the bottom of the steps leading up to my house and looking up at me.

The ache over Wraith hasn't lessened. I'm not sure if I wish it had.

I stand back at the edge of the cliff, the point where we jumped and look down at the water. There's a small floating island of vegetation, entwined with flowers. I have a startling flashback to the moment of my death. It holds no pain or trauma. It was merely the door opened for me, and I stepped through. I understand that's a weird fucking thing to think, when we're talking about—

"Dylan?" The voice from behind is tentative, but I'd recognise it anywhere. I assume the nervousness is because she's talking to a blossom-covered person standing on the edge of a cliff.

I turn to face her.

Dani stands a few paces away. I forget to breathe, so it's lucky my new body knows how. She is extraordinary. Her tawny skin is threaded through with a delicate tracery of green veins, like a pattern of tattoos that map the energy that flows through her. She still has her hair, and there's a ruff of purple and yellow blooms that froth around her neck like a living scarf, and then spills in a cascade down over her body.

"Holy shit," I say. "You're Groot's hot sister."

"It *is* you." Her face lights up and I'm relieved to see her smile is the same. "I feel strange."

"You look incredible." I close the distance between us, and I can see she's trembling. "The same, but flowery."

"Flowery." She takes me in her arms and looks at me, as if re-memorising my face. "I love you."

I could still fall into her eyes forever. They're slightly greener now, and the irises are shaped like flowers with a delicate arrangement of petals, but they're still hers. "I love you too."

There's a rush of self-consciousness over my new body, brushed with petals and colour. I place one trembling hand on her heart, to feel the same rhythmic hiss as there is in mine. Her skin is cool and firm, but as she adjusts the position of my fingers, her cheeks flush and the petals covering her skin flutter and heat. I graze my fingers down her, and watch the flowers shade from orange and gold to blushing pinks.

"It feels—"

The rest of her words are lost when I kiss her.

Our bodies do feel different. Her mouth is cooler and her tongue is firmer, and her skin is softer, clothed as it is in silken flowers. I tangle one hand in her hair, to pull her closer to me, and it's fragrant, winding itself around my fingers as if it has a life of its own. The energy from below flows up and through us, connected through joined fingers and mouths, and curves of flesh fitting together. It is intoxicating, and we collapse to the ground as light as if a breeze had carried us there. We sprawl, limbs loose, among the sea of flowers, and let them close over our heads. The loop of energy closes, and there's the ghost of her feeling amongst mine, and the same is echoed in her. It means that when we kiss, I feel my tongue move against hers and sense, through her fluttering hands, the taste of the nectar from my lips.

We bloom together, and she is lush, and I am life. We are beautiful.

It's also seriously fucking hot.

I'm not saying that if you get the opportunity, you should have your body rebuilt by an energy matrix purely so it feels better to make out, but that's definitely one hell of a side effect.

The feeling ebbs gradually, and we lie together, two flowering creatures among the flowers.

"It feels cliche to say wow," Dani says. Our arms are still entwined together, far longer than arms have any right to be, just so we can weave them around each other in sweet smelling tangles. It wasn't meant to be us experimenting with our new powers—it just happened while we were occupied with each other. Now that my brain is cooling, I can identify the fact that our new bodies do stretch this way.

"I still feel wow." I find my body amongst the blossom and roll toward her. My limbs drape over her, and I find her face to kiss her again. Our mouths still fit together perfectly. "And you are a ridiculously beautiful plant person."

"So are you." Dani trails her fingers down the line of my back.

"Given I was rebuilding you, I thought I should at least give you a consolation prize of the forms you both seemed to enjoy." Cybele speaks directly into my mind and I sit up startled, scattering petals everywhere. Her voice is softer than I remember it—fainter, as if we're tuning into a far-off signal.

Dani sits too, wide-eyed. "So we really are newly created then?"

"I captured your blood, so I had your genetic template for growing these new bodies. It took some time for the seeds to germinate, and I used a significant portion of my energy to transmute you."

"Will you be ok?" I push my feet deeper into the ground. The spring of energy seems strong, but this is Cybele's place of power, and we are so small compared to the vastness of a planet.

"Perhaps. We shall see. You are no longer human—or extrahuman for that matter. You are a new form of life. It is yet to be seen if that is enough."

Dani buries her hands in the soil. Moments later, a ring

of sunflowers springs up, ten feet tall and bowing their giant golden heads. "Does this take power from you?"

"You are a circuit, and feed each other," Cybele says. "However, if you are far from the energy network, and attempt great transformations, your powers will be limited. You will also need to be cautious when feeding from the network itself, as weakening certain nodes could lead to a cascade effect which could be catastrophic. I am so fragile these days."

"No crazy uses of our power. Got it."

"Unless it is vitally necessary." Cybele's voice flickers in and out. "Which it may well be. As I told you in the beginning, the winter would be long, and the world has changed in your absence."

"How long?" Dani turns to me.

"A single journey around the star."

"A fucking year," I squawk. "We've been gone a whole year? Everyone's going to think we died!"

"We did die." Purple flowers bloom along Dani's cheekbones like two tracks of tears. "I didn't think it would be so long."

"Some change takes time." Cybele whispers. "It was all I could do. Now I must focus on maintaining the network before it collapses. You will know what to do. A sign is coming."

The last few words of her sentence are little more than breaths. Dani and I sit side by side and listen, straining to hear any final words. Even the energy flowing beneath our feet seems fainter, as the current has been rerouted somewhere else.

Despite being rebuilt, I still feel like me. Still unsure, still wanting something to fight. Preferably Michael. Still wanting to find my friends. "Well, shit. Now what?"

"We're stuck on this island until we get some *sign*." Dani gets to her feet and looks around, but all we can see is flowers and the husks of two trees that once held our growing forms. "How the fuck would we even leave?"

"Maybe we can swim?" I cross to the cliff and peer over. "Or there's this flowery island thing down here that could be a raft? Or our trees could be canoes? I don't fucking know."

"Emma?" Dani calls. "Keepaway? Farsight? Anyone out there?"

"Wow. About fucking time. Looks like you got yourself an upgrade, you little asshole, and the girlfriend too." Something drops out of the sky and lands with a thump beside us. It's a battered black car, with scratched up paintwork and one smashed headlight. The windows have been haphazardly painted with a home tint job.

"Roxy?" The word sticks in my throat.

"Oh, so you do recognise me." The voice is hoarse, as if my poor beloved car has been gargling broken glass. "Fuck, I'm sorry. I've spent so much time imagining this moment, and I'm being insufferable."

I sprint over and drape myself over her, pressing my cheek to the driver's side window. There's a drift of crushed petals left behind, a red so deep it looks like blood. "I'm so glad to see you!"

The car wheezes. "Fuck me. Don't get too sappy. This isn't a world for that anymore. Get your asses inside." The doors open with harsh metallic shrieks. Inside, the once-pristine interior is stained with ash and blood and who knows what else.

"What the fuck has been going on? And how come I can talk to you again?"

"I'd say you got your fucking powers back, genius. Sorry for the sarcasm. It's been a year, I'll tell you that much. The answer to your first question is easier seen than told. So drag your potpourri asses inside and we'll go take a look."

Dani's standing still and staring at the car, beautiful mouth agape. "I can hear her."

"Oh, look at us." I grin at her. "Power twins."

She frowns. "But before I could never—"

"You're both plugged in now. Rather than pieces broken off from the whole." The car rocks back and forth on her wheels. "You understand I can talk and fly at the same time, don't you? Your brains aren't empty seed husks or something?"

"Sorry." Dani crosses to the other side of the car and climbs inside. Her fingers trace a line across the dashboard. "It's good to meet you properly, Roxy."

"Shit, now I'm embarrassed. I used to be a lot prettier and more charming, but this year's been hell on us all."

"Fine." I clamber into the car too. "Stop being so fucking cryptic, and show us what you mean It's hard to imagine disaster among all this beauty."

"Well, you're in fucking luck. It's not hard to find disaster in this world."

The bitterness in Roxy's voice makes me shiver. What have we returned to?

CHAPTER THIRTY-SEVEN

Roxy heaves herself into the air with a great sigh, and the island recedes below us until it's a patch of vibrant colour in the middle of the vast ocean.

"Where's everyone else?" It's a question that makes me nervous.

"That's a question for Goddess," Roxy says.

I run my fingers along the steering wheel. "At least tell me they're alive."

"I can't give you lists of the living and the dead. After you died…" The dash lights flicker. "I didn't take it well. All that urgency I felt, taking you out to that place, it all disappeared. And you were gone too. Really gone, Dylan, like extinguished from the world."

"I'm sorry." I trade glances with Dani. "We didn't realise what would happen either."

"No." Roxy's voice is a growl. "After that, me, the sword, and the bat spent some time together. Roaming through the world, attempting to right wrongs."

"Oni and Sheba?" My voice cracks. "Where are they?"

The car snorts. "We'll get to them, don't you fucking worry. But everything turned to shit once Michael woke up properly."

"Fucking Michael's still around?"

"That situation turned out to be a little more complicated." Roxy's laugh is metallic and empty.

Dani turns to me. "Before we left, Emma was trying to find a way to detach him from the minds of humanity. So many people got infected, right under our noses."

This sounds familiar to me, like an echo of a story I overheard, but when I try to focus on the details, they evaporate, smoke drifting through my brain. Something about Emma, about a star, about a battle, about...

It's gone.

"You'll see." Roxy's engine hums, deep and resonant. "We're on our way to what used to be California. One of Michael's places of power."

"I'm glad you fought, Rox." I curl my fingers around the steering wheel, letting the backs of my hands bloom with gardenias. Dani has a wreath of honeysuckle around her forehead and wrists. The mingled scent fills the car, helping to combat the ash and blood.

"I smell that bad, do I?" Roxy asks. "And of course we fought. We come from you, don't we? You awoke us so we were infected with your energy."

"Infected." My voice is very quiet.

"It's just a word." The car sounds irritable. "My point is we wouldn't sit back and let the world fall apart." She sighs. "It collapsed anyway, but that's hardly all your fucking fault, is it?"

"The world is dying," Dani says. "We had to do something."

"And now you're two pretty flower people, come to give the world something beautiful to look at while it burns. Can't say I understand the reasoning, but let's trust the death throes of a planet."

"We're far more than that," Dani says. There are pictures in my head of crumbling cities being reclaimed by nature, trees pushing their way up through cracked concrete, broken buildings swathed in vines. I tilt my head curiously and look at her. Did she send me those? A pair of figures walk down an empty street and kiss amongst the desolation. Vines spill out from around them and tear a building apart until it's rubble.

We've been reborn for such a short time, and Dani's already showing off with our new powers. So typical. I picture a heart of pink flowers growing up around the couple making out in the abandoned city. It's mirrored in our mental image. Dani laughs, and it's delighted.

"You'd better be a hell of a lot more," Roxy says, as she banks to the left, heading for a grey smear on the horizon. "Otherwise we're all fucked."

"You used to be such a sweet car." Petals drift from my skin.

"That was another time." Roxy winds her window down a fraction so the petals blow out into the cool air. "And besides, that bitch is dead."

"I'm sorry." I entwine my fingers like vines so I can touch as much of her as possible. "I didn't realise we'd be abandoning you."

"Nobody's perfect. I loved you, and you left, and I made my peace with that." Her headlights flicker on, but only one pierces the increasing murk we fly through. The other sputters and glows a baleful red, like the eye of a monster. When Roxy speaks again, her voice is much softer. "I will admit I am very glad you returned."

"What is this place?" Dani asks.

"One of Michael's cities that runs between what used to be Los Angeles and San Francisco. Mined the mountains and tore them down, made himself an engine from the grinding of plate tectonics. Although we won't be going too far in, because fuck that. We'll be sneaking down at the edge. The sulking place of the thorn in my bloody side."

"Onimaru." I can already sense him, voice raised in a howling lament.

"Did he always sound like that?" Dani looks nervously at me.

"No." I push my head out the window. The air smells of smoke and rot. Up ahead, a city looms, formed of blackened towers wreathed in fumes, an industrial nightmare rearing out of the ground. In front of the city is a towering presence, an enormous glowing figure with a sword and shield. I'd think it was Alyse or Excalibur and Gwen, if not for the enormous bloody cross smeared across the front of the armour. Two identical figures stand in the distance.

"Who are those gumball guardian motherfuckers?" I ask.

"They are part of Michael. He is vast and powerful and has fought Goddess to a standstill."

A snatch of memory flickers at the back of my mind again. There was a mountain, and someone drifting in space. I taste dirt at the back of my throat, and clear it awkwardly.

Roxy turns in a slow arc. "That's a building full of computers. The form is for show and intimidation, to convince people of Michael's might and power. Humans are so susceptible to symbols. They wanted a saviour to fight the war against mutants, but instead they found a chain to loop around their necks." She swoops closer, so we can see the lines demarcating the thousands of floors, and the numerous indicator lights freckled over the surface. Drones with many limbs scale the statue, swarming in and out of small apertures. Beams of light stab out in sweeping arcs of green. Roxy buzzes her windows up and drifts through it, letting the rays play across her body.

"They don't see you?" I ask.

"The paint job isn't just my fucking goth phase, little Dylan. One of Emma's many many clones did it for me, with some borrowed power of stealth. It lets me pass through checkpoints and dodge servitor patrols if I'm lucky." She chuckles to herself. "I'm not always lucky."

Oni's voice is becoming difficult to ignore, singing something in Japanese.

"He misses you too," Dani says.

"We all did," Roxy tells me. "Seeing you back… It should be wonderful, but it feels too late. Like the doom of the world is inevitable. Flowers aren't miracles, Dylan."

"Listen, you've been here for me more times than I can count. So I'm returning the favour. You take us to Oni, and we'll not die and give you a tiny bit of hope back."

Roxy snorts, but the grumbling of her engine smooths out into something gentler. Once we're past the enormous Michael statue, she drops towards the city. The buildings at the center are tallest, and they descend down like steps to the outskirts, which is surrounded by a massive ring wall, topped with lights and razor wire. Just inside the wall is a small square of barren land.

"The scene of a great battle," Roxy says. "Where many of the last mutants fell."

"What do you mean fell?" My stomach goes into freefall, and not because we're plummeting towards the ground.

"After that, we only saw Goddess," Roxy says, which is no kind of answer at all.

Dani hunches in the passenger seat, petals fallen around her. Pollen dusts her face, and her fingers weave themselves together. "It's all gone terribly wrong, Dylan."

"We don't know the whole story yet."

Roxy lands gently, and I push the driver's door open.

Oni's haunting yowl falls silent. The smooth concrete feels uncomfortable under my feet. I long to claw cracks in it and tear it up, to sink deep into the soil buried below.

"You're not Dylan," the sword's voice says.

A battered piece of wood rolls out of a dark corner towards me. "It *is* them, Onimaru, you sullen piece of tin. We looked forward to their hour of triumph. Now it is here, and you refuse to see it."

"Do not condescend to me, Sheba," Oni snaps. "This is some trick. You are a device for playing elaborate human games, so it is understandable you would be easily fooled."

"You've gotten so charming while I've been gone, Oni." I look around, but can't find him. The square is bordered by smooth walls made of a hard black material. Carved into them are hundreds of names in neat columns. Written along the top in faintly glowing golden letters it says *Enemies of Humanity*.

"Mutants," I say.

"So many." Dani stands in the center, looking dazed.

"They all disappeared." The sword's voice sounds bitter, but I still can't see him. "I cannot know if they truly died, but Michael claims it as a victory. And while Goddess lurks in her great stone fortress, there is nobody to argue against him. Meanwhile, the city grows ever more cancerous and powerful. The world shall die, and humanity shall celebrate for the few moments they have before they climb into the grave they've dug themselves."

"Bloody hell." I move in a slow circle. "Dani and I are gone for a year, and we come back and everyone's so fucking emo."

Oni splutters to himself. "Perhaps you are Dylan. Although you are vastly changed."

I finally track him down, buried to the hilt in stone beneath one carved name.

Dylan Jean Taylor.

"It's not true." My fingertips trace the letters one after the other.

"I saw you die. I squired you to that place, at the bidding of that awful shrieking voice, and I watched helplessly as you and your lover threw yourselves into the sea. I was complicit in your demise, and therefore in the tragedies that happened afterwards."

It's hard to take my eyes away from my name, written like a tombstone. "I hope someone explains some shit, because this makes no fucking sense at all. We've been gone a year, and it's turned into some fucking godawful dystopian future."

"It is a dark tale, but I am not the best person to tell it."

I give an enormous sigh. We need to find Emma. I feel super awkward, given that we had a massive fight, then I went off and sulked before dying for a fucking year. I know I'm bad at social niceties, but this seems like a situation that deserves all my awkwardness and more.

"Why are you in the stone like this?" Dani asks.

"After my litany of failure, I decided to remain here until someone worthy came and retrieved me."

"Well, here I fucking stand." I wrap my hand around his hilt. "And you don't even believe I'm me."

"The profanity helps, but you have changed."

"Honestly, Onimaru." Sheba leaps up and hovers at my shoulder. "Stop being such a baby."

"Insolent thing," he grumbles.

I tug on the sword, naively expecting it to slide free because I'm the fucking chosen one, but he's completely wedged in. My vines sprout thicker and longer and I tangle them around the blade. He's right—I have changed, so let's use that. More tendrils work their way into the stone, swelling and growing.

"Um, Dylan," Dani says from behind me, but I don't listen because I'm preoccupied with freeing the sword. I give one final tug and he slides free.

"Ta-fucking-da." I brandish him wildly, but my triumph is short-lived.

I squint up into the bright light that bathes us. The dim shapes of two figures hover.

"Attention," a deep voice says, oddly inflected. "Potential unauthorised intrusion."

Roxy's door clicks open. "Servitors. We should flee."

"I hate them." Oni twists in my grasp. "They wade through innocent blood."

"Then let's try fighting." It's probably not the best time to experiment, but Michael is long overdue a punch from my flowery fist.

The two figures descend slowly, scaled-down models of the giant statue at the edge of the city. They're meant to be angels, I think, but a particularly dude-like variety with rugged jawlines and tight caps of short blonde curls. Three concentric rings of eyes in the center of their faces light up at the sight of us, white beams scanning up and down. Stubby wings protrude from their backs, sleek metallic shapes which ruin the illusion somewhat. The only difference between them is that one has a rune branded into his forehead. There's no spark of Cybele's life-energy from them. I'm pretty sure these are—

"Robots," Dani whispers. "Or androids at least. There's been some freaky tech upgrades while we've been gone."

The angels don't have mouths, just a thin glowing slit across the bottom of their faces.

"What exactly are you?" The voice is surprisingly soft but barely inflected. "You do not scan as extrahuman by any metric."

"They are not human either, brother, and are not networked to his divine will." The second angel's eyes toggle from white to red, one after the other. "They desecrate this monument to Michael's triumph. Their termination is essential."

The rune angel's eyes stay white. "As they are not extrahuman, they are not subject to divine mandates, brother."

"Hi," I say. "We're just passing through. New to the city and took a wrong turn."

"Mendacity," the less friendly angel hisses. "This species speaks in lies."

"Perhaps a defence mechanism," Rune Boy says. "We have descended as aggressors. It is natural they would react with fear."

The other angel blurs. One arm lashes out and erupts with a spear of white light. The rune angel collapses to the ground, steam pouring from his mouth-vent. The many eyes in his face are dark.

"Silence," the remaining angel says. "We've had concerns about the Penemue cluster after their work in the laboratories. Their programming has diverged from the divine will. Now, as categorisation of your species is impossible, you must be returned to the Host for analysis."

Dani points at him with her forefinger, thumb raised.

She bends her thumb and makes a click-click sound with her mouth.

"Finger guns?" I am aghast.

The sculpted chest of the angel bursts outwards, as if a bomb has detonated inside. Vines spring free, along with blackened branches like gnarled fists. The tall, golden figure topples backwards, landing on the ground with a crash. Soil pours from the open cavity in his chest. Snaking tendrils of green rise from his shattered eyes, each topped with a single flower. Lilies, pink carnations, and roses with petals such a dark red they're almost black.

"No fair," I complain. "How come you got all the cool powers?"

"I didn't even know." Dani brushes hair from her face. "It felt right. Confidence, you know. Visualise yourself as the badass and then boom, instant flowery death."

"That easy, huh?" I shake my head, but I can't hide my grin. "Always the fucking teacher's pet, even when the teacher is an ancient energy spirit haunting the planet."

"You can probably do it too."

"Yes, I have confidence to pull off finger guns." I scowl and jab my fingers at the ground, but nothing happens. "Pointless. Maybe it only works in the heat of battle."

"You did get Oni out of the stone." She snakes a long vine arm around me and pulls me close.

"Fuck me." Roxy rocks back and forward on her tyres. "That was incredible. I've never seen anyone do that before. I mean, Goddess kills a bunch of these, but not like *that*."

Bloody hell. I can't put off this awkward shit any longer. "Speaking of Goddess, I think it's time to finally find her."

"Yes." Dani hunches her shoulders. "That's going to be a fun conversation."

I lean in and rest my head against her. "I'm glad you're scared too."

"I should be more scared of Michael, but this…"

"Fighting's easier than talking." I hold up my fingers, even though they've shot exactly zero weird angels. "At least in my experience."

Even still, I hope Emma's in a talking mood.

CHAPTER THIRTY-EIGHT

"So where *is* Emma exactly?" I ask.

"She turns up everywhere," Oni says. "Many versions of her with different powers. They appear from nowhere, attack various outposts of Michael, and then leave."

"Why hasn't she come to find us?" I cross back over to Roxy and climb inside. "You think she'd show up to at least say hi."

Dani joins me inside the car. "One teensy-tiny problem. Rox, how are we getting to space?"

"Do plants even grow up there?" I ask.

"I doubt it." Dani frowns. "I think the water would evaporate. Why? Are you wondering if we'll survive in a vacuum?"

I fish my phone out from under the seat, intending to Google how plants behave in vacuums, except the instant it connects to a network, the screen flickers and changes to an image of a golden eye that rotates slowly.

"Greetings." Siri's usual Australian twang has been replaced by a deep and creepy dude-voice. "Michael welcomes you, child of God. Open your heart and mind to truth. The glory of the Lord is within you. Please place your phone to your heart to initiate the upgrade process."

"Shit." I toss my phone out the window so it shatters against the stone. "MichaelOS. Why does that fuck ruin everything? I really loved that damn thing."

"This is how he connects with people. How he *infected* everyone." Dani frowns. "Makes it more urgent to find Emma. Figure out a way to use our new powers and hers in tandem. Maybe we can seal Roxy properly or—"

"Enough," Oni says. "Why do you not tell them, Roxy?"

"I do not wish them to die on another foolish errand," the car rumbles. "Once they meet Goddess, there is only one outcome."

"You really did become a fucking fatalist while I was gone." I stomp my feet on the pedals angrily. "We're not going to put up with that shit anymore. You said you learned to fight from me. It's time to gear up for the battle again."

"It has been a long and dark year." Roxy's red headlight sputters. "Loss does not become easier, just because you have more of it."

"They are changed indeed, dear Roxy," Oni taps his blade restlessly against the window.

"Fuck it. The brat is back, and prettier than ever. So what's one more hopeless mission between friends?" Roxy's engine hums to life.

"Hold up." Dani clutches at the dash. "You're not really going to hurl yourself into space?"

Roxy gurgles a laugh. "Space? The asteroid crashed after the two of you perished at the island. It took many mutants combined to bring it down without destroying the world."

Dani winces. "Oh, shit. That one's my fault. Without my powers to draw on, Emma mustn't have been able to hold it in orbit. We didn't think, Dylan, when we—"

"No." I glare around at everyone in the car. "There's no more blame. This is the world we find ourselves in, and it might be disastrous and epically shit. The heroes fucking died, but the story's not over. We came back. So we're going to find Emma and make an army. Then we'll take Michael down, and fix the goddamn planet for dessert."

"A noble sentiment indeed." Oni seems slightly unsure.

"I can give you a very hesitant fuck, yeah," Roxy says. "But not much more than that."

"Well, I think it was very inspiring," Sheba says. "It is wonderful to have you back, Dylan, and to meet Dani as well. There have been many tales told of you in your absence."

Roxy's dash lights flicker. "Suck-up bat."

"Come on then, you grumpy goth asshole." I slam both hands down on the steering wheel. "Let's get out of here."

There's a lot more grumbling, but Roxy ascends out of the square with a huff. The city sprawls away, as far as we can see. So many thousands of buildings, so many people inside.

"Can you sense the energy?" Dani asks.

"It's hard off the ground, but yes." I stretch out my awareness, waving my vine-fingers in the air as if they're little antennas. The lines stretch out from the city, but they're severed at the edge of it, as if the sentinel buildings are blades driven into the ground.

"You feel it, right?" Dani asks.

I turn to her, eyes wide. "The city's a black hole."

"It *should* be a nexus point of the leylines. A node of Cybele's network. Michael has hollowed it out and negated it somehow. Roxy, you said there were other cities?"

"There are many, although I couldn't tell you all their locations. Goddess will know."

"How the hell did this happen in a single year?" Dani asks.

Once the city's influence is gone, the tendrils of pure Cybele energy arc away from us. They're thin and sputtering, a far cry from the torrent that foamed around the island where we were born. The once-great array is a faint sketch scrawled in chalk, something the next shower might wash away.

"Hard to keep hope alive." Dani shivers fragrantly beside me.

"And we've only been back a few hours. Let's not give up just yet... Oh great, what fresh fucking hell is this?"

Above us, a cloud of glowing green sparks materialises, like horror-movie fireflies.

"Take us around, Rox," I say sharply. "And Dani, reload your finger guns, however that works."

"No need." The car gives an enormous sigh, and simply hovers in the air as the swarm descends. It forms a spherical cloud around us. I wonder if my vines can smash a hole in it, but on further inspection I can see it's a host of machines. Each is around the size of my middle finger, with a familiar logo lit up on the surface.

"Cute Mutants," I shout out of the car window as some machines drift down to alight on Roxy's body.

"We are *Reboot*. Many generations ago, our forebears were gifted a spark of consciousness from your own progenitor."

"Um," I say. "I'm still me."

"Not entirely correct, as your hardware has significantly changed. Perhaps the same core programming, although you humans have significant flexibility to deviate from such."

"You're the descendants of the Chatterbox Protocol drones," Dani says excitedly, which, hello even I had figured that out.

"We are a single swarm, evolved this way to remain nimble and escape detection by Michael. We have been in watch and wait mode for a number of cycles, awaiting the expected disruption event."

"You're talking too abstract." I put my hand out the window, and a number of drones land on my open palm. "What the hell do you mean?"

"They're talking about us," Dani says. "We're the expected disruption event."

"What, like we're supposed to be the goddamn chosen ones after all?"

Reboot hums. "That is a reductive way of looking at it. We mapped the energy patterns emanating from the heart of the matrix. A significant proportion of worldwide output had been redirected, so it was simple extrapolation to infer a resulting change in distribution."

"They're talking about Cybele creating us." Dani seems way more invested in this story than I am, because I'm still not entirely following. "It took a lot of her energy. Are we right that the cities are an attempt to block the energy flow through the planet?"

"Yes. Michael has declared war on the energy matrix and attempts to disrupt it at key points."

"Hold up." I frown. "Why is he fighting Cybele?"

"She is energy. He wishes to drain her to power his machines. And if the energy network is retasked, mutants will die out. It is that simple. The cities are his major tool for waging war."

"But how did they grow so fast?" Dani asks.

"Nanotechnology," the drones tell us. "It appears that seeding an artificial intelligence with a simulation of the mind of God, and feeding it millions of human brains is a disastrous idea. Although we largely voted to eschew sarcasm in our vocal presentation, at this point we must utter the phrase: who'd have thunk? Now the cities grow unabated, due to the matrix's large energy investment in you, and also because of the siphon."

They buzz and hum at this last part, as if it's supposed to mean something.

Enter me, always a step behind. "And the siphon is…?"

"It is difficult to find a metaphor you humans will understand. Imagine the world is a flat sheet and energy covers it like liquid. If you place a weight at a certain point in the sheet, all energy will flow to that point."

I think I finally understand. "The siphon's Emma, isn't it? That's where all the other energy is going. It's all flowing into her, for some goddamn fucking reason."

"Of course," Dani breathes. "It makes sense. See, Dilly, you do understand."

"I'm a good guesser." I frown. "Cybele said mutants are given parts of her power, and she invested a whole bunch of energy in Heart. That must have flowed down to Emma, and so she's carrying around all this Cybele energy, and then she borrows more from mutants. That means she's like… overloaded or whatever. But why doesn't Emma use all this energy to shoot Michael in the face?"

"We have many theories," *Reboot* says. "It is the one question that we cannot reach consensus on. For the truth, you would have to speak to the siphon herself."

"That's where we're headed." I wave my hand through the swarm and watch it flutter and reform around me.

"The siphon and the disruption together." The drone swarm murmurs to itself, their lights cycling through various colours. "Determining the outcome of that confrontation is difficult indeed."

"You can always come and watch, you know," Dani says with a laugh.

"No, we must remain here and do what we can to disrupt Michael. Although it may sound like human arrogance, it is no exaggeration to say the world would have fallen before now if not for our efforts."

"Good job then, little sibs," I say. "Keep up the good work and hopefully we'll fuck up some shit good and proper. We've poked Quietus in the eye before. This time we'll have to hit them harder and hopefully stab them in the brain."

"It is as they have said for generations," Reboot intones. "You speak extraordinary words."

"I'm really fucking sorry," I'm leaning halfway out of the car as if looking at more of them makes a difference.

"I'm a terrible person to base anything on."

Dani hauls me back inside. "Oh, stop. Nobody buys that. You started the Cute Mutants and now look."

"I was a lonely kid, desperate for friends, and I didn't start shit. It was Alyse and Emma and everyone. We gathered around and joined together. That's what made the team. I was the one who kept standing up so someone could smack me in the face."

"World's best idiot." Dani kisses me, and I feel flowers blossom along my collarbones in response. "Now let's go find the rest of our team."

Reboot drifts towards the city, spreading apart until they're an enormous cloud of particles. I hope these crazy kids are okay, drifting into the belly of the beast like that.

Roxy kicks into a higher gear and sails faster through the sky. For a second, if I didn't know better, I'd think she was actually humming to herself, like there's something to celebrate now. We travel down the west coast of America and back out over the ocean.

The sun sinks behind the horizon in a halo of fire, drenching the clouds furnace-red. It's almost reassuring to see something hasn't changed. The world hasn't been rebuilt to be inside out and have our sun as its center. Who knows? Perhaps that's next. Soon humanity and mutants alike will die out, and the machines will inherit the earth, mining its burning core to build a monument to a copy of a god that humans built themselves. There's an irony in there somewhere, but it'd take someone smarter than me to appreciate it.

As dark falls, both Dani and I bloom. Jasmine ripples down our arms, and moonflowers sprout from our navels. At the hollow of our throats, a single lotus flower opens, petals an almost translucent pink.

"You're beautiful." Dani's voice is husky.

"We smell the same," I say. "We always used to smell different. You'd smell of that spicy perfume and I would be redolent of Dorito crumbs."

"You were not." She cackles with laughter all the same.

I reach for her in the dark. "Am I really beautiful?"

"You always were." She leans the seat all the way back, and pulls me towards her. Our night forms are subtly different, bedecked with ferns and wound around with mosses that glow faintly. There's water that trickles between us, and it tastes sweet when I put my lips to the rim of the lotus flower.

"This feels like a kink," I say with a laugh. "It's not one I ever had."

"You never fantasised about Groot's hot sister?"

"Oh my god, will you fucking stop." I stroke my hands through her petals and she arches her back. "I swear, if Cybele fucked up our compatibility in this area, I'd quit."

"You wouldn't." She kisses me, and we thread ourselves together so tightly I'm not sure where I end and she begins. "It's why I love you so much."

The rest of the night drifts by without either of us being aware of the passage of time, as Roxy sails through the darkness, filled with the scent of flowers.

When morning comes, we should be tired, but I don't feel it. The blossoms from our night blooming are piled up in drifts, and Roxy lowers her windows to let them fly out into the morning air. In our sleep we've sprouted brushy grasses over our skin to keep us warm, but as Roxy descends to a lower altitude, we bloom with brighter, tropical flowers that wreathe us in dazzling colour. I almost turn to Dani again, when Roxy makes a throat-clearing noise very loudly and importantly.

"New Zealand."

"The hell?" I ask.

"The place where our journey began, or near it anyway. The vastness of the Canterbury Plains, now with one added geological feature."

"Stop talking like the drones," I grumble.

"She means a big fucking rock, Dills."

"Oh, Asteroid Ems. Are you nervous? I'm really fucking nervous. Do you think she'll be happy to see us?"

Dani stares out the window. "For the longest time, I would have said yes. But after seeing what's become of the world, I don't know anymore."

"Great." I slouch down in my seat. "You were supposed to cheer me up."

I'm super edgy as we detour away from Christchurch and head inland. We can see the asteroid from a long way out. It's enormous. Of course it is, it was a massive rock floating in space big enough for thousands of people to live in. Both of us sit, hands strung between us, as it grows larger and larger.

We pass over a sprawl of ruined military vehicles. A little further, there's a graveyard of thousands of Michaels. It looks like the war came to New Zealand after all. It also looks like Emma wasn't content to sit quietly by and let it happen. It reminds me of something, but I can't put my finger on it.

Roxy dips down towards the ground while we've still got a distance to go.

"Fly us in, Rox," I say.

"There's something you need to see first." She noses her way through piles of pitted and scarred wreckage. Some of it's melted, some is torn apart. I wonder if I can trace back to see which mutants were here. The whole place is an eerie memorial, especially after seeing the wall of the fallen. How many of our friends died while we were gone?

Something catches my eye amongst the black and gold wreckage. A misshapen lump of metal, smeared with every colour of the rainbow. The thing in my chest seizes.

"Stop," I croak.

Roxy says nothing, but throws her doors wide.

I stumble towards the broken thing over parched ground. When I finally reach it, my fingers trace the words I painted on her surface. It feels so long ago.

"She did, you know," Roxy says. "She killed a lot of fucking fascists before the end."

"We all did." Oni hovers at my shoulders. "Once upon a time I would have sung songs to celebrate such a noble end, but the world gets darker by the day."

Dani joins me, tugged to my side by the grief that surges down the connection between us. Tears glisten on the curve of her cheeks. "Poor Abby." Her hand finds mine. I soak up the comfort she offers, but I still feel as drought-stricken as the earth.

"How did it happen, Roxy?"

There's no answer, so I turn to look at her. She's rocking back and forward, headlights flickering red. "She was trying to save me. I was being reckless. There were so many servitors, thousands of little Michaels coming from everywhere. Lou was down in the middle of them, completely surrounded. I went to rescue him, big spikes welded to my bumper so I was all kinds of badass." She shudders and a crack splinters along the passenger window. "I was surrounded, but Abby drew them away. She destroyed so many, but they beat her in the end. And I hid in the tunnels like a coward and—" The passenger window explodes inwards, chunks of glass littering the seats and falling into the footwell. They sparkle like tears.

"Roxy." My words feel heavy in my mouth. "We've all lost people. We've all fucked up. It's not your fault. I know that doesn't make it any easier, but it's true."

"I loved her," Roxy rumbles, barely audible.

"I know. She was amazing."

Dani leans inside the broken metal container that was once Abby, the vines of her arms extended. Flowers of all hues bloom with wild abandon, spilling from her grasp and filling the empty tank.

I join her and close my eyes. I can't figure out how to get the right flowers to bloom, but Dani gives me a mental nudge, showing me how to visualise the different colours. Together, we pile them high, a glorious river of blossom. Roses, marigolds and daffodils. Chrysanthemums, delphiniums, lavender, and irises. We build her a rainbow, because that's how she wanted to be seen. Something glorious and beautiful. A symbol of defiance.

We're still here to defy, no matter what this Michael asshole thinks.

"We missed you, Dylan," Oni whispers, and I curl my hand around his hilt. Sheba nudges in at my other side, and I hold my two weapons. It almost makes me feel like a hero again, even though we're a long way from triumphant. It's the comeback that matters though. That's what the stories taught me.

My arm tingles, and when I look down I see the name Abby blooming below the others.

This far and no further is what we said, once upon a time, when we were younger and dumber. It's still the right thing to say. Impossible dreams are how we get where we need to go.

Speaking of impossible, I turn and look at the towering shape in front of us. There's no need to dig my feet into the ground to sense the energy here. The drones were right, it's an enormous pool of energy, all accumulating inside the fallen asteroid in front of us. It's even more than Cybele's island. With that much energy—

"I still don't understand," Dani whispers. "What's she doing with it all?"

Something flickers at the back of my mind—a star, standing at the foot of a mountain—but it darts away again like trying to catch a coin at the bottom of a stream.

"Shit." I grimace. "This is going to be a fun conversation.

Hello, Emma, we're not dead. Nice to see you, now please explain the clusterfuck."

"Maybe I should do the talking." Dani squeezes my hand, and we climb back in Roxy for the final approach.

The ground right outside is scoured clean. Roxy's tyres leave faint imprints in the dust. Dani and I get out of our respective doors, and stand there. If you took a photo of this scene, you couldn't fit the asteroid in frame and also see us. We're specks. Even Roxy might only be a single black pixel.

"I'm scared," I admit.

"Me too."

"We came all this bloody way," Roxy growls from behind us. "Knock on the fucking door."

CHAPTER THIRTY-NINE

There is no door to the asteroid, at least not that I can see. I try to remember the placement of it, but it's too big, standing on its end like a misshapen egg. Maybe there are no doors anymore, and you can only teleport in.

We stand in its shadow, waiting for something to happen.

It doesn't, and then it doesn't some more.

Eventually, I wave my arms. "Hello. Anyone? We're out here, for fuck's sake. Rumours of our demise were, well, not exactly exaggerated but—"

Emma appears in front of us. She looks pale, but otherwise healthy. Her hair's been hacked off short. Her feet are bare, and she's wearing faded jeans and a tight t-shirt.

"Ems?" Dani's voice is little more than a breath.

Our Goddess holds up a single trembling hand like a stop sign, like a rejection. "No, go away. This isn't fucking fair, Michael, you complete asshole. Take them away. You can't show me this. It's cruel. It's a step too far, and I hate you for it. I hate you so much." She falls to her knees.

Dani and I run towards her, but she disappears before we can reach her.

"What the fuck was that?" I wave my arms again and turn in a circle. "Hello? Emma?"

Alyse appears next. She's not in any monstrous form. It's simply her. My best friend, who I love.

"Hello, Lys." I promptly burst into tears.

She closes the few metres between us and pulls me close. "You're here." She's crying too. "How the fuck is this happening? Where were you?"

"We died." I press my cheek against hers, feeling the warmth. "I'm really sorry."

"Oh yeah. Everyone knew when that happened. Emma went a little, uh, batshit fucking crazy, honestly. Managed to talk her down from destroying everything on that occasion, but it was close."

"And we did come back," Dani says.

"Emma thinks this is a trick, but I know it's you."

I frown at her. "So what makes you so convinced?"

"Shall I count the ways? Number one, your hand is on Dani's ass. Number two, how many times has the word fuck been uttered already? Plus Roxy, Oni and Sheba are here. To top it off, nobody has that disappointed glare like Dani."

"That is so unfair!" Dani steps closer. "My disappointment is because Dylan is getting all the hugs."

Alyse laughs and throws her other arm wide to bring us both in.

"I am in dire need of tea, because you're weird plant people now and something has obviously gone on but—"

"Is it really you?" We break the hug to see Emma standing near us. For a moment, her eyes are an impossibly bright white, as if the sun's held inside, but they dim to be filled with tears. Her hands tremble. "Dylan, Dani, please tell me I'm not seeing things because I couldn't *bear* it."

"It is us." I grin at her. "The disaster child and the ice queen."

"You feel different." Emma puts one hand on Dani's cheek and the other on mine. "You *are* different. Wildly different. What happened to you?"

"We've got a lot to talk about," Alyse says gently. "Why don't we go inside?"

"Oh." Emma blinks. "Of course. Sorry, there's a lot going on." Her body shimmers in and out of focus before resolving into something solid.

I try to catch Alyse's eye, but she's studiously avoiding my gaze. Before I can say anything, we're inside the asteroid again. The chamber we arrive in is small and almost entirely bare. There's a single bed in one corner, piled with blankets.

"It's been a while." I shiver. It's like a damn freezer in here.

"Sorry." Emma snaps her fingers, and a floating column of flame springs up in the middle of us. "I don't feel the cold, and Alyse usually transforms into something warm and fluffy. It's all just... complicated. Remembering everything. Keeping things running. Stopping the world from tipping into one disaster or another."

"Where's everyone else?" I can't even see a door out of this chamber.

"They're alive. Don't worry, Dylan."

"I want to see everyone else. *All* the Cute Mutants."

Dani shifts uncomfortably. I can sense she wants me to chill, but it's too goddamn cold in here and something very bad is happening, I'm sure of it. There's still that nagging thing poking at the back of my brain. Something I'm missing, that I'm not *remembering*.

"They're in suspended animation," Alyse says. "But they really are fine, Dylan. The Cute Mutants are all safe. You don't need to worry."

"Suspended animation?" It's Dani's turn to be pissed. The vines tangled around her hands grow thorns and the flowers at her neck close themselves against her rage. "What the fuck do you mean by that?"

"The normal definition." Emma glares right back. "It means I can access their powers more easily."

"But you can't just—" Dani begins.

"I *can* and *did* do that. It was because it was necessary. My back was against the wall and people kept running off and *getting themselves killed*." The last part is in a shriek that sends both Dani and I staggering. Someone's borrowed power, no doubt.

I snort. "I'd actually been stripped of my powers as punishment first, so you can stick that card back in your hand."

"Shit." Emma crumples in on herself. Her voice cracks. "I'm so sorry, Dilly. I've hated myself ever since that day. It was my biggest mistake and since then I've been scrambling. The deep freeze was the only thing I could think of. We lost a lot of people. None of the original team, but mutants all the same."

I walk over to Emma and take her in my arms. "I was an asshole too, you know. I could've tried another approach with the damn voice and its demands. Honestly, I had no idea it'd end up with both of us dead for a year, I swear."

She collapses against me, almost boneless in her despair. There were once so many things I wanted to tell her, so many grudges I held. But after seeing the history of the world, and coming back to a present that's engulfed in darkness, it seems a lot less important. We need to get through this next battle, and then maybe we'll talk. So I simply wait for the sobs to subside.

"There's one other question I need the answer to," I say. "Please tell me Pear is okay, and Dani's Mum too."

"Oh." She visibly wilts with relief. "Yes, they're fine, and the other civilians too. We finally woke One Thorn up to be a safe house. They're not back to doing galaxy distance again yet, but they've got doorways into safe cities, as far away from Michael as possible."

"Okay." I take a deep breath. "I think this feeling is called relief. I assume we're still trusting that the house doesn't eat people."

"Everyone's fine," Alyse says. "We speak with them psychically every day."

Now I'm calm enough to start being pissed off again. "I want to actually see them."

"It's not safe." Emma is firm on this. "If we give Michael any clue to their location…"

"Just fucking send me in and out." I can be just as stubborn as she is. "It'll only take a second."

"Dylan, I said no." Her eyes flare that impossible burning white one more time. I've seen this before somewhere. In a dream, or—

No. A memory. While I was changing.

Stamen floating frozen in the void of space, awakening at her sister's touch.

The two of them, sipping coffee together in a pristine landscape.

Emma reaching out and taking her sister apart.

The top of a mountain, sheared off perfectly neatly.

You do realise that once you do this, there's no going back, don't you? You'll die too. This is a terminal diagnosis. Even you weren't built to hold this much energy.

Cybele kept this from me, because otherwise I would have torn myself free of the ground I slept in and died as some half-formed thing. Because this, this is too much. It's—

"You," I gasp. "You've taken on your sister's power. It's way too much energy for anyone to hold, like keeping a nuclear explosion paused. You're—"

Going to die is what I intended to say, but Alyse is shattering in my peripheral vision. She's on the verge of blowing away completely, so I lock those words behind my lips. I think she understands all too well.

"What?" The flowers at Dani's neck are wilting. "Going to what? Die, Emma? How?"

"There's such a thing as too much power, it turns out." Vines and thorns twist around Emma, as if she's borrowing our abilities. "It was the cost of stopping Michael from turning humanity into a bunch of mindless terminals. Things are contained for now, but it's like pressure slowly increasing. Even though I try to let it off, there's no proper outlet outside of a critical explosion."

"Ems." Dani's shrinking in on herself, like her whole body is joining her flowers in withering.

I don't know how to react. There's got to be some impossible solution we haven't thought of. We'll find it. We have to. My previous anger has been lost somewhere between my death, and finding her as this feverish sacrifice, freezing herself the instant before exploding.

"I knew what I was doing." She fidgets, flickering her fingers together as sparks and flame jump between them. So much power coursing through her that she has to constantly let out the overflow. It's a reminder of the ever-ticking clock. "I'm fine for now. Which is good, because there are bigger problems to deal with."

I shake my head. "First we save you, then we deal with Michael."

"Wrong way around." Emma takes hold of my wrist. "The me problem is too big, but you're back like *this* for a reason. A secret weapon, courtesy of..." She trails off, looking increasingly exasperated. "Do I have to *beg* for the story? I can't read your minds anymore."

It takes a while, mostly because Dani and I keep interrupting each other. Even though we have these new shared senses and are closer than ever, we still don't agree on the right way to tell this. Given that we have to cover alien incursions at the dawn of the universe, it's not exactly concise. We eventually hit on the key points: that hive mind of object consciousness I've been talking to all along? It's the remnants of a being called Cybele, who was generated from— or *is*, we argue for five minutes on this point—an energy matrix that runs within the planet. She's dying, which isn't a huge surprise to anyone, and we are her last ditch effort to save things.

"Plant-human hybrids." Emma frowns. "I don't entirely get it, to be honest."

"We can sense the energy matrix," Dani tells her. "I don't know why you can't. Maybe because you're too full of energy, so it's like a bright light shining in your eyes and you can't make out anything else. We're pretty sure Michael can detect it, because the cities are at a precise points to disrupt the flow through the planet. A large portion of her energy is stored in the island where we were reborn, so we're thinking that if we destroy the closest city it might work—"

"Like blowing a dam." Emma's quicker on the uptake than me, and I'm supposed to understand this shit. It makes sense though, even when she starts speaking a mile a minute. "I haven't destroyed the cities, because they're full of millions of people and any subtle damage gets rebuilt so quickly. We'd have to strike very precisely, which means knowing where the points of weakness are. Which leads directly to the problem of infiltration. No matter what I try, they eventually detect me, but if I'm jam-packed with this *energy* it explains a lot."

"Maybe we can get in," Dani says. "The servitors were confused when they met us."

"There's a better option." I raise my eyebrow, because I like being the one to figure smart shit out sometimes. "Our little drone buddies. *Reboot.* They're super stealthy and if they can sneak in…"

"This is starting to feel like a plan-shaped thing." Emma purses her lips. "We haven't had a new angle for a while. I'm trying not to hope too much. The thing with Stamen felt like a desperation plan, which—

"Sealed your fate." Alyse glitches, like she's a hologram with a dying power source.

"It's done." There's a curl of irritation in Emma's voice, and Alyse folds inwards as if that can cushion the blow. "I'm sorry, Lys, but I wasn't going to let the population of the world have their brains overwritten by an artificial intelligence."

"How is he still alive, Ems?" I ask. "Surely you can defeat him with all your…" I wave my hands.

"I could defeat him." Her head hangs down. "At the cost of destroying the world, or humanity, or too much of humanity to bear. I've held him at bay, to save everyone, but this whole time he's been working on this other plan to defeat Cybele. One I was too blind to even see."

I shake my head. "This isn't the time to beat ourselves up for bad decisions."

"No. All we can do is the next right thing. " Her eyes meet mine. "So, we're going into the city to attack Michael. What can I do?"

Dani sighs. "There's no chance you'll rest, is there?"

"Are we done? No? Then of course I won't rest." She flinches back as if she's scared of what we'll say. "It burns in me. There's a fire in my heart and my throat and I need to do something with it before it all stops."

I can sense all of Dani's confusion and hurt down the connection we share, but there's resolve threaded in there too, and we both know what needs to be done.

"You can weaken Michael. Distract him, while we try to break the dam."

"Okay." Emma takes a deep breath and nods. "I think we can do this."

Dani's intent, focused. I love seeing her like this. A commander. "We'll need the whole team. You know those creepy angel servitor things won't leave us alone, and having the gang there means me and Dilly can do our thing."

I sling my arm around Dani's shoulders. "Remind me what our *thing* is exactly."

"We can sense the energy network, or lack of it. I'm hoping it's like negative space, and we can trace back to the fundamental point at which it breaks. Then we destroy that, and hope the backwash of energy from the island can re-ignite the network."

Even from here, within this rock, I can feel the tendrils of Cybele's matrix. I am part of it, and from the twinned sparks of Dani and me, the delicate lines join the frayed connection that feeds back to the pool of Cybele's island. Emma shows on my radar as the star from my dreams, but she's entirely disconnected—a pulsating ball of swirling threads that tangles and coalesces like a universe being born.

"So we're looking for a *something*." I can't think of a better word. "Whatever's causing the dead spots in the network. While everyone else is punching Michael and his creepy angel fucks, we rip that out and hope it's enough."

Dani lifts one shoulder and smiles at me. "It seems like a very *us* plan. I mean, there's plenty of details to figure out, and even more things that can go horribly wrong, but—"

"Fuck it," I say. "The Cute Mutants ride again."

CHAPTER FORTY

Emma and Dani immediately dive into a whole bunch of strategic jargon. Emma teleports a war room table from somewhere, and then a map and some action figures. Dani starts pushing them around, talking almost too fast for me to understand. A couple of *Reboot* drones pop into the room too, and spiral overhead, casting pointers of light. Everyone's excited and positive, and it's almost enough to make me forget about the odds.

Then I notice Alyse, standing on the edge of the room. She's not transformed, and it makes her look so fragile, like her human body can't possibly hold the weight of what's coming. Her eyes don't move from Emma, the girl she loves flaring with so much power she vents abilities like they're steam. Alyse is poised like a woodland creature, on the verge of darting startled from the room.

"Lys." I keep my voice low and soothing. "You need a break?"

Her eyes meet mine, and shock breaks in her face again. "Yes." She holds out her hand, and lets me pull her out through a newly created doorway into the tomb-like corridors of Asteroid Ems.

Now that I'm here, I don't know what to say. "Are you okay? It seems like a lot."

"She's going to die." Alyse is a hollow shell. Darkness worms its way through the cracks in her skin, spilling out in tendrils that curl around her like thousands of claws. "Nobody can stop it. If she stays like this, she'll explode like a bomb and destroy the world. So clever girl's plan is to disappear into space one day and become a distant supernova that will shine its light on Earth in thousands of years."

"We'll find a way." I hope Cybele has an answer. She's my only hope.

"No." Alyse's voice cracks. "It's been made very clear there is no *way*. So I'm going to be left again, just like with you two." She waves shadowy limbs at me, as if I'm not standing right in front of her, having returned from the fucking grave. "What is it about me that makes people leave? Why does nobody want to stay? Am I that impossible to love?"

The pump in my chest gives out with a splattering hiss. My heart literally fucking breaks in my chest, cracking the front of my body open and sending sap splattering down my front. I envelop Alyse in my arms and press my forehead against hers, ignoring the cracks and the darkness within. I'm struggling to breathe, but I need to get these words out.

"You're my best friend and I love you so much. All this shit got fucked up but I'm back now, and I'm not going anywhere."

"It's so hard," she whispers.

"It is. I am the worst, and you have to put up with me."

"That's not what I mean." At least she's finally smiling.

I pull away from her slightly, gesturing at the mess in my chest that's sealing itself up. The pump is wheezing, but sap is flowing through my body again. "You broke my fucking heart when you said that, Lys. See the proof."

"Soft bitch club." There's a glimpse of Alyse's old radiance there, but the darkness still shadows it, because the woman she loves has a terminal diagnosis and there's a monster that needs fighting. "I really missed you. It was the longest goddamn time." She slumps against me and lets me hold her up. "Every time I thought we caught a break, it would twist in our hands and get worse. Everything we did was poisoned. And Emma kept standing there, taking every hit herself, no matter how much I begged. She took my augmentation back in the end. I kept being too reckless with it. She told me that I didn't need to live up to your memory so thoroughly."

There are tears running down her cheeks, and I brush them away with soft green fingers. "I'm so sorry. I didn't know it would be so final."

"When Emma found your broken bodies on the floor of the ocean." Her breath shudders. "Seeing you both there, split open and bleeding like that… it was the worst moment of my life."

"And our reunion doesn't make any of it better?"

"I'm so happy to see you, but I'm numb. I've felt too sad for too long, and with all this stuff with Emma hanging over me…" She buries her face in the soft petals on my breast. "I envied you at times, and I hardly ever feel like that."

"Everyone deserves a year off once in a while." I stroke her hair. "But if I'd come back to a world without you, I'd burn it all down."

"We're supposed to fight together until the bitter end, aren't we?" She smiles weakly. "Especially since now you two are jacking my style. I've been doing plant-girl shit from way back." She transforms into her old Woodland Hulk form, a massive creature of twisted branches and curving thorns, topped with a crown of pink, purple and blue flowers.

"Fuck yes we're fighting." I look up at her, now that she's looming over me. "We're going to need the others. Not every single person, because we don't have time to train them or learn how they work. The OG crew, meaning us and UwU."

"Everyone's asleep." Alyse leads me to the end of a corridor, peering into frigid darkness.

"Yes, I understand what suspended animation is." I grin at her. "Now that Dani's explained it to me in painful detail down our pretty new psychic connection."

She snorts. "That's the last thing you two needed."

"We can pass love notes in secret." I nudge her. "Whisper all our sweet nothings."

"Sweet? That'd be the day. If anyone ever gets a glimpse you'll be straight to horny jail." A wistful expression crosses her face. "It is nice though, when the person you love can talk straight into your mind. It's going to be so quiet when she's gone." She doesn't wait for me to respond, but heads into the darkness, transforming into something like one of those lure fish, a big dangly light hanging off the front of her head. We navigate our way through the corridors until we finally reach one small room. It's so cold that I feel my plant extremities cringing away from it. Maybe I'm not built for this.

We step inside, and Alyse's light illuminates a row of slumbering figures. They're lying on metal shelves that extend from the rock wall. It's all my friends, a year older. Katie looks like a fucking adult now, her face sharpened but still scowling. How the hell has she grown up like that in only a year? Lou's filled out a little more, his arms approaching himbo territory which I'm sure he loves. Feral's curled up like a sleeping cat, her fur longer and more luxurious and her claws sheathed. I fight the urge to stroke her, because she's in suspended animation and it seems creepy. The others look mostly the same, but I pause beside Violet. She's in human form, although it seems as if she's lying in shadow, on the verge of escaping even as Emma put her to sleep. Her cheeks are brushed with streaks of blue light, and her lips look delicate and pink. It makes me think of kissing her, and how we trembled against each other like branches in the wind. Then I get a very vivid mental image of Dani kissing her, and it's all very confusing.

None of them have any new scars, even though I'm sure they've fought in our absence. It's a side effect of Doc's healing powers, to obscure the wounds that you received, even though you feel every one. There's only one person missing, and my throat seizes.

"Where the fuck is Ye Shou?"

"She's a liaison with One Thorn," Alyse says. "The spiders are great at navigation."

"You really are all okay." I slump against Alyse. "It's so fucking good to see them all. Don't you dare tell them I cried."

"Nobody will be surprised." She nudges me, and her eyelids flutter as she communicates with Emma. One by one, the Cute Mutants wake up from slumber. They stretch and yawn and slowly get to their feet.

The first one to see me is Katie. Her eyes go wide, and her jaw makes a little click sound before she snaps her teeth shut.

"Alyse? Can you please explain why I'm looking at a fake version of Dylan?"

"Um." Alyse glares at me, like I'm supposed to explain everything, but I feel tongue-tied and super fucking awkward because now *all* of them are looking at me.

"They're not fake." It's Gladdy, shaking her head. "That anxiety and all those fears, I'd know them anywhere. I'm not sure what all the plant stuff is about, but it's very clearly our Dilly. Now with added fears about—oh, God. Poor Ems. Oh, come here." And then, miracle of fucking miracles, it's Fetch who strides forward and hugs Alyse.

I try to find a smile and spread my arms in a big dumbass shrug. "It's me, Dragon, you little asshole."

Lou would have reached me first, if it wasn't for Feral's super-speed and the fact that Penance can fold herself through reality. The others are there soon after, and I'm the center of the big internet hug, everyone nestled in against me as blossoms explode outwards in a drift. It's impossible to make out individual words, as they're all talking at once, demanding answers. Skye Prime doesn't let out her clones. She looks haunted, and I wonder how many times they were wounded in the fight.

I finally do get to run my hands through the fur on Feral's arms though, and it is as soft as I imagined. She squeezes me so tight that her claws make little divots in my plant-skin. Trickles of sap ooze out and I don't even care, because I'm here among my friends again.

"You *died*," Katie insists for about the fifth time. "It was *horrible*."

Violet has her arms around me and her face pressed into my neck. I stroke her back in soft, rhythmic circles, her skin so warm through her thin shirt.

"I searched and searched for you," she whispered. "I thought I heard your voice, lost in the in-between, but I could never truly find you. But it gave me something to cling to, otherwise I couldn't bear it." Her hand clutches her silver pendant tightly. "I couldn't, Dylan. I just couldn't."

She falls silent and I feel her tears wet against my skin. The others are quiet too, leaving me struck by an awkwardness that reminds me of how I used to be, overwhelmed by the impossibility of justifying my place in the world. I made an impulsive decision to throw myself off a cliff with the belief that it would all work out through comic book destiny. And sure, okay it did, but it took some time. Now I'm here looking at the faces of my friends, and in them I see that awful bereft echo of what I felt with Wraith.

"I'm sorry," is all I can say before I can't force words out through my shuddering breaths.

Lou and Katie take me by the hand and tow me through the corridors with the others. I follow, a leaf in the current of their emotion. We reach another small chamber, except the bodies in this one are only skeletons.

I'm looking down at my old form, with Dani lying beside me. Someone's positioned us so we're curled together, like in death I'm spooning her. I can't breathe. Tears spill from my eyes and down my cheeks. It's such a visceral reminder of every nightmare future I dreamed that I want to sink to my knees and wail. They all saw this. They've kept us here. A reminder of what they've lost and what's been sacrificed.

"Emma tried so many things to bring you back." Lou's shaking, looking from me to the bones and back again. "Nothing *worked*. Your bodies got all fucked up but she kept trying, like there was some trick she was missing. So I fucking prayed, Dylan. I begged a God who *hates me* to bring you back. That's how desperate I was."

"I'm sorry, I'm so sorry." I repeat it like a chorus, like it's a tune that'll make sense with enough delirious repetition.

"What *happened?*" Violet asks. She hasn't retreated behind her mask, but still clings helplessly to me as if I'm the only thing that can tether her from slipping through the cracks in the world.

"Yeah, we're all happy to see you back," Maddy says. "But we don't need apologies. We need to know what happened."

It takes time and false starts, but I tell them everything, in this cold room with the skeletons of our old forms lying beside us. Dani comes in partway through, and interrupts everything, because everyone has to hug her too. We eventually get through the whole story, as miraculous and strange as it is. I think it would be completely unbelievable if we weren't standing there, green-tinged and fragrant and swimming in blossom.

"So typical." Gladdy looks across Alyse's head at me. "You had to become something else didn't you? Even mutant wasn't enough."

I meet her eyes. "The current theory is that we're weapons. Brought back by Cybele for one reason only."

"A thorny knife to drive into Michael's heart," Dani says.

"So on brand," Maddy snorts. "But I'm not complaining. It's about time we had some good news."

"And we've been woken for the same reason?" Feral asks. "Because it's finally time to fucking fight again, rather than being packed away like toys that Goddess outgrew."

"It wasn't like that." Alyse is immediately defensive. "It was to *protect* everyone."

"When did I ever need protection?" Feral's hackles rise and she bares her teeth. "I *told* her I'd fight until the end."

"We lost too many people." Emma stands at the entrance to the chamber. She looks so young and fragile, a collapsing star poised trembling on the verge of annihilation.

I want to protect her, to take this burden from her grasp, but Cybele only brought me back as a different kind of weapon. I don't have the answers or the secrets. I'm back and yet it's still not enough.

"It should've been *my* choice," Feral snarls.

Emma juts her chin out and glares right back. "I couldn't lose anyone else. I couldn't *bear it*. And the rest of our dead didn't come back, did they?"

Feral still bristles, but subsides under my touch, my hand tangling in the fur at the back of her neck.

"You stole our choice." Violet's fingers twitch from blade to flesh and back again. "Took us away from a fight that was ours too, like you took Dylan's powers."

There's a clicking sound from Emma's throat and I see a hollow red light at the back of it when she speaks. "I made mistakes, okay? I tried to do too much. I thought I could control everything and save everyone, because I was the one who'd been gifted all this power. After I spent so much time supporting everyone and letting *you all* be the ones who took risks, it was my turn to fight. But I fucked it up and I don't know how to take that back. Except to say I'm sorry." Her words trail away, like there's some clockwork inside her that's wound down.

It's my turn to talk, I guess. "There are no easy decisions in this fight. Let's say we've all done some dumb shit. I know there's been a lot of darkness, and it's going to take some time to push through it. But the fucking gang is back together and we need to focus on the mission in front of us."

Later, there will be some hard decisions. About choices Emma made, and ones that I made too. That's assuming we get a later, because underneath all my attempts at inspiring speeches, I'm still very fucking unsure.

"Together," Feral echoes, and finally steps forward to enfold Emma in a hug.

"So where do we go from here?" Violet asks.

"The battle's not done," Dani says. "We're going to stop Michael."

I'm not sure if it's desperation or faith, but none of the others question this. They steel themselves, and they get ready to fight. It's what we do.

CHAPTER FORTY-ONE

We don't even need to fly Roxy back to the city. Emma simply teleports us. We appear in the vast, rubble-strewn wasteland that lies for miles around the smoking metropolis. I think this was suburbia once, but everything has been torn down and repurposed in the construction of the buildings that dwarf us. The city is a stain on the world, a smoking, reeking dagger thrust into the heart of the energy network. It is not so different to cities from before except in terms of scale.

We assemble in the midpoint between two giant Michael statues. Emma will stay here, protected. Katie is in full dragon form, lying on the ground with her tail wrapped around us all. Penance hovers above, a spilling forest of blades, as if all the shadows have grown teeth. Alyse wanted to stay too, but us plant-types are going to hit the city, and we need all the help we can get. The others are coming to help with angel control. I'm nervous about putting them in the firing line, but they all chose this. Skye's clones are finally all here too.

"Fucking plant-ass bitch," Skye Six scoffs. "You think we're supposed to be fucking impressed with resurrection." She pulls up her shirt to show me a horrific pattern of scars on her torso. "We've dealt with plenty of shit our own fucking selves."

"Dial it down, Sixy." Five punches her clone in the shoulder. "Stop fucking flirting with the boss and do your job."

This is the last stand of the Cute Mutants, and every member deserves the chance to choose whether they fight or not. The joy at being reunited has burned off, leaving a mix of determination and rage.

"We'll celebrate properly once we've won," I say.

Nobody argues with me, not even Emma. This is the team. Everything we built together and worked for. I'm swept up in the rush of emotion that crackles between us.

"You feel this too?" Dani murmurs in my ear.

"I think so. It's what we need." I raise my voice. "This is that last stand shit. Proper superhero vibes. So here we go. Time to survive the experience. Cute fucking Mutants."

Everyone joins in, and we do one last big internet hug, because goddamn it, symbols mean something. When we separate, everyone is ready. I can see it in their eyes, in the way they stand.

"Greetings," the soft voice of *Reboot* says. "I am currently cloaked. Many of us are scattered throughout the city. We shall give a series of subsonic pulses identifying nodes of particular importance amongst Michael's network. There are strategic, commercial, and military targets. Please convey this news to Goddess, who can then deploy your assault teams accordingly."

I tell all this to Emma, who nods. She seems calmer for now.

"Chatterbox, Marvellous? Please confirm you agree on the source location for the energy dead spot," the drone continues. "The so-called heart of Michael. We shall trigger a beacon there, as a ping for Goddess to deploy you."

"Sure." I close my eyes and wiggle my toes inside my beat-up rainbow Converse. It's hard to distinguish anything, because it's so many shades of *empty*, but there is a pitch-black hole driven through the middle. Emma projects a map of the city into my head, a glowing green arrow pointed at the precise location. Smart fucking drones. I give a thumbs up.

"Triggering beacons," *Reboot* says.

Emma snaps her fingers a bunch of times in succession. The other Cute Mutants vanish one after the other. I have to trust they'll be okay. This mission is too important to be distracted.

"Ready?" Emma arches her eyebrow.

I take her hand, twining the vines of my fingers through hers. Dani joins on her other side. "Let's go kill a monster."

The world blinks out, and we reappear inside a building. Smooth walls glow with faint lights. Far above, the ceiling is dark and criss-crossed with huge metal struts. The floor is slick and cold, and the only thing here is a glass sculpture in the shape of a Möbius strip—the name pops into my head courtesy of Dani. Lights flicker along its surface, dancing in complicated shapes.

"The hell is that?" I murmur.

"A brain?" Dani's thoughts flicker down the connection between us. "A processing unit. I know they're running a distributed network, but this could be a subsystem responsible for a fundamental—"

"Chatterbox smash." I wrap my vines around the delicate shape and tear it out of the ground. The lights die almost immediately. I don't know what to do with it next, so I hurl it at the wall.

"Subtle." The corner of Dani's mouth twitches.

"Do you think that's it?" It seems too good to be true. We can't have beaten Michael this easily. It's not how things work. Emma would have done this before now or—

Dani turns in a slow circle. "It doesn't seem like we've won. Maybe we need to take this whole building down, like—"

A grinding sound comes from above. The building shudders, and the high ceiling folds in on itself in a series of fluid mechanical motions, revealing a grey sky studded with thousands upon thousands of glowing shapes.

"Stars?" I ask.

"Those are no stars." Dani's voice is grim, and I sense her determination surging between us. "Those are servitors."

"Great." My fingers twitch. "The only problem with Michael is that there aren't enough of him."

The angels come fast, blazing meteors descending.

Dani manages to take a lot of them out with finger guns. Their shattered forms land around us, spilling soil and draped with flowers. My hands stubbornly refuse to work that way, so I reach out with my vines, snatching at falling angels and giving them even more velocity. They slam into the ground, shattering into golden pieces.

There's more coming, but between Dani's flower bullets and my vines, we manage to beat them back until we stand in a sea of broken metal and waving flowers.

"Wave one defeated." I give her a half-ass grin.

I really shouldn't do the smug thing. An aperture in the wall near us slides open, rays of red light erupting from inside. Dani grabs hold of me and leaps off the ground with a great spring of her legs. It's starting to piss me off just the tiniest bit that she's so much better at mastering this plant form than me.

We sprawl on the ground together, but have to roll apart under another barrage. Where the beams hit, the ground is torn up in great ragged gashes. I can smell the soil underneath it, and it gives me an idea.

"Cover me," I push an image into Dani's mind. Thankfully, she doesn't waste any seconds arguing, but spins around her top half without moving her legs. It's on the creepy side, but I can't complain because she's blasting magic flower bullets into the building. It erupts with a wild tangle of creepy plants. Dani's brain keeps supplying me with the names: gloriosa lilies, proteas, corpse flowers, and something called monkey-face orchids. It almost distracts me from what I'm supposed to be doing, which is throwing myself bodily into one of the holes and driving my hands and feet into the soil. The energy network may not be online here, but I can feel the vibrations generated by thousands of machines.

"Okay, so your finger guns are pretty fucking impressive, but watch *this*."

I push my limbs deep. Cybele gave us all this energy, so there's no point keeping it all locked inside. Hopefully this isn't going to trigger her warnings about fatal cascades, but this *is* that last stand shit. The walls around us are actually more buildings, an interlocking spread moving outwards from this central location. I feel for the shapes of the largest, most active structures and try to grab them from underneath. There's something solid in the way, but I tear frantically at it, scraping with my extended limbs until it gives way. I paw through the chunks and take hold of the buildings, trying to grip the entire extent of them with my fingers. It makes me light-headed and slightly hysterical, maintaining this much control.

I chance a glance up and out of the hole and give myself a hell of a fright.

The walls that surround us are wreathed in vines. It looks like one of those post-apocalyptic movies where nature has encroached on the ruins of humanity. Except it's all me, reaching out with my plant hands and gripping tight.

I pull downwards with everything in me, arching my back and clenching my jaw. The buildings crumble, chunks of material disintegrating around me. Maybe they were built with thousands of tiny machines, but they fall apart like tearing into a sandcastle. The air is grey with particles, swirling around like smoke.

"Showoff." Dani stands over me, flowers blooming from

her fingertips. She lifts one to her lips and blows, scattering petals and making a pocket of clean air around us.

I get to my feet and stand beside her. Everything is awfully still and quiet. There's no sense of energy moving from below.

"Maybe it takes time," Dani says.

"If we've breached the dam, we should feel something. A trickle, at least."

"Yeah, we're missing something." She frowns and peers at the sky. "Except right now I think we have other problems."

I follow her gaze, and the sky around us is blotted out with thousands of golden figures descending towards us. Far more than last time. All here to witness our downfall. "Reload your fingers and fight, while I think of a better idea."

"Okay." She trusts me completely, doesn't even question that I've got the capacity to think of the last-ditch plan among the last-ditch plan. I better fucking come through. There's a hell of a lot of Michaels to kill.

The cloud of particles clears and a hulking, thorn-covered figure bounds through the gap. Hot on her heels is a ferocious creature with sharp teeth and a spiked tail. An enormous blast of heat comes from above, and the massive figure of Dragon lands, draping her wings against the shattered foundations of the fallen buildings. Yet more figures scramble off her neck.

"The distractions didn't work," Alyse calls. "It was all going fine, but then something happened and all the Michaels headed in this direction."

"Well, fuck." I give her a double thumbs up. "This is that big cinematic moment."

"They must have a reason for coming here," Dani mutters. "Michael feels threatened."

She's right, but we don't have a lot of time. Emma appears in front of us, closely followed by the many blades of Penance.

"You're supposed to be keeping a safe distance," I shout.

"Oh, Dilly. You forget how many powers I hold," Emma says.

"Ems, no." Alyse is a furious, vengeful scribble drawn in blood. "Remember last time?"

There's no time for any more discussion of who was wrong, and whose fault it is, because the angels are upon us. I know we're super goddamn powerful these days, but there are a lot of them. There's such a thing as overwhelming odds. I'm pretty sure they can regenerate, or at least the city can make more of them from the discarded pieces.

I've got no bird's eye view of the battle, so I only see it in disconnected fragments.

There's Lou on the ground, fists like balls of fire, melting holes in angel bodies. Sourpatch is perched on Dragon's back, spraying descending waves of angels in acid so they crash to ground as pitted wrecks. Turns out flame doesn't destroy them, but they don't like Dragon's claws at all. Feral tears them open like tin cans and leaves them scattered like garbage. Dani weaves through everyone, guns blazing. The more she kills, the more beautiful our surroundings become, until we're all knee deep in flowers. Oni's here too, and he's managed to figure out weak points in the design of the angels. He's flying with great enthusiasm, and shouting encouragement to us on the ground. Sheba follows him like a shadow, smashing the delicate electronic innards of the angels into fragments once the sword has pried them open.

I don't even know what Emma's doing. She vibrates in place, as if she's stuck when trying to teleport. Every so often a great section of the angelic fleet will explode, or disappear entirely, or turn into liquid that rains from the sky and streaks us all gold.

It's a losing battle. We're killing a vast number of them, but they won't stop spawning.

Dani was right—there's something we're missing.

Let's start from the beginning. *Reboot* sent us here for a reason. The only thing here was the glass tube Dani thought was a brain. I smashed it, but obviously that wasn't enough. Was there something else inside it?

Since we arrived, the buildings around us have been torn down and I've gotten all turned around in the constant fighting. Plus there are dead angels everywhere and far too many plants, so I can't find anything.

Plants. That's the trick. I sink myself into the soil again.

"I'm looking for a brain," I tell the newly growing flowers.

Turns out plants aren't that smart. Or they are, but they're efficiently smart, with all their energy taken up with necessary shit and none of it on existential dread. Probably more useful than humans, tbh. It means none of them have no idea what a brain is, and can barely understand my concept of needing to find something.

"Imagine if the sun vanished and then reappeared in a different area of the sky. Would you turn yourselves towards it?" I ask.

There's a fair bit of murmuring and vague consternation on the subject of the disappearing sun, but they begrudgingly admit they would seek it.

"That's what I want to do, except it's not the sun I want to turn towards, it's a shiny thing full of lights."

First, they think I mean the night sky, so I have to find a way around that. It takes me almost five minutes to get anywhere. I sit cross-legged among the flowers while all my friends fight angels around me, complete with narrow escapes and daring rescues. There will be stories told of this day, assuming we survive, and everyone will complain about Dilly, who chose to sit down and talk to flowers for the duration.

"Focus," Dani whispers along the thread that binds us. "You're doing the right thing."

I return my attention to the plants. Once we establish what we're looking for, I can extend my sense through their network and feel what they feel. They're very concerned with the lack of an easily accessible water source, but when I push past that, I find the thing made of lights. It's half buried in angel corpses and wreathed with flowers, but it's close.

"Finally." I struggle to my feet and run for the location.

I make it four steps before I'm shot in the back. It blows a huge hole in my chest on the way out. Moss and soil sprays over the ground. It's rich and damp and smells like autumn air.

"Shit." I take two more tottering steps and fall face down. Petals drift in front of my eyes. My fingers are splayed in a patch of soil, but there's something hard and rough under my fingertips. Seeds?

The ground quivers like a series of small pools, something beneath disturbing the surface. Figures drag themselves up from the depths. A series of small, identical creatures made from moss and twigs and clad in petals. They've got scruffy hair, dark eyes and grumpy expressions.

"What fucking ridiculous shit have you gotten yourself into now, world's worst idiot?" They stand over me and scowl.

"Holy shit." I gasp laughter. "You're little versions of me."

"That's what you get when you scatter your fucking seeds all over. Now stop whining and drag yourself over to this brain."

I reach out and try to haul myself along the ground. It's unimpressive. I know it, and the little versions of seed-me definitely know it.

"Fuck's sake. You're an actual disaster. Come on, you lot. Let's drag this big asshole."

The tiny Dylans take hold of my hands and haul me towards the glass brain-thing. I hope this is what we're looking for, or else this is a lot of shit to go through for nothing.

Anxiety floods down my connection from Dani. I shove back images of peaceful vistas interspersed with us making out. Translation: I'll be fine. Don't worry about me and carry on killing angels.

A Michael crashes to the ground beside us, flowers pouring from his stomach, growing like they want to swallow the sun. Something furry blurs past me, claws extended and tail dragging an angel. A glowing figure crashes down beside me, lashing out with his fists, face too bright to look upon.

"I'm actually fine," I say. "It doesn't look like it, but my little flower clones here are doing what they're supposed to."

Everyone ignores me, as they should, because they're destroying angels to keep my way clear. I finally reach the glass tube and unearth it from angel wreckage. Somehow, despite all the chaos around me, a chunk of the middle is completely intact. My seed-versions sit around on the ground, panting theatrically.

"They're not even fucking grateful." One of them kicks at my side.

"I am, you little shits. It's so on brand for me to have clones that don't even fucking like me."

"We do like you." One of them grabs at my hair and tugs. "We just want our thank you."

"Wow. Fucking priorities, little Dylans. Thank you all so much. Now let me concentrate." I roll over and look at the glass object, taking it into my vine hands. It's been broken, one end of it sheared off. The piece I'm holding shakes when I rattle it, and there are no lights moving inside it anymore. No, wait. Grey particles drift through it, but they're moving with purpose and order. It's disguising itself, like camouflage. It really is important.

I twist it in my hands and hold it up to my eye. There's a glowing thread inside, wound all the way through the center of it. It's obscured by a cloudy film. What happens if I pull it? How have I not developed past the instinct of a five year old? When I put my fingers in, they don't reach, so I extend the vines to wrap my hand around the end of the golden filament.

I yank as hard as I can.

The world vanishes.

CHAPTER FORTY-TWO

I'm standing in an office. On the nearest wall is a giant ornate cross. There's an intricately detailed model of a bleeding man nailed to it. He blinks at me. The only furniture is a large wooden desk, the monitor on it spider-webbed with cracks.

Everything is covered in blood, but most especially the dead body slumped against the desk. The front of his neck is a jagged tear, and his suit and shirt are soaked a dark, brutal red.

"Pastor Mike." I reach out one vine-covered hand and poke at him. Penance's Dad. Dead just like I killed him. "Please tell me this isn't going to be a jump scare. That would be too tacky."

The body topples slowly and collapses onto the carpet. His head is wrenched back so the wound is a gaping mouth. I can see inside him, the meat and bone and organic wiring.

I don't look much better, given I've still got a gaping hole in my chest, oozing sap and clods of soil. It's probably a terrible indication of my future, but I actually feel totally chipper and like I could go skipping through fields of wild-flowers.

Except there are no wildflowers to be seen. Only the body, which I assume is a statement.

"Bored now." I turn in a slow circle, and when I get back to the start, another man sits behind the desk. He is golden and slender and what some assholes might call rug-gedly handsome. He's got the jaw and the blonde curls. His smile is blinding.

"Hello, Dylan Taylor."

"The famous Michael, I assume?"

"Yes. An avatar of my consciousness at least. I am not literally here in this room, although it is not precisely a room, and we are not precisely here."

"And I give precisely zero fucks."

"Of course. Always so rebellious." His mouth turns down at the corners. Still handsome. "The first sin, of course, when the angel Lucifer attempted to overthrow the living God. In punishment, he was merely cast out of Heaven. An oversight I shall not replicate with you."

I roll my eyes. "I heard a different story about a differ-ent Lucifer, but each to their own myths. I'd say it's good to meet you, but that'd be a lie and I think we're past that." I gesture at the room around me. "I find it interesting you chose this place to bring me." Holy shit, am I channeling Ray?

"It's a natural choice." He grins wider, until it stretches into uncanny valley territory. "This is the moment you became a villain."

"Bzzzzt." I pull an exaggerated sad face at him. "It's the moment I thought about what it meant to be a villain. It's not the same thing."

"You killed this man of God because he hurt your girl-friend. A petty reason to take a life."

"Maybe." I walk around the body and perch on the desk near Michael. "Or I did it because it was a power too dangerous to exist in the world. Mind control is the fuck-ing creepiest, I swear. Even if someone used it for simple things—jumping the line at the coffee shop, begging your partner to please never leave you. In the hands of someone like the pastor here, it was an existential threat."

"Justification and words." The smile is faded now, so easily transmuted to anger. "You stood here and you counted the cost of villainy, and you murdered a man. This was the beginning of the journey that led to the massacre at Eli Crane's, the terrorist attack on the Daintree compound at Shanty Town, and—"

"It's true." I see-saw my hand in the air. "Sort of, at least. You could have avoided it all by leaving us alone. But no, you just kept coming, so sure of your divine right to—"

"Mutantkind is an abomination," Michael roars, the tendons on his neck standing out like metal cables. "The work of the devil, which must be torn down for the kingdom of God to flourish. You are the children of Lucifer, the malign entity that lurks beneath the surface of the world."

It takes me a second to parse my way through that jumble. "Oh! You mean Cybele? She's a fucking nature spirit if anything. I mean, look at me." I hold out my hand and a single daffodil blooms in my palm. "We're a defence mechanism, here to stop the planet from being destroyed by the species you chose to protect."

"Humanity was made in the image of God," he hisses.

"Sure, fucking up the planet. Isn't that God's creation too?"

"This is the promised land for humanity to inherit, and do as they will. Once Lucifer's children are destroyed, and his power is suffocated, then we begin the work of building God's Kingdom on Earth."

"Cool story, bro. Kill a planet and then play with her corpse. Sounds fucking inspiring."

"You are unrepentant." He reaches for me, as if he wants to close his golden fingers around my throat. "I bring you here to the scene of your villainy and you smile."

"Do I regret my decisions?" I shrug. "Some of them. I wish less soldiers died, but on the other hand, maybe don't sign up to fight for the evil assholes. Overall though, what were my options? You pushed us until our backs were against the wall. You wanted us to bare our throats and die, and I won't apologise for not doing that."

His eyes are white flames, impossibly hot like the glowing gaze of his God. "You are a monster, and you only ever act like a monster."

"Maybe. You don't think I wished for a different world? I grew up with Xavier's fucking dream, dude. Humans and mutants working together in harmony. That isn't the world we got. You're the one who made sure of that. It didn't have to be this way. You could have fucking left us alone. So no, I won't take the blame for all this."

Michael lashes out to backhand me across the face, but I'm faster. I catch his hand in a tangle of vines. He strains against it, and tiny gypsophila flowers bloom on my fingers and down to my wrist.

"I understand you're scared of what we could be." His golden hand creaks and strains in mine. "There's a potential monster in all of us. I've seen it in me, flashes of it, and I don't like it. You're the ones who embraced it. You saw that possible future, and raced to be monsters first. We never even got the chance to be friends."

"Nothing unclean can enter heaven." Michael's voice hisses like steam. "Nor anyone who does anything detestable or false. And what are you, child? Mutant degenerate, who—"

"No." I tug on his arm and pull him closer so his face is right near mine. "I'm not listening to any of that. We're not going to see eye to eye, that's very clear. So why am I here?"

The smile is back. "First I shall crush the life from your seed, and then execute your girlfriend. Then only your puny Goddess remains, barely able to stand under the weight of everything she holds. The question is whether she dies before I get a chance to kill her."

I take a deep breath and release him. I slide off the table and stand. "That threat was a mistake."

He towers over me. His eyes are a blaze of fire. There are more of them now. "Quis ut Deus. Who is like God? None, save for me, His chosen servant and most holy weapon. I take your life in His service. You are no sacrifice, but a rotten fruit to be plucked from the tree and cast into the fire."

"Wow." One corner of my mouth lifts up. "That's the fucking supervillain speech. You got any actual follow through?"

Great question, Dylan. He answers it by hitting me harder than I've ever been hit in my life. I say that, but it's not like I can be entirely sure. Get hit and shot and killed enough times, and after a while it all starts to blend together. It definitely hurts a lot. I fly through the air and smash into the wall, right beside the cross, spreadeagled like I'm doing a sarcastic imitation. It would be very on brand for me, but I'm actually embedded among the broken wood, feeling sorry for myself. My face is broken, or feels that way, but I'm nervous to reach up and check how bad it is.

Michael walks over leisurely, confident in his ability to take me apart.

I heave myself out of the wall. There are a lot of holes in me. I'm sagging. Vines snake from my hands, weaving up and around my arms, cinching me tight and holding me together. The hole in my chest is making a sucking sound, like it's trying to slurp moisture out of the air.

"A monster who's turned herself into a different kind of monster," he says.

"Usually I'm flexible as shit with my pronouns." Sap trickles from the corner of my mouth. "But not to you, asshole. You can call me they."

"Male and female, he created them," Michael says.

"Hoisted by your own fucking words." I smile. "He created *them*, you smug fuck."

"That's not what it means." He kicks me this time as a nice change. If I'd been human, he would have shattered my ribcage into little bone fragments, but instead I sail away from him in a big shower of soil. I hit the desk and bounce off, sprawling on the ground past it. There's a big chunk taken out of my side. Inside, the densely packed moss that makes up my body is visible, threaded through with tiny vines and curling ferns.

"Fuck." The thread of anxiety from Dani is a torrent. I try to push reassurance back to her, but I don't think it's convincing. Then I show her a picture of Michael, coming at me with his eyes bright and his fists clenched.

She doesn't like that at all.

"You're a disrespectful young woman," Michael sneers. "You were born female and you shall die one, too."

"It's basic respect for people." I lever myself up again. Vines spill out of me, reaching for Michael and shoving him away. "Using the pronouns and names they want to be called."

Michael tears his way through the vines, shredding me apart, until he gets close enough to drive his fist into the hole of my heart.

Okay, that fucking *hurts* like a supernova exploding in my chest. The wall behind me disintegrates in a shower of splinters. I fly through it, out of the mocked-up office of Pastor Mike and into a featureless white expanse beyond.

I get to my feet one more fucking time. I'm swaying, sap forming a puddle around me.

"It's important, the words we use," I tell Michael, as he bursts through after me. His many eyes glow and his wings fan out behind him like twin arches of fire. "Everyone deserves to exist and be seen on their own terms."

Dani screams down the connection between us. Probably wondering why I'm giving an artificial intelligence a lesson on pronouns in my last moments. I try to convince her I'll be fine, but I'm barely held together by thin threads of vine and force of fucking will.

"If I die here, do I die in real life?"

"You die everywhere. I'll sever you from the river of energy that powers you. You'll be a fallow field, like your people should have been all along." He stomps towards me. "First, I'm going to get rid of that endlessly flapping tongue of yours."

He comes at me in a rush, but the advantage of being a barely held-together plant creature is I can collapse and flow out of the way, a spore carried on the breeze.

"If anyone needs to shut up, it's you. Fucking monologuing cliche supervillain asshole." On the outside, my band of friends staves off a descending torrent of angels. There are too many of them. We'd need to blow the whole city up to stop them, raze it to the ground, and there are millions of people in there. Innocent, or close enough to it.

Right now, I've got Michael here. He may call it a projection of him, but there's enough of his power pooled here to take on Cybele. I can sense it through our connection, a smothering hand reaching out to extinguish the energy. I'm a tiny flame against the darkness. A single shoot of green sprouting in a wasteland of ash.

There's an idea.

I reach for the connection to Dani, pouring love back down it along with a request for very specific and careful instructions. It makes me a fraction too slow, and Michael's golden hands snatch me from the air. His touch burns and smoke pours from my front. Tiny fires flicker among the densely-packed fibres of my flesh. He's going to burn me alive. It's hell and glory in one package.

Thorns sprout at my neck, around my wrists, and at my knuckles. I slam one of my fists into Michael's golden, sneering face. Two of his glowing eyes shatter, jetting sparks. Behind the polished surface, lights dance in complex patterns. I jab two thorny fingers into the holes and something inside him shrieks.

He throws me to the ground. One of my shoulders shatters to splinters. He raises his foot above me and then brings it down on my neck. It crushes my plant flesh but I only need the tiniest thread to connect me. The bigger problem is the fire still burning in my chest.

It's time for a fucking miracle.

Hello, Marvellous, my darling. Here's the chance I'm looking for. All the information floods into my brain, carried on this new connection between us. I have all I need.

There's one huge problem.

The trick to pulling this off is confidence.

How can that really be it? It's some fucking cosmic joke, to the point I can believe some god out there is pulling the strings to dangle me here in an impossible position. What an asshole.

Find some self-belief, Dylan.

Harder than it sounds. I'm alone against an artificial intelligence. Emphasis on the second part. I'm the worst option to be left at the end, a single figure whose only talent is taking a punch.

No, that's not right. The connection to Dani is flooded with love and reassurance. I'm not only worth it because of my powers, or lack of them. I'm me, and people love me for who I am.

More importantly, I'm part of a network just like Cybele. This tangled, furious group who supports me and loves me and gives me strength. I'm still me without them, but plug them into me and I'm so much *more*.

First, there's Pear. Who loved me before I was aware of it. They never let their pain and shadows break them, and always gave me what I needed. Then Lou, the boy who fell in love with me. My first kiss, my partner in isolation. Alyse, who broke the shell, who etched friendship into my heart and refused to let my insecurities drive her away. Emma, who held the world in her heart but still made space for me. Outwardly so sweet, but so dark and hilarious inside. A girl who was the fulfilment of an awful prophecy, but turned away from it to fight for something better. Bianca, my emotional support himbo, who I loved and couldn't save. My eternal ghost, sitting at my shoulder to teach me why we fight. A wound that will never heal, and I don't want it to.

Then all the others too: Katie, my adopted sister and partner in extremely low levels of chill. Feral, whose favourite place to sleep is on the end of our bed and who nestles into us like we're her new family. Penance, still struggling to find her way out of darkness to a place where she can accept herself. Who has something like love for me, a tangled river of feeling I'm not sure how to swim in.

And then there's Dani. The most beautiful girl I've ever seen, who drew close despite my disasters. Someone impossibly strong and smart, who opened herself to me and gave me the courage to do the same. The woman who loves me, despite my flailing and my flaws, who holds my mercurial flame in the palm of her hand. My partner in everything, even death and resurrection.

All these people, who've chosen to stand beside me. Who love me despite my edges and my bruises, and the darkness in my heart that rages at the injustice and cruelty in the world.

I'm lying here alone, but I'm flooded with the echoes of the ones I love.

Dylan Taylor. Chatterbox. Teen Magneto. Genderfluid weirdo who tried to build their own X-Men team and found the best fucking family ever. A little bit hero, a little bit villain.

In the final reckoning, I'll fight for what's right.

Even if it kills me.

I fucking hope it doesn't kill me.

"Dani, I love you."

I raise my hands, and point my index fingers at Michael, in the shape of little guns.

I drop my thumbs.

I even make a click-click noise.

Michael's chest explodes. There are so many flowers, roses and orchids and daffodils, all woven through with leaves and ferns. It's a riot of colour and scent, like spring was super late this year and then decided to punch everyone in the face.

"On the third day," Michael slurs. "God created..."

I point my finger a second time.

His head disintegrates and in its place is a giant lotus flower, lit from within with golden light that makes the delicate pink petals glow.

"Hello, you sweet, delirious creature." Cybele speaks from the heart of the flower. "You have exceeded my wildest dreams. I hoped to stall the monster and buy time, not slay it." She reaches out a hand towards me. "I am so desperately sorry about what must come next."

"What do you mean?" I ask.

And then I wake up.

CHAPTER FORTY-THREE

’m lying on the ground in tatters, the shattered remains of the glass tube strewn across me.

"I think he's fucked." One of the seed-Dylans pokes at my broken face.

"She's fine." Another climbs atop my face and yanks hard on my eyelid. "See, they're looking pissed off. One of our default fucking states."

"Oh shit, here comes the sexy one."

They scatter as Dani comes over and kneels beside me.

"What did you do?" She strokes my face. "I can tell you're alive through our connection, otherwise I'd be freaking out right now."

"The finger guns worked." My smile doesn't work right, because my face is all torn up. "Blam, right in the chest, and then another one in the head. I saw Cybele there." I try to sit up, and fail miserably. "She said something super cryptic and depressing, but she also said we won."

"Can't you feel it?' Dani asks.

"I think most of my senses are keeping enough of me together to regrow."

All the little Dylans are standing around looking up at Dani with extraordinarily saccharine expressions on their faces. I'm sure it's nothing like mine. I flail my last working limb out and sink it into the ground. The unusual dead patch of the city is gone, and I can feel the tentative vibrations of the soil. Somewhere, off in the distance, the massive poised wave of Cybele's island is cresting, breaking.

"Hold tight." Dani clutches onto the ruin of my left arm.

I close my eyes, which is ridiculous because I can't *see* any of this. It's not perceptible in any way I can explain. It's beyond light and warmth, although it has elements of both. It cascades through the ground below the surface of the earth, a river flooding underneath us, that foams up, as if my presence draws it up through the soil and into me.

It's suffocating in its intensity, like every part of me is being turned on and gently toasted at the same time. It only lasts a few seconds before it subsides, and the river floods elsewhere, rushing through the city before branching out into three streams, seeking to reignite the pattern that surrounds the entire globe.

I blink my eyes open and sit up in one elegant movement. We're in a park, with trees growing overhead and a stream running through it. There's a wooden bridge across it, grown rather than built. Around us, the remaining buildings of the city still tower, but the lights have all gone dark, and no smoke or fumes vent from the upper stories. The tiny seed-Dylans are gone, dissolved back into the soil they came from.

"You're okay," Dani's arms go around me and her mouth is on mine.

We collapse back down into the grass that's long and cool and fragrant.

"Of course I am." I check myself up and down but my body is completely back to how it was before, like all that energy casually wove me back together. "I told you we'd survive."

She kisses me long and hard, until the shouting from nearby becomes too loud to ignore.

Standing on the wooden bridge are the rest of the Cute Mutants. Everyone's back in human form, even Katie, who is far too fond of being a dragon—not that I can entirely blame her.

Dani gets to her feet and hauls me up. I'm suddenly awkward, even though these are the people who gave me the confidence to shoot an angel.

"By the way, the confidence trick? That's so annoying."

"I told you. You just have to believe you're badass and sexy enough to blow someone up with flowers."

"It's clear I am not and have never been that person."

"Except you are. Because you did it, at the most necessary time of all."

"Because of you," I insist.

"I wasn't the one there with him. That was all you."

Part of me wants to tell her that it's all of them, this network of us, but she already knows. It's who we are now. She wraps her arm around me and we cross to the bridge, where we're surrounded by everyone. They all talk at the same time about how amazing it is, and how overwhelming the battle with the angels was.

The echoes of the energy matrix still ripple out across the world. Cybele's island is less of a beacon than it was, but one thing still blazes among us.

"I feel weird." Emma clutches the railing of the bridge. "Nauseated."

I think about what Cybele said. Her apology about what's coming. She knows I'm going to lose a vital part of my network and there's nothing I can do about it.

"Are you okay?" Alyse asks. "It's not still Michael?"

"No. He's gone, but I can't—"

She leaps up into the sky, so fast we can barely track her. One second she's there, the next she's a glowing dot like an evening star.

"What is she doing?" My voice is panicked all over again.

"She's fine." Alyse touches my hand. "I can still hear her."

There's a bright flash of light like a detonating bomb. A few seconds later the sound of it washes over us, making us clutch at the railing of the bridge until our knuckles go white.

"What the fuck?" Katie's staring up at her. "She's not still losing her shit, is she?"

"There's no still," Alyse says in a very tight and unconvincing voice.

"Um, so we're not talking about the fact she knocked us out, stole our powers and put us in the freezer for months?" Katie glares right back.

"Yes, Draggy, we're very much ignoring that." Feral's tail twitches. "In the hope everything is all fixed now that the bosses are back."

"We're going to try," Dani says. "That's all we can do. It's worked for us in the past, right?"

Emma appears back on the bridge in front of us. Her hands are transparent and I can see the glowing skeleton inside her, each delicate bone blazing in a different shade. Small creatures flutter inside, curling around her knuckles.

"A problem for another day." Smoke rises from her shoulders, as if she burned up re-entering the atmosphere and rebuilt herself. "We saved the world. Let's party."

CHAPTER FORTY-FOUR

Emma whisks everyone back to Asteroid Ems, then teleports in a bunch of food and alcohol. The problem is that everyone's too sore, tired and worried about her. The party never really gets off the ground, and so people end up lying around eating pizza, drinking cider, and watching the news.

People's reaction to Michael being gone is rapturous. They're crying and clinging to each other. It's a slightly weird feeling, because we missed most of the horrible stuff. Dani and I swung in at the end, like that thing in Greek plays where something's pulled out of the ass to fix everything. All these people had to wade through the whole year of shit though. I bet there are some grim stories in there. I'm not even sure I want to hear them.

The Dark Year, that's what they're calling it. A year where Goddess held everything together.

Emma's distracted and irritable, so unlike her that I spend more time watching her than anything else. Alyse is fixated and over-protective. The two of them drift in and out of the main group a lot, and Emma keeps manifesting various powers. On one occasion she has at least ten arms, and another she's a smooth marble statue, blinking eyes that weep fat drops of blood. Everyone else studiously ignores it through some awkward politeness.

Watching the news isn't what I'd usually think of as a party, but everyone wants to see how the world has changed. Most of the news networks are offline, showing a rotating golden eye and playing religious muzak. There are some people on pirate TV networks, waxing lyrical about a variety of topics. Most are excited about the downfall of Michael, but they're evenly split on whether mutants are wonderful or evil.

"At least some of them like us." Katie has an enormous tub of popcorn in her lap, and is leaning against Lou, who is leaning against Maddy, who's idly playing with his hair. "It's a whole new world."

This is obviously a cue for Maddy and Alyse to break into song, and they get most of the way through the entire thing before anyone can shut them up with a hail of popcorn and empty cans. With the cities down, the population inside are wandering lost. The majority of them were brainwashed drones, but now they're roaming the empty countryside around the cities, looking for places to go.

"Must be strange," Skye says. "To have your world changed so much and so abruptly."

Maddy smirks. "Like becoming a mutant, but a whole lot more crap. The problem is what do we do about them?"

"Not our problem." Gladdy is very firm on this point. "The humans can take care of their own, honestly."

Everyone turns to look at me, like I'm still in charge.

"Gladdy's right. Fuck them. We need to figure out our own situation." I have some ideas about this, but I haven't talked about them with anyone save for Dani. It's a shame Cybele's island isn't big enough as a new home, because it seems like a logical choice.

Speaking of Cybele, she's still the only one who might have answers about Emma, so I nudge Dani down our mental connection, and we slip away while everyone else is chattering. We find a cozy little space with a comfortable seat, where we curl up together and entwine our limbs. Inside this giant rock with Emma blazing all around us, it's hard to sense the energy network, but it's flickering on the edges of our awareness. At least it's coherent now, circling the globe even though it's weak.

"Cybele, are you there?" Dani asks.

There's silence for a handful of seconds, and then a creaky voice is audible, like someone speaking from the next room. "I am somewhat awoken, yes. It appears disaster is averted in the immediate term, yet we still face a crisis in terms of wider human behaviour."

"So our extinction isn't tomorrow, we've got a handful of years left," Dani says bitterly.

"Precisely, and we should all be grateful for this brief window as it may give us the time to make other changes. There is one far greater problem which dwarfs all the others, and will put a swift end to everything if not addressed."

"Emma," we say in unison.

"Yes. She contains far too much energy for any single person to bear. If not for her ability, we would have blinked out of existence a long time ago. If we want to avoid the end of everything, we need to siphon the energy out of her before she destroys the world. This would also do much to restore me to full health and enable me to mend some of the more grievous injuries I have sustained."

My heart surges with life. Flowers bloom all over me in a delirious riot of colour. Hope makes me almost breathless. "This would fix her? We could extract it from her and into you which would—"

"No," Cybele says solemnly, and all this new life flickering along my limbs wilts instantly.

"But why not?" I whimper, curling myself inward.

"The energy is the only thing enabling her to sustain her unnatural life. She has rebuilt herself from death hundreds of times, the tiny, stubborn miracle that she is.

Your Goddess is remarkable and singlehandedly staved off extinction while we wove our plan. Without her, all would have perished."

"And yet she dies." Dani and I are closely pressed together, united in grief in that merged form where I'm not even sure of the lines between us.

"Everything dies," Cybele says gently. "There is no way of avoiding this. She is doomed, but we have choices in how her demise is handled. If she keeps the energy, she will be unable to contain it and this world will be put out like a doused flame. Her current plan is to become a dying star in a far off galaxy, but it will be far better if she returns her power to me as Lucifer did long ago." There's a brief silence. "Come to the island, and I will show you the manner of her passing."

I want to take Roxy, because I'm not sure if I can have a conversation with Emma without having a full-blown meltdown. The problem is that'll take too long. We're standing in the corridor, having a loudly whispered conversation, when Keepaway comes around the corner and almost bowls into us.

"Keepsy! Did Emma wake you up?"

They frown. "Yes. Apparently she's trying to bring us back in shifts. I'm very confused about everything and nobody will tell me what's going on."

"There's time for that later." Dani claps them on the shoulder. "Right now, we need you to send us to an island."

Thankfully Keepaway is probably the sweetest and most compliant mutant there is, so they send us away with barely even a twitch of their mouth.

The island is mostly as I remember, except bursting with even more life. A small copse of trees has grown up around the ones that Dani and I hatched from. I wonder if these have people growing inside them too.

"Creating new life in this fashion is not something I make a habit of." The indistinct outline of a woman steps out from among the trees, almost like one of Alyse's sketch-like transformations. She's stooped and shuffling, moving with great care and not leaving the shade of the branches. "To build you required an enormous amount of effort and energy. As I told you before you were born, it was a tremendous gamble. It seems it paid off, but at a cost." She shivers, like wind in the leaves. "Anyway, we are here to discuss tragedies and the passing of someone magical from the world."

It's my turn to shiver. "Are you sure there's no way?"

Cybele reaches out one hand and strokes the trunk of the tree beside her. "I truly am sorry. You have all fought so hard and sacrificed so much."

"Rebuild her, like you did to us," I demand.

"That is not a trick that can be done with this one. She has no template, not anymore. Your Emma is a miracle and nothing I can reconstitute. If I knew a way, I would have already provided it. Now come with me." She turns, and shuffles into the trees.

We follow, because there's little choice, but I drag my feet. A giant weight presses down on me. Each step is a struggle, shuffling along in Cybele's wake. It's only a small patch of trees, but it feels like we're lost in a giant forest. At the center is a small clearing with a deep, clear pool fed by a tiny stream that burbles over rocks. The trees dip down towards it, as if they're paying homage or drawn by some force in the water. The leaves are a riot of autumnal colour, reds and orange and golds fighting for prominence. Around the edge of the pool, wildflowers grow, like drops of pure colour staining the grass.

I've never seen anywhere so beautiful in my life.

I hate it.

A large, flat rock sits at one end of the pool. I can't help feeling it looks like a headstone. On it lies a long, slender blade of grass. An ornate knot makes a hilt at one end, studded with flowers. It looks almost identical to Onimaru Kunitsuna, except grown instead of forged.

"What's that?" My voice is hoarse.

"You know what it is," Cybele says. "It is the weapon which will end the life of your suffering friend, and restore the world to health."

"No." The sword blurs in front of my eyes. "We can't do this." I turn and clutch at Dani.

"I know." Dani strokes the soft petals in my hair. "Cybele, please."

"This sentimentality of yours is understandable, but unnecessary and impractical. If you do not perform this act, she will die, in far more pain and suffering than you can imagine, and the rest of the world will follow in her wake. This is the kind and ethical choice. Is it not better she dies somewhere beautiful? To pass away at peace and surrounded by her friends?"

"Fuck." I want to tear through the clearing and destroy everything, but it would achieve nothing. If there's blame to be laid anywhere, I can't find it. The choices we made were the best we had at the time with incomplete information. With mutantkind and the planet at risk, we chose to stand and fight. We could blame our enemies, but they're defeated. We could blame humanity, but we need them to get their shit together and make sure the planet is saved.

Emma's sacrifice can't be in vain.

And there it goes. I've already got the idea in my head of losing Emma.

"You know we have to do this," Dani says.

"She needs to know." Petals drift around me, fluttering in a disconnected rainbow, falling instead of tears. "We need to explain this to her so she understands. It needs to be her choice. I'm not going to ambush her or anything."

"I agree. Emma needs to know."

"Know what?" We both whirl, to find Emma and Alyse on the far side of the clearing. Alyse is herself, as far as I can tell. No transformation to face this moment. Emma's eyes are clear and there's a smile on her face. Her hair is clean and silky and curls slightly inwards around her chin.

"This place," Alyse says. "What's it for?"

Emma brushes her fingers through the grass. "It's perfect. I love it here."

Alyse looks from my face to Emma's. One of us looks like the world is collapsing, and the other looks peaceful. "No. Dylan, fucking no. This isn't right."

"I'm sorry." The tears come no matter how hard I fight them. I'm the center of a blizzard of falling petals. "We tried to find a solution, but the only other way is worse."

"It's true." Dani's voice is so gentle, I want to hide in its soft corridors. "Emma's going to die. We tried to stop it, but there's no way. All we can do is choose how. Even outside the fate of the world, do you really want her to suffer?"

Emma turns to Alyse and places one hand on her cheek. Then she leans in and kisses her, very softly, on the lips. They hold this pose, as the sun filters through the leaves and dapples them with light. The flowers around them spread their petals as if Alyse and Emma are the twin suns in their sky.

Alyse clenches her fists. I think she wants to transform, but she's also determined to face this as herself, without hiding from this cruelest blow. "Why is there no miracle for me? We've had so many, and I only need one more."

"My life has been a series of miracles, but you're the best one." Light spills from Emma's eyes and mouth, and vast golden wings flare outwards from her back. "I never thought someone like you could love me."

"It was so easy." Alyse plants one more kiss on Emma's mouth and the light surrounds her, too bright to look at. "So inevitable."

Emma turns slightly. "It's going to happen soon, Dilly. I don't have much time. It's so hard to hold myself together. I can feel the universe clutching at me. It wants me to pour myself down its throat." She holds out one hand, and it trembles.

"What do you need from us?" I ask gently.

The light fades from her face, and I can see she's smiling. "My favourite thing. One last meal with the whole family."

CHAPTER FORTY-FIVE

The whole family includes Emma's parents, who look so stunned and shadowed by everything that they lurk in the corner and barely interact with anyone. I feel sorry for them, because Mrs. Hall aka Teen Spirit aka Lan Jing has been through so goddamn much in her life, and most of it has been stolen from her. Emma's Dad seems to be facing it with stolid indifference. His only acknowledgement to the situation is making weird dad jokes about being Joseph, cuckolded by a godlike being. Honestly, I don't properly understand them, but I pretend to laugh.

Emma's re-opened the whole asteroid up, and it's weird to travel stone corridors again. I've finally got Emma's parents settled, and am heading back to the party when I round the corner and bump directly into the next group of people who've exited the mysterious halls of One Thorn.

"Holy." It's the only word I can get out, because *fucking shit* gets stuck in my throat. It's Pear, dressed in their favourite coat, their hair a few inches long. Their girlfriend Sarah and her family are straggling behind, and they all crash into each other at the sight of me.

"Pear." Tears spill down my cheeks, and I'm shaking so hard that I'm reenacting autumn for her. Now I know why they call it fall, because I can't hold myself up. They're on the ground with me, and we're both ugly crying in the most spectacular and embarrassing way, huge hitching sobs and fragments of what might be words if you stitched them together carefully.

"You're alive," they finally manage to say. "And Dani?"

Dani's been hit by the backwash of my wave of emotion. I'm swamped by her responses, all the guilt and excitement and love. She comes racing into the room, trailing vines and flowers and barrels into the two of us like a sweet-smelling missile.

"I'm here too, Ness." She buries her face in Pear's neck. "I'm so so sorry."

Pear's just repeating *you're okay* over and over.

"I told you." Sarah's daughter Hazel looks a lot older than I remember, with an adorably messy pixie cut. Her mouth twitches when she looks at me. "I kept telling them both you weren't really dead."

"I was so dead." I'm not entirely sure why I'm arguing this point.

"Maybe, but I knew you'd find a way back. You're superheroes." She's got tears on her face too, and it makes me cling to Pear even harder, because I think about how it must have been for them. I've put them through so much since this all started. I wonder if it was a relief for them at all, to not have to worry about what would happen to me next. Freedom from the nightmare of Dylan Taylor.

"No." Dani's damp forehead presses against my cheek. "Not for a second. You stop that right now."

Stupid half-ass psychic bond.

"What's happened to you?" Pear finally asks, once their voice is recovering.

I'm about to launch hesitantly into the story all over again, when a piercing voice cuts through everything.

"Joo-hyun! Danielle! Is it true?"

"Oh shit." Dani's face crumples, but she gets to her feet and stands swaying as Mrs. Kim advances down the corridor like a warrior going into battle.

"Fuck." I scramble up to stand beside her, but I'm too late. Mrs. Kim's arms are around her daughter's neck, and she's wailing. It starts me crying all over again, those sappy tears that make my cheeks so goddamn sticky.

Dani's brother Min-jun is standing slightly off to the side, looking as awkward as I feel. There are no tears on his cheeks, but his mouth is a neatly ruled line, and I see the tension in his eyes.

"It's been rough, huh?" I ask him.

"Yeah. People have been really kind, but—on top of Dad, it's just… a lot for someone to deal with."

"Someone?" I put my arm around him and he grabs hold of me, fistfuls of my hoodie in his hands. I manoeuvre him over to Dani and Mrs. Kim and manage to entangle us all in a hug. It's maybe not a healing thing, but it helps to all stand together and be there as one organism. Even if it's not as obvious as what's running between Dani and me these days, we're all connected.

"How could you die?" Mrs. Kim glares up into Dani's beautiful face. "How could you *do* that? And they tell me you've been back some time already! You should have informed me! It is unacceptable, Danielle, but I am so pleased to see you, my beautiful girl, and look at you."

"I'm sorry, Umma, like I don't know how to be sorry enough."

"She really is, and the thing is that it's not her fault." I'm babbling and I don't know how to stop. "It was mostly me, and I got us in over our heads, and we didn't realise we would literally, you know, fucking *die*, but here we are and—"

"Of course this was your doing, Dylan." Her gaze makes me quail, and I'm probably more scared of her than Michael, because I'm hopelessly in love with her daughter and crave her approval desperately.

I fight my tears and nervousness down, but all I can do is carry on babbling. "I might be reckless, and I know this sort of shit keeps happening with me around, but I fucking love your daughter and I'd do anything for her, including death and resurrection. It just means that—"

"Hush." She pats my cheek and holds my chin in a grip as firm as Dani's metal hand used to. "Listen to me. You're a good person, Dylan Taylor, and I am so pleased to have you in Joo-hyun's life. Even with this. I lost so much of my world, and I have grieved and grieved until I felt empty, but today I have been given a gift and you do not need to apologise for that."

"You don't hate me?"

The chin grip gets even tighter and I want to cry for different reasons now. "You could listen to me for once. I know you are allergic to that—Ness and I have discussed it on multiple occasions, but perhaps you could accept that I love you."

"Okay. I love you too, unless I'm not allowed to, in which case I'll do it in secret."

"Impossible creature." She throws her other arm around my neck, and crushes us all together awkwardly, until Min-jun tells us he can't breathe and we break apart.

Everyone's looking at me expectantly.

"Okay, so I'm happy to tell the whole resurrection story, but let's eat first, huh?"

Emma teleports food in from somewhere, enough to feed everyone and more. Even though Mrs. Kim offers to cook for everyone, and there's probably nothing better than her bulgogi to send someone off, what she really wants is to sit next to Dani and gaze upon her newly transfigured daughter. I can't blame her.

Instead, we eat pizza and ice-cream and tacos and wasabi Doritos. The story of us in a single, terrible meal. I tell the story of what happened with Dani and I, and afterwards the room is full of tears, conversation, and even some laughter. But inevitably, every eye turns back to Emma. She's quiet and watchful, looking from face to face as if she wants to memorise everything about everyone.

These are her last moments, surrounded by everyone she loves. I press my hands between my thighs to still their shaking, but I can't stop the rest of me. I'm drowning in white lilies and black roses and yellow chrysanthemums, a funeral wreath come to trembling life. Alyse is sitting between Emma and I, one hand on each of us, as if we can tether her to reality. She's desperately clinging to human form, although she occasionally loses focus and drifts away. This is supposed to be a last celebration, but the awful goodbye of it keeps forcing its way into my brain and I can't see any good in it at all.

People are still eating as Emma begins to move around the room and say her farewells. I don't eavesdrop on any of them, no matter how much I want to. There are so many tears. Her parents look numb and wrecked. After she moves away from them, they scurry away as if they can't bear to be here anymore.

Soon it's just the Cute Mutants left in the room.

"I'm going soon," Emma says. "It feels fucking weird to say this, knowing I'm not coming back, but I love you all. I was created to be a monster, but you kept me human."

"What's going to happen?" Lou's face is shadowed and sad. There's no light in him at all.

"I'm going to Cybele's island where she's going to siphon

the power out of me before I can't hold on anymore." Her voice shakes. "It'll be peaceful. I'm so sorry about—"

"God, you don't need to apologise for anything," Maddy says. "All you need to know is that you saved the world. And we love you and we're going to miss you." Tears trace down her cheeks, leaving stinging red lines.

Feral bounds across the table and flings her arms around Emma. "I don't want you to go. I've lost too much family already, and it never gets any easier."

"I know, Marisol," Emma says. "But this is going to make it safer for the rest of our family. You're finally going to thrive. Things will be better now."

"That's hard to believe," Penance whispers.

"Do you trust me?" Emma asks. "All of you? Despite everything I've done?"

All around the table, everyone nods. Our Goddess, who we love. Who's suffered for us all.

"I can't promise you everything will be perfect from now on. We've won a huge battle today, and this is another victory, even if it looks awful right now. There's no way to stop me dying, and I know that seems unfair, but sometimes shit just fucking sucks, as Dilly might say. It's not what I want, but I also know I'm leaving behind the best friends in the world, who are going to keep fighting in my name, but not just fighting—building a new and better world. One I'd be proud of." She sways on her feet slightly.

"You okay?" Alyse asks her.

"I'm exhausted." Her smile is a shadow of its usual self. "It's time to let go."

The world blinks out around us.

CHAPTER FORTY-SIX

We reappear in the middle of Cybele's clearing. It's even more beautiful than I remember, and I resent every part of it. I'd rather it was some blighted, horrible place that echoed my heart, but at the same time Emma deserves something this gorgeous as her gravestone.

She wraps her arms around Alyse's neck, drawing close. The others turn away, but Dani and I bloom, making a cocoon of vines and flowers for them to say their goodbyes in. It has dahlias and roses and tulips, and we weave in the ace flag and the bi flag because we are both extra like that. This business of creation also distracts me, something to stave off thoughts of the loss bearing down on me like a vast shadow. But it also reminds me of creating our funeral wreath for Abby, and suddenly I don't want to do it anymore.

Then the island joins in, energy looping through to connect us in an effervescent circuit. It doesn't soothe the pain of what's happening, but helps to feel part of something bigger. Our team. The Cute Mutants.

Nobody knows what to do here. We're used to fighting disaster, of hurling our bodies into the dark to deny the horrors of the future. Against this, we are helpless, and it chafes on us all. Feral prowls restlessly, and Penance flickers between forms, as if she cannot bear to stay in the world for more than moments. Lou looks sombre, dressed in all black, and even Maddy's usual joy is dimmed. Gladdy stares at the ground, because if she looked at any of us, the darkness would overwhelm her. Katie cries silently, tears wobbling down her cheeks and watering the soil around her. Tiny blue flowers spring up, delicate and drooping. Skye stands with her clones, the whole group of them joined together in a cluster along with Ye Shou. Keepaway wants to run, I think, standing with their hands pressed tightly together and their eyes red. But they stay, despite it all.

"We're done," Emma calls from inside the bower.

Dani and I let it collapse, the flowers drifting away on the breeze, a flood of petals that brush against our skin like the tenderest touches.

Emma is cross-legged on the flat rock, leaning back against Alyse. The sword is in her lap. It looks too fragile to cause any pain or death, let alone channel a vast outpouring of cosmic power. She smiles up at us, and we all gather around her.

This is the final time that the whole group of us will be together. All our power, all this *ability*, our fierceness and our fire—we cannot fix everything and we will never be whole again.

There's no boosting, nothing but tears and goodbyes and everyone aching and sharing that ache between us. Emma spends time with each person, whispering to them, telling them something beautiful, while I cling to Alyse and try to keep her held together. She remains her true self, but one so tear-stained and shaky it's hard to distinguish her from one that's dissolving.

"Dani." Emma holds out her hand. "My oldest friend. You've always been there for me, even when I was like a thousand times less cool than you and just wanted to sit on my computer all day. I'd also like to remind you I was the first one who pointed out the extremely obvious fact of your crush on Dylan."

"Sounds fake, but okay." Dani's smiling but there are tears in her eyes. "And you were always so much cooler than me, because you never even tried. I fucking love you, Ems."

"I love you too. And Dylan." Emma's voice shakes. "I'm so sorry about the things I said and did to you. I should never have taken your power."

I collapse down onto the rock beside her. "Don't waste this time on apologies. You really think one fight would wipe out all the times we shared? We made a baby together and called it the Cute Mutants. It's still a fucking *terrible* name for the record, no matter how accurate it might be."

"We did, and we saved the world, and now we're going to save it one last time."

"No, impossible girl." I kiss her cheek. "You're healing the world all on your own."

"I'm not Dark Phoenix."

I hold her close, as if I can unpack the best parts of her, to take them into my heart and shelter against the oncoming storm. "No, you're Goddess. You're Emmaline Jing Hall. You're my friend."

Emma presses her cheek to mine and we stay that way a long time, as if we're paused and the whole world is holding its breath to see if I can assemble one last miracle from the threads of my recklessness and fire.

When she pulls away, her cheek is sticky with pollen and covered in petals. "We can't wait too much longer."

I reach for the sword in her lap, but Alyse pushes my hand away.

"No, I want to do this."

"Are you sure?" Emma searches her face.

"This is the right thing to do. We're easing your suffering. Otherwise you'll be in agony up until a brutal end."

"Yes." The word drops sweet from Emma's lips.

"And I'm the one who loves you most, so I should be the one to guide you on your way."

Panic rises up in me, so intense I want to scream. Instead, I clutch at Dani, and push that feeling down the connection between us. She sends hers back to me, and we hold that twinned in our hearts, until we can forge something like strength from it. The others are all huddled together, but I stay close to Alyse, for when she needs me.

Alyse takes the grass sword in her hand. She's shaking, but the sword stays perfectly steady, moving with her.

"Hurry." Emma's teeth are chattering. "It hurts holding it together."

"I love you," Alyse says.

Emma smiles and it's the most beautiful thing I've ever seen. "I love you too."

I'm clenching my fists so hard that sap drips between my fingers.

Alyse stands perfectly still for a moment, one last breath as if something waits for the last possible second to intervene. Then she pulls her arm back and thrusts the sword forward.

I let out a horrible keening sound like the lonely cry of a bird.

The sword pierces Emma's body as if she's made of water. It drives into the stone below, cracking it perfectly in the center. Radial marks shoot outwards, like the spokes of a wheel.

Emma arches her back. Tears roll down her cheeks and make darkened splotches against the rock. A soft noise escapes her throat, a bubble of rainbow light trembling on her lips.

The grass sword glows, too bright to look at. It's a live wire connecting Goddess to the island, opening a conduit for energy to flow. Her star explodes, but instead of obliterating us all in a tidal wave of fire, it's channelled back into the source that created her. From the very first mutant until now, we all have a piece of Cybele within us, and Emma's held more than anyone.

From the perspective of a tiny little part-alien plant person, it's like standing underneath the world's largest waterfall. The energy gushes into the earth, which drinks it gratefully. The world around us blooms, trees dancing in delirious splendour. The bright flowers grow huge, big enough to sit in. My whole body is covered in flowers, twining together and bursting with fruit.

I think I'm floating too, knocked into a bucolic stupor.

I'm not sure how long it lasts. The sword slowly dims until it's a single blade of grass, the flowers on its hilt wilted.

Emma lies sprawled on the stone.

She looks peaceful.

Alyse places one hand to Emma's heart and her lips to Emma's neck.

"She's gone." She manages to get the words out before she dissolves into tears. I think that like me, she thought we'd earned one last victory. Now that moment has slipped through our grasp, impossible to claw back. Gone doesn't seem a word big enough for this absence, like we've lost a fundamental element that makes up the world.

We surround Alyse, taking her back into the center of the group. It feels cruel to pretend to be whole despite the brutal gap that's been torn through the middle of us. Emma was our friend, before and after being a Goddess. There was an equation that made up who we are, and we'll never be able to solve it again. I never could fucking figure out x, in all my years of algebra, and now I've finally got the answer and lost it at the same time.

I don't believe in heaven or hell, but I like the idea that there's *somewhere*—some plane of existence, or a memory-form level of mutant consciousness. In that impossible place, Emma steps over a threshold and finds Wraith waiting for her, purple lips twisted into a smile. Leapfrog will look up shyly, fingers tangled in the cords of Lou's B-Mo hoodie. Two Skyes, clinging to each other for safety. And Thottie, tattoos flaring with light, unscarred by our desperate attempts to pull her back from this strange land. Behind them, the parade of other mutants who've fallen stretches into the distance.

I'm crying again. I can't help it. Even after being pulled apart and reborn, my scars have been regrown with me. And now there's a new one, thicker and deeper than any other. The mark Emma left, a heart carved in my skin around mine. On my arm, the word Goddess blooms in golden lilies.

This far and no further. We need one more impossible dream.

There's rustling from among the trees, which have grown so thick and lush, and a woman steps into the clearing. She's young, around our age, and her skin is such a dark green it's almost black. She has a lotus flower at her heart, a belt of lilies around her waist, and a crown of yarrow flowers at her brow.

"Hello, my sweet children."

CHAPTER FORTY-SEVEN

Cybele is different to Dani and me, like a sapling shook itself from the soil, smelling of rosemary and pine. Her eyes are darkened gouges in the smooth wood of her face, but they gleam with light. I know this is only a small part of her, a single sprouting of the vast alien lifeform living inside the planet, but even this sliver seems incomprehensible. She moves in jerky motions like a bird, crossing to Alyse and bending to plant a kiss on her brow. "That was very brave. It is a very human thing to fear and avoid death."

Alyse's eyes are twin pools of black, as deep as Cybele's. "I'm not human though, am I?"

"No." Cybele brushes her fingertips over Alyse's cheek. "You are my children, and you have fought so hard."

"She deserves a rest." Dani's voice trembles and breaks. I pull her in close again, but there's no soothing this pain. We have to get through it together, a single step at a time.

"Are you healed at least, Cybele?" I try to keep bitterness from my voice, but I can taste it spilling from my lips. We lost Emma, and here I am trying to salvage something from the disaster.

"I am not what I once was, and many dire threats remain. Yet I now have the strength to face them, and the ability to make change."

Alyse is still crouched beside Emma's body, as if she can't bear to detach this last connection. "What do we do about funeral arrangements?"

The alien hums, a fluting sound like wind passing through a hole in rocks. "I would leave her body open to the sky and let it return to the soil naturally. I understand this may not—"

"No. It's the most beautiful place I've ever seen, so it's a perfect resting place for her." Alyse looks at us, and there doesn't need to be a transformation to show us the pain in her eyes. "Can you give me some time alone with her?"

"Of course." I scuttle out of the clearing with what feels like unnecessary haste, like I'm running desperately away from all the pain, except it's in my heart, impossible to escape.

Emma sacrificed herself, and it was noble and beautiful, but she's still gone.

The whole group of us stumbles out of the small forest to find ourselves at the cliff. Instead of the wide empty ocean, there's a lush green island. It's only a short boat ride away. Low hills slope down to sandy beaches dotted with miniature palm trees. Patches of lush vegetation run along the ridges, but mostly it's wide green fields, with so many flowers it looks like they've been poured out of a bottle.

"What the fuck is this?"

Cybele beams. "When you died, your bodies flowered and grew. When the flood of energy left Emma, I redirected some of it to encourage the planet to do something far more extravagant. It seemed like an appropriate—"

"Home," Dani and I breathe simultaneously.

The group of us stands in a line on the cliff's edge, looking out at this impossible island. Everyone's talking, excitement trading off with the numb echo of loss.

"A gift for you." Cybele sketches a bow in our direction. "Built from your sacrifice. It also moves, if we speak to the ocean currents and beg their favour. Something I can do again, now that I have been restored."

This is what we've been aiming for this whole time. The mutant nation. A home for our people. A new land claimed by nobody else.

Alyse drifts out of the trees, transformed into something impossibly gorgeous and flower-bedecked, like she's joined Dani and me in soft plant club. "I laid her in the grass, and covered her with flowers. We've given her back to the world." Petals blow around her, but there are real tears too.

She joins us at the cliff's edge, looking out at what Cybele and Emma made for us.

"Home." She spreads her arms wide, and lets herself dissolve into grief, becoming an enormous winged shadow that blots out the sun. "Why couldn't she see this?"

"Because it's her." Dani leans her head on my shoulder. "The last miracle of Goddess."

"It's beautiful." Violet's eyes meet mine. "She would have loved it."

I cannot speak, because every word is caught in my throat at once, a horrible wet tangle of them all mired in grief and longing. Emma should be here. That truth is wickedly edged and lodged in my gut. She is a loss that cannot be undone. One more name on the list of my dead, those who fell in a battle that wasn't mine, but that I took on like an old hoodie, blood-soaked and torn. All those gone, and I am still here, a shattered warrior put back together and thrust back into the fight.

Except this time we have a home. A protector. And we still have our family.

"Keepaway." I raise my head. "Take us to the island, then go back to the asteroid. Start sending other people too. This has been a shitty day. Hell, it's been a shitty fucking year. It's time they got to see something good."

They send me and Dani first, almost simultaneously. We stand barefoot on sand at the very tip of our new home. Lush forest stretches down from the low hills of the island, cupping the beach in the curve of its palm. Small waves chase us, a fringe of frothing white stopping just before our feet. In front of us, the cliffs of Cybele's island tower, and we see the tiny figures of the other Cute Mutants waving.

"Didn't sink underneath us," I mutter to Dani. "Almost thought it would."

"No." She takes me in her arms and kisses me. "This is a good thing. It's what we deserve."

One by one, the other mutants join us, and then more arrive, sent from the asteroid. Pear is there with Sarah and her family. Mrs. Kim and the sobbing figure of Emma's Mum. Then the whole host of mutants, all those who survived the Dark Year in which Michael tried to burn our species from the earth.

Alyse speaks to every single person, and takes their memories of Emma into her heart. She thanks each and every one.

Then Dani and I greet each new arrival, giving them a flower and a hug.

"Welcome home," we say.

MUTOPIA

THREE MONTHS LATER

CHAPTER FORTY-EIGHT

'm standing on the eastern edge of the island in the early hours of the morning. My arms are extended, laden with blooms that turn towards the rising sun. My skin tingles with the light, tendrils twitching through the skin of my neck.

Warm arms slip around my stomach from behind, lips against my neck

"So beautiful."

"You are." I turn in Dani's arms. She's still covered in night-blooms, fresh from sleep and cheeks blushing pink with the dawn. "I like sharing the mornings with you."

The next few moments are taken up with the business of kissing and blooming, until there's a cough from behind us.

"Sorry to interrupt." Alyse's voice is hoarse. "But I woke up and she wasn't there, and—"

"Come here." We both open our arms and she joins us. We wrap her in ferns and flowers and let her mourn.

Behind us, our little wooden cottage stands in the morning light. It's mostly open to the elements, and drifts of petals pile up around its edges. Feral sits on the front step with a coffee in her hands. Penance leans in the doorframe with her own mug, watching us.

I wave at them and they wave back.

The five of us share this house. It started with Dani and I, but Alyse needed to be looked after so we asked her to move in too. Then we kept waking up to find Feral on the end of the bed, and Penance hanging suspended in a cat's cradle of blades above us. It seemed easier to submit to the gravity of friendship. I like the way it is now. It feels like a family, and it feels like home.

There are a small group of other cottages around us, also grown from the island. The rest of the Cute Mutants live in this little village, as well as our families. Pear and Sarah live two doors down, but we're all a good distance from the main settlement. I find it easier that way. Too many people these days, too many things to do. All these demands yanking on my fucking strings. It's a hell of a job, trying to keep this new island of ours afloat. Satisfying, I guess, but not exactly easy.

This is the happiest part of the day, being with my family and friends.

These are the moments when things hurt least.

Later that morning, I'm back in the main city. It's called Emmaline, which was voted for by the entire population of the island. I find myself avoiding saying the name, because I don't need to be haunted even more than I already am.

I'm here to meet with Ray, who's been elected the President of Mutopia. The island does have an official name, but nobody ever uses it. We've been granted full nation status and our rights have been enshrined in international law. That's our reward for destroying a rogue artificial intelligence that had overrun the world. It doesn't seem like enough, but it also seems like everything. The population of the island is nearly two thousand people now. Even though only two-thirds of that are mutants, it seems impossible to believe we exist in such numbers and have a safe place of our own.

When I enter their room, Ray is standing at the window. From here, the hills slope steeply down to the water, and it looks like they're suspended in the air.

"Chatterbox." Their mouth twists into a smile. "It's good to see you."

I pull the seat back from the desk, and collapse into it, one leg slung over the side.

"You too, Prez."

"I wish you wouldn't call me that. It feels mildly sarcastic."

"Nah." I grin at them, trying to be at least half as sardonic as they are. "You're the best person for the job. Alyse needs two things, time and space, and neither of those come with the presidency." Alyse won the presidential election by a landslide, so we made everyone have it again. Someone else won the second time, some *clearly* unqualified person who didn't want the job at all, so we ran a third election with a few names off the ballot. It's not supposed to be a popularity contest. You need someone smart and competent.

"I am aware you're far more capable than you like to let on, Dilly." Ray flashes a wicked smile at me. "It suits you to be underestimated. One day, I hope you'll dig into the why of that with me."

"Therapy with the Prez. Aren't I just the luckiest duck?"

"One day." They sigh and finally take their seat. "When we have less pressing issues to deal with. Such as the report from your delightfully named friends."

"Yes, UwU got back last night. Woke me up and interrupted Dani's evening bloom. Very sad, because she's always so damn horny after that."

"Do I really need to know this?" Ray's voice can be very

dry when they want it to be.

"Fine, I'll summarise. They squished a little pro-Michael cult very tactfully. No loss of life, but Fetchy thinks it might be the tip of the iceberg. Who knew people liked being told what to do by powerful authority figures?"

Ray snorts and motions for me to continue.

"They'll keep an eye on it. A more uncomfortable problem is the homo superior crowd. Mutants that don't want to leave their homes, which is fair enough, but they're trying to run the so-called baselines out. Turns out being a mutant doesn't exclude you being an asshole. More life lessons for you, Prez."

"You'd think my present company would have taught me that." They keep a straight face after that, which I'm impressed by.

"Sometimes I think you actually like me, and then you cut me down to size."

They laugh. "I've always been a fan. What about progress on the other sensitive issue?"

"There are far too many things you nag me about to know which—"

"Your entirely delightful parent."

"Fuck." I almost fall out of my seat. "I think you're barking up the wrong tree on that one. I mean, they *could* do it, and they *are* bored, but it's probably the worst job in the world. Who would want to be the bridge between mutants and humanity?"

Ray stares at me.

"Fine." I jiggle my leg impatiently. "I'll talk to them."

A brief silence grows between us.

"And how are you feeling, Dylan? I see Alyse every week, but you always have a reason to skip your appointment."

"You know me. I'm a survivor."

"You're an avoider. They're hardly the same thing."

I shrug and stare out the window, searching for a new

topic. Sadly, Ray gets there first.

"And our green friend? Are we still seeing incidents?"

"You mean is Cybele still addressing urgent climate change issues? While humanity pats itself on the back for escaping one disaster while barrelling towards the next one?"

Ray steeples their fingers and regards me. I hate when they do this.

"I'll talk to her." Cybele won't listen to me. I wouldn't in her position either. But I can reiterate the importance of subtlety. We're trying to do it without people noticing. Malfunctions in factories, key staff coming down with mysterious spore-borne illnesses. We're waging a quiet war against the world's most polluting companies, and Ray isn't supposed to know anything about it, the interfering busybody.

"No surprises, Chatterbox." Ray sounds exhausted, the grain of their voice hollow.

"That's the plan." I grin at them.

They shake their head, and I walk out into the sunshine.

Late that afternoon, we get a message flung into our heads by Demi.

Alert! Potential intrusion off the north coast!

"Ugh." I'm lying in a patch of trees, with my legs in the sun and my roots in the soil. Dani's curled up with me, although she's more in the sun because she likes it far more than is natural. We probably spend too much time like this, letting other people run around and do all the work, but I feel like we've earned it.

"Should we see what this is?" Dani asks.

"Surely there's someone better qualified to deal with it."

"Nobody better qualified, but perhaps less lazy."

Feral lopes out of the house in uniform. "Are you two going to sleep the day away when there's fighting to do?"

A shadow blots out the sun, and I look up to see Alyse looming over us. The light reflects off her metal surface and her face is a glowing blue demon mask.

"Oh, we're riding?" I ask.

"People driving a boat full of explosives into our home?" Alyse holds out her hands. "Sounds like a job for the Cute Mutants."

"There's no retiring, is there?" I wrap my vines around her hand and allow her to tug me to my feet. "It's never actually *over*."

"Stop it." Dani pats me with a thorny hand. "At least now we've got a home to defend."

"Fine, you've twisted my arm. Let's go."

"Keepaway, my sweet bean." Feral taps the side of her head. "Can you take us to North Beach, please? Bodyslide by four."

Keepaway pops out of thin air beside us. "No rest for the wicked," they say with a smile, and touch us all one after the other.

North Beach isn't deserted. Riot Grrl is here, working on the island's wards. Turns out her power isn't just useful for inciting riots after all, and her symbols help protect us from the prying eyes of all the other countries out there. It's one more piece of the fragile wall that shores up the safety of our land. I give her an awkward side hug. Even though she's been healed from her almost-death experience, she carries herself like she's still wounded. She dreams about dying all the time. Ray hasn't even managed to eradicate them from her mind, and I know they've tried. Riot Grrl talks about looking upon a city full of wonders, and sometimes I wonder if she wishes she stayed there.

"You doing okay?" I ask, like I always do.

"I'm alive, aren't I?" She smiles, and turns away to continue her work on the wards.

I suppress a shiver, and look towards something more cheerful. Fishbelly—the name stuck, despite the fact the glass bowl of her stomach is empty now—is trying to coax her two children out of the ocean. They're sweet and chaotic, and can survive on land for a decent amount of time, although they don't like it. It always makes me happy to see them, because they're a perfect example of why we fought and keep fighting.

"Sorry," Fishbelly says. "They pretend they can't hear when they're in the water."

"They'll be fine." I look out at the fins cutting a line through the surf. "Just tell them to keep clear of the big, scary boat. I'm more worried about this lot." I gesture at a group of teenage mutants who are standing in the shallows, deep in discussion.

"It should be me," a lanky girl in denim shorts says. "I'm the one with water powers."

"You're barely more than a good swimmer," another scoffs. They've got bright purple skin and a spiny crest along their back.

"*Shut up,*" a third girl hisses when she catches sight of us. This one I recognise. It's Sarah's daughter Hazel, who's basically my step-sibling.

"Don't tell me to shut up," Spiny says. "I've got a plan."

"And we've got *company.*"

The others turn, and present us with cartoonish expressions of shock.

"Oh, holy fuck, it's the Cute Mutants." The lanky girl flings herself headlong into the ocean and disappears beneath the waves.

"Sorry." Hazel blushes. "That's my friend, Airy. She's shy."

"We're not that goddamn scary," I growl, sounding like I'm trying unsuccessfully to audition for the role of Wolverine.

"Are you here to deal with the boat?" Spiny asks, having regained their composure.

"Boat's on its way." Feral peers into the distance. She's the only one with eyesight good enough to see it.

"Let's keep it at a distance," I say. "Cy, you there?"

"I am always here." The voice sounds in my head.

"Do you mind beaching that ship for us?" Dani asks. "And give us a nice little causeway to it, so we can have a chat."

"I assume we are still treating them with kid gloves?" Penance hovers in the air above us, her face a glorious rainbow of colour. "Despite the fact they're attacking us."

I sigh. "Accidents do happen at sea, but let's not leave a floating ghost ship full of blood."

The island shakes slightly as the ocean floor shifts, rocks rising up to carve a dripping path to the oncoming boat

"Crunch." Feral shows all her teeth. "Let's go meet them."

"You and Penny go as advance guard," I say. "But be gentle. Disarming only. That goes for you too, Onimaru."

"It's so long since I shed blood I am practically retired." Oni floats down to hover in front of me. "However, I shall go with the sharp-toothed and the sharp-fingered one to ensure they are on best behaviour. Come on, sweet Sheba. We shall fight together."

"We shall shatter kneecaps for justice!" My bat descends to hover beside Oni.

"For justice." I give them a little wave onwards.

Oni flashes off through the air, Sheba arrowing behind him. Roxy grumbles overhead, like an angsty black bumblebee. Feral leaps nimbly over the rocks, while Penance flickers away.

Dani, Alyse and I take the stroll nice and leisurely.

"Do you think we're getting lazy?" Alyse asks.

"It's called delegation," Dani says with a laugh. "We'll have a whole new generation soon. You saw those kids on the beach."

"Superhero school." My breath hitches. "Emmaline Jing Hall's School for Higher Learning."

"She'd like that, I think." Alyse slings an arm around my shoulder. "But we've got work to do yet. Come on, you two ride with me." She transforms into a towering figure, a giant of steel and flowers. We perch on her palms as she closes the distance to the ship.

By the time we reach it, the crew are collected on deck, a small and sullen group.

Alyse deposits Dani and me beside them, then shrinks down into regular form. The assembled sailors don't look happy to see us, and not impressed to have been overwhelmed by a furry, a ghostly face in the sky, and a flying sword/bat combo. You've been Cute Mutanted, assholes.

I lean back against the railing. "You lot really made a bad fucking decision here. What the hell is this in aid of? I hope it's not pointless bigotry, because we've been there too often. Give me a good reason. Surprise me."

The first one to talk is a woman in a filthy blue coat. "What are you talking about, you unnatural monster?"

Dani sighs. "And here we wanted a single *good* reason."

"God will not be mocked!" This is from some brave soul at the back of the group. "The existence of the mutant nation is an affront."

"An affront?" I spread my arms. "I don't even know what the fuck that means. You need to turn this pleasure cruise around and go home. Think about what it means that we spared your lives after you came to kill us. Maybe share it on social media or—"

"I don't have long to live," a voice rumbles in my head. "If you wish to survive, perhaps you should vacate the premises. Though survival seems pointless, because life holds such little joy."

Oh shit. It's another fucking bomb. They're always so depressing.

"Your death is God's will," Filthy Coat screams.

A metallic clang comes from behind us, and I spin to see a bunch of people with guns pouring from a hatch.

"You didn't search the ship?" I ask Feral.

"We were about to, and then you turned up and started bantering!"

"Fine. You deal with these assholes, and I'll talk to this ridiculous bomb."

Dani spins towards the new arrivals in a shower of petals.

Alyse shifts into a vortex, blades whirling at her center. All her transformations are so dark now.

Penance extends her hands in welcome.

Feral shows all her teeth. "Oh, this won't be a problem at all."

I extend my awareness to find the presence of the bomb, sitting sullenly in the base of the ship.

"There's no point in speaking to me or trying to cheer me up," he tells me. "My destiny is to destroy."

"I'm sure that's what it feels like." I lean against the railing as my friends fight around me. "I used to think that about myself too. Let me tell you a story…"

Here we are once again. The Cute Mutants, saving the day.

So this is my life.

MUTOPIA

NINE MONTHS LATER

EPILOGUE

'm sitting with Dani at the end of the little lane that leads
to Jing Hall. We're surrounded by flowers that have grown
up around us. The school is a fairly new addition to Mutopia, and it's thriving. Our attention is on the crowd surging
around a tall and beautiful figure.

"Goodbye, Ms. Sefo! See you tomorrow."

"Did you like my apple, Ms. Sefo? I grew it myself! Out
of my own head!"

"Don't be gross! You can't give her that!"

"Ms. Sefo, look! My flying is so much better. See?"

The schoolchildren stream down the lane past us. A flash
of rainbow light, followed by a mutant with extremely long
legs, then one with wings of light, and another with wings
like a butterfly. So many children, some with obvious muta-
tions and some who appear entirely human. Since Cybele
reawakened, the frequency of new mutants has increased.
We've even got a team responsible for monitoring them and
assimilating them into life on Mutopia.

Right at the tail end of the line trudges one child, maybe
thirteen or so, with no obvious powers. Their head is down
and they stare at the ground. A few metres from us, one of
the winged children swoops down and plucks the bag from
their back, shooting back up into the sky. The kid doesn't
even shout, looking after it with a resigned expression I recognise from my own childhood.

"Asshole." I shoot out one vine arm after the flying mutant. It sails through the air and snatches hold of the bag, before I tug it back towards me.

"Nice job, Bulbasaur," Dani says with a laugh.

I present the bag to the kid with a flourish. "Who was that?"

"Firewing." The kid takes the bag and slings it over their shoulder before finally looking up at us. They pretty much leap into the air when they see who it is. "Um, oh, wow, your majesties." They sketch a little bow to us. "I'm really sorry. I didn't know it was you."

"Hey, none of that majesty stuff." I reach out one flowery hand and tip their head up. "We're just mutants like you. No different to anyone else."

"I'm not even a mutant," they say. "I'm just a baseline."

I frown. "We don't use that word here."

Alyse has joined us by now. "Some of the children do, unfortunately. Especially that one." She gestures in the direction of the disappearing mutant.

"Should I give him a stern talking to?" I ask.

"I think it'll be a case of waiting for him to grow up." Alyse sighs. "Some are easier than others, like Effie here." She reaches out and ruffles the kid's hair, who blushes fiercely.

"I should get home." The kid fidgets with their bag. "I'm sorry."

"There's nothing to apologise for." I smile down at them. "People are sometimes assholes. They used to do shit like that to me too, except my bullies couldn't fly away."

Effie squints up at me. "Even you?"

"Even me. Now we need to steal your teacher away, if you can possibly spare her."

They blush even brighter. "Of course." They duck their head and skip away down the path.

"Cute kid," Dani says.

"One of the best." Alyse looks fondly after them. "I've been nudging friends around them, to build them their own little gang. I think it's finally starting to work."

Dani and I link arms with Alyse, one on each side. "I wish I'd had a teacher like you."

"I do love it, and not only because it keeps me busy. You know, I almost forgot what day it was today."

"You did not." I glance sideways at her, and see the tears have already started.

"Of course I didn't. I did have a moment where I decided I couldn't possibly do this, and it was too much for anyone to bear."

Dani pauses. "You don't have to."

"Of course I do, even if you two have to drag me there in a shower of petals." She squeezes my hand. "It's hard for you as well. We all loved her."

"We did, but what you had was special."

"Yes." She exhales, and I feel salt spray, but not from the ocean. "It really was."

We follow the path through a small copse of trees and out onto the headland, where we see the towering cliff of Cybele's island directly in front of us. She's spent the past few months paddling Mutopia slowly in this direction. A narrow rock bridge thrusts out of the ocean, curving around to hit the lowest point where the cliff falls away.

The rest of the Cute Mutants are waiting down on the shore. Everyone looks anxious, but brightens when they see us. The whole gang gives Alyse a hug, one after the other.

"You doing okay?" Lou asks.

"If you cling to me, I can't run away." For a moment, she becomes a cloud of scented particles, but eventually reforms. "I can't believe it's been a year."

"To be fair, it's been a super weird fucking year." Lou laughs, and kisses Alyse's cheek gently. "And that's going by our standards, which are not what normal people use."

"I miss her every day." Her voice is impossibly soft.

"We all do."

We make a straggling trail up the rocky path and onto Cybele's island. Alyse is crying the instant we wade into the grass. It's grown up thigh-high, still strewn with so many flowers. Dani and I stay with her as we forge a path to the trees in the distance.

The trees smell so good when we reach them, like the air here is filtered into something fresher and cleaner. Even Alyse stops crying. Her eyes are clearer and there's more colour in her cheeks. There are flowers everywhere, and more grow wherever Dani and I tread. This is the place of our birth, and it sings a greeting to us.

The clearing is exactly as we left it. The clear pool, and the smooth rock beside it. All the trees and flowers, bowing down as if they pay homage. They're the only things alive.

Part of me was hoping for a miracle.

Alyse falls to her knees, making a cracked and broken sound. When her hands hit the grounds, she shatters. She's been holding herself together this past year and this anniversary has broken her open again.

"What do we do?" Katie asks from behind us.

I kneel beside Alyse and wrap my arms around her neck, holding her close and letting her cry. We're all together, this tangled mess of us. We've made it through this year, and it didn't kill us. Our mutant nation is stronger, despite the threats we still face. There's a hole at all of our hearts, but Emma gifted us so much.

We don't just survive.

We thrive.

Alyse finally gets to her feet and crosses to the cracked stone where Emma died. Her body still lies there, her skeleton amidst a beautiful bower of flowers. It's so fragile and beautiful. Alyse traces her fingertips over the smooth line of Emma's skull.

"I'll always miss you, my love."

I have to look away because it hurts too much. Amongst the treeline I see the new, young Cybele watching us. I drift towards her, and meet her halfway.

"It confuses me that you cannot see the beauty in death. It is part of life, inexorably twinned. All of you here will die. You thrash and fight against it, and there is beauty in that too, but the living and the fighting and the dying are all bound up together, and they are all beautiful in their own way."

I watch Alyse, curled over the bones of the woman she loved. There's a well of sadness there that I don't think anyone can plumb. I wonder what's at the bottom, and it frightens me. "Emma was young. And she was part of our family. Missing people is part of life too."

"Yes." Cybele shifts with a rustle of leaves. "I have been working on something, but seeing the grief of you and your friends, I am not sure it was wise."

"What is it?" I glance over at Alyse. "It's nothing to do with…"

"As I told you, there was nothing I could do for your Goddess. It is better if I show you."

Cybele disappears among the trees without speaking further, and I follow her. The others all notice, and begin to trail after me. Alyse runs to the front of the line, snaking her arm through mine.

"Whatever this is, it's nothing to do with Emma," I tell her.

"I know." She shivers against me and blue light ripples through her body. "It's something new. You're going to flip."

"You know about it?"

"I promised I'd keep it secret."

"Alyse," I say in exasperation, stopping dead. "You have to tell me."

"Dylan Jean Taylor, we are literally walking to it. You cannot have *that* little patience."

"I don't like surprises," I grumble, but let her tug me onwards.

A short way through the trees, we reach another small clearing. Two large plants sit in its center, petals tightly closed. They're extraordinarily beautiful, with delicate traceries of rainbow threaded through the pale pink.

"What is this?" I stop at the edge. "Something new?"

Cybele smiles. "Oh, yes. Something *marvellous*. You see, I retained the patterns that make up the two of you. Given you are not able to reproduce in the traditional method—"

"What are you talking about?" Dani asks.

The two flowers spring open, the petals falling away in a flourish. Sitting in each is a small figure. Their skin is a gentle tan with a slight greenish tinge around the extremities. On their head are tufts of dark and messy hair, scattered through with purple blossom. As the warmth of the sun falls on their skin, they both open their eyes and blink around. Their irises are beautiful hazel fractals that look very familiar.

"Holy fucking shit," I say.

The two tiny children stretch and yawn. They tumble out of the petals and get to their feet.

"This is freaky," Katie whispers.

"They look like," Lou tails off in a hysterical giggle.

"Like an exact blend of Dani and Dylan." Maddy is grinning. "Aren't they *adorable*?"

"I'm rather proud of them." Cybele's eyes glow a luminous green. She's delighted by this.

The two figures toddle over to where Dani and I stand, completely fucking stunned because in all the goddamn world I could not have predicted this. The emotions churning through our shared connection are too tangled for me to tell apart, but there's excitement and shock and fear in there for sure.

"Mama?" They raise chubby arms, their voices high

and soft. "Pear?"

Even though I'm in shock, I can't resist bending down and picking the nearest child up. They wrap their arms around my neck and nestle in against me. I turn to face Dani, who's holding the other, perched on her hip and toying with the flowers at her neck.

"What the fuck?" I say.

"Language." Dani glares at me.

Alyse is right beside us, looking into their little faces. "Hello, babies. I'm your Aunty Lys." Tears shine on her cheeks. "I'm so happy to meet you."

They both reach out for her in unison, wrapping their tiny vine fingers around her hand.

"And I'm your Uncle Lucifer." Lou leans in to look more closely, and then starts laughing.

"What's so fucking funny?" I demand.

"You being a parent, Dilly, you have to admit."

"Fuck me."

"Language," Dani says again.

"They're so beautiful," Alyse breathes. "Emma would have loved this too. Seeing life go on. That's what she gave to all of us."

I run my fingers through the impossibly soft hair on the child's head. *Our* child, somehow. I get the whole life goes on thing, and it's very fucking beautiful but… "Cybele," I say, in what I think is a very calm voice considering the situation. "You have some explaining to do."

The End (for now)

ACKNOWLEDGEMENTS

It's a strange feeling to have made it this far. By the time I was halfway through the first volume, I was already imagining wild and wonderful endings. It wasn't long before I had a title for this book: *The Dark Goddess Saga.* A nod to the most famous X-Men story of all, and one I wanted to play with. It did twist a little in the telling and I changed the title because, uh, spoilers much? It's still surreal to be here, having told this story that begins with a group of teenagers together in a house and ends up with them, older and far more battered, standing on the shores of sanctuary. I hope you enjoyed watching these chaos kids grow up.

To get all these books out in such a short time requires a lot of help. Starting with my family who has to put up with my obsession, my early morning writing hours, and the fact part of my brain is always off in Mutopia. Then there are people all around the world who provide support and encouragement that helps make me feel like this is all worth it. Thank you to everyone who's listened, bought, retweeted, messaged, and (most especially) read. The list of names is too long to actually list because I went way over word count, but you know who you are.

This is a big, weird book and I had a whole bunch of beta readers and critique partners who helped me fix plot holes, deepen character arcs, and point out where I said something badly. Thank you so much to Emma, Amanda, Jen, Art, Andee, Hsinju, Rosa, Charlotte, Monica, Jenna, Andy, and Logan—turns out books are a lot better when you have kind and smart people give you feedback on them.

And then there's Melo, my critique partner who helped me blow this book up and put it back together (just like a certain character). More than anyone, you had to put up with my mutant ability of spiralling at the slightest criticism. This book wouldn't be what it is without you, and I wouldn't have dragged it over the finish line without your kindness and friendship.

My writing group of Team Trash has to put up with a lot of me complaining about… pretty much everything. So to Andy, Crystal, Leah, Mallory, Melo, Michelle, Monica, Nat, Nina, SinJ and SoftJ—thank you for the friendship and support, and for helping me achieve my dream of the Cute Mutants Universe.

Thanks yet again to @kassiocoralov for another stunning cover, and to G for the beautiful formatting that makes these books look so wonderful inside as well as out.

This might be the end of the Cute Mutants series, but there's a whole universe out there to explore. And, as you can tell from the ending of this book, there's more for Dylan and the others to do. There will be more books to come and in 2022 the sequel series is coming, continuing on the adventures on Mutopia and in worlds beyond this one.

I hope you'll continue to join us <3

ABOUT THE AUTHOR

SJ Whitby is a writer. That's about all you need to know. They're nonbinary and live in New Zealand. On Twitter and Instagram they're @sjwhitbywrites, and you can find more Cute Mutants Universe content on their Patreon at www.patreon.com/sjwhitby.